UNBROKEN THREADS
JENNIFER KLEPPER

Unbroken Threads

Red Adept Publishing, LLC

104 Bugenfield Court

Garner, NC 27529

http://RedAdeptPublishing.com/

To mothers and grandmothers.

CHAPTER ONE

"**A**re you Jessica?" The receptionist placed the phone receiver on her shoulder and pulled a folder from the top of a pile on her desk. "Leslie isn't here today. Here's the case file. You can go ahead to the meeting room. I'll bring the client over." She motioned toward a room to the right of the legal clinic entrance as she handed over a manila folder.

Before Jessica could follow up with any questions about how in the world she was supposed to do this without a staff attorney, the woman resumed her phone conversation, speaking in a language Jessica didn't understand.

Jessica smiled hesitantly at the two Hispanic women sitting in the metal chairs by the social services pamphlets. Children played at the women's feet, silently pushing plastic cars and buses along the curved lines woven into the faded carpeting. Pale curtains framed the empty street visible through the security bars on the window, but the waiting room was otherwise unadorned.

The meeting room wasn't much better, and it certainly wasn't like the conference rooms at Highland & Cross, with their shiny, in-laid mahogany tables and original American artwork. But the International Asylum Project wasn't a high-powered DC law firm, and nonprofits took what they could get. Here, in a sketchy part of Baltimore, that meant a wood laminate table with mismatched chairs, flat white paint on the walls, and patriotic stock photos mounted in cheap plastic frames.

The legal clinic clearly had money for the electric bills, though. Jessica shivered at the air conditioning, glad she'd worn her new jacket. She hadn't practiced law since her sixth grader was a toddler, and she didn't even know how to look the part anymore. Somewhat jokingly, but somewhat not, she had referred to television legal dramas for sartorial inspiration before heading to Nordstrom to buy some updated professional attire.

Today's cropped houndstooth jacket and flare-legged trousers were perhaps a little stiff for IAP, but they conveyed the confidence she needed in taking on something completely out of her comfort zone.

Jessica pulled a wheeled chair away from the table, cursing when she twisted her ankle and stumbled, the chair sliding away in the process. The four-inch heels might have been too much.

After straightening the chair, Jessica reached into her pocket and pulled out one of her new business cards for reassurance. *Jessica Walter Donnelly, Attorney*. IAP didn't provide cards for its volunteers, but Danny had surprised her with a stack when she'd finished the training. *A good catch, that sailor boy.*

Despite having taken on this volunteer position somewhat reluctantly—entirely reluctantly, to be honest—she'd had butterflies, the good kind, about it. Sure, she already had a full résumé of volunteer roles, but this one had more substance and would be more impressive than the others. She was in a suit, after all. Today should have been an opportunity to show off her admittedly rusty professional skills to the staff attorney, who was ten years her junior, but who was counting?

Unfortunately, a shiny rectangle of paper and a new suit weren't going to help make up for the fact that her supervisor hadn't shown up for her first client meeting or that the *pro bono* attorney training had been on the light side. Maybe the receptionist would be tied up on the phone for a while longer and Jessica could cram in a quick review of the file. She opened the folder to the client information sheet, and her stomach dropped.

Name: Amina Hamid

Gender: Female

Date of Birth: 07/20/1989

Languages: Arabic, English, French

Country of Origin: Syria

Syria. As in red lines and barrel bombs, ISIS and beheadings, terror and jihad.

She had expected to be sitting there with a staff attorney, maybe an interpreter, and a client like one of the women or children in the waiting room, not a Muslim woman from the Middle East. Though maybe she wasn't Muslim. Jessica scolded herself. *That shouldn't matter.* She had never thought of herself as prejudiced. In fact, taking this *pro bono* position to help immigrants should have been proof she wasn't. But in the pit of her stomach, she felt otherwise, and it felt ugly. She shook off the unexpected sense of dread, marking it up to nerves, and flipped to the next page.

A knock interrupted the cram session too soon. Turning toward the door, Jessica caught her warped reflection in an eagle-adorned photo and smoothed her auburn waves, which had been caught off guard by an unseasonal autumn humidity.

As the receptionist walked away, closing the door behind her, Jessica gestured toward the table, inviting the client to sit. The woman stood significantly shorter than Jessica, even accounting for the new heels. Her slate, long-sleeved blouse, matching wrap, and flowing black maxi skirt accented her petite stature.

A plum scarf, expertly draped around the woman's head and neck, framed her face. She would certainly stand out in Baltimore. Being so conspicuous in a new country had to be uncomfortable. Thank God Jessica hadn't gone with the sexy TV lawyer look Danny had advocated. The contrast with the demure Muslim attire would have been embarrassing.

The woman had an unnerving stillness about her. Jessica had never spoken with a woman in a hijab before. She had of course seen countless photos of Muslim women in headscarves. In her mind, the photos showed a sea of sameness—masses of women subjugated into hiding themselves away from the world and homogenizing their appearance.

Jessica reassessed. The woman sitting across from her, small and shrouded in her traditional clothing, seemed more striking because of it. The headscarf hid the woman's hair and ears, but it served as a bold frame that highlighted her features.

The tenseness of her brow formed three vertical lines between her eyebrows. The lines still had that woman-in-her-twenties transience, but they looked as if they had been invited to stay too long and might take up permanent residence. The eyebrows themselves turned up slightly at their inside ends, betraying sadness, but they were perched above piercing black eyes that undeniably screamed "don't fuck with me."

Hoping to break the ice, Jessica forced a sorority-rush smile and introduced herself. "First of all, I want to say that I just received your case file when I walked in the door, so I haven't been able to go through all of the particulars at this point. You don't need an interpreter, though, correct?"

The woman answered with a curt nod. Stillness. It wasn't serene, placid stillness but more like the stillness of a lioness calculating when to pounce on a gazelle. Or perhaps it was the stillness of an injured lioness calculating how to protect herself against an attack.

"What can you tell me about your case?" Jessica deflected her eyes and paged through the paperwork. "It looks like you've already filed your application for asylum." Jessica would have expected to be preparing that application right now, not backfilling it.

"Yes, I hired a lawyer to prepare my original paperwork. He was very expensive but said I would have no problems. When I read the application he prepared, the information was wrong." Amina spoke with a crispness—each hard consonant taut and deliberate—that made each word sound considered. The accent was distinct, but it didn't overpower the woman's English.

Jessica fought the urge to shift in her seat. "What do you mean by 'wrong'?"

"What it said happened to me was incorrect. What it said happened to my family was incorrect. He told me what he wrote was the way to get approved, that he knew the stories that worked. I did not trust him. He was only doing things for the money. But I had already paid him and had no money for a new lawyer. So I completed my application myself and submitted it." Amina's stiff monotone delivery betrayed an anger that hadn't subsided. Her narrowed eyes remained fixed on Jessica.

Jessica felt a bit like a gazelle, still hesitant to move. She really did hate lawyers sometimes, and stories like Amina's were why. The industry of nonattorney *notarios* and even licensed lawyers preying on immigrants and submitting fraudulent paperwork, or no paperwork at all, was hard to police since the victims were reluctant to draw attention to themselves by reporting the crimes.

But Jessica represented the good-guy attorneys. And Amina was clearly no pushover. She had to have uncommon confidence to take back an application from a lawyer in a foreign country. *So much for the stereotypical submissive Middle Eastern woman.*

"IAP is different." Jessica crafted what she hoped was a sincere, reassuring expression and decided not to mention that the staff attorney who was supposed to be there to lead the case had bailed out that morning. That wouldn't inspire confidence. "I'm a volunteer. I'm not doing this for the money—any money, really." She turned up her palms reflexively. Hopefully, this fact would allay any fears Amina might have that she was going to get screwed again.

Amina raised her chin slightly. "Then why are you doing this?"

Because I would have come off as selfish and uncaring if I had turned down the IAP director? That response didn't seem likely to engender trust.

"You deserve someone to help you gain asylum. I have the skills to help you." The nonanswer followed by what was possibly a non-truth left Jessica's mouth dry.

Amina relaxed—just a bit. The lines between her eyebrows disappeared, but her eyes narrowed, pulling a lone freckle below her left eye upward ever so slightly. "How many asylum cases have you won?"

Shit. Keeping her shoulders squared and her eyes steady, Jessica responded without hesitation. "None." She hastened to add, "But I haven't lost any, either. I'll be working with a staff attorney here at IAP, so I'll have access to all of the help I need." The new suit had better be conveying some confidence because that was about all she had going for her right now.

Amina stared at Jessica without breaking eye contact. Jessica willed herself to exude competence.

She clearly needed to work on her exuding. Amina stood abruptly, clutching her bag and appearing taller than when she'd entered. "This was a mistake. My cousin wished that I would come here, and so I did. I can do this myself. Thank you for your time."

Jessica rose from her own chair. Before she could get any words out, Amina had turned away from her.

Jessica spoke anyway, her words scrambling over each other in an attempt to beat Amina to the door. "I can assure you that we have the resources to provide you the best assistance so you are prepared for the rest of the asylum process." She hadn't been able to read through the application, so she couldn't call out anything in particular that Amina definitely needed help with from an attorney.

Amina pivoted, the steadiness and determination in her voice adding a bulk to her stature that layers of clothing did not. "I already had a lawyer who almost destroyed my chances. I will succeed or fail on my own. That is best. Again, thank you for your time."

The door closed softly behind Amina, leaving Jessica standing in a cold white room with crappy furniture, holding a single business card out to no one.

AFTER FIRING UP HER Audi, Jessica flipped over to the eighties station, hoping some nostalgic tunes might trick her into a better mood on the drive back to Annapolis. But her mind reeled with internal debate and analysis, and the New Wave music couldn't compete.

Thank God there had been no witnesses in that cold room. No one had ever doubted her abilities before, and now two people had: a Syrian woman who didn't even know her and, worse, Jessica herself.

Maybe she'd waited too long to go back to something substantial. All those PTA and community do-gooder jobs had kept her busy and showed she cared, but they hadn't kept her sharp. As a result, a woman had just rejected her offer of free legal assistance. A Muslim woman seeking asylum from a war-torn nation had rejected her help. And yet a rush of relief hit Jessica when Amina had walked out that door. Maybe it was all for the best, considering Jessica hadn't exactly sought out the role to begin with.

Months before, Jessica had run into the IAP director at a law school alumni gathering. She and Rosalie had stayed in touch since graduating from law school, but the relationship had diminished to Christmas cards and an occasional shout-out on social media. Rosalie had forwarded the alumni event invitation, urging Jessica to come to an event "just this once." Danny's business travel and late nights had picked up considerably, a hazard of success in the booming cybersecurity industry, so Jessica had taken advantage of the opportunity to mingle with some fellow alums.

She hadn't been to a networking-style event since she'd left her firm, and she'd found the private bar teeming with attorneys to be a hedonistic throwback to those law firm days. The receding hairlines in expensive suits were opportunities to upgrade from a current law firm or government agency to a new and better-paying opportunity. The bright eyes taking advantage of the sponsored buffet were a reminder of the rush she'd received from those big post–law school paychecks before the reality of houses and kids and life had set in. But without a professional goal in mind, it was hard to mix at those sort of networking events, and Jessica had found herself at the open bar with Rosalie, who wasn't looking to upgrade and had never desired the rush of a big paycheck.

The "refugee situation" and the influx of unaccompanied minors from Latin America were pretty big in the news, so Jessica had politely inquired how Rosalie was handling the workload in her new role as IAP director.

As Rosalie answered, Jessica's mind had drifted, fascinated by the solid streak of gray that cut through Rosalie's otherwise sensible bob. The spark of edginess contrasted with her practical department-store pantsuit. Rosalie got caught up in explaining the effects of immigration policies and global unrest on refugees in America, her words tumbling out with the rapidity of a teacher attempting to give as much of the lecture as possible before the bell rang.

The "And what have you been up to?" caught Jessica mid-sip. Since leaving her corporate law position at Highland & Cross, with its name-droppable clients and prominent reputation, she hadn't been able to give a solid answer to that question. Explaining what she'd been "up to" as a stay-at-home mom was even harder when talking with an impressively employed fellow grad. Kids, husband, school, house responsibilities, blah, blah, blah. Jessica had no grounded response even though she was quite busy, or at least had been until recently.

As Jessica fumbled, Rosalie pounced. "You have to come to the IAP information session." She placed her hand firmly on Jessica's upper arm, as if readying to pull Jessica back to the IAP offices that very moment. "Our next introductory session for *pro bono* attorneys is next month, in fact. You don't have to worry about doing a series of training sessions, just a couple up front. Then we assign you to a case with a staff attorney who can show you the ropes. Even though we're overflowing with requests for assistance, our volunteers only have to carry one case. This helps with our volunteer attorneys who are working regular jobs, so in your case, you might find you can carry more than one."

Ouch. Jessica shifted her stance, successfully prompting Rosalie to release the hold she had on Jessica's triceps. "Rosalie, I know it's been a while, but you *do* recall that I worked at H&C in securities compliance? If your refugees are planning to take a company public or are closing a venture capital round, I'd be pretty qualified to help once I brushed up on things a bit." She would need more than a *bit* of brushing up, but still. "Immigration, asylum, and all that weren't my area."

Rosalie was undeterred, words pouring out again unapologetically. "That won't be a problem at all. Most of our volunteers practice in areas completely unrelated to asylum. We have tax attorneys, divorce attorneys, patent attorneys, you name it." She extended her arm Vanna White–style toward the assembled collection of lawyers, who were getting louder as the bartenders poured more free drinks. "You'll be fine. And didn't you write your *Law Review* article on due process in eminent domain cases?"

Jessica had an inkling now of why Rosalie had invited her. "That's not immigration." She signaled for another cabernet. The event sponsor had sprung for a vintage Jessica would only buy if she was in need of fine liquid comfort.

"No, my point is that you clearly haven't limited your scope of knowledge to securities law. You'll pick things up quickly. I know you do a lot of volunteer work, and this comes closer to your training. Listen, it's a great way for attorneys to give back, and the people you help are wonderful. The mentor program is strong, and you'll learn everything you need to know before you get your first solo case. We have some retired attorneys who take on cases, but most are practicing, and they have no problem working the IAP case in with their full-time jobs."

She'd spoken as though Jessica had already signed up, and of course Jessica would, because that was what she did. For the past ten years or so, askers had benefitted from Jessica's need to say "yes" to every request for her to take on a volunteer position, even when she hadn't wanted to.

She wondered if that lack of desire *might* explain the shameful sense of relief that had washed over her when the Syrian had left the room that morning. Perhaps more shameful, and more likely the reason for the relief, though, was the gnawing discomfort in her gut when she'd discovered the identity of her client—a Muslim from Syria. *Give us your huddled masses, yearning to be free—just not the ones who scare me.*

Jessica took the on-ramp to the highway, squinted at the city in her rearview mirror, and asked her phone to dial Rosalie so she could tender her resignation for a job that had never really started.

CHAPTER TWO

Back in Annapolis on her neighborhood's tree-lined streets—streets free of *notarios* and barred windows—Jessica pushed the unwelcome inner dialogue out of her head. Having blocked off her day for meeting her new client and doing research for the case, she now had the day free. She didn't want to spend it arguing with herself about her capabilities and her possible prejudices, especially now that she had left a message on Rosalie's voice mail that she was done at IAP. "It's just not a good fit," she'd said.

A mature sugar maple, on the verge of exploding into fall colors, marked the Donnellys' century-old bungalow, a welcome view in any season when turning from Poplar Avenue onto Sycamore Street. Today, however, the tree cast a shadow on a yellow moving truck parked at the curb.

Jessica pulled into the driveway and checked her watch, though it wasn't going to tell her it was tomorrow, which was when the moving truck was supposed to arrive from Iowa with the remnants of her grandmother's estate. A man wearing a blue uniform was standing in front of the Donnellys' historic association-approved Revere red door, further confirming the truck was there for her. She slumped against the steering wheel then slowly peeled herself out of her car.

The man was wide in a way that wasn't fat. He was sturdy, as if he was built for balancing heavy furniture with his low center of gravity. He wasted no time after Jessica approached him. "Ma'am, we were just about to leave. Been waiting here for some time." He didn't mask the irritation in his voice as he folded and pocketed the note he had been taping to her door.

"Actually, you're a day early," Jessica said, not quite *un*masking her own irritation with the man's righteous tone.

"No, ma'am. We called." He waved toward the truck. A tall man, perhaps matched as the squat man's partner to provide an extra foot and a half of reach, exited the truck and walked toward the back.

"I didn't g—"

"Can you show me where you want us to put everything?"

Jessica resigned herself to replacing a day of law with a day of movers and stepped around the man to unlock the door. The lubrication-challenged hinges protested with a grating squeal when she pushed open the heavy wooden door.

Gracie, a labradoodle, more doodle than Lab, barked once at the man with the clipboard then nuzzled Jessica's hand, knowing, as dogs do, what her owner needed.

Jessica shooed Gracie away and directed the man to the parlor to the right of the front door.

The man peered into the room then back at Jessica. "We're gonna need some open floor space, ma'am. There's a lot of boxes out in the truck."

"To reiterate, I wasn't expecting you until tomorrow, so I hadn't cleared any space yet." Jessica set her purse by the stairs and moved to the parlor. "But we can do it now." She started to move the ottoman, sofa, and end tables out of the way, chucking her heels toward the stairs after nearly tumbling into a corner lamp. She had apparently been presumptuous with her use of the word "we," expecting that a moving guy would help her move things, but he just stood in the entryway, watching the amateur.

He nodded when she finished, as if approving a child's first attempt at a new task. "Should work. We'll get started." The man propped open the front door with a rubber doorstop he pulled out of his back pocket and walked toward the man standing at the back of the truck.

"Thanks for your help," Jessica said sarcastically, though not loud enough for him to hear, before picking up her shoes and her bag. Heading up the stairs to change out of her fancy lawyer clothes, Jessica ran her hand along the smooth handrail, reflexively rubbing a spot halfway up where she had used the wrong-colored filler to cover a nailhead. Danny swore no one else noticed it, but to Jessica, it looked like some half-assed job done on one of those DIY shows. It had been one of her earlier projects, and she had since learned to match fillers and stains properly.

The buzzing phone in her purse bumped DIY lamentations out of her mind. Seeing "Betty" on the screen, Jessica stopped on the top step. She answered on the fifth ring, just before it switched over to voice mail.

"Hi, Mom," Jessica said.

"Is the truck there?" her mom asked.

"Yes. How did you know? It's a day early."

"They called me to let me know they were ahead of schedule." Her mom paused. "Shoot, I meant to text you and completely forgot."

Jessica closed her bedroom door so she could change. "I wish you had let me know. I had a client meeting this morning and would have missed the truck if... if it had gone on any longer."

"A client meeting? For what?"

Jessica hadn't told her mom about the *pro bono* job and didn't want to, especially now that there wasn't one. "Just some volunteer stuff I'm working on."

"I figured it would be okay. You indicated last time we talked that you were around during the days now that you have another driver in the family and you're not in charge of the fall gala and most of those school committees."

"I do have other responsibilities, believe it or not." Jessica put the phone on speaker and set it on the dresser so she could hang up her slacks and jacket. "I still think it's crazy that I'm the one doing this. I get that Oma wanted me to be the executor of her estate because of the lawyer thing, but to ship a truck full of her things halfway across the country..." Jessica didn't need to remind her mom that she was far away. Jessica had put twelve hundred miles between them when she left for law school, though she'd added the real distance later. "Surely Kenny or Jason or you could have gone through it all."

"Your brothers don't have the time, and I simply don't have the space now that I've downsized. I guess you haven't seen my new condo. Well, not new." And there was the dig. Her mom had moved four years ago, and Jessica hadn't visited.

An uncomfortable silence filled the room through the speakerphone. Jessica grabbed a pair of jeans off a shelf and shoved her feet through the openings.

"I don't know that we'll have the space, either. I don't have an attic like Oma did."

"No one said you have to keep everything, or anything."

Jessica bristled at her mother's tone, trying to decide whether it was exasperation or disappointment she heard. Probably both.

"You are welcome to throw it all out. She just wanted you to go through it all and distribute or donate as you see fit. Maybe you'll find a treasure or two."

As a little girl, Jessica had loved to tag along with her grandmother to get something from the dusty alcove hidden by the door in the ceiling. Oma had always seemed to be reorganizing her things, sorting them in meticulously labeled boxes. Whether it was a box of old children's books, a stash of county-fair ribbons, or a board tacked with old campaign buttons, all were treasures to a curious child.

A shout muffled by the closed bedroom door interrupted her mental trip to the attic. "Ma'am? Can you help with the dog?"

"Shit. Mom, I need to go. Gracie is trying to guard all of the treasures. I need to go get her before the moving guys kill her." She threw on one of Danny's regatta T-shirts and opened the door.

"I understand." Her mom sounded far away, as though she'd turned away from her phone to attend to something.

Gracie barked, sending an echo up the stairway and prompting another call from the mover. "Ma'am?"

"Gotta go, Mom." Jessica slid the phone into her back pocket and got to the stairs just in time to see the movers bash a trunk into the wooden framing around the parlor entrance.

Gracie barked. *Good girl.* Gracie knew all the work that had gone into this house.

"Let's go, girl." Jessica grabbed the dog by the collar and led her past the dark stairway. Jessica had originally wanted to paint all the dark wood in the house to lighten things up and maybe give the place the beach-cottage look that was so common in the area. She had envisioned white wainscoting against walls painted the colors of sea glass. That style was not unlike the suit that now hung in her closet, a style that would have been wholly unfamiliar to her before she'd left small-town Idaville, Iowa.

But having three kids while working in a white-shoe law firm left no time for home improvement, and by the time she left H&C just over ten years ago, she had grown to love the Arts and Crafts styling of the house and had learned to appreciate the sturdiness and structure of the dark beams and moldings.

She had refinished the wood herself while getting her stay-at-home-mom "degree" in woodworking online during nap times and when the kids were at school. The amount of woodwork in the home was impressive, but once relieved of lawyer's hours, Jessica had not only had the time but had also welcomed the intense and sometimes intricate task of refurbishing the wood. The original craftsmanship that had gone into the details revealed itself even now as Jessica moved from the stairway back to the kitchen, admiring box beams and built-in benches.

Thanks to a prior owner who'd removed a wall, the kitchen was open to the family room, complete with its original drafty brick fireplace. The open room was the typical family gathering place, which would explain the mess that faced her as she walked in. Tuning out the sound of the movers' steel-toed boots on the wood floors in the entryway, Jessica attacked the dirty dishes in the sink, the newspapers strewn across the counter, a couple of green-clover marshmallows on the floor that Gracie's canine nose had somehow failed to sniff out, and some dirty soccer socks curiously placed on the kitchen table.

Each completed task pushed thoughts of the meeting with Amina further away.

Jessica scanned the room and ran through her mental checklist to make sure she hadn't missed anything. Green apples sat above red apples in the fruit bowl, and fresh sunflowers from the garden had replaced their droopy predecessors. The newspaper lay folded neatly on the end table next to the couch, and the dirty soccer socks had disappeared. The kitchen table glistened, and the smell of lemon zest lingered in the air. It was almost as if the morning had never even happened, at least if she didn't think about what was being unloaded into the parlor.

Jessica had missed out on one last attic visit when Oma broke her hip about seven or eight years ago and had to move into the assisted living facility. When Jessica thought about it, she realized she hadn't been in that attic since before she'd left for college. She had no idea what Oma had ended up keeping. After Jessica had gotten a place of her own and began taking pride in the simplicity of her space and not accumulating things for the sake of accumulation, she wondered if Oma might have been a bit of a hoarder. The mere fact that these things had been tucked away in an attic suggested there was no reason to keep them.

"Ma'am? We're done."

Jessica jumped, surprised she hadn't heard the boots approaching. The squat man with the clipboard leaned in through the kitchen doorway.

That hadn't taken very long. Maybe Oma had gone through a decluttering phase and the mover had overestimated the floor space they would need.

Jessica walked to the entryway. *Holy shit.* Oma had not decluttered. The moving guys were just really efficient. Stacks and stacks of boxes greeted her, some even placed in the dining room off the entryway and opposite the parlor. A jagged gash scarred the doorframe. The culprit, a vaguely familiar trunk, sat lodged among the boxes. Each box declared its contents via black Sharpie: *My Mementos, Mother's Dishes, My Glassware, My Quilt. Betty.* The box with her mom's things probably should have stayed in Iowa.

Oma had clearly been busy before she went to the assisted living facility, having done one last reorganization. And all of that reorganization disrupted the order Jessica had just reestablished. This unboxing was going to take longer than she had anticipated, though the morning's events cleared up her schedule considerably for the foreseeable future.

The man handed Jessica the clipboard. She reviewed the delivery invoice, which included a detailed list of the boxes and the contents as noted by the black marker, and scanned the rooms to compare. She took her time, partly because that was what she would normally do—dot the i's and cross the t's—but mostly to be passive-aggressive toward the man who stood fidgeting next to her. After everything checked out, Jessica signed the form and handed it back.

Jessica turned slowly as she creaked the door shut, facing off against the box-filled rooms flanking her. She would open one box, just to get an idea of what she was dealing with, then come up with a plan of attack.

Poking among the boxes in the parlor, she spied a smallish box marked "Open this box first." It triggered thoughts of *Alice in Wonderland,* but it did make the decision easy. After grabbing a pair of scissors from the kitchen, Jessica carefully sliced the clear packing tape that sealed the box, hoping not to find a bespectacled white rabbit inside.

The floral notes of Elizabeth Taylor's White Diamonds perfume wafted out of the box as Jessica folded back the cardboard flaps. *Oma.* Jessica's jaw muscles relaxed at the scent. She must have been clenching her teeth since she'd left Baltimore.

At the top of the box sat an unsealed lavender envelope.

Oma's handwriting was unmistakable. Each tiny letter was schoolhouse perfect, and each line was written as though she had used a ruler as a guide. The "Dear Jessica" with the tree-stump r and flowing J made Jessica recall countless letters she'd received in college, law school, and beyond. Most of Oma's letters had included a newspaper clipping of a story from home that she thought Jessica would like or coupons from the Sunday circular. Those letters had always included a return envelope, stamped and addressed to Oma. Jessica hated herself a little bit at the memory of throwing a stack of those out at the end of every term.

Dear Jessica,

These boxes contain my memories and memories of my mother, my grandmother, my great-grandmother, etc. I could never get rid of these things, even though I couldn't take them to the 'Old Folks Home' with me. They are full of history. I've included notes in each box. I never wrote my memoirs, but maybe these notes are little bits and pieces!

Oma

Under the wadded-up yellowed newspaper—Canned Yams $.69 at Family Grocery!—the "Open this box first" box revealed a plain metal box.

The smell of stale cigars and aged paper caught her off guard as she removed the lid from the container. She closed her eyes and inhaled. Oma was clever, starting her off with this box. Jessica opened her eyes and started to leaf through the newspaper clippings inside. Then she gasped, and her eyes filled just enough that she had to blink to staunch any tears from falling. The headline read, "Local Employee Recognized by Postal Service." The bald man with the jug ears was grinning in the photo. The gap between his front teeth and the Kirk Douglas chin triggered a smile of remembrance. Jessica rubbed her own dimpleless chin. *Loved it on you, Gramps.*

He stood next to a wooden desk, with his right hand, as always, in his pocket. It was one of those old oak desks found in any government building back then—nothing fancy, no shiny lacquer or inlaid ebony, but it was heavy as hell and built to last. Gramps was just that: nothing fancy but solid and reliable.

That particular wooden desk was the one he would sneak Jessica and her brothers back to when they visited him at the post office. He would get fired, he'd told them conspiratorially, if anyone found out he let anyone in the back office. But they were worth the risk, he would say. The top left drawer had always been full of Brach's caramels. They would each get one. Well, the boys would get one, and Gramps would palm an extra to Jessica with a wink. "Cuz you're my *other* good-luck charm. You're the prettiest and the smartest, and I know you'll show your brothers a thing or two someday."

Jessica and her brothers would sneak out of the office, opening the caramel wrappers as they went. Just looking at the photo, Jessica could feel the creamy meltiness of the caramel as it dissolved in her mouth. Grinning, she remembered how devious she'd felt, knowing that she had another one she could enjoy alone in her room after they got home.

At the bottom of the container, she found a large coin so worn and smooth that she knew the denomination only because she had seen Gramps with it so many times. She picked up the silver dollar and held it between her thumb and two fingers. She could trace the barest outline of a head, but she couldn't make out the date.

Ruefully eyeing the boxes that surrounded her and cluttered what had been a decidedly uncluttered space just an hour before, Jessica could only think of what she would have to show for her own life one day. She had left Idaville so she could do important things, achieve things that were impossible to do in a small town in the middle of nowhere. The boxes were no longer a distraction but more of a warning.

Jessica found herself reflexively rubbing the smooth silver from the box and put the coin in her pocket. Based on today's events, she might need it.

CHAPTER THREE
AMINA

Amina breathed in the exhaust-tainted air as she shed the feel of the IAP offices. The somber facility was stifling enough, but the windowless meeting room with propaganda on the walls had felt more like an interrogation room than a place to seek asylum. Seeing the lawyer pull in her breath so sharply when Amina walked in the room had set Amina on edge even more. She could still feel the tension in her own brow.

Although the lawyer had tried to say the right things, she'd looked at Amina through eyes that didn't understand. The lawyer had borne a practiced posture of strength, her square shoulders and long neck asserting innate power, but her eyes had shown weakness in the way they couldn't quite meet Amina's. Walking out of the office had reminded Amina of her own strength, and moving through the city streets bolstered the sense of independence she knew she needed to survive.

As she approached the next intersection, Amina squinted at the sunlight reflecting off the windows of a building up ahead. The cityscape blurred, and Amina could almost envision home. Almost. The warm sun on her face was the same elixir. But even with the outlines of the buildings blurred, Baltimore was no Aleppo.

Silent pedestrians plugged into headphones replaced men chattering loudly in Arabic. Impersonal storefronts replaced the vibrant and social markets she had loved to visit with her mother. Mostly, though, there were no mortar explosions, no sniper shots, and no screaming women calling for their dead children.

But that had been later.

She had reserved much of the day for the meeting she'd just walked out on, so she didn't have to be to work until late afternoon. The unexpected freedom meant she could get to the library for the first time in weeks.

She had discovered the Enoch Pratt Free Library shortly after filing her asylum claim. Initially, the wealth of books had drawn her in, limitless possibilities contained in shelf after shelf of inquiry. But as the war in Syria continued and grew in intensity, the library had become her haven of knowledge of a war she could no longer watch on television.

The quick-edit flashes of video, the cracks of the bombs, the stressed commentary of embedded journalists, the images of injured children and sobbing mothers—all were broadcast here in a country that couldn't make any of it stop. She didn't need to be brought back to the horror via satellite.

Though she couldn't bear to watch her country's demise on television, she devoured the newspapers at Pratt so she could stay informed about her home. True, she had fled the country and could not return, but it would always be home. Between the *Post*, the *Times*, and the *Wall Street Journal*, she could read about the horror and choose not to turn the page, and she didn't have to hear the sounds of death or watch her countrymen moving about as ghosts among rubble that used to be bustling city streets. The thought of her family as ghosts, whether dead or alive, still darkened her heart, and every image that wasn't one of those who might still be alive pulled her further away.

A blaring horn brought Amina's attention back to America. A taxi driver yelled at her in a language not her own. She held up her hand in apology and stepped back onto the curb. Fluttering hands and a hijab to the left caught Amina's attention. A woman not much younger than herself, wearing a light floral scarf with her modest blouse, fashionable jeans, and Chuck Taylor sneakers, descended the stairs of a brick building ahead, chatting animatedly with a young man. The woman was American, Amina deduced, based on the un-accented English. She seemed so comfortable, her arms flowing in a visual melody punctuated by her laughter. A hunger filled Amina's gut, a longing to move her own arms that freely again. They had been weights at her side, holding her back, for too long.

She hoped to catch the young woman's eye, to learn a bit of her melody, but the couple turned away from Amina, caught up in their own news of the day. A lost opportunity for connection, the moment blended in with the everyday reality of the streets. Sometimes Amina would catch someone sneaking a peek at her or even blatantly star-ing, but most people were too focused on where they were going next to interact with those around them. Lack of connection was better than conflict, perhaps, though it was probably a lack of connection that led to conflict.

Rounding the corner past the Baltimore Basilica, she saw the massive library that occupied a city block. Amina considered the late Enoch Pratt's vision that she'd read in the lobby: a library for "rich and poor without distinction of race or color." The quote accurate-ly portrayed the library today. Amina herself fulfilled much of that vision as she entered through the tall metal doors. Today, this poor woman from Syria would be researching for her asylum case.

One of the great frustrations of the asylum process had been the absolute uncertainty of timing. In limbo for over two years, Ami-na had been both relieved and fearful when she'd read the newly re-leased asylum office waiting times that indicated she could hear from the office in as soon as a few months with an interview date. She was no immigration lawyer, but she knew that if she presented a good case in the interview, she could be approved and not have to go before a judge, where approvals were even less likely.

She was in control and would be prepared, and she would start with staying up to date on the current political and martial state of Syria.

Amina joined the job seekers needing to print résumés, the homeless regulars seeking reading material or air conditioning, and the others for whom the Pratt was a refuge. The *Washington Post* awaited her, and she took a spot at a table in a corner below a window.

In a midpage headline, the *Post* revealed another broken ceasefire. Amina didn't need to read the paper to be reminded of the endless series of broken promises. The Syrian regime had promised change during the protests and demonstrations of the Arab Spring, and the world had promised support for Syrian civilians. But the regime decided to go to war against its own people, and the world stood by. A broken ceasefire didn't seem like such a huge breach of trust anymore.

Nor was the news in the politics section a surprise. Congressional action would increase refugee review and immigration enforcement requirements without increasing funding or resources. This was one of the reasons asylum cases took so long already. Diversion of even more resources meant that Amina and others like her could expect their state of limbo to be indefinite, and the interview notice could be potentially put on hold forever.

IAP materials advised asylum seekers to "live your life as though you are staying in America forever." That was easy for them to say, but for someone in America due to broken promises, it seemed almost suicidal to make efforts that could lead to further disappointment.

Amina replaced the *Post* and picked out the *Wall Street Journal*. Finding two students conferring at her table when she returned, she headed to a different section of the library to find a quiet spot.

As Amina walked through the atrium, a woman passed with a young child. Amina silently guessed at the girl's age. It was a sad game she couldn't keep from playing when she saw young children, thinking about lost opportunities to have her own family. This little blond girl, whose mom wore a matching dress, looked about four and a half. Amina smiled at the girl, whose eyes opened wide as she stared up at Amina.

The little girl tugged on her mom's hand and, without taking her eyes off Amina, urged, "Mom, Mom. Look."

The newspaper crinkled as Amina clutched her bag to her chest like a shield. The mom gasped sharply then hushed the girl and scurried away. Amina didn't want to decide whether the woman's expression reflected shame over her daughter's staring or aversion to the object of her daughter's curiosity. What mattered more was that the little girl was learning to associate that reaction with the woman in the hijab.

A connection was severed, and limitless possibilities started to look more limited. But Amina had endured worse than the shocked face of a mother in a library.

CHAPTER FOUR

At the squeak of protesting hinges, the dog started barking again. Jessica set down the half-diced onion and checked her watch. It was close to dinnertime, and the kids were due home anytime.

The whistled melody drifting into the kitchen triggered a smile. It wasn't the kids, but it was proof that something good had happened today.

Gracie bounded into the room, followed by her sailing partner. Gracie wasn't particularly helpful as crew, but she loved to lap at the spray when the wind was high, and Danny was happy to bring her aboard.

"Wasn't expecting you home so early," Jessica said. Late nights at the office had been the norm for Danny this year. His increasing hours somehow made Jessica's diminishing responsibilities more apparent to her, though he had been too busy to notice. He might notice her tension after today's events, though, and could hopefully help her work through it.

He, on the other hand, moved as if he hadn't a care in the world, which certainly wasn't true. Staying calm under pressure had always served him well on a sailboat, and it translated well to business. "Hope you don't mind, hon." He tilted his sun-streaked head slightly in the direction of the front of the house. "We seem to have some boxes that weren't here when I left this morning." He set his laptop case on the table and grabbed an apple.

"They were a day early, and yes, there are a few more boxes than I expected. You'd think Oma would have gotten rid of everything when she moved into the facility, right? But I guess if you live through the Depression... ugh. I just don't know what I'm going to do with it all." Jessica picked up her knife and started chopping again.

"You might want to make sure no one else names you executor of their estate." He took a bite of the apple. "Otherwise, we might need to bunk up with the kids to make room for another load of boxes." His blue eyes twinkled. "And we don't want that." He leaned in for a kiss, running his hand from her shoulder to her lower back. He pulled his head back, maintaining his hold on her. "Do we have time for a little..." He arched his eyebrows mischievously.

The front door squeaked open then slammed shut, closing out any chance for a rare afternoon tryst that would have taken the sting off of the morning's events. The door squeaked open again. She really needed to WD-40 the hell out of that thing.

"Hey," yelled a prepubescent voice. "Why'd you shut the door on me?" Footsteps pounded up the stairs, then a door slammed shut.

"Clearly not. Isn't Conor being an ass lately?" She wasn't sure Danny had been around enough to notice Conor's attitude.

Fortunately, their kids weren't all angsty teenagers. Her curly-haired eleven-year-old burst into the kitchen and threw his backpack on the table. The bucktoothed grin indicated that he had already gotten over having the door slammed in his face by his big brother.

"So..." Jessica prompted. "How did the speech go?"

"It was crazy!" Mikey's wild-eyed expression shot back and forth from Jessica to Danny, who had moved to the couch in the family room, as though wondering which one of them to tell.

Jessica walked to the couch when he picked Danny, and the words came tumbling out.

"We were giving our speeches, and Andy Franklin, do you know him? He got up and got totally freaked out, and then he threw up.

Not a whole lot, just a little. But it was on the thing you give the speech from."

"Lectern. It's called a lectern." Jessica motioned for Mikey to continue, hoping she could keep up with him.

"Right, so the *lectern* was all gross, and they moved it off the stage so they could clean it up. I had already given my speech, so I didn't have to go up there after him. The rest of the people had to hold their speeches in their hands, and the principal held the microphone for them."

"Did Andy get the sympathy vote?" Jessica could certainly sympathize with nerves and a sick stomach.

"I'm not really sure what you mean by that, but he did get president. And I got vice president!" Mikey grinned, giant dimples forming as if to provide more space for his joy.

"Just a heartbeat away from the presidency, son," Danny said. "Or an upset stomach away, perhaps. Be ready to take over." He ruffled Mikey's hair then pulled his phone out of his pocket and started scrolling down the screen—the parent hand-off signal. Danny might have been home from the office early, but that didn't mean he was home from work.

"We're proud of you, Mikey. It takes guts—no pun intended—to get up there and speak in front of your class." Jessica picked up the backpack from the table and held it out. "Even vice presidents have to do their homework, though. Get going. Can you tell Conor dinner will be ready around six thirty? Cricket should be home from swim practice by then."

"Got it." Mikey stopped in the doorway and hollered to Conor.

"Well, I could have done that." Jessica sighed. "Looks like we've got a little more time alone. Do you want to help with dinner?" *And tell me I'm not a failure?*

Danny glanced up from his screen. "Sorry, hon. I've got to go take care of something. One of our customers got a hacker scare today. The software did its job, but their CTO is panicking. I should be done talking him off the ledge by dinnertime."

So much for some alone time together. But if anyone could talk someone off a ledge, it was Danny. He always looked and sounded relaxed in that way sailors do. It was deceptive. She knew he was always on the alert, whether for a change in the wind or a security threat at work. But he exuded the calm and cool that reassured everyone around him that they would get through the storm.

He had been exactly what Jessica needed when she'd first fallen into those bay-blue eyes. And today, she had hoped to talk to him about her own morning and get a neutral and reassuring perspective. But work took precedence. She understood. Her morning wasn't of critical importance.

The outside corners of Danny's eyes crinkled when he smiled, more today than they had back then, but they still sent her insides spinning. "I'm sure you've got everything covered." He kissed her as a promise for later and sailed out of the room.

CRICKET'S hair was still wet from practice, her auburn curls piled into a bun atop her head, but she completed the group to allow for a proper family dinner. With Danny's late nights and the kids' crazy schedules, people had gotten used to throwing together a plate from what Jessica put out, and they now hovered near the kitchen counter like vultures.

"Have a seat, people." Jessica shooed them toward the table. "We're doing this old school. A good old-fashioned family dinner. Leave your phones over here." She tapped the granite counter with a serving spoon, eliciting groans all around.

Three phones soon lay on the counter, one already vibrating with messages. "Set it on Do Not Disturb, please, Crick." Jessica tapped the counter again, feeling like a schoolmarm. Cricket grudgingly changed the settings and joined everyone at the table.

Jessica brought over the platters and started passing them. Danny looked relaxed in a tattered golf shirt and plaid shorts. He must have talked the client off the ledge. Jessica searched his face for a clue and was rewarded with a wink. Danny then turned off his own phone and placed it on the counter with the others.

Conor ate silently, his heavy eyebrows shielding his occasional glances around the table, while Mikey and Cricket argued about who they would have on their zombie-apocalypse team. Their dad made the team not because software development skills would be essential but because zombies couldn't swim and Dad could sail them out of reach of the dead hordes. The argument centered on whether they would bring Gracie. Ever the pragmatist, Cricket was on board with the dog because, well, "We might need to eat her." Mikey wanted to bring Gracie as a companion but not if his sister planned to make dog burgers out of the poor thing.

"I wouldn't make dog burgers." She shook her head at her brother's naïveté. "We have to plan for the long haul. I'm thinking we would make dog jerky." She tented her fingers and placed them to her lips. "Then we could pack her up and have protein snacks that wouldn't spoil." Now she was just pushing Mikey's buttons.

Jessica jumped in just as Mikey's reddening face threatened to burst. "Did you hear Mikey was voted vice president today, Conor?" Jessica prodded her oldest, hoping to pull the glowering teen into conversation.

Conor ran his fingers through his golden hair, standing it up in faltering spikes. "The student council doesn't do anything in middle school. They all say they're going to add more dress-down days and have pizza delivery days in the cafeteria, but all they end up doing is decorating signs for the spring social." He sneered in Mikey's direction. "Make sure you have some sparkly markers, Mikey."

Red embarrassment replaced red anger on Mikey's face, and Jessica's youngest trained his focus on the salad he was pushing around his plate with a fork.

Jessica gave Conor a death stare for being a jackass, but he wouldn't give her the pleasure of looking in her direction. "Mikey, we're proud of you for going out for the student council. Right, honey?" She nudged Danny with her psychic powers, not wanting to be the sole defender against sibling rivalry.

Danny obliged. "Of course. Congratulations, Mikey. Conor, we'd love to hear about *your* latest successes."

Conor had no response, but Mikey sat a little taller now.

Zombie-apocalypse planning resumed then morphed into updates on everyone's day. Swim practice was grueling, the math quiz was easy, the sixth grade was having a bowling social next week, and everyone wanted to know if there was something for them in all those boxes from Oma.

———— ❦ ————

ONCE the kitchen sparkled again, ready to be destroyed afresh in the morning, Jessica headed toward the stairs so she could pick up with Danny where they'd left off when Conor and Mikey had interrupted them.

Movement in the parlor stopped her at the base of the stairs. Someone must have taken her up on her offer to open a box or two.

Jessica stepped into the room. "Hi."

Cricket sat on a chair that Jessica had pushed next to the doorway earlier. A tan leatherette jewelry case sat open on her lap. "Jewelry," she said simply.

Oma had kept her few pieces of fine jewelry with her at the assisted living facility, and they had gone to Jessica's mom, to be divided among the granddaughters someday. "It's probably just Oma's costume jewelry. But you can have it. I bet there's something in there you might like."

Cricket held up a silver cross embedded with rough squares of green stone. "I really like this. It had a note with it that said it was Oma's grandmother's. Grandma Margarethe?"

In the lamplight, the color of Cricket's eyes, a green deeper than even her mom's, glinted as if they were reflecting the stones.

Jessica stepped forward for a better look. "So pretty. I think I might have a silver chain that would go with it. I'll check upstairs."

Cricket placed the cold cross in her hand. Surprisingly heavy, the cross invited Jessica to embrace it in her fist.

Cricket left the room, taking the jewelry case with her. The collection of boxes didn't look any less daunting than it had earlier in the day. It just looked like a lot of work. But maybe there would be more than a couple of gems among Oma's things.

———— ❧ ————

"Why, Jessica, have you found religion?" The mirror above the vanity reflected Danny's feigned look of sincerity. Mussed hair lent to his air of earnestness. They weren't regular churchgoers, though Danny had been raised Catholic.

Jessica laughed. "Oma's grandmother, the kids'..." Jessica set the cross on the vanity and counted out on her fingers. "Great-great-great-grandma Margarethe, I guess. Crick found it in one of the boxes downstairs. I'm sure I have a chain that would work with it." She lifted the lid of a chestnut jewelry box.

"Celtic."

"Pardon me?" Jessica didn't look up from the jewelry box. The tangle of silver knots made it hard to see if she had a chain long enough for the pendant. The silver dollar already had its spot in the corner, catching light from the lamp on the dresser.

"This is a Celtic cross. See the etchings?"

She picked it back up. "Ah, and the circle. Of course." Jessica hadn't noticed the etchings in the lamplit parlor, but they were distinctly Celtic, with dense, interwoven lines between the green stones. "Remember when we got married and Oma cornered me in the church?" Jessica put on her best northern Iowa accent. "'Since you're marrying an Irish...' I loved how she always called you 'an Irish.'"

"Makes me sound like a dog." He glanced over at Gracie, who lay at the end of the bed. "No offense, Gracie."

Gracie didn't lift her head, but her tail wagged in acknowledgment.

"She said we had some Irish in our family, but it was something that just wasn't discussed. You know, like cancer or homosexuality. I figured it was just a bit of fun because of my green eyes, especially considering my great-grandma's references to the 'dreaded papacy' when I was a kid." She jabbed Danny playfully.

"I was an altar boy, I'll have you know. Even thought about becoming a priest." Danny raised his eyebrows, daring her to challenge his qualifications.

"You would have been the 'hot priest.' That's for sure." She brushed away his wandering hands, which had found their way from her shoulders to her hips. "Though I don't know how you would have been able to keep your vows." Jessica finally freed a chain from the knotted mess and threaded it through the loop on the pendant. "In any case, I like it. Oma seems to have a few surprises up her sleeve. Do you think I'll look like Madonna, circa 1985?" She held the necklace over her chest.

"Only if you wear it with your cone bra."

He didn't seem to remember her plans for the day, so Jessica asked him about his. "I didn't get a chance to ask you how your meeting went today. You seemed to be in a pretty good mood when you got home." Jessica flicked off the light before sliding under the covers.

The bed creaked as Danny climbed in beside her. "Things are moving along. I met with our contact at the Department of Defense, and he said Binnacle's proposal is really strong. None of the other firms have the encryption capabilities that our team has put together. From there, it's just a matter of politics."

This was a big deal, possibly the biggest in Binnacle's history, and not because the company wasn't already successful. An encryption software patent and a charismatic founder who put in crazy hours ensured that it was. But this deal, with both its scope and its high profile, would propel the company into the vanguard of the industry. It was why Danny had been working so much this year and would likely continue to do so if they got the contract. "What exactly are they buying from you?"

"If I told you, I'd have to kill you." Danny's steely eyes bore through Jessica before he cracked a smile.

It still made her laugh. Early in their relationship, she had learned he couldn't tell her about some of his work, and he knew she couldn't tell him about hers, back when she was a practicing attorney, anyway. She thought about her earlier client meeting and cringed at Amina's rejection of her and of her own relief in the rejection.

"But I can say that the table you made for my office out of that old ship hatch door made quite the impression when he came in today, hon. He's a naval officer, and he knows good work when he sees it. I know I always questioned you leaving those remnants of the original naval gray paint on it, but that's what pulled him in. He's convinced it's from a World War II ship. Between your workmanship and our product, the meeting went really well."

"I'm glad somebody had a good client meeting today."

"That doesn't sound good. What happened with yours?" He placed his hand on her cheek, the warmth helping ease the lingering ache from the clenched jaw.

"I showed up expecting Leslie to be running the show, but she ghosted." She rolled over and turned off the lamps, first on her side of the bed, then on Danny's side. Then she decided that even the dark wouldn't make giving him a play-by-play less demoralizing. "Let's just say it didn't go well."

"You'll bounce back. You always pull things together." He ran his hand past her cheek and through her hair then pulled her closer.

She was on no ledge, but she'd hoped he would at least sense her self-doubt, ask more questions, and say something to validate her internal conflict—the fear of leaving behind nothing but boxes, the memory of the failed meeting that morning, and her sick feeling about not being as open-minded as she thought she was. Instead, he caressed her back and kissed her softly on her temple.

She may not have wanted to be in that office this morning, but this could be worse, to be so dependent on someone else to validate her feelings. If she started to unload on him now, it would prove a reliance on Danny's imprimatur or confirm that she was a failure, or both.

Jessica rested her head on Danny's bare chest as he pressed the full length of his body against hers. She would need to figure this one out herself.

CHAPTER FIVE

"Jessica, I am so sorry about the mess the other day. If I hadn't been at the conference, I would have been able to help out." Rosalie sat behind a desk that seemed much too cluttered for someone who was the director of the IAP.

"It's fine," Jessica replied. "It was just unexpected, having to go in there myself." *And be faced with a defensive woman from Syria rather than a sweet, scared child from Guatemala.* But she couldn't say that out loud.

"I hope you'll reconsider volunteering, though. I know you said in your message that this isn't a good fit for you—"

"Forget I left that message. I called in the heat of rejection. I've had some time to think about it." That, and she'd had time to realize that if she gave into self-doubt and other weaknesses, she wouldn't like the person she became. "I'm still on board."

"Great." Rosalie clasped her hands together and leaned forward, her brow furrowed. "So, what happened in your meeting?"

"I met Amina Hamid, and she fired me." Jessica shrugged to mask the remnants of her earlier embarrassment.

Rosalie pursed her lips in commiseration. "Yes, you mentioned that. Any reason? What did she tell you?" She put on red-rimmed reading glasses and then, somehow knowing which of the hundred or so folders on her desk was the right one, pulled out the Hamid file.

"She didn't tell me anything. She just didn't like the idea of having me as her attorney. We really should have rescheduled for when

Leslie was available. I think Leslie could have explained to her the challenges of not having an attorney and what IAP can do to help. Is she back?"

Rosalie drummed her fingers on the desk, staring intently at Jessica. "Leslie isn't coming back for a while."

Jessica caught herself tapping her foot against the chair leg and stopped. "Oh, okay, that's fine. I can shadow her replacement or some other attorney. I'm flexible."

Rosalie squinted, drawing Jessica's eyes toward hers. "Believe me when I say I would love to have a replacement lined up. But I don't have a replacement lined up. It's tough as a nonprofit to fill some of these staff positions. It's hard to compete with the law firms and the corporations." She locked onto Jessica's gaze, and Jessica restrained herself from squirming.

In law school, Rosalie had distinguished herself as an outward-thinking progressive on day one, joining the indigent legal clinic and assorted service-oriented student groups before graduating and heading to Thailand to do human rights work. Meanwhile, Jessica had joined so many of her classmates, heading off after graduation to make serious money at a big law firm without leaving much of a community service mark behind her.

For Jessica, it wasn't about the paychecks, though they were nice. It was about the bigger and better things she had promised herself when she'd decided to leave Iowa. Working at a big firm and representing international clients on multimillion-dollar deals was heady stuff—the kind of work that a kid who'd worried she might never leave Idaville couldn't even have dreamed of doing.

Yet somehow, Rosalie had just made Jessica feel personally responsible for making it difficult for nonprofits to hire attorneys.

Rosalie pulled her keyboard forward. "I can assign you to shadow a different attorney on one of their open cases. Let's see..." She opened a spreadsheet populated with tiny, anonymous font.

Jessica interrupted Rosalie's scrolling. "What about the Hamid case?"

The corners of Rosalie's mouth turned downward. "If Ms. Hamid doesn't want us on her case, we're under no obligation to pursue it. We can't force ourselves on her. Besides"—Rosalie waved her arms, highlighting not just the files on her desk but also the ones on the file cabinet and on the floor next to it—"we aren't hurting for cases."

It made sense to focus on the people who were happy to accept IAP's help, and there seemed to be an endless supply. But Jessica couldn't shake the feeling of smallness she'd had when Amina walked out that door two days before. She had to prove she could handle this case—to Amina and to herself. "I want to do Ms. Hamid's case." She almost surprised herself with the definitiveness of her assertion, but the resulting jolt of confidence in her chest confirmed the veracity of the statement.

Rosalie brushed her fingers through her gray streak, mixing it with the dark strands around it. She flipped the first few pages of Amina's file. "We always give our newest volunteers uncomplicated cases so we don't scare them away. That's why I assigned you to this one." She spoke slowly, letting her thoughts form before the words came out. Rosalie threaded her forefinger behind the gray, and the colors separated again. "It should be manageable. Ms. Hamid speaks English, and she has her application submitted already." She closed the file. "You would just need to help her through the rest of the process."

Jessica knew there was no "just need to" in asylum cases, and she noted the "you" that Rosalie employed seemed to be singular, as in singular to Jessica. "Assuming Ms. Hamid agrees to go with IAP, when will you know who her staff attorney is?" she asked, dreading the answer.

Rosalie placed the file back on the pile in front of her, removed her glasses, and twirled them thoughtfully. "We are being overrun. You can handle this case yourself. Of course, I and the other staff are here to help you, and you know we have a resource library here and access to extensive online materials. If you'd rather handle a case with a staff attorney, I would honestly rather put you on a different one than burden one of our staff with another case."

Shaking her head, Jessica privately resolved never to attend any law school alumni event ever again, lest she run into someone who might rope her into another *pro bono* position she didn't have the balls to say no to.

Jessica expected to see an air of triumph on Rosalie's face for having converted a reluctant volunteer into a champion for the persecuted, but Rosalie remained pensive. "I'll take the headshake as confirmation that you want to do this yourself." Rosalie patted Amina's file. "The application does look pretty thin. If what's in there is accurate, then your job—if you can convince her to work with you—will be to help flesh out her story, pull together documentation, and get her prepared for her interview, because her interview could come at any time. I'm guessing four to five months based on the current backlog. You'll have to be on your toes to pull everything together and get it to the USCIS."

Rosalie leaned back in her chair. "It's worth going over a few things now, especially considering some of the things I learned at the conference. When you came in for introductory sessions, you met a lot of children and families from Latin American countries."

"Right," Jessica said. "And I expected an unaccompanied minor. Where the hell did you find a Syrian? It's not easy to get into the States from over there... Can you even get into the States from over there?"

"You're right. There aren't many Syrians seeking asylum, and that's because it's so hard to get into the country. But after the civil war began, a lot of Syrians with means were able to leave Syria, some before the travel restrictions. Others with means had connections that helped them even after the restrictions. Most went to Europe or other Middle Eastern countries. But a small number ended up here. Amina's one of the few."

"Lucky me."

"Lucky her," Rosalie corrected. "Though she'll need more luck. There are always political arguments around immigration in general, but the public rhetoric against Middle Eastern refugees is off the charts, and politicians are feeling the heat about tightening restrictions and reviews. I'm sure I don't need to tell you that. But here's something you might not know yet." She leaned forward again, inviting Jessica into the immigration lawyer fold by imparting special information. "The US will be accepting a wave of Middle Eastern refugees by the end of the year, with even more after that. This is going to make it hard for people like Amina. There will be a lot of political pressure, and the bar for Muslims—probably anyone, to be honest—seeking asylum will be higher, even if the USCIS doesn't admit it."

A wave of second thoughts washed over Jessica, triggering her foot to tap against the chair leg again. She uncrossed her legs and anchored each foot to the ground.

"You have to emphasize the importance of honesty, consistency, and evidence with her." Rosalie's attention diverted again, this time abruptly, to a pile next to her computer, and she selected the top folder. "We just brought on a case for a man from Venezuela who was smuggled by a coyote. A *notario* charged him five thousand dollars to put together his application, and the application was a complete fraud. The immigrant doesn't speak English and had no idea what was going on, but he signed the application and let the guy file it. He's barred now. Deportation is imminent. We can try to file for reconsideration based on the circumstances, but..." She shrugged.

With Amina's unwavering stare still vivid in her mind, Jessica paced through what she knew. "Ms. Hamid seems pretty savvy and tenacious. She speaks three languages. She managed to get the asylum filing done accurately and on time. She has a job. She's educated. She probably could follow the process by herself, though with the increased scrutiny, I imagine her odds of success are slim without an attorney."

"Are you trying to convince me or you?" Rosalie displayed a hint of the triumphant air Jessica had missed seeing earlier, though maybe it was just supportive amusement.

"Ms. Hamid's the one I need to convince. I'll follow up with her and see if I can get her to meet with me. I don't have any delusions that I exude charm—I leave that to Danny. But I'll review her file, do some research, and try to talk with her. She'll have to open up for me to help her, though."

"Let's give it a week. If she's on board by the end of next week, great. If not, we'll reconsider assigning you to a different case."

Jessica gathered her bag and case file and stood up to leave.

"Jessica, I think you have a tiny bit of charm." Rosalie rose from her chair, grinning mischievously. "I seem to recall a law student sweet-talking her way into a presidential inaugural ball without a ticket."

Jessica felt her cheeks flush a bit. "Why, I don't know *what* you're talking about. But I'm sure that law student you speak of was just seeking to understand the electoral process more deeply."

"In a ball gown at an open bar." Rosalie arched an eyebrow knowingly. "Seriously. I think you'll make this work. She might see that you are pretty savvy and tenacious yourself."

Rosalie's comment sounded gratuitous, but that didn't diminish the trace of confidence Jessica had felt earlier. After all, Jessica had convinced both herself and Rosalie to take Amina's case, and she took a little pride in that. But wanting to take the case was just the first step. While the hardest part would be building Amina's case for convincing the interviewer, Jessica knew she first had to build her *own* case for convincing Amina.

CHAPTER SIX

White ceramic bowls of fresh guacamole, chopped cilantro, lime crema, and pico de gallo decorated the kitchen table in red, white, and green. Only the roasted corn broke the color coordination of Jessica's fish-taco buffet. Jessica had hit the grocery store after her meeting with Rosalie that morning, hoping to pull off a second family dinner for the week.

"You sure you won't join me, Danny? It's a little uncomfortable eating by myself with you sitting there watching me." Only Danny and Jessica sat at the table. Only Jessica had a plate of food in front of her. Cricket and Conor had begged off family dinner, filling plates as quickly as Jessica could put the food out, then headed to their rooms. Mikey's soccer practice had been rescheduled, and he wouldn't be home until later.

"I like watching you eat."

Jessica searched his face for a smirk, the twitch of an eyebrow, or some other indication of sarcasm. All she saw was a face utterly relaxed in its sincerity, so she obliged by taking a giant, messy bite of a fully loaded taco. That, satisfyingly, elicited a smirk.

"That's what I'm talking about, hon. As I was saying, we're meeting up at Lewnes' for dinner, otherwise I'd be on my second taco already. They remind me of that trip the two of us took to San Diego." Distractedly, his eyes moved from her eyes to lower on her face. "You've got some... right here." He reached out his hand and wiped his finger slowly across Jessica's lower lip then put it in her mouth so she could lick off the lime crema.

"When's the last time your high school group got together?" Jessica asked before taking another bite.

Danny furrowed his brow. "At least... seven or eight years. Dave took that job in Hong Kong about that long ago, so it can't have been more recently. I'm impressed he was able to get us all together this time. It was pretty last minute." His eyes moved to her mouth again. "More lime crema? Are you doing this on purpose?" He wiped her lip with his finger again, eyeing her with suspicion.

"Maybe." Jessica leaned in for a crema kiss. "I'll wait up for you."

Danny finished the kiss and ran his fingers through her hair. "Better not. We're likely to be out late. Gotta make up for the years. Who knows when we'll see each other again?"

You and the guys, or you and me? She felt guilty the moment she thought it since he rarely went out with friends, especially lately, and his busy schedule hadn't stopped her from her regular girls' nights.

"Gotta go, hon." Danny stood and stretched. "I'm sure the kids'll keep you busy tonight."

AFTER PUTTING AWAY the remnants of dinner, Jessica made her way to the second floor to collect dirty dishes. The stairs creaked with each step, so familiar now that she could identify the stair based on the sound. An old house had things to say. It drove Danny crazy. He thought that surely Jessica had learned enough by now to fix the steps. She could fix a loose tread, yes, but she couldn't eliminate a century's worth of creaks even if she wanted to.

Cricket's door hung open, and Jessica could see feet bopping to the beat of some unheard music. Pushing the door open wider, she smiled, seeing her daughter, pencil in hand, working through math problems while listening to something on her headphones. According to Cricket, listening to hip-hop while doing math helped her synthesize the concepts and establish a deeper understanding of the material. Something about the beat structure.

Danny, the math whiz, was pretty technical in his analysis of their daughter's study methods. "Whatever works," he'd said, even if "what works" came with horribly misogynistic and violent lyrics. Jessica surprised herself that after her own free-range childhood, she would be the stricter of the two parents, especially with Danny coming from a military family. She relented on the music thing, though, since Cricket's report cards backed up the beat structure hypothesis.

Light streaming through one of the house's three remaining stained-glass windows decorated the room with an ever-changing mosaic of colors. A younger Cricket had "helped" Jessica refinish the window seat in her bedroom, doing a little bit of sanding but mostly making crayon drawings of the designs created by the light.

Lying on top of a funky boho comforter, surrounded by decorative pillows and a couple of tattered stuffed animals, Cricket seemed oblivious to the colors dancing around her.

Jessica bent over to pick up the empty dinner plate sitting next to the bed and a T-shirt and shorts lying nearby.

Cricket moved the headphone off her right ear. "Hi, Mom. What's up?"

"Just cleaning up. Whatcha working on?"

"Precalc." Math was Danny's thing. Cricket knew not to get too specific with her mom about what they were learning in class. It was all gobbledygook to her.

"What else do you have tonight?"

"History. I have to work on a digital presentation due next week." Cricket counted out the classes on her fingers. "Lit. A lot of reading, and I need to write a response essay. Spanish. Some conversational work online. I already did my chem lab report."

Clearly, the two of them would not be watching old TV shows like they used to or going through another one of Oma's boxes together in search of a new treasure. "Anything I can help with? I'm happy to proofread your essay or help you out with the presentation app." It wasn't as though one of the kids would need her help with anything digital. They didn't even need their dad's help, and he ran a software company.

"I'm good. Thanks, though." Cricket put her headphones back on. Her feet bopped, and her pencil scribbled letters and numbers in equations that formed yet another language Jessica didn't understand.

Jessica tossed the dirty clothes in Cricket's basket and closed the door on her way out.

She took the few steps toward Conor's closed door and raised her hand to knock. She stopped then lowered her hand. Mikey would be home from soccer soon. Maybe he would need someone to quiz him for an upcoming test.

Until a more receptive offspring arrived home, the boxes downstairs were sure to be more than welcoming to Jessica.

WITH A PARLOR FULL of boxes to the left and a dining room with overflow to the right, Jessica stood in the entryway brandishing a box cutter and her laptop. The laptop was open to a spreadsheet, complete with columns for item information: Item Name, Description, Photo, and Letter from Oma. She had also listed the item disposition: Consignment, Donate, and Keep. The spreadsheet offered an ordered balance to the cardboard chaos in front of her. She scanned the room, trying to decide where to start. The trunk peeked out from behind a stack of boxes, beckoning her.

Jessica had a vague memory of seeing the old trunk in Oma's attic decades ago, tucked in the back like a forgotten memory. Before her now, with its frayed leather handles on the sides and cracked leather straps with buckles securing the lid, the trunk screamed transatlantic steamer voyage. The wooden slats were so dirty that she couldn't get a read on what type of wood they were, but probably oak. Dents in the metal bracing hinted at bumpy journeys, steamer ships, trains, and wagons. She ran her fingers over the dull gray metal, cringing when she turned her hand to find four blackened fingertips.

"Ooh, a treasure chest!" Mikey walked in the room, his huge grin leading the way. The WD-40 had clearly worked. She hadn't heard Mikey come in through the front door.

"Hi, sweetie! I'm so glad you're home!" She went to hug him but held back so she didn't cover him with black trunk grime.

Mikey looked right past her, not noticing the holdback on the hug, let alone showing any resulting disappointment. "Did we have pirates for ancestors?" All those years of playing pirate seemed to be flooding back and filling his face with a mixture of hope and... perhaps a bit of pirate greed.

"Ah, no." Jessica shook her head apologetically. "No pirates. Sorry."

The pirate excitement fell from Mikey's face, replaced by a twitch in his nose. "Is that me?" He sniffed at his armpit.

"How about you throw your jersey straight into the washing machine?" She paused, remembering the kitchen table from a few days before. "Your socks, too." Before she could ask him to come back after he'd changed, he was gone.

Jessica slid the trunk from behind the boxes, undid the buckles, and folded back the straps, watching bits of rotten leather flutter to the carpet as she did so. Lifting the lid, she caught the feminine notes of Oma's perfume flirting with the faintly toxic smell of old mothballs. She had to use both hands to push the heavy lid back far enough for it to stay open. The trunk was definitely pre-Ralph Nader. There were no child-protective hinges, and the lid would've had no problem taking off a hand if it were to fall back shut.

And inside... no pirate booty. But she did find lots of linens—crisp white linens. Jessica sat back, perplexed, wondering what one does with a trunk full of old linens. This was most likely a cache of "Donate" items.

After a quick trip to the powder room to scrub off the antique dirt from her fingertips, Jessica opened the lavender envelope Oma had left in the trunk.

"Linens from the farm. Gr. Margarethe and Gr. Bertha did the embroidery on all of the table linens. Gr. Margarethe did all of the white-on-white embroidery. Gr. Bertha used color in hers. Even when there was little to put on the table, Gr. Margarethe made sure the table looked nice."

Tonight's taco bar had filled the Donnelly table, but even if Jessica had had lovely linens to accent the dinnerware, no one would have been there long enough to notice.

Jessica removed all of the items and placed them on a blanket she had spread in the entryway, handling the items carefully to avoid antique grime contamination.

The embroidery was intricate and beautiful, three-dimensional and throbbing with life. Flowers and birds' nests and corn and wheat graced the fabric. The white thread on white linen, which seemed as though it would be mild and staid, had a complexity and layering of stitching that made the pictures more vivid than a full-color photograph.

Mikey appeared back in the entryway, balancing a taco plate in one hand and a jar of salsa and a water bottle in the other. He eyed the spread of linens with bewilderment.

Jessica raised her eyebrows. "What do you think? Treasures?"

He rolled his eyes. "Uh, no, Mom. I was thinking more like gold doubloons, pearls, gold cups, you know, like in *Pirates of the Caribbean*. I kind of hoped we had some cool criminal ancestor."

Jessica gestured for Mikey to set down his food. "Come over and take a look." She wouldn't delude herself into thinking that a boy was going to be thrilled to see Grandma's linens, but she could still show him. The selfishness of this triggered a pang of embarrassment, but she would get at least a few more minutes with him, so it was worth it.

"These are all old linens. Look at the embroidery. Wait, are your hands clean?"

Mikey held up his hands, and Jessica nodded her approval, handing him a tablecloth and a stack of cloth napkins. "Your great-great-great-grandmother embroidered these."

Mikey tested a box marked "Cigar Boxes," decided it could hold his one hundred or so pounds, and took a seat. As he unfolded and turned over the cloth and napkins, the realization of discovery filled his eyes. "Here's a bird and a bird's nest. And this tablecloth has little clovers scattered all over it. And here's corn and a butterfly and—what's this round bumpy thing?"

Jessica ran her fingers over the embroidery. The "round bumpy thing" was a cluster of individually stitched balls, all comprising a greater round object with a display of broad leaves at its base. Jessica searched her memory, the threaded mystery quickly solved. "It's a hedge apple."

Mikey scrunched his face in disgust. "A bumpy apple?"

"Not apples. They grow on what's called an Osage orange tree. But they're not oranges either, and you don't eat them. My brothers and cousins and I used to collect them into piles and have huge wars." Jessica smiled at the memories of hiding behind the barn and pelting the boys with slightly rotting hedge apples.

"Got it. So she embroidered the plants and animals by the farm. Here's an acorn, another clover, and is this a baby pig?" Mikey smiled. "It's like playing 'I Spy' or... oh, oh... 'I-owa Spy.'" Mikey gave a self-satisfied nod.

Jessica grinned. "I see what you did there."

Mikey handed the linens back and picked up his food.

"Can I join you for your dinner?" Jessica heard the neediness in her own voice, grateful Mikey was too naïve to pick up on it.

"Science test. Gotta study." He pointed up the stairs with his water bottle.

"I can quiz you if you want." She struck a casual tone just in case he wasn't actually that naïve.

"Thanks, but I got this new app. I can make my own flashcards online and quiz myself. I don't think I'll need your help with the quizzes anymore."

Jessica looked down at the stack of napkins in her hands, wondering how long it must have taken to stitch a single hedge apple. "Oh, okay. Well, let me know if you need anything. I'm happy to help."

She checked her watch as she heard him creak up the stairs. It was only seven o'clock, and Danny wouldn't be back until who knew when. She seemed to have time to stitch some hedge apples, if only she knew how to embroider. For now, the linens went back in the trunk, and Jessica sought out Amina's case file. If the kids didn't need her help with studying anymore, she could do some studying of her own.

CHAPTER SEVEN

"This isn't enough." Jessica slammed the folder shut, creating an unsatisfyingly weak "whoosh" when she would have preferred a loud slap.

Gracie, ears pricked, looked up at Jessica from the rug in front of the fireplace. Realizing Jessica wasn't offering food or a walk, she rearranged herself, pulling the rug here and there into a proper dog's nest, and went back to sleep.

Jessica had cleaned up the impressive taco mess her youngest had left in the kitchen and now sat curled into the corner of the couch with her laptop, paging through Amina's thin application and typing notes. Unfortunately, but perhaps not surprisingly, Amina's application read the way Amina spoke—clipped and devoid of detail, guarded.

To be fair, considering the debacle with Amina's first lawyer and the fact that asylum applications have to be filed within one year of entry into the US, it was likely that Amina had prepared the application in haste to beat the deadline.

Jessica clicked on the browser tab that displayed the asylum law's text. Amina had to prove that she could not return to Syria due to "persecution or a well-founded fear of persecution on account of race, religion, nationality, membership in a particular social group, or political opinion." It was one thing to learn about this in a short training session but another to apply the rule to a woman's story.

Amina had no criminal convictions. It would have been a rough, no, impossible road if she had. She was married, but the location of her husband was unknown. There were no children, but the form didn't ask if she'd ever *had* children.

Jessica skimmed past the benign things again, like Amina's college degree, university employment as an accountant, and her involvement in a women's study group. These added shades of normalcy, but the rest of the application twisted that into shades of darkness. There was a father, interrogated and assaulted; a sibling, murdered; and a husband, kidnapped and missing. All descriptions were light on detail and devoid of documentation. Then there was mention of the Syrian Armed Forces and the Free Syrian Army, both somewhat familiar names, but *Mukhabarat* didn't ring a bell.

Jessica had hoped she would learn about Amina's history from the application and see if, at the very least, she could give a little guidance to the woman who wanted to do this herself. But mostly she learned that she had a lot to learn. It was like another pile of boxes. She didn't know what was inside any of them, and in this case, there was no "Open this box first" box.

She did know that Amina was from Syria. And everyone knew that Syria was a shit storm. She watched the news and knew to associate the country with the Arab Spring, Assad, and ISIS, but she wouldn't even be able to find Syria on a map.

That box was the first she should open. Jessica's laptop hummed in the background as she typed "Syria" into the Internet browser.

A map opened on the screen. A red dot marked Syria, which was nestled between Turkey, Iraq, Lebanon, Israel, and Jordan. It didn't take many clicks before Jessica was mired in the history of a former French Mandate damaged by colonialism and a religion torn between two elements disagreeing over divine guidance and spiritual authority to the point of genocide.

Political and religious shifts, both from within and without, affecting borders, regimes, and alliances, proved that unrest had deep roots that spread mindless of artificial borders.

Jessica typed and clicked then read and typed and clicked some more. She opened her notebook and drew a circle diagram. Referring to her computer screen and its ever-increasing number of open windows, she tried to follow the dynamics of dictatorship versus democracy, the Assad regime's fight against the Free Syrian Army, the invasion by ISIS and religious extremism, and the involvement of Iran, the Kurds, Russia, Turkey, and the US.

The diagram started elegantly, but soon, a new spreadsheet seemed in order or maybe some of Mikey's flashcards. What she had was a mess of big circles, little circles, lines, and arrows. Her own attempt at bringing some order to the chaos was failing graphically. Sunnis versus Shia. Sunnis versus Sunnis. Allies fighting shared enemies but not always. Enemies fighting shared enemies but supporting each other's allies. Centuries of bad blood.

Everyone had stances that were as clear as mud. And of course, all of this was subject to change in the winds of war and politics and religion. The common denominator was that the people of Syria suffered, and the number of refugees continued to grow.

Jessica stood up and stretched, her joints cracking in protest, muscles thankful for the fresh rush of blood. She didn't need to solve the problems of Syria, but she did need to figure out how Amina fit into all of it and how all of it would support Amina's asylum claim.

After pouring another cup of coffee, Jessica returned to her computer, scrolling through photo after photo of bombed Syrian cities. Buildings in Amina's hometown of Aleppo stood exposed, whole walls peeled away. She wanted to look into each shell of a building, peek around every corner, and flag down each of the poor souls wandering through the wreckage. Clicking on one image led to another, and eventually, the concrete shells gave way to bloodied bodies twisted from torture, bloated heads lined up on poles, and kneeling men facing away from the guns held up to their heads. All of these recent atrocities stemmed from protests over the regime's treatment of some young people who spray-painted antiregime graffiti on the walls of their school.

Spray paint. Millions of refugees.

Settling back into her corner of the couch, Jessica felt chastened and small, something this case was beginning to make common. Leaving her own home in Iowa had seemed so monumental, so brave—a small-town girl going out into the big world. That and feeling for years as though she could not go back seemed trivial now, though the damage had been done. But this wasn't about her.

Jessica picked up Amina's application and studied the woman who fit into this history in her own way and who now had to prove a basis for her fear in order to stay in America, using an attorney who had just learned where Syria was on a map.

Just knowing Syrian history wouldn't win the case, nor would endless Internet research. Jessica needed to get Amina to open up about what could be a harrowing story and let Jessica in. Jessica checked her watch. It was too late to contact Amina tonight, which gave her time to work up the nerve and the pitch for a call tomorrow.

CHAPTER EIGHT
AMINA

Amina dried the last dish and put it in the cupboard, lifting the door slightly so the loose hinge would reset as she closed it. The muscle memory of the action reminded her that it had been well over two years since she'd arrived in Baltimore.

In that time, memories of her home country, once so vivid, had faded under the glow of news images of fighters and destruction. It wasn't *her* Syria they showed, the Syria that she remembered. Her Syria was from before the war, where the ruins were from millennia ago, not a year ago, where a girl could dream of a bright future, not of finding a way to survive. The news images, with their gray and dusty sameness, seemed to turn even her good memories to rubble, making her connection with home ever more fragile.

Small giggles and grunts interrupted her fading memories, and Amina turned to see a jumble of black hair and matching Spider-Man pajamas rolling on the rug outside the kitchen doorway. She walked toward the two brothers, her socked feet quiet on the linoleum floor.

Amina stood over the mini-wrestlers until one, then the other, looked up and caught her eye. She must have looked very stern from down on the floor, because the giggling, writhing oneness quickly unraveled into two little boys lying flat on their backs and saying nothing. If Talib were not three-quarters the size of Khaled, a stranger would have been forgiven for thinking they were twins, with their matching cherubic faces and deep-brown eyes wide with wonder.

Her life today, so far away from Syria, included helping take care of these two packages of joy. They grounded her in this house, though their faces were high-resolution reproductions of faces from home. Through them, she felt a tangible connection with home, where family had been her stability.

She clapped her hands, eliciting blinks from matching long eyelashes. "Guess what? I went to the library the other day." She emphasized "library" as she would "circus" or "Legoland." It had the anticipated effect, with both boys widening their eyes and dropping their jaws.

"Did you get us some Thomas books?" Khaled asked. "Talib likes those."

Amina had checked out every Thomas book from their local branch multiple times, first for Khaled then again when Khaled had insisted his little brother wanted to check them out.

"No, but next time I will," she assured them. "This time, I found a special book that they don't have at our library. I got it at the big library." She spread her arms to indicate the block-sized Enoch Pratt. She checked the clock above the sink. "Where's your baba?"

The smallest boy rolled over and pointed awkwardly toward the front door with one arm pinned under his belly.

Big brother Khaled translated. "Still at work."

"I'll let you stay up a little bit late tonight so you can see my book," she said conspiratorially. It wouldn't be that terribly late, but the mere idea of staying up after their mom had gone to bed early made the boys giggle. Amina ushered them onto the brown chenille couch in the dark living room and turned on the matching floor lamps at either end of the couch. The boys immediately started fussing over who got to sit where, each wanting the full couch to himself yet not able to bear being apart from the other.

She stared at them, pulling her eyebrows inward in an attempt to recapture her earlier stern visage without breaking a smile, until they stopped fidgeting. "I will sit in the middle." She lifted her bag from the coffee table and pulled out the book before squeezing between the two boys at the center of the couch. She set the book on her lap ceremoniously. "This... is a book with some magical pictures."

Khaled gasped, causing Talib to gasp.

"Pictures of Syria."

Khaled's gaping mouth morphed into a frown, as if he'd been tricked.

She reassured him. "Your mama and baba are both from Syria. You know that. That makes it your home, too. Think of how exciting it is that the big library has pictures of your home in it."

She opened the travel guide, a book that had once served to introduce adventurous travelers to an old and exotic location but was now a devil's mockery of an unrecognizable place. The boys' minds were pristine, though, protected due to their age from the news she refused to watch.

She hadn't been thinking of the boys when she'd checked out the book earlier that week, but now she felt inspired to share it with the living visions of home sitting next to her. Perhaps their joy and innocence would weave their way into her own memories, regenerating the connection that was crumbling into the rubble.

On the first page, aged pillars stood dark against the sky, separating an orange-gold setting sun from the deepening blue sky it was leaving behind. "These are ruins at Palmyra. They are over two thousand years old." She opened her eyes wide to indicate that they should be astonished. "Do you know how old Baltimore is? It's less than three hundred years old. Baltimore is like a little baby compared to Palmyra." She leaned in and touched noses with each of them before turning the page. "This church is almost two thousand years old." The rough stone walls of the Chapel of Saint Ananias glowed in yellow light, while a plastic fan marred the solemnity of the chapel.

"I thought you were Muslim, like us."

"I am, but Syria is like America. There are Christians and Muslims."

Khaled seemed satisfied with her response and turned the page to a scene of crystal-blue waters washing up on a beach dotted symmetrically with grass umbrellas. "Did you go here?"

"Yes. I went on a very special trip to that beach once." Memories of windblown hair silhouetted against a watercolor sunset and of sand in the sheets of a wedding bed stung her eyes. She turned the page. "But I liked to play in the snow." She pointed at a winter photo in the countryside. "Are you excited for winter?"

Both boys nodded like one of the bobblehead dolls on the shelf above their beds. She turned page after page of a ministry of tourism's glossy vision of a Mediterranean destination, with sweeping views of green landscapes, ancient castles, and busy, bustling marketplaces. She closed her eyes and could feel the places, breathe the aromas, and be there again in its not-always-glossy but always-familiar and deep-rooted reality.

The two heads leaning against her shoulders brought her back to the present. It was bedtime. She closed the guide. The front door opened, and Fayiz closed it slowly behind him when he saw Amina hold a finger up to her lips. He set a black bag on the ground, removed his square-toed black shoes, and lined them up next to the other shoes by the door.

One small head swiveled upward toward Amina, deep brown eyes struggling to stay open long enough to ask a question. "This is your home now, right?"

"I hope so," Amina said.

Khaled burrowed his head into her shoulder. "Do you want to go back to Syria?"

"I do someday. And I hope you can visit, too."

"Why did you leave?"

She turned toward Fayiz with sad eyes. The boys were so young, too young to understand why millions fled the home they may never know, yet almost old enough to feel the pain of being an outsider in the only home they did know. "Because I wanted to meet you two." She hugged them both but not hard enough to break the spell of twilight.

Fayiz extracted the boys from Amina's embrace and carried them upstairs to their room, his strong arms allowing enough security for the two little boys to fall asleep in transit. Soft footsteps on the stairs receded, leaving Amina alone in the middle of the couch, illuminated by two overlapping circles of light.

She opened the guide again. This was the Syria she wanted to return to, her home, not the Syria shown on TV and in the newspaper. As much as she knew she'd had to flee, the emptiness of loss hung heavy with second thoughts and regrets about those she'd left behind, those who had helped her escape what they could not.

She'd been wrong. The boys' closeness to her, their warm bodies and soapy postbath smell, hadn't enhanced her memories. It had accentuated her loneliness and her faded dreams of building her own family, dreams that were once in vivid color when imagined from beneath white sheets in a room overlooking the Mediterranean Sea.

CHAPTER NINE

The GPS told Jessica in its sexy British accent that her destination was ahead on the right.

Three phone calls and two text messages to Amina had gone unanswered. She'd spaced them out so she didn't come across as a stalker, but she wasn't entirely disappointed Amina hadn't returned her calls.

However, the dread of talking on the phone with a Syrian who didn't trust lawyers was being replaced by the dread of going back to Rosalie after a week and not even having spoken with the woman Jessica had insisted on pursuing. She only had a couple more days to get the situation worked out, so she had to be more forward.

According to the file, Amina worked at a Baltimore restaurant called Bathanjaan. Middle Eastern cuisine was not a thing in small-town Iowa, where Jessica had grown up. In fact, Jessica couldn't remember any kind of "cuisine" back home. Spaghetti was about as exotic as it got in Jessica's little spot out there in flyover country.

Finally, she spotted her destination—a ground-level restaurant in a three-story brick building. The faded painting of a watch on the side of the building proclaimed that the structure had once been the home of a watch store. In this newly gentrified neighborhood, the architectural and design elements of a bygone era lent a comforting credibility to the businesses that served a new world. "Bathanjaan" was printed in script on a large picture window, through which Jessica could see a busy lunch crowd.

Jessica thought back to her days at H&C, both the busy time and the lunches. For an associate who came into the office at 7:00 a.m. and didn't know if she would leave at 7:00 p.m. or midnight, lunch was the adult equivalent of recess. And recess in DC had allowed this Iowa girl to indulge in all kinds of "cuisine." She'd particularly loved a pho restaurant just a block away from the firm's building and a million miles away from Iowa. Between daily lunch outings and night after night of delivery for the overworked associates, Jessica had made up for a lifetime of cuisineless living in just a few short months. She couldn't recall any Syrian restaurants close to her old office, though, so this would be a first.

A bearded man, fully engaged in checking his cell phone, held the door for Jessica. The thoughtless act of thoughtfulness allowed Jessica to laugh to herself and release some anxiety. Scanning the room unsuccessfully for Amina, Jessica's eyes turned almost involuntarily upward. Colorful strips of cloth gracefully draped the ceiling, complementing the complex aromas and intermingled conversations that filled the restaurant. The dining tables around the perimeter of the room framed a waiting area in the center of the space. No, it was more a gathering spot than a waiting area.

Jessica bypassed the hostess stand by the door, drawn almost magnetically to a table placed in the center of a circle of cushioned chairs. The low table was actually the stump of an unfamiliar tree. Irregularly shaped around the diameter, with bold waves and asymmetric juts, the tree spoke of a gnarled and lengthy life. Its caramel tone, interwoven with vanilla and mocha, seemed to be an image of a barista's masterpiece. It looked almost like a cross section of brain, with cavities coursing through the swirls. Actually, it was more like a damaged brain—the "after" images they showed to ward people away from doing drugs—with black nothingness where vibrant gray and white matter used to be.

It made for a less than practical coffee table. A misplaced cup wouldn't stand a chance of staying upright for long, but the table had a gravity to it that seemed to be holding the building itself in place.

Just as she reached out to graze her fingers across the burly slab, Jessica felt a light touch on her shoulder. A woman with Middle Eastern features, wearing a Western maternity dress and leggings, rested a menu atop her swollen belly.

"Just one?" asked the heavily accented woman.

Jessica followed the woman to a round two-top by the window, glancing back at the table, trying to take a mental picture of it. She had worked a lot of wood at her home. The more interesting pieces carried a generation or two of meaning that emerged as she sanded and refinished. The last owner of the Donnelly home had had a big dog, whose claw marks on the front door Jessica had sanded smooth. Another owner, the original family, had notched their children's heights in a closet doorframe every year. Those marks she didn't touch, letting the children live on. This table, though, carried more—more generations and more stories.

Jessica had looked up the Bathanjaan menu online before her visit. Feeling adventurous and not afraid to try lamb for the first time, Jessica ordered the kibbeh arnabieh. Before the woman left the table, Jessica asked if Amina was working today. The woman stiffened and shook her head before beelining for the kitchen, as if Jessica was with Immigration and Naturalization Services, doing recon for a raid.

The lunch crowd was a metropolitan mix. Some elderly men looked Middle Eastern, but they were outnumbered by white, hipster-looking twentysomethings and more professional types of all ethnicities. An old woman sitting in the corner alone caught Jessica's eye and smiled. She had a plate of bread on the table in front of her and held a book.

Jessica wished she had brought her own book, which she needed to finish up for book club that night, but she'd only been able to get it from the library a few days before. Finding some online book spoiler summaries for the month's selection, *All the Light We Cannot See*, would have to do. With no sign of Amina, Jessica clicked on her phone and started typing.

She soon found herself deep in an Internet rabbit hole that led away from a promising summary of Anthony Doerr's book. Instead, she was reading about something that had nothing to do with books or any form of intelligent thought, so she jumped when a man said, "Hello."

The man bowed slightly toward her and set two dishes on the table. "I am the owner. I understand you were asking about Amina Hamid." His accented voice was gruff, but his face was mild and inquisitive.

Jessica fumbled her phone into her purse. "Yes. Is she working today?"

"I'm sorry. She is not here." His cautious response didn't quite confirm that she worked there or that he even knew her. "May I ask why you are looking for her?"

Jessica wasn't sure how much the owner knew about Amina or that she was seeking asylum. Jessica was already skirting the rules of confidentiality, and the owner's circumspect comment inspired wariness on her part. "I'm a friend. Can you tell her that Jessica Donnelly stopped by?" She didn't hand over her business card. Amina might not like that she referred to herself as a friend, but she surely wouldn't like Jessica presenting herself as an attorney.

"Certainly. Please enjoy your meal and let your server know if we can get you anything else." The man bowed again and turned to walk away.

"Sir? The table over there." She pointed toward the center of the room. "What kind of wood is it?"

The man's smile started with his eyes, waterfalling down to his lips. "Olive. The olive tree is from my grandmother's home. It was many hundreds of years old before it died."

Untold memories, or maybe even dreams, seemed to pass through the man's mind as he paused wistfully.

"It was not easy to get it to America." He bowed again and moved to another table, his arms open wide in greeting.

Jessica adjusted the napkin on her lap and surveyed the dishes, wincing. If she had looked up pictures of kibbeh arnabieh online before ordering, she almost certainly would not have selected it. It looked like giant sea slugs floating in a milky sea.

But it was the order she'd made.

THE number on the phone showed it was Amina. Nervousness and indecision seemed to have gone on hiatus following Jessica's trip into the city, giving her a welcome boost of unencumbered confidence. She stopped stripping Mikey's bed and accepted the call. "Hello, this is Jessica Donnelly."

"Hello. This is Amina Hamid." She sounded as steely over the phone as she had been face to face, resulting in the end of the hiatus.

Jessica sat on the exposed mattress, taking a deep breath to center herself. "Thanks for calling me back, Ms. Hamid."

"I am calling because you came to my work. My employer does not want any trouble. I didn't ask you to come to the restaurant."

This was not starting off well. "I am so sorry if I put you in an uncomfortable position. I couldn't reach you by phone, but I wanted to talk with you about your case."

She hoped the silence on the other end of the phone was good. At least Amina hadn't hung up yet.

Jessica stood, continuing. "I know you had a bad experience with your first lawyer. I'm really impressed with what you've already done, so far as submitting your application. Really, I am. You prepared a complete application, and everything seems to be in order. But, to be honest, complete doesn't mean detailed or persuasive."

Jessica caught her reflection in Mikey's mirror, seeing her younger attorney self pacing the H&C office while advising a client. She had once cut off a Fortune 500 CEO mid-sentence to tell him in no uncertain terms that the deal he was about to sign would land the SEC on his doorstep and she had no intention of joining him on a perp walk.

Amina, however, was not a corporate executive, so Jessica softened her edges. "You didn't include enough information or documentation to support your case. I believe you need to do a significant amount of preparation in order to succeed in front of the asylum officer. I would hate for you to be in that interview alone and unprepared. If you want to do this on your own, that's fine. But why not meet with me one more time? I've been through your application now and have some ideas I can pass along."

Jessica stopped pacing. She moved the phone so she could see the screen to make sure the line was still open.

"I will meet with you one more time."

Jessica fumbled the phone back up to her ear. "Okay, then. Great. I can come to your home or the restaurant."

"Somewhere else." Amina's response wasn't a sharp chastisement, but its quickness sent a clear message that Jessica had pushed as far into Amina's personal life as she would allow.

Jessica made some suggestions, and the two settled on a coffee shop a couple of bus stops from Bathanjaan. "I can come to pick you up—"

"No. I can get there on my own. I will see you tomorrow morning."

CHAPTER TEN

The kids were fed, homework was in progress, and most importantly, no one was engaged in killing either of the others, so it seemed safe to leave for book club. With Danny on an unplanned trip to Seattle to meet with a potential new customer, Jessica didn't even feel guilty about the self-indulgence.

Heading out the door for the short two-block walk, she ran through the earlier call. Amina had offered to meet "one more time." The woman hadn't sounded as though she'd warmed to Jessica, so this could simply be a meeting at a neutral public spot, where Amina would tell Jessica once and for all to leave her alone.

Jessica had used that tactic herself with a law school boyfriend—boyfriend was a stretch, but he'd seemed to think he was, so Jessica had had to end it cleanly—and she didn't relish the idea of being on the receiving end.

She didn't owe Amina anything, as Rosalie had stated, and Amina owed Jessica nothing, either. So the best road could be for Jessica to give Amina some basic advice and bow out. But something about that didn't feel right. Jessica felt as though she did owe more, but she didn't know what or to whom.

She wanted to shake her mind free of all things *pro bono*, at least for the night, and Nari's beautiful home helped.

Architecturally lit from the foundation to the widow's walk, the white three-story home stood like a wise sentry on the corner of Walnut and Sycamore, an exemplar of the homes that made up the Sycamore Street neighborhood. Thankfully, historic-preservation regulations had spared the outside when the Grants did extensive renovations on the home, transforming the aged interior into a model of contemporary style.

Nari had come across an antique boat hatch cover in her attic during renovations and had promptly brought it to the Donnellys' house. "Jessica, you should have seen our decorator's face when I showed it to her and said maybe we could incorporate it into the interior design! I thought she was going to quit on the spot. Anyway, I thought maybe you could use it. I mean, you have kept your house so historical."

Jessica hadn't minded the backhanded compliment. With sturdy pine and unadorned metal edging, the hatch cover had looked battered but impeccably intact. Its history was unknowable beyond sea voyages that had somehow ended at a port in Maryland, but Jessica had spent countless hours using her newfound woodworking skills to ensure its future as a restored maritime relic in the office of a certain cybersecurity company's CEO. She wasn't sure if Danny had been serious about the restoration serving a role in landing the Defense Department contract, but she took unashamed pride in the possibility.

Walking into Nari's home without knocking, Jessica could hear the women before she could see the group. She glanced in the mirror in the front hall and smoothed her hair. Her grandmother's cross, which she hadn't quite stolen from Cricket but was certainly sharing custody of, looked just right against her flowy black top. She didn't look like Madonna at all.

Hearing the clink of a wine bottle against the rim of a glass, Jessica oriented herself toward the kitchen.

"Jessica! I'm so glad you could come!" Nari accepted the bottle of cabernet sauvignon offered by Jessica and added it to the collection on the white marble island that separated the kitchen from the great room. "You just missed Charlie. He said to say hello and that he wouldn't be back down."

"I guess he learned his lesson last time," Jessica said, laughing.

Nari tied an apron around her waist, accentuating her thin frame and her decidedly non-housewife outfit that was more Manhattan than Annapolis. "No, he did not enjoy being the 'man's perspective.' He's just lucky that wasn't the month we read *Fifty Shades*. Oh God, can you imagine? In any event, he won't be through here again tonight." She motioned toward the great room. "Please, help yourself. Open bottles and glasses are at the bar. I'll be over in a sec." She pulled on a monogrammed oven mitt to retrieve some miniature crab cakes from the oven. The elegant anesthesiologist had outstanding skills in the kitchen, and the ladies from Sycamore Street never ate dinner before book club when Nari hosted.

Eight women were gathered loosely between the island and the bar. Occasionally, all twelve members would attend, especially now that everyone's kids were getting old enough to be left home alone. Over the years, the group had changed little. Well, the women had gotten older, the houses had gotten nicer, and the inside jokes a little bawdier. By all accounts, the group had gotten better with age.

Jessica poured herself a glass of cab and edged into the circle of women, already a world away from Syria and her involvement, such as it was.

Tonight's book researcher, Denise, was talking, but not about this month's historical fiction selection. "I never should have agreed to move away from here, away from you guys. But I thought being closer to his work would let us be together more. Turns out that's not what was keeping us apart." She pushed her hands against the sides of her face, pulling the skin taut and temporarily erasing the despair that had physically etched itself into her face over the past year.

The women shook their heads in support.

Denise continued. "The trial separation is over. No more therapy. *We're* over. I don't know what I did wrong." She reflexively reached her right hand toward her left ring finger. It was bare where it was once ringed for eternity.

"You did everything right, Denise," insisted Mary Anne, who stood to her left. Mary Anne was the loudest of the group, the most unfiltered. But she was also the most loyal and always the one Jessica would want to have her back. "He's the one who fucked up, with that—" She stopped abruptly upon seeing the glares from the other women. Bringing another woman—the *other* woman—into the discussion was not a good idea. She sipped her wine in lieu of finishing her sentence.

"I almost don't even mind losing him. It's losing *me* that I didn't expect. I have been at home almost our entire marriage. Being a wife and a mom was everything to me. You guys know that." She twisted the nonexistent ring on her finger and whispered, "He knew that." Tears started to fall. "Even the mom part is cut in half now. I'm a quarter of the woman I was before, and I have no idea what comes next."

The other women were still, letting her get all her words out.

"I don't want to keep shrinking." Blond highlights covered her eyes as she leaned forward. "I don't know what I'm going to do." She looked back up at the women, challenging them. "What the hell am I supposed to do?"

Nari appeared in front of Denise, holding a goblet filled with chardonnay. "The first thing you're going to do is drink some wine."

Denise waved away the goblet. "No. I have to drive home."

"Why?" Nari asked, placing her free hand on Denise's shoulder.

"Why what?"

"Why do you have to drive home?"

"Because I always have to drive home now that I live in fucking Bethesda."

Nari placed the goblet in Denise's hand. "You said he has the kids tonight. So you're staying here. With us." Her strong bedside manner came through with her firm yet compassionate cadence. "You can get up early and drive home. Tonight, you're ours. We're going to talk about the book, and we're going to drink wine, and we're going to tell you how much we love you. Even though you moved to *fucking* Bethesda."

Denise's unexpected laugh brightened her splotchy face, allowing the rest of the circle to breathe fully again.

Jessica grabbed Denise's hand, intertwining their fingers. "Nari just dropped the f-bomb. You'd better do what she says, or who knows what will happen next." She clinked her glass against Denise's, the pure tones rising from Nari's fine crystal goblets putting an end to the discussion.

Nari ushered the women toward the cushy white couches and camel chairs that flanked them. Jessica always marveled at the woman's nonchalance about the red wine and other threats to the upholstery. Maybe having a job like Nari's, in which she held the balance of a person's life in her hands, allowed her to block such mundane worries from her mind.

It seemed easier not to get white couches.

Taking her own place on a camel chair, Jessica gulped a healthy slug of her cab, hoping it wouldn't take much wine to stop her from thinking about whether she, too, was shrinking.

CHAPTER ELEVEN

The dark interior of the coffee shop was a small blessing for the unrelenting pounding in Jessica's temples. *I shouldn't have had that last glass of cab.* Book club had talked late into the night, strategizing about Denise's future, before falling into their regular gossip, and Jessica had wobbled home well after even the teenagers had gone to bed. Short of sleep and long on hangover, all Jessica wanted right now was a freshly brewed cup of anything strong and full of caffeine.

Amina was hard to miss, her poppy-colored hijab standing out against the decor of dark barrels and the rows of coffee bean–filled burlap bags. The anti-Starbucks authenticity of the small-batch roast shop lent a sense of privacy to the scattered tables. A public breakup didn't loom as large as it had after the phone call yesterday.

Jessica smiled as she approached Amina, wincing when the movement of her facial muscles triggered another round of pounding. "Thanks for meeting me here—you're early! This is certainly more comfortable than that awful meeting room at IAP. Can I get you a coffee, tea, or something to eat?" Jessica reached into her purse for her wallet.

"No, thank you."

"Really, my treat. Are you sure?"

Amina nodded tightly. "Yes, thank you."

They couldn't take up this table without ordering something, even if the place was empty, *especially* if the place was empty. Plus, she needed that caffeine.

Jessica ordered a coffee and a breakfast sandwich and returned to the table. Her fingers burned even with the cardboard coffee-cup sleeve protecting them. If Amina weren't regarding her with such intensity and what looked like a touch of impatience, Jessica would have gone back and asked for an ice cube so she wouldn't have to wait so long for the coffee to cool.

Jessica removed the lid, releasing a balloon of steam that momentarily obscured Amina's face. "As I said on the phone, I apologize for any problems I caused by coming to the restaurant. I didn't say anything about you or your case, if you're worried about that. I just mentioned that I was a friend."

The muscles in the hollows of Amina's cheeks tensed slightly. *Right. Not a friend.* Amina was a woman of few words, but Jessica was beginning to sense that maybe the woman simply didn't need a lot of words.

"By the way, it was amazing. The restaurant, I mean. I got the—and I'm sure I'm going to mispronounce this—the kibbeh arnabieh?" Jessica looked questioningly at Amina, who obliged with a nod. "So. Good. I mean, when it came to the table, it didn't look all that appetizing. I've never had Syrian food before and didn't know what to expect." She barked a pathetic laugh, instantly regretting her impolite words.

Amina's face hadn't so much as twitched.

"Anyway, it was fantastic. Any chance the owner would give out the recipe?" She'd blurted the request without thinking, her nerves getting the best of her.

The corners of Amina's mouth tilted up for a split second, quickly returning to the sterner status quo. "The owner would be happy to hear you enjoyed your meal, but he is very protective of his kitchen." She pierced Jessica with a stare that made it clear Amina had no interest in small talk.

Jessica accepted the unspoken directive. "Let's talk about your Form I-589 filing." She handed Amina a copy of the asylum application. "It looks complete but only in the sense that you put something down for each question. A bare-bones application is acceptable to file, but it's not enough at this stage, ahead of your interview. There isn't much detail, and there's no documentation. The United States Citizenship and Immigration Services—the USCIS..." Jessica searched Amina's face for an acknowledgment that Amina knew the name of the government entity.

Amina clenched her jaw in response.

"Right. You filed the application with them yourself." Jessica admonished herself silently. "The USCIS wants detail and documentation to support your claim of persecution, and there's just not a lot of that here." She was repeating herself and slowed down to focus. "I think you have set out the bare foundation for a good case. We—sorry, you—just need to sell it." Jessica shook her head, releasing a pounding behind her right eye. She was flailing. This had been a mistake. "Not sell it, sorry. What I mean is that you need to be able to present a strong case."

Clarity broke through the fog of last night's wine. The sole reason Jessica had come to this coffee shop today was to present her own case to Amina, and she wasn't going to shrink away from that. "The good news is that we can gather more documentation and evidence and work together ahead of your interview so you're well prepared to present your case. That is, if you want to use me as your attorney. Of course, you can still try to do this on your own." Jessica paused to determine if she had the latitude to continue.

Amina's eyes didn't waver from their attention on her.

Jessica leaned in to challenge Amina's stare. "You originally hired a lawyer who clearly didn't know who he was dealing with." Amina's eyebrow twitched, and Jessica drove forward. "But even though you were able to complete and file the application on your own, I'm afraid the statistics don't support your success. Only around eleven percent of asylum seekers without an attorney win their case. If you lose—" She paused, thinking of the scenes of Syrian destruction. "If you lose, you will be deported."

Amina continued to sit, attentive and unreadable.

Jessica dug in. "I used to work with a law firm in Washington, DC. I worked in securities offerings and compliance."

Amina tilted her head slightly, eyes questioning.

Jessica clarified. "I worked with corporations in financings, capital market transactions, and compliance with state and federal securities laws. Making proper disclosures, complying with insider trading rules, corporate governance—" Jessica clamped her mouth shut to end the digression. "The bottom line is that I was good at it. But I stopped working to take care of my kids—I have three—several years ago."

Amina's suspicious look reemerged. "You are not an attorney anymore?"

"No, I *am* an attorney. I just took time off, and now I'm volunteering with IAP, which has experience and resources to support me and the person I'm working with. I will have only one case. One. Yours."

Amina's eyes darted to Jessica's left as a shop employee set a still-sizzling breakfast sandwich on their table. The grease oozing from the pressed sandwich puddled on the brown plate, turning Jessica's stomach and disrupting her mental flow.

"How old are your children?" Amina asked, taking advantage of the breach in Jessica's monologue.

Jessica's serious lawyer face gave way to a smile, and she felt her neck muscles loosen and her shoulders soften. She hadn't realized she was so tense or that the thought of her kids would be soothing rather than stressful.

"Sixteen, fifteen, and eleven. My oldest is Conor." Jessica hesitated to divulge too much. This wasn't about her. But Amina's newly receptive demeanor encouraged her. "He's a junior in high school, and boy, he is testing the limits these days. But he's a good kid. Looks just like his dad did at his age. Cricket is fifteen. She's whip-smart and so confident. My other son, Mikey, is eleven. He's the baby of the family, but I'm not sure how much longer that will last. He has more energy and happiness than the rest of us combined." Hissing followed by a whistle sounded from behind Jessica, indicating someone had just ordered a latte or maybe a cappuccino. Jessica dropped her smile and mindlessly rubbed the pendant hanging from her necklace. Raving about her family to a woman who'd left hers behind seemed insensitive.

Mercifully, Amina changed the subject again. "It's a beautiful necklace. It looks very old."

Lifting the cross with the tips of her fingers, Jessica admired the patina and the texture of the green stones. "Thank you. Cricket found it in my grandmother's things. My grandmother passed away earlier this year, and we're just now going through the things she left behind. She got this from her own grandmother."

"A lovely family treasure." The silence at their table grew contemplative, soft. "I will use you as my attorney. I can change my mind later?"

Jessica let out a laugh.

Amina didn't smile. She wasn't kidding.

"Yes, you can change your mind later." Pressure lifted, but it was time to move on. Amina was checking her watch. "We'll have to go over your application in detail. We don't need to do it all at once or even today, but we will need to get the details down and then see what kind of documentation we can pull together to support your claim. Are you okay to do a little now?"

"I have some time."

The door to the shop opened with a jingle. Jessica glanced over to see two young women, likely college students, carrying backpacks. They were chattering and waving their hands about emphatically as they walked into the shop.

Jessica turned her attention back to Amina and her application, starting with the easy stuff—where she was living and making sure she had the resources she needed. "We'll first want to confirm everything in your application is accurate—"

"It is accurate."

Okay, then. "So you are still living in Baltimore."

"Yes."

"Are you living with anyone?"

"Yes. I live with my cousin, Fayiz Darbi, his wife, Sama, and their two sons." Her dark eyes softened.

Having family here already was good. That meant Amina had a support system and stability. "Great. How long have they been in the US, and what is their immigration status?" Jessica kicked herself. That was rather presumptive, or racist, or something bad, she was pretty sure.

Amina didn't seem to take offense. "They are US citizens. I do not know exactly the date. Fayiz came to America before the events of September 11. Sama followed several years later. Their children were born in America."

An immigrant family growing in their new country reminded Jessica of some of the "soft" advice she'd learned in training. "As you know—painfully, I'm sure—the asylum process is a waiting game. IAP urges our clients to live life as though they will be here permanently. Jobs, housing, life in general." She shuffled the application pages to the employment section. "You were an accountant in Syria. What are you doing at a restaurant?" She regretted the wording as soon as she'd asked the question. She should have used "the" instead of "a" to avoid sounding condescending or making it sound as if she didn't realize that educated immigrants had trouble finding jobs in their chosen fields.

Amina didn't pick up on the nuance in Jessica's article misselection. "I work in the office with the phone and other things, including the books. I work in the front if they need me. Even before I got my work permit, I helped. Now I have my work permit, and Sama is pregnant, so I am working every day."

Jessica wanted to make a joke about Amina being so wordy all of a sudden but decided against it. "I don't understand. Why does Sama's pregnancy mean you need to work more?"

"She cannot work the hours at my cousin's restaurant she worked before, so I am helping more."

Jessica nodded in realization. The pregnant waitress was Sama. The owner with whom she'd spoken must have been Fayiz. The cousin. They would have known all about Amina's status and probably that Jessica was not the friend she'd claimed to be.

Amina continued. "I will need to find another job for after the baby arrives."

"Why is that? Won't Sama be spending a lot of time with the baby?"

"The townhouse is not big enough for all of us and a baby. I must leave, and Fayiz cannot pay enough for me to rent an apartment."

Jessica made a note to talk to Rosalie about IAP housing and employment resources. "Now could be the time to look for a job that fits your education and what you want to be doing going forward. We have employment resources at IAP."

"I will let you know if I need assistance."

Based on the dismissiveness in Amina's voice, Jessica wouldn't hold her breath. She returned to the application, opting to skip over some mundane items in the interest of time. "I'd like to talk to you about your family. Your father, mother, siblings. Your husband."

Amina rose in a single fluid movement. "I must leave now. I must be at the bus stop to go to the restaurant."

"Oh, I'm sorry. I thought we had more—" Jessica fumbled reaching for her purse, nearly knocking over her coffee in her haste to keep up with Amina. "Can I give you a ride?"

"No, thank you." Her response was terse but polite. Amina started to turn away but stopped and looked over at the two young women at the counter then back at Jessica. "After the fighting began and the extremists came in, the buses stopped running. I could not go out alone."

The door jingled as Amina left the shop. Jessica took a sip of her coffee, promptly searing half of her taste buds and setting off a new round of pounding behind her eyes, reminding her of the wine, shrinking women, and the fact that she still had so much more to do.

CHAPTER TWELVE
AMINA

A fall breeze ruffled Amina's scarf against her cheek as she waited for the walk signal to turn white. She would never have imagined that abrupt exits would come to define her, but she had made two with the lawyer, and the greatest abrupt exit of all had brought her to this country in the first place.

She'd surprised herself with her reaction to the lawyer's question about her family and her own inability to answer or even remain at the table. Maybe the upwelling of suppressed emotion came from sharing the pictures of home with the boys or the new prospect of permanency or a relative stranger asking personal questions. Or maybe she simply wasn't ready to process everything that had happened.

The bus stop was just a block down to her right. Instead of turning, she clasped her bag and followed the crosswalk straight ahead. She would walk to the restaurant today. She had time due to that early exit, and she doubted the lawyer would see her and question why she wasn't taking the bus. Jessica had probably never even ridden the MTA and wouldn't know where the stops were. Amina certainly had never seen anyone dressed like the lawyer on the bus. Though she had to admit that today's outfit was a strong improvement over the American TV lawyer look the woman had worn the day of their first meeting.

What a woman like the lawyer would never understand was the tense instability of life as a refugee. It was like sitting at a bus stop in a barren desert for years, staring at the horizon and not knowing if a bus would ever even arrive. The sense of hopelessness that brought was overshadowed only by the sense of fear that when a bus finally did arrive, it would take her back to where she'd started, with no opportunity for a return pass.

Amina knew she was fortunate in her situation, which made leaving behind others to face the horror more shameful. She had shelter, food, income, and family, distant though that family may have been. So many million others did not. But as with those millions, she craved security. Everything she had could once again be taken from her.

Despite that hopelessness, Amina had begun to see dust billowing on the horizon, a bus possibly in the distance. She didn't know what had prompted the vision. Maybe it was instinct or perhaps just baseless optimism. Either way, the dust had already prompted her to do exactly what the IAP and the lawyer had advised.

She stepped out of the pedestrian flow and into the recessed area near a bank entrance then reached into her bag. She unfolded what was merely an internship flyer but what could be a ticket to her future.

A trip to the Enoch Pratt over the weekend to return the travel guide had led her to the Job and Career Information Center, where she'd found a notice for an accounting internship program starting in January. She met—no, exceeded—the requirements of experience and education. A preference for traditionally underrepresented minorities made the opportunity seem perfect for her. A Syrian woman in *Syria* was traditionally underrepresented in accounting, after all. She'd submitted her application just yesterday. An internship would be a step down from her blossoming career in Aleppo, but it would give her a foundation on which to build.

A steely pride filled her chest. She hadn't needed a lawyer to tell her to pursue a fitting job. She still was not sure about needing a lawyer for the rest of it, but with so much at stake, it couldn't hurt to have good people on her side. She had been foolish to trust the first attorney, an immigrant from Lebanon.

It had seemed prudent to use a lawyer who spoke her language and knew her culture, who wouldn't look at her the way so many Americans did, like an apparition that could be wished away or a creature untamed. But he had treated her with condescension. He'd flashed an expensive-looking watch and bragged about his law practice, how successful he was, and all the immigrants he had represented. She should have followed her instincts. She didn't have to come to America to know that lying and cheating transcended borders, cultures, languages, and religions.

Amina's mother had always told her, "You can tell if you can trust a man by how he talks about his family." Amina hadn't heeded that message when she'd hired the first attorney, who had dismissed his "foolish" daughters for marrying imbeciles. "But they never were very smart, just like their mother," he'd said. On the other hand, the woman lawyer's face had softened and glowed when Amina had asked about her children, triggering a painful longing in Amina. Gaining asylum wouldn't cure that pain and the guilt that accompanied it, but going back wouldn't, either.

Amina's mother was the wisest person she knew. She spoke little but always with gravity. Amina refolded the flyer and stepped back onto the sidewalk, edging along the curb to avoid passersby. Her bag thumped against her hip with each step, reassuring in its regularity.

A desire to feel her mother's hands rubbing her back and to hear her mother's soothing words overtook her and wouldn't succumb to the distractions of the city. She reached into the bag to pull her phone out from beneath the internship flyer. It was an old model, the one she had purchased when she first arrived. Accessing her saved messages, she took a deep breath before clicking to listen to the last message from her mother.

"Amina, it will be hard to reach us. The bombs are falling again, and services are unreliable. We take comfort that you are safe. Your father—"

The hit felt slight, but Amina's hand whipped forward, empty. She yelped a pitiful cry, unnoticed by the people passing her on the sidewalk. A young man, newly possessed of her old phone, was already at the next block, pedaling fast as he dodged parked cars. He would be disappointed with the early-model Samsung littered with Arabic, perhaps even a little scared by that latter fact. Amina's despair merged with a grim recognition that her status could be snatched away just as that phone had been.

Her scarf fluttered again, and she reached to hold it still against her jaw. She had despaired back then, when she'd seen she missed her mother's call and was unable to reach her parents again. The recorded voice had sustained her since, but now it was possible her mother's voice could only be heard through Amina herself.

CHAPTER
THIRTEEN

Jessica pushed back from the dining room table, silently cursing Rosalie.

A few days before, her former classmate had been blasé about Jessica's success in convincing Amina. "Of course she's going to use you. You'll do great." Then she'd handed Jessica a stack of black, numbered binders and pointed at a larger stack of even more. "Read through these. Let me know if you have any questions." Jessica had had to make two trips to haul the stacks out to her car in the lot around the corner.

Those binders now lay splayed out in front of her. Reading through laws and government regulations two days in a row would be mind-numbing under any circumstances, but scouring through old cases detailing humiliations, imprisonments, rape, torture, and death and attempting to parse how those details did or did not lead to a grant of asylum made the research exhausting.

Jessica's subconscious began to weave the anonymous images from her earlier Syria research with the more intimate, personal stories of former IAP clients in the binders, creating a tapestry of terror in her mind. She had barely scratched the surface of Amina's own personal story but was starting to gain a better understanding of the woman's situation.

Jessica's own insensitivity came into focus. Her judgments about Amina's attitude and demeanor hadn't been terribly kind. The trau-

ma of Amina's story—not bitterness or arrogance—and being disconnected from the people she loved could explain both Amina's reticence to speak and her swift exit from the coffee shop. Jessica closed
the binders, stacked them, and placed them in boxes under the table.

More boxes. Just what I need. What she *did* need was some balance among the chaos and some progress.

"C'mon, Gracie. Let's do something easy before I go get groceries
and the kids get home." Gracie gamely trailed Jessica into the parlor.

She scanned the labels on Oma's boxes: *My Mementos, Mother's
Dishes, My Glassware.*

My Quilt. That looked simple and sweet. No beheadings there.
Jessica sliced cleanly through the tape and opened the box. The now-
familiar lavender note and scent of White Diamonds instantly separated her from the stress of her research, the ruminations on her relationship with Amina, and even the piles of boxes that continued to
taunt her.

She unfolded the note.

*"Enclosed is an antique quilt. The design is 'double wedding ring.' It
was made especially for me for my Hope Chest. Hope Chests were usually cedar at that time, but my Gr. Margarethe gave me the trunk that
her parents brought to America. The blocks in the quilt were made from
scraps of material left from flour-sack dresses and aprons of mine and
my mother's. As you will see, all the tiny, even stitches are so delicate. Gr.
Margarethe was known for her fine workmanship."*

The note continued with washing instructions. Surprised Oma
hadn't enclosed a coupon for detergent, Jessica double-checked the
envelope just in case. While she couldn't recall a "double wedding
ring" quilt at Oma's house, the promise of more of Margarethe's
artistry piqued Jessica's interest.

She folded back the tissue paper that surrounded the quilt. One
side of the quilt was solid yellow. The other side had colorful squares
stitched together to create a design of interlocking rings on a back-

ground of white. A different fabric made up each colored square. There were pale-blue leaves on white, bright-yellow lemons on orange, and cottony-white flowers on lavender. Jessica felt an unexpected flash of regret that she hadn't kept any of the sweet gingham jumpers Cricket had worn before she'd insisted on choosing her own clothes.

"Tiny and even stitches..." Oma hadn't begun to describe what Jessica saw. The stitches were almost microscopic—thousands and thousands of them. And they weren't just utilitarian, connecting the squares and attaching the front of the quilt to the back. They were mathematical, like something that might have been graphed from Cricket's equations.

Jessica ran her finger lightly along a line of stitches, randomly following the left then the right branches as the stitches created a complicated yet perfectly symmetrical repeating design. A starburst of patterns with lines radiating from center points and intersecting with what looked like a Spirograph design of interlacing arcs covered the entire queen-size quilt. She flipped the edge of the fabric and couldn't spy a single knot. It was as though it were sewn with a single thread.

This. Was. Done. By. Hand. Jessica admired this woman, who had spent unknown hours of labor and love to add such beauty to discarded scraps of fabric. The wood surrounding Jessica represented endless hours as well, but she hadn't created anything. The ship table she'd made for Danny came close. But her joy with that project wasn't so much from creating something new as it was from bringing the history of the piece to life.

Jessica tabbed the cursor from column to column on the spreadsheet. Consignment. Donate. Keep. She marked the last column and closed the laptop. Then she folded the quilt carefully and set it across the arm of the chair.

JESSICA pulled into the driveway with a car full of groceries just as the kids were arriving home.

"Great timing, guys!" Jessica opened the trunk invitingly.

Mikey and Cricket hauled in as many bags as they could carry, while Conor made a show of turning off his car, checking the mirrors, collecting bits of trash, opening and closing his trunk, and walking ever so slowly over to Jessica's car.

She handed Conor a gallon of milk and a gallon of orange juice. "You think you can handle these? I don't want to overburden you." The insincerity dripped from her voice like the condensation dripped from the gallon jugs.

Conor wordlessly took the jugs and walked toward the house as Mikey ran out to get another load.

Back in the kitchen, Mikey and Cricket competed in telling Jessica about their day and their weekend plans.

"We're studying continents, and I got Australia, which is really cool because I love koalas, so I get to include them in my presentation." Mikey had his arm up to his elbow in a bag of potato chips. Gracie sat patiently at his feet, awaiting the inevitable cascade of oily crumbs. "Did you wash my soccer uniform? I need it for the tournament this weekend."

Cricket grabbed an opening when Mikey shoved a handful of chips into his mouth. "Mom, Mrs. Harriman is so mean! She made Ella cry today." Her eyes widened with incredulity. "It made me so mad. But it *is* AP," she conceded. "So Ella should have known there would be a lot of homework. I'm so glad I don't have a swim meet this weekend. I have to work on a paper applying Machiavelli's *The Prince* to a contemporary ruler. I haven't even picked out my ruler yet."

Without thinking, Jessica offered, "Bashar al-Assad." She'd gone from not being able to find Syria on a map to having its dictator at the top of her mind for trivia.

Cricket twisted her mouth and looked up at the ceiling, considering the suggestion. "He did choose to have people fear him rather than love him, but he didn't manage to avoid the people hating him part. Thanks, Mom. Good idea." The kids were a little more in tune with world events than Jessica had been at their age, perhaps more than she was even now.

Mikey ran off, yelling something about going outside to play basketball, while Cricket wandered out of the room, glued to her phone. She was no doubt messaging with her AP class about how mean Mrs. Harriman had been today.

That left Conor, who was making a sandwich but was probably wishing he had snuck out ahead of his brother and sister instead. These one-on-one moments had been precious bonding times when he was five or eight, but now they felt tinged with the desperation of a mother who could see a door still ajar but couldn't get to it before it closed.

"So... how are things going with you?" Jessica was fishing, buying time.

Conor wasn't biting. "Fine."

"Classes going okay? Do you like your teachers? How is that photography elective? Do *you* get to do a project on koalas?" Perhaps levity would hold the door open.

He probably rolled his eyes, but since he refused to make eye contact, it was impossible to know.

Jessica could feel the cords in her neck pull taut as she clenched her jaw and held back the words she wanted to say—that she was his mother, goddammit, and he couldn't continue to ignore her. Instead, she kept her tone calm, imagining how a therapist would speak. "You don't want to talk? Okay. But you didn't finish up the last school year in stellar fashion." Maybe a therapist wouldn't have made a negative comment like that, but it wasn't a secret that Conor's grades had fallen second semester. They hadn't fallen by too much, but he'd received a few low B's that would have been A's had he put in his regular efforts. His teachers' reports on his classroom apathy were what had signaled a potential downward trend.

Conor finally eyed her with what looked like disdain.

"If you need help, just let your dad or me know. We're here for you. No judgment." That was what a therapist would say. "We were teenagers. We know what it's like."

Conor exhaled sharply through his nose, a condescending message that she was too far removed from today's reality to comment.

She took a stabilizing breath, inhaling so much that she shuddered as she over-filled her lungs. "Whatever it is, school, sports, girls—"

He threw his head back as if it were a trunk lid on a hinge. "God, Mom. Everything is fine." He grabbed his sandwich and stomped out of the kitchen.

Jessica stood impotent in the middle of the room. Maybe it wasn't that she was too slow to reach the door to her son. Maybe she was taking the wrong path. They had hardly seen him over the summer. Danny had offered him a summer internship position at Binnacle. It would have looked great on his college applications. But the kid who used to want to spend every waking hour with his dad—hell, he'd wanted to *be* his dad—had decided he would rather sell tickets at the movie theater all summer.

"He's got to find his own way," Danny had said. If he'd been hurt by the rejection, he'd given no indication. "And he still has basketball."

In any case, Conor had spent the summer working the two o'clock-to-ten o'clock shift, sleeping late, and coming out of his room only for sustenance.

Jessica agreed that Conor needed to find his own way, but it had better be the right way. She didn't like the way she was seeing right now but didn't have a clue as to how to direct him. Her arms hung heavy with the powerlessness of that realization. Basketball season couldn't come soon enough to inject some discipline, structure, and social life back into Conor's world.

"Lamb?" Danny must have come in the back door just after Conor left the room. Jessica turned to see him holding a meat-department package that he had pulled out of one of the grocery bags.

"Yeah, I know. Weird, huh? Thought I'd try something new this week. You know me, crazy kitchen adventuress." Jessica waved her hands in mock wackiness, her heavy arms protesting the farce.

"Sounds good." Danny moved toward her with a mischievous gleam in his eye. "I like when you're an adventuress, though maybe not in the kitchen so much as elsewhere." He wrapped his arms around her waist and kissed her on the neck. "Sorry I'll miss dinner tonight. I've got a conference call and some documents I need to get out. I'll be in my office. You all set?"

Jessica looked around her own "office." "All set. I'll take care of dinner and the kids. You and I can meet up for adventure later, after you're done with Binnacle stuff."

"That's my girl." He grabbed the newspaper from the table on his way out and lightly whacked it on Cricket's head as she passed him on her way back into the kitchen.

"You're back," Jessica said.

The freckle-faced beauty opened the pantry, foraging for a snack. "Had to get my backpack. I've got a ton of homework. We finally got our tests back in world lit, and the scores were so bad that Mr. Harvey decided our current unit will include both a paper *and* an in-class debate."

"Based on fifteen years of arguing with your brother—"

"And winning." The cocky grin that proved she was Danny's daughter lit up her face.

"Mostly, yes. Based on that, I imagine you'll do pretty well in a debate." With feigned nonchalance, Jessica offered, "You know, if you need any help, I *am* a lawyer. Just sayin'."

"Got it, Mom. Anyway, I have trig homework and a lab report due in chemistry, plus a ton of reading for lit."

Cricket arranged a tidy plate of pretzels, carrot sticks, and hummus then put everything away. If only Jessica could get the boys to do that.

"Hey, Crick. Before you head upstairs, I want to show you something I found in one of Oma's boxes. I don't think the boys will be terribly interested, but you might. It'll just take a minute." Jessica grabbed her laptop and led Cricket to the parlor, then she handed her daughter the handwritten note that came with the quilt.

Cricket started reading the note out loud. The honors student was suddenly a first grader, sounding out each word phonetically. "Enclosed is an an... an... What's this word?"

Jessica grabbed the note, sighing. Damn schools didn't teach cursive writing anymore. "Antique. It means really old."

Cricket rolled her eyes. "Oh my God, Mom. I know what antique means."

Jessica waved her off. "Enclosed is an antique quilt." Jessica read the full note aloud while Cricket lifted the quilt from the chair.

"What's a flour-sack dress?" Cricket fingered a quilt square of bright red with white stars.

"I had to look it up myself. Apparently, flour used to come in big cloth bags, not paper sacks like we have now. Women used the cloth bags to make dresses and aprons. Can you imagine?" They gaped at each other in mock horror. "The flour companies were smart, though. They started making the sacks out of colorful prints. Your great-great-grandma made all of Oma's dresses out of different flour sacks. And here they are."

Cricket touched one square after another, hopscotching across the quilt. Jessica steered Cricket's finger to a square of cornflower blue covered with white trellises and red poppies.

Jessica opened her laptop. "Look at this. It's Oma as a little girl. I pulled this photo from her obituary page." She showed Cricket a faded black-and-white photo of a pigtailed girl holding a basket full of kittens. The little girl wore a dress covered with white trellises and poppies.

Cricket's eyes sparkled in the lamplight. "This square is from that dress! That is so cool. Good thing flour comes in paper bags now. I wouldn't want to wear a flour-sack dress you made... or any dress you made. No offense." She frowned, her eyebrows pulling together.

"You'd better be nice to me, Crick, or I may just make your prom dress all by myself. In fact"—Jessica picked up the quilt—"this looks like just enough fabric—"

Cricket grabbed the quilt from Jessica. "No! Mine!" She hugged the quilt to her chest. "Can I have it?"

It had been in a box for who knew how long, and Cricket's pleading eyes could win Jessica over any day. "Yes. I think Oma would have liked that. Just, please, be careful with it. No food, pop, whatever." Jessica remembered the marshmallows on the floor. "And keep it away from Mikey."

Cricket rolled her eyes. "I know, Mom. It will be fine. I love it." She wrapped the quilt around herself and tromped up the stairs toward her bedroom.

"Thanks, Oma." Jessica was not completely helpless with her teens after all. She knew she could find a way to reach Conor. She just needed to keep looking.

CHAPTER
FOURTEEN

Jessica arrived early at the coffee shop and sat at a table by the window farthest from the entrance. This time her coffee would have time to cool, but she already regretted her decision to go with decaf.

It had been hard to schedule a follow-up meeting with Amina. First, there was something about a lost phone. Then Sama went on bed rest, so not only had Amina's hours at the restaurant increased, but so had demands at home. Today, Amina had the lunch shift off, so the two should be able to have a productive meeting.

On the up side, the delay had given Jessica a few extra days to scour those binders and learn more about immigration technicalities and how the intricacies of asylum law might be applied in this specific case. She had printed out and read the entire USCIS Asylum Officer Basic Training Course, and she had an empty ink cartridge and achy eyes to prove it. She'd read case law online and had tagged relevant passages and opinion summaries for future reference. When it was all said and done, she figured she could probably substitute for an asylum officer in a pinch and do a pretty good job at checking the boxes, judging credibility, and applying the law.

Danny had taken notice of the efforts, finding her in the dining room, working through some recent guidance Rosalie had sent. "Looks like you're back in law school, hon. Didn't they teach you this stuff in training? Or are you off on one of your 'do more than I need to do' tangents?"

Jessica felt vulnerable surrounded by the open binders and piles of papers, not to mention the boxes from Oma that still encroached on the space, and Danny's subtly mocking tone put her on the defensive.

"Okay, Captain, imagine if I took an introductory 'How to Sail' webinar without stepping foot on a boat."

Danny smirked. He knew she hated sailing.

"Right, I know. That'll be the day. Anyway, just say I did. Would I be able to jump on a J-22 with an inexperienced crew and make it to the bay? Would I even be able to make it out of the harbor?" Jessica acknowledged Danny's comical look. "Of course not. So in this situation, it's like I read the materials from a training session months ago, and now I'm finally on the boat. And even though I read about what to do with which rope—"

"Line," Danny corrected, "not rope."

"Right! *Exactly my point!* Even though I learned that it's called a 'line' and I read what I'm supposed to do with it, now that I'm on the boat, I just see a bunch of ropes. I know I can sail this boat eventually, but I'm going to have to be very deliberate about learning while I'm sailing."

He had nodded sagely, no longer mocking her. "Just remember that it's not always about simply knowing what's in the book. Sometimes, you have to go with your instincts."

This morning, looking ruefully at the closed folder resting on the coffee-shop table in front of her, Jessica's instinct was telling her she'd better not sink this boat.

The front door jingled, and the draft from the door opening sent the rich, dark smells of fifty varieties of coffee beans swirling around the tables. Sneering at the decaf in front of her, Jessica inhaled the aroma, hoping somehow to absorb some caffeine as Amina approached the table.

After again rejecting Jessica's offer of a drink or pastry, Amina positioned her chair a bit away from the table, as though she were attempting to make it clear that she was not joining in any coffee klatch. Or maybe she was ensuring the ability to depart quickly.

Jessica pulled Amina's asylum application from the folder and set it next to a yellow legal pad displaying a handwritten checklist for today's meeting. "I'm so glad you were able to meet me. I'm sure those boys are a handful. Is Sama doing well?"

"Yes."

"Are you working at the restaurant every day now?"

"Yes."

Those questions weren't on the checklist, and they weren't helping to ease into the discussion they needed to have. Amina's dark stare, coupled with her body positioning, telegraphed an intent not to get comfortable. Amina was clearly not interested in small talk, but Jessica wanted to develop some level of comfort, if only for herself. She would pivot.

"I really did enjoy my lunch at Bathanjaan. I know I told you that already. But did I tell you I tried to make my own kibbeh?" Jessica inferred from the look on Amina's face that either she hadn't mentioned it or Amina simply didn't care, or both. She wouldn't tell Amina what a disaster it had been. Actual sea slugs in a milky sea would have been better.

Pivot. "I haven't asked you, what else do you like to do? When you aren't working or helping the Darbi family, that is."

"I am very busy." Amina's raised eyebrows and pursed lips indicated this was not an answer but rather a statement of the current situation.

Jessica needlessly shuffled the papers and picked up her pen. She would just work her way through the asylum application. She handed Amina the copy that Amina had left behind at their last meeting.

"Can you check through the first two pages of this and make sure the information is still accurate?" The first and second pages were full of identifying information about Amina and her missing husband. The third page asked for information about children. Amina had left that page blank.

Amina ticked off each entry on the application, one by one. She paused about three-quarters of the way down the first page before checking the section off and moving on. Jessica glanced at the duplicate form in front of her. *List each entry into the US, beginning with your most recent entry.* Amina had visited the US twice before, when she was school-aged. It was long enough ago that it wasn't likely to raise eyebrows with the USCIS, but something about it struck a note with Amina.

After checking the last completed block on page two, Amina looked up at Jessica. "Everything is still accurate." She raised an eyebrow. "I did tell you that last time."

Jessica forced herself not to sound defensive. "Yes, I understand. But it's important to make sure we take note of anything that changes. I will ask you to go through and check again before you go in for your interview. Can you check page four as well?" That page asked for places of residence, education, employment, and immediate family.

Tick, tick, tick. After checking the boxes by family members whose whereabouts were marked "Unknown" and by the sibling marked "Deceased," Amina set down her pencil. Her mouth opened slightly, but she didn't say anything for a moment. Her impatience won out over her reticence to speak, though. "It is all accurate."

Unfortunately, now they had to get into the horribles. *What horrible things happened to your family? What horrible things happened to your friends? What horrible things happened to you? What horrible things will happen to you if you return?*

Jessica had thought this through ahead of the meeting. She was not a therapist. She would go at this dispassionately. Questions needed to be asked, and she would ask them. She would check off one item and move to the next, marching through the horribles but not stopping to stare.

She took a slow sip of her coffee. Her racing heartbeat assured her that she hadn't needed the caffeine after all and that it might be hard to stay dispassionate. She scanned the room. The two of them were tucked away in the corner, alone in the shop save for the barista, who took advantage of the downtime to restock the bagged coffee.

"Let's start with your parents. You note here that you don't know where your parents are. When did you lose track of them? When did you last communicate with them?"

"When I arrived in America." Amina hadn't adjusted her posture, but her hand clenching tightly around the strap of her bag broke the veneer of calm.

Jessica double-checked the application. "But that was well over two years ago. You haven't been in touch with them at all since then?" Even Jessica spoke with her mother more frequently, though her mother didn't live in a war zone.

"No."

Jessica really needed to stop asking yes-or-no questions, or this would take forever. "How have you tried to reach them?"

Amina pulled a napkin from the center of the table and centered it flat in front of her. "I spoke with them by telephone when I arrived. But their number stopped working. I have not heard from them." She seemed to be talking to the napkin.

"Where were they living when you left?"

"Aleppo."

Amina's last address in Syria was in Aleppo. The images Jessica had seen of the city showed bombed-out shells of buildings, first responders tending to the injured, and dead victims of Assad and rebel attacks. "Did you live near them?"

"Yes."

"How long had they lived there?"

"They lived there my whole life and before that." She folded one edge of the napkin, pressed the crease from edge to edge, then folded it again.

Jessica tore out a piece of yellow paper and slid it across the table. "Can you write the address on this?"

Emotion flashed behind Amina's bold eyes. But it didn't last long enough for Jessica to tell if it was anything other than impatience.

"What are you going to do with it?"

"To be honest, I'm really not sure right now. But when I'm pulling together evidence, I might need it. We need all the documentation we can get to support your case."

Amina eyed her warily but wrote out an address and handed the paper back to Jessica. Jessica noted the elegant swoops and heavy straight lines in the script. It was as if the handwriting had a Middle Eastern accent.

"Can you tell me about your mother?" Now Jessica did feel like a therapist, but she hoped she might find an opening here in which she could get Amina to make an emotional connection.

Amina's hand went to her jade scarf, her fingers moving slowly along the edge that draped across her shoulder. "She is traditional."

Is. That could mean hope. "Traditional? How?"

"Everything she does is a testament of her commitment to her faith."

"You mean in clothing? Like hijab?" Jessica made a slight gesture toward Amina's scarf as if Amina needed to be reminded what a hijab was.

Amina ignored the gesture. "Everything. Raising the children. Keeping the home. Honoring her husband."

"How about your father? You note here that he's an economics professor." *And that's why he was arrested and tortured.* "Where is he a professor?"

"He taught at the University of Aleppo."

Taught. Jessica took a deep breath and exhaled slowly. "Please tell me about his arrest. Who arrested him? Why? What happened to him in custody?" She set her pen down and folded her hands together, leaning toward the table. "I know this can be difficult, and I'm sorry we have to talk about it."

Amina adjusted in her chair. "He taught global economics. There was an uprising in 2011."

"Yes, the Arab Spring. Was your father a part of that?"

"No. 'An economist cannot be a politician,' he said. Assad's soldiers detained him and questioned his teachings. My father thought they were..." Amina seemed to be grasping for a word. "They were ignorant. He did not think they understood his teachings." Amina leaned forward, placing her hands on the edge of the table. "My father was proud of Syria. It is an ancient country that has faced both terrible times and times of peace and prosperity. After the Arab Spring, Assad said the government would make changes." Amina exhaled and shook her head slowly. "My father believed him."

Jessica endured the abrupt silence, hoping Amina would continue.

"My father believed that he was helping our country by teaching his students how Syria's changes would allow it to regain its promise and sit among the powers of the world. An informant in the class reported my father to the regime. We didn't see him for five days." Amina's fingers pushed into the table, her knuckles whitening.

"Do you know who took him?" Jessica asked.

"The *Mukhabarat.*"

Jessica repeated the word in her head, attempting to hear her own voice say it. She had read about Assad's secret police and the state terror they'd perpetrated, though she hadn't heard the term spoken aloud.

Amina continued. "After he returned home, the bombs came. Assad, our president"—Amina almost spat the title—"he sent bombs to our city, to his people. I believe that hurt my father more than the beatings he endured. My father never again spoke of our country rising as a world power. He no longer wrote. He stopped teaching."

"Do you have any kind of record of this? An arrest record or any affidavits?"

Amina's squint reflected her incredulity with the question. "The *Mukhabarat* does not provide documentation other than the scars they leave on your back."

Amina's phone buzzed, breaking a brief but uncomfortable silence. After hanging up, she placed her phone in her bag and straightened as if to leave. "I must go to the restaurant. The hostess called in sick."

Jessica regrouped. "A couple more questions if it's okay. I'll be quick." Jessica checked her notes. "You said you spoke with your parents right after you arrived here but you couldn't get through after that. Have you tried to find them online, Facebook, a refugee locator site? How about your brother?"

"I see pictures on newspapers, on the television. It is never their faces. I look at some websites, but I have been careful. We could be tracked and targeted."

"I'm sorry, I don't follow. Tracked and targeted?"

Amina pursed her lips. "It is best that we not bring attention to ourselves. Too many communications with Syria or too many Internet searches might make the American government think we are terrorists."

That was something Jessica hadn't considered.

Amina stared at some unseen image over Jessica's shoulder. There would be no unexpectedly abrupt exit today. There was no question the conversation had reached its conclusion.

Jessica couldn't help but feel the boat hadn't even left the dock yet.

CHAPTER FIFTEEN
AMINA

The door jingled as it closed behind her, and Amina walked away from the restaurant without a backward glance despite another offer of a ride from the lawyer. It was enough to hire IAP, answer the lawyer's questions, and work with them until this was over. She didn't need to add the complications of anything beyond that. She'd had enough complications.

Amina slowed to avoid bikes chained to signposts along the sidewalks and fell in with the pace of the other pedestrians. Stopping at a crosswalk, she looked up above the brick buildings surrounding her and closed her eyes, letting her hand rest on her bag.

Life had seemed uncomplicated, even charmed, before the conflicts. Her father had traveled to economics conferences outside of Syria, sometimes bringing Amina. He'd never brought her brothers. She and her father had shared a special bond, talking endlessly about economics, world affairs, and the rights of women. They were conversations that had occurred only abroad or in the cocoon of their home. Not because they'd advocated rebellion or opposition, but because, in Syria, one limited conversations to pleasantries when outside a trusted circle. Later, Amina had learned that even trusted circles weren't always safe. But alone with her father, anything could be said, and anything had seemed possible.

The memory was as vivid to her today as it was in 2000. She'd stood, an awestruck teenager, with her father at the top of the Sears

Tower, marveling at the city of Chicago below. The sun bounced off the glass buildings, illuminating a view so new and so vast. The reflective structures rose like great swords from the ground, promising strength and progress.

"Amina," her father said, waving his hand in a grand gesture over the city below. "This is beautiful, but it is not our Syria. We have a richer past, and our new president will bring a brighter future. Keep studying, and you will be a part of it. That is what will lift our country," he'd said. "Education."

She missed her father, misguided though he had been that the son of the former cruel dictator would not follow in his own father's footsteps. Her father loved Syria, and for that, she could not fault him. It was her country, too.

She opened her eyes and turned to a window to see a reflection of a scarved woman with blank eyes, standing at the base of a low brick building in a country that wasn't hers.

The walk signal turned white, and Amina headed toward the bus stop on the next block. Her shift started soon, so she would take the bus today.

The MTA signpost hosted a disconnected party of three, or maybe four if the jittery woman shouting short bursts of expletives into her phone was waiting for the bus and not just stopping to assure full focus on her argument. Two African-American men, one wearing a cap, the other with loose hair and a wispy beard that he stroked mindlessly, spoke in low tones. An older white woman, plump and tired looking, guarded a large, bulging plastic bag at her feet.

The man wearing the cap swiveled his head in Amina's direction, catching her eye for a split second before his gaze shot beyond her shoulder. Amina turned to see the arriving bus just as her phone buzzed, the vibrations tingling the fingers that held her bag against her side. She pulled out the phone and saw an unfamiliar but local number on the screen.

Since the day her phone had taken off on a bike, Amina hadn't recreated her full contact list. She hadn't had a lot of contacts, just the restaurant, the boys' school, Fayiz, a few others, plus some that no longer existed. That could have been why she hadn't taken the time to create a new list. She preferred the old list.

She answered and heard a woman's tinny voice, one unconnected to any of her lost numbers.

"This is Julie Meyer from KLP. I'm calling about your application for the internship program." She had the lilting voice of a twentysomething-year-old American. Each sentence ended as if it were a question. Amina heard this cadence when she occasionally waited tables, always wanting to respond to "I'd like the kabab?" with "Yes, you would like the kabab" but thinking better of it.

Amina hadn't expected to hear from the program so soon, and her heart accelerated as the bus in front of her slowed to a stop. She asked the woman to hold a moment as the brakes screeched and her heart pounded. Two people exited the bus, and the two black men climbed on. The older woman struggled with her plastic bag and followed them. The jittery woman hadn't broken from her argument but held a hand over her free ear to drown out the noise. The bus driver raised his eyebrows at Amina and the arguing woman. Amina waved him off. He closed the door and pulled away, dark-gray exhaust leaving a trail along the curb.

Amina turned from the street before taking a deep breath. "Thank you for holding, Ms. Meyer. I am glad to hear from you."

"Ms. Hamid, thank you for sending in your application. We are super excited to see that you would like to be part of our diversity leadership program."

Amina squeezed the phone. Professionally a step down or not, the possibility of getting this position thrilled her, almost enough to take her mind off the things she and the lawyer had discussed.

"All we need from you to complete the eligibility review"—the woman managed to add a question mark mid-sentence as she paused—"is a copy of your college transcript. You reference your ac-counting degree, and we need the transcript to confirm course com-pletion and satisfaction of our requirements."

If it had in fact been a question, Amina would have responded, "No. No, you don't need the transcript." Instead, she said, "You need a transcript from my university... in Syria." It was not a question, coming from her. She spoke as if she were reciting an item from a to-do list, not as if she were suppressing a primal scream, which she was.

"Right! We require the college to send it directly to us. They can send it to the same address you used for the application. Do you need that?"

"No. I... I do not know that I can get a transcript sent. There's a war."

"A war? Oh, hmm, yes. Maybe we can make an exception if you already have a copy of your transcript. We don't usually accept that. Potential fraud, you know. I can't promise."

I didn't travel with my transcript. Her father had been smart not to include anything that would arouse suspicion when he sent her away. Future employability in the event of an extended civil war had not been on his mind. "I'm afraid I do not have a copy. Thank you." She clicked off the phone. She didn't want to hear any more ques-tions.

"Education will lift our country." Amina mouthed her father's words and laughed out loud, drawing a glare from the jittery woman. In fact, she thought ruefully, machetes could cut off the head of an educated man, and a single barrel bomb could kill a school full of children. And since she hadn't traveled with a transcript, it was as though her education had never even happened.

CHAPTER SIXTEEN

Jessica hustled about the kitchen, chopping, preheating, and setting out condiments, while Danny relaxed, feet up on the coffee table in the adjacent family room, reading the paper. The law school graduate in Jessica tried to argue that this was criminally old-fashioned. But after all these months of Danny working late, she was the one who wouldn't be home for dinner. Playing the happy homemaker assuaged some of her guilt. It also distracted her from worrying about how Amina would respond to the meeting they would be attending together that night at the IAP offices.

Amina had been visibly agitated at the end of their last meeting. Talking about her parents must have been a trigger. When Rosalie had called yesterday, asking Jessica to bring Amina to the IAP offices to join in discussions about incoming Syrian refugees and maybe even talk about her own experiences, Jessica had predicted that Amina's answer would be a hard no. The fact that Amina had not only said yes but also seemed eager to attend placed pressure on Jessica to ensure the meeting didn't serve as another trigger. She felt a growing need to protect her Syrian client, who not so long ago seemed to be someone from whom Jessica thought she might need protection.

"What's this meeting about?" Danny didn't look up from his paper.

Jessica set the timer on the oven and opened the cabinet to remove a stack of plates. "There's a group of Syrian refugees coming to the US at the end of the year. Rosalie led the efforts to open the way for Maryland to take some of them in, so the governor reached out to IAP to assist with resources. Rosalie invited me to the meeting about how the process will work. It's not a huge meeting, just a few people from housing and employment resources." She shrugged. "Should be interesting."

Danny snapped the newspaper open, spreading it wide so he could fold one side over as he moved to the next section. "I wonder if it's a good idea. Opening the way."

"What do you mean?"

He let the paper fall back on itself, exposing his bay blues. "Seems to be inviting trouble, letting in people from a country full of zealots who want to kill us all."

"I'm pretty sure the goal is not to let in those particular zealots."

"It's not just that," Danny said. "It's an inefficient use of resources. There are, what, hundreds of thousands of displaced Syrians—"

"Millions."

Danny raised his eyebrows. "Supports my point even more. The cost to resettle and support a single refugee must be, I don't know, tens of thousands of dollars when you figure in social services, education, food stamps, and housing assistance. That money would be better spent on humanitarian aid in the region. Services cost less over there, you have economies of scale, and people get to be closer to their home, families, and culture. People don't get to feel like do-gooders here at home, but we end up helping more people."

His analytic tone, absent of political tinge, was far too clinical to come off as reactionary. He sounded entirely reasonable, in fact, though it stung to hear her efforts deemed frivolous and self-serving.

He added, seemingly as an afterthought, "And we don't have to worry about terrorists claiming to be refugees so they can infiltrate our country."

Jessica set the plates around the table, continuing her happy-homemaker routine, resisting the urge to get argumentative and instead adopting her own analytic tone. "The review process is pretty intense. Multiple government agencies do extensive background checks, biological screenings, and detailed interviews. It can take twelve, eighteen, even twenty-four months to get cleared to enter the US as a refugee. I doubt many terrorists are going to make it through that review or even be willing to wait that long."

Danny pushed the paper down. "It's happened before. Don't you remember those al Qaeda guys from Iraq in Illinois? They came in as so-called refugees. You think they're the only ones?"

"The process has improved."

He waved away her statement. "We don't need the process if we focus humanitarian efforts over there. I know there's a lot of suffering, but we just can't trust them."

"Them? That's quite a generalization. I'd expect you to be more nuanced than that." She hadn't told him about Amina. She couldn't recall making a conscious decision not to, and he had never asked. It seemed normal, a throwback to her days at the firm when "don't ask, don't tell" was the house rule about clients. She had originally withheld the information—after Amina had fired her and she was filled with relief—out of concern that she would betray her own bias. And here it was Danny who was biased. She shouldn't judge, though, recalling her own initial reaction to Amina.

He tilted his head and smiled condescendingly. "Hon, I know Rosalie has sucked you into her world and its tunnel vision on immigration. And I agree it's different with a lot of the immigrants who are already here. Those"—he motioned toward Jessica as if she were surrounded by immigrants—"unaccompanied minors, for instance, that IAP is working with. I'm pretty sure we don't need to worry about them."

Jessica searched Danny's bay-blue eyes. She could have heard those same words come out of her mouth not so long ago. "We have to trust the process, I guess."

"You don't know the things I know. As closely as Binnacle has worked with the Defense Department and some of our international customers, I know the threats out there. These people want to take us down. We can tighten the system and try to stay a step ahead, but you can't outwit people who feel they have nothing to lose and everything to gain in the afterlife. All it takes is one coming in."

"You're right. We know different things." Such as the fact that more Muslims than non-Muslims have been killed by extremists.

He nodded as if she had agreed with him. "There's too much at stake to risk ourselves. Good thing you're working with kids."

Jessica opened her mouth to respond then shut it. *Did I tell him that?* She supposed she had prior to meeting Amina. Since IAP was so heavily involved with the kids, she'd assumed that would be her assignment. But she hadn't lied about anything. In the interest of marital harmony, she decided it was best not to say anything now. Who knew what Danny would say if she told him she was representing one of "them."

She motioned toward the oven. "The pasta will be done in twenty-five minutes. I shouldn't be too late."

Danny folded his paper. "Be careful, hon."

CHAPTER SEVENTEEN

"You're sure you don't want a ride home?" This routine was getting old, but Jessica had to ask, especially since the meeting had gone long. Afterward, she and Amina had lingered to go over some outreach materials that Rosalie was hoping Amina would translate into Arabic ahead of the refugees' arrival.

Amina shook her head.

"If you say so. But you can't stop me from walking you to the bus stop. It's over by the parking lot, right?" She felt as if she were talking to Conor.

Dark eyes rolled ever so slightly, confirming that Amina was indeed a stand-in for Conor at that moment, but she didn't protest. Jessica knew that even the stolid Syrian recognized the neighborhood was dicey at night.

Amina wrapped a thin woolen cape around herself and led the way out of the IAP offices.

The evening was cold but clear, and the crispness of the late-fall air complemented the bright pinpoints of light in the sky above. Craning her head upward, Jessica could make out Orion, though the city lights drowned out many of the lesser constellations that had graced the endless skies of her childhood.

The sidewalks were quiet, and the commuters were home by now. Jessica winced at the exhaust from a passing delivery truck and watched the red lights as the truck turned at the next intersection.

Nighttime quiet without nature was still jarring to Jessica, even after all these years. Quiet nights back home meant that the farm animals were asleep. Darkness hid the crops, while the absence of the sun exposed the universe above. Quiet nights in the city hid unknowns and exposed little.

Amina walked silently next to her as they neared the bus stop just around the corner.

"Well, what do we have here?" The low voice carried as though it were part of the urban darkness, but its mock joviality seemed to cloak something sinister.

Jessica's heart skipped a beat as she saw three men in heavy jackets approaching from the corner. The one in the middle, the most imposing of the three, had his coat collar flipped up against the chill. He pulled his hands out of his pockets and displayed his palms. "I was talking to you."

Out of the corner of her eye, Jessica could see Amina stand taller. Jessica held eye contact with the man in the middle, attempting to size up his intention. The women could turn around and head back to the offices, but she didn't want to give these guys the pleasure of seeing her display fear. Plus, she wouldn't be able to see them if they were behind her.

The men stopped a few yards in front of the women, and the one in the middle stretched his arms out just enough to create a wall for his friends to form next to him and show he was the one in charge. The one on the right flicked a cigarette down by his side. The ugly smell of cheap tobacco drifted unimpeded downwind to the women.

Amina and Jessica stopped, instinctively closing the gap between themselves. Jessica wasted a second, pondering this reflex, wondering if the instinct was to make themselves seem more imposing by becoming a single, larger target. She then took a second to assess their surroundings, hoping a car or human would appear on the desolate street. Amina's hand moved to rest on her bag. Jessica couldn't remember who had been in the office when they'd left.

"Looks like a Mooslum whore to me," said the man on the left. The smallest of the three, he wore pants so long he'd had to roll them up at the bottom. He sniffed at Jessica. "And a sand-nigger lover." The last words felt like a slap to Jessica, but Amina didn't flinch.

The man in charge stepped forward slowly, the rest of his wall moving as one with him. He still held his palms facing out, as if to assure the women that these three thugs stalking toward them on a dark street while referring to them in derogatory, sexually charged terms meant no harm.

Jessica felt her senses heighten. Her instincts were not deceived by the gesture. The men must have been able to hear her heartbeat or at least see the thumping in her chest. She exhaled in an attempt to press her ribcage against the galloping muscle, to slow it before it exploded. She couldn't see the building on her left, but she could almost feel it, sensing the brick barrier only a couple of feet away from her.

The orange tip of the cigarette pulsated as the man on the right flicked it. The men still stood more than an arm's length away.

"We're just heading home, guys." Jessica couldn't tell if these were drunk, belligerent guys or simply belligerent guys. It didn't matter. She kept her face calm, even threw in the hint of a smile, in hopes of staunching any escalation.

"We'll decide where you're heading," the one in charge said.

Jessica followed his gaze toward Amina. Her stillness seemed almost practiced, betraying no fear or emotion.

"We'd like to have a word with your, um, your friend here." He gestured toward Amina, his eyes darkening.

There was no time to defuse the situation. Jessica pivoted to the right. They would be safer out in the street. But the middle one dropped his outstretched left arm, and the man on the right closed in to block their escape, backing both women up toward the brick wall.

Flick.

"So, what's under that, uh, that—" The middle one disdainfully flapped his hand toward Amina's head.

"Hijab," Amina said drily.

The little man on the left was starting to get twitchy. "Don't speak your Ay-rab around here, bitch! Why don't you go back to your cave in the desert?"

The one in charge stilled the twitchy one with a glance. "I think we need to show them what we do to terrorists here in America."

The three men moved close enough that Jessica could smell the beer on their breath. Her heartbeat filled her ears, accompanied by the whoosh of the blood violently coursing through her veins.

The one in charge leaned forward conspiratorially and whispered, "We fuck them up." He had his eyes on Jessica, as though trying to decide if the white American was culpable as well.

Flick. Out of the corner of her eye, Jessica saw the orange glow catapulting toward the street, pinpoints of tiny embers trailing, before hitting the ground and going dark.

Jessica's head hit the brick wall hard enough that the sound of the impact was more startling than the bolt of pain. Only one of the men—the middle one—had pushed her. The other two flanked Amina, and Jessica couldn't see them through the flash of pain and the bulk of the man pinning her to the wall. But she could hear hissed Arabic coming from the struggling woman to her left.

Then she heard the sound of a car, no, a truck. A door opened, and the three men spun around and ran. Jessica turned to her left to find Amina clutching her bag with one hand and tightening her scarf with the other. Black strands of hair were out of place, strewn around her face.

A man in a food-service uniform stepped down from the cab of the truck, seemingly torn between chasing the three men and checking on the women. But the men were gone already.

Jessica wanted to grab the truck driver and hug him out of gratitude, fear, and relief, but something about the way Amina held her composure made Jessica feel weak for even considering it. Instead, she reached up to check the back of her head, wincing as her fingers discovered the point at which it had struck the wall. A goose egg swelling with hot blood resisted her touch.

"You ladies okay?" As the man got near and his eyes focused in on Amina, he flinched. "I'm going to call 911." He took out his phone.

"No." Amina's command offered no compromise.

The man froze.

Jessica placed her hand on Amina's arm. "Amina, we need to call the police to report this."

Amina pulled away. "No. We will not contact the police." The finality of her statement seemed abrupt and unconsidered. But the vulnerability that flashed across her face paused Jessica's impulse to call in the heaviest government force available.

She took Amina aside. "Why? We need to report this. It's—"

"No police." Amina grasped Jessica's arm. "Promise me."

Jessica searched Amina's face, ignoring the distraction of the stray hairs caught in the breeze. Then Amina's fears revealed themselves. Assad, the *Mukhabarat*, an economics professor tortured, a pending asylum case. Even if Amina were comfortable dealing with law enforcement in the US—and she might not have been after her experiences at home—there was still the consideration of not wanting to draw more attention to herself while she pursued permanent residency in the country.

Jessica might have disagreed with that assessment, but she wasn't the one with so much at stake. Turning back to the man from the truck, Jessica thanked him and spoke with a confidence she didn't feel. "We're fine. There's no need to call the police. They're gone. We didn't even really get a good look at them."

"If you say so." He looked off in the direction the three men had run then back at the women. "But let me walk you to your car."

CHAPTER EIGHTEEN

Jessica jerked awake, her every muscle contracted as if ready for impact. The numbers on the clock glowed red in the darkness. It was only 4:13 a.m. She could feel Danny breathing steadily behind her and relaxed slightly.

He'd been asleep already when she'd arrived home after dropping Amina off at the Darbi home. She hadn't wanted to wake him, nor had she wanted to talk, so she'd whispered goodnights when he stirred mid-dream. But just because she wasn't talking about what had happened didn't mean it wasn't replaying in her mind.

Maybe she could convince herself that three drunk assholes had just said some mean things to two women on the street, and that was it. Maybe it was best to move on and forget about it rather than make a big deal of it. She didn't know the half of what Amina and her family had been through. Maybe this seemed like nothing to Amina. Maybe getting the police involved really would have been worse in some way.

Sure, she could aspire to convince herself of that, but her body screamed otherwise. Adrenaline had her in self-defense mode even while she was safe at home, in bed with a man so comfortable in his security that he could sleep through the monstrous pounding of Jessica's heart. She rolled over and looked at her husband. Even in his sleep, Danny moved to embrace her as she burrowed her head into his chest.

The minutes ticked by in slow motion. She feared closing her eyes and seeing the men again in her dreams, where she had no control over what they might do. She couldn't keep events from replaying while she was awake, but she could freeze-frame them, questioning each word she'd spoken and every move she'd made—from not calling the police to not turning back to walking out of the office alone to taking Amina's case in the first place to not telling Danny.

She should tell Danny. *Wake him up right now and tell him.* He would hold her and tell her she was safe, that he would protect her. Or he would be angry she hadn't told him about Amina.

He would—and in this, she had no doubt—insist she call the police. And she had promised Amina she wouldn't.

There would be no more sleep tonight, and the men in her head, the noise in her head, needed to be tamed. All of it was just more disorder, more disarray in what, not so long ago, had been a well-ordered life. She slid out of bed.

"We have an iron? What else have you been keeping from me?" Danny looked deadpan at Jessica, who stood behind an ironing board, next to a growing pile of freshly pressed napkins and tablecloths.

She muted the TV news that had been distracting her from replaying the night over and over.

Danny nodded approvingly at the coffee maker. "Now that's what I like to see." The sole early riser in the family, Danny was usually in charge of the coffee. "Why are you up so early? And why the, uh..." He waved his hand at the linens.

She shrugged. "Couldn't sleep."

"Is everything okay? I don't even know what time you came in last night."

"I'm fine. The meeting went late." On the TV, images of a refugee camp in Turkey replaced the sports results on the screen.

Danny's eyes followed hers. "Oh, that's right. You were talking about the refugees. So, they really are going to resettle some in Maryland?" He shook his head. "I still think it's a bad idea."

Jessica nodded noncommittally, the bump on her head pulsating in response, inviting trouble. She flicked off the TV.

Danny laced up his running shoes. "I'm going for a quick run, then I've got to get out of here. You all set with everything?"

She realized she hadn't made eye contact with him yet this morning. She forced a smile and did so now, hoping he couldn't see the still-untamed chaos behind her eyes. "All set. Thanks."

By the time Danny had exercised and showered, Jessica had finished the ironing, made the kids' lunches, and pushed the old trunk on a blanket from the parlor to the back door.

Danny poured himself a to-go cup of coffee and grabbed his laptop bag. "What's with the trunk?"

"Thought I'd take it out to the shed and do some work on it." Her greatest arsenal for managing chaos lay in the shed, and even if all it accomplished was distraction, it would be better than the ruminations that threatened her sanity.

"Ah, that's why the ironing. It's all coming together now. Great idea, hon. Glad you have a new project. It's been a while since you've been out there. Let me help you get it to the shed." He started to set down his things.

"No." The "no" had come out more sharply than she'd intended. "I've got it. I don't need any help. My project, right?" She mockingly flexed her biceps.

Danny adjusted his laptop bag over his shoulder. "You know, every time someone comes into my office for the first time, they comment on that table. I love telling them that you made it. Lawyer-wife turned PTA president slash DIY-er. What's the inspiration this time? Extra time now that Conor is driving?"

"I guess. Yeah." He was close. Extra time would mean more opportunities for events to replay in her mind, and that was the last thing she wanted.

Danny's phone buzzed. "Shit. I don't have extra time. I gotta go, but I'll be home early tonight. Have a great day." He pecked her on the lips and was gone.

Jessica's body started to relax from the façade she'd been presenting, but the sound of feet on the stairs pulled everything taut again.

The kids whirlwinded through the kitchen, as usual. Ever since Conor had replaced Jessica on morning driving duty, she'd felt bittersweet about it. Extra time for herself didn't quite make up for the lost time with her kids. But today she was relieved she didn't have to be in the car with them.

She felt separated from the action—from herself, even—as she watched the blur of a familiar morning passing before her. Her curly-haired boy spilled Lucky Charms and milk from his plastic container yet again on his way out the door. Her freckle-faced girl checked her lunch to see if Mom had packed it correctly. And her sixteen-year-old driver sullenly chastised the others for running late, which they weren't, but why deviate from the morning routine?

As the front door slammed, Jessica sensed the rumbling of an oncoming rush of emotions. The fear, anger, anxiety, and guilt all wanted to take advantage of the empty house and attack. She fought back. Focusing intently on the trunk, Jessica shoved her phone in her back pocket, propped open the back door, and braced herself.

Reaching to the right and the left, Jessica could just get her hands into the cracked leather handles on either side of the trunk. She tested their strength and felt the leather strain but hold against the weight as she lifted. The cold metal pressed against her upper arms.

Even empty, the trunk was heavy, built to withstand time, travel, and abuse. Sensing the tension in her own legs as she lifted the heavy piece, Jessica welcomed the stress on her muscles. Steadying the trunk, she swiveled her body toward the back door, using the fronts of her thighs to stabilize the bulky piece as she waddled sideways through the doorway. It should have been a perfect fit. But a bent metal hinge on the back of the trunk proved otherwise and made itself known by scratching straight across the doorframe. The ruler-straight gouge was oddly mesmerizing.

Once through, Jessica set the trunk on the grass next to the walkway and gauged the distance to the shed. The shed was a miniature reproduction of their house, with soft gray siding, ivory trim, and a historically accurate Revere red door. The outbuilding was small enough not to be over the top as a child's playhouse but just big enough that she had claimed it for herself as a workshop before the kids had gotten too attached.

An image of the men from the sidewalk invaded her mind again, and the bump on her head throbbed in opposition to the memory. The shed seemed like a sanctuary now, a place where her sole focus could be this trunk, and there would be no room for anything else. She pushed the trunk forward, the grass impeding her progress.

The shorter man with the cigarette.

She fetched a rope from the garage and tied it around the trunk. Danny would not be impressed with her knots, but they held as she pulled the trunk across the yard. Tripping on the shed's threshold, she grunted, interrupting the silence of the morning. She dropped the rope and looked at her hands. They were filthy.

Open palms.

After tossing the rope to the side, she lifted the trunk again with a groan and sidled through the doorway.

Orion, flicked embers.

Standing in the middle of the shed, she balanced the trunk against her thighs, looking for the right spot to place it.

Danny asking if she's okay.

Was she right in not mentioning it to him? Should she have insisted on calling the police? What was Amina doing right now? *Oh my God, Amina. I should call her.* But she didn't want to call her, because then she would have to talk about what had happened. She focused again on the trunk.

The weight of it pulled at her shoulders and her hands. The space seemed smaller than she remembered, and the walls felt as if they were closing in on her. The metal edging of the trunk dug into her quads, and she felt the strain of every muscle balancing her body against gravity and fatigue and the heft of the trunk. Any adrenaline she'd had in reserve was now depleted, and without the hormonal crutch, she became vividly aware of how tired she was, how hard her head was pounding, and how utterly, vacantly sad she was.

The sudden vibration in her back pocket shot through her like a Taser, shocking her nervous system and freeing her muscles from her control. The trunk fell forward with a smash. Jessica reflexively grabbed at it, instantly regretting the motion, then crashed to the floor herself as balance lost out to gravity. She felt pain from hitting the floor and pain from a sharp metal bracing slicing through flesh, but it was the dam burst of emotions that crushed her. Jessica tossed the still-buzzing phone out the open door and let the tears wash over the fear, exhaustion, and pain.

CHAPTER NINETEEN

Gracie nudged her nose under Jessica's hand. Jessica opened her eyes, squinting against the sunlight. Dust danced slowly in the air. The angle of the light had changed since she had first stumbled into the shed with the trunk. Gracie nudged Jessica again.

"Okay, Gracie, I get it." The dog had squeezed in between Jessica and the trunk at some point, lying patiently as Jessica's breathing slowed and the tears stopped flowing. But now the dog wanted some love. Jessica obliged, petting Gracie with one hand and wiping her face with the other. The stinging pain in her upper arm brought her fully awake. She eyed the metal bracing dusted with rust. Images of a dark sidewalk and a looming brick wall shoved aside concerns of whether her tetanus shots were up to date.

Jessica pressed her eyes shut to end the scene. "Gracie, let's see what this old trunk has to say." She stood up and brushed off her jeans, wincing in pain. She pulled the waistband down enough to see that she would soon have an ugly bruise on her hip to go with the sliced arm and the bump on her head.

From a cursory glance at the trunk, Jessica was relieved that it seemed to have fared better than she in the crash. If it had acquired any new dings or dents, they were indistinguishable from the ones it had accumulated over the rest of its lifetime. That would really have made her day, to destroy a trunk that had traveled thousands of miles over a hundred fifty years, only to meet its demise on the floor of a potting shed posing as a wood shop.

Jessica turned and jumped at a ghostly glimpse of her face reflected in the dusty window. Black smudges on her cheeks destroyed her trails of tears. She reflexively raised her hands to wipe her face again and sighed when her blackened fingers came into view.

Gracie nudged her again.

"Sorry, girl." She scratched the dog behind the ears and patted her on her back then sized up the trunk. "Move along. There's not enough room for the three of us in here."

Gracie obliged, finding a spot on the grass where she could monitor the shed and the squirrels in the yard.

Jessica squared her shoulders and faced her supply shelves. Everything was in perfect order, just as she had left it after her last project, which she was beginning to think was too long ago. Tools hung arranged by type and size, nestled together like a woodshop jigsaw puzzle on the wall. Stains were organized by shade. The narrow counter was clear, ready for staging. She reached for a wire hand brush.

Inch by inch and piece by piece, Jessica brushed the metal elements of the trunk. She took care not to brush the oak with the wire brush, saving the wood from getting ripped away and blackened by the wires.

The softly grating swish of metal brushing metal became a rhythmic mantra, pausing only when Jessica stopped to wipe her work with a blue shop cloth. Clearing the accumulation of dirt, grime, and corrosion, Jessica felt her focus sharpen as if she were zeroing in on the individual dots in a pointillist painting. Her concentration left no room for other concerns or memories, only the concerns and memories of the piece in front of her.

She meticulously brushed around nailheads, each turn and each edge, noting the large dents on the corner bumpers. The trunk had been dropped many times before today in untold events in someone else's life. Only the piece that left its mark on her arm fought Jessica's efforts, struggling against the clamp she used to force it back in place.

Wiping up the last of the bumpers, Jessica stood, grimacing as the waistband of her jeans rubbed against the bruise. The blue shop towel was mostly a black shop towel now. Jessica tossed it into a bin in the corner and turned back to the trunk. The wood looked to be intact and in decent shape, though there were rough spots, more dents, and splinter danger zones. She would work on that next.

She lifted the trunk's lid to see what work lay in store on the inside and groaned at what she saw. The middle piece of wood framing on the bottom of the trunk was cocked off-center. It hadn't been at 4:30 a.m. She would have noticed when she was taking out the linens.

Apparently, she was capable of damaging this stalwart piece of family history. She slumped and looked down at her filthy clothes and blackened hands. Her still-shiny wedding band reminded her that Danny would be home early. She should at least be clean when he walked in and found her in her own damaged state. Closing the trunk carefully, Jessica glanced in the window again, commiserating with the woman reflected back at her.

THE washing machine beeped three times, and water started to fill the drum. Jessica walked through the house unclothed. With the dried blood on her arm, the growing splotch of thunderstorm gray on her hip, and the streaks of black on her face, she must have looked like one of those images she saw in her Internet research. Except she was safe in her historic home on the way to a hot shower.

She didn't wait for the water to get hot before stepping under the showerhead. Even the cold water felt embracing, and she closed her eyes as she tilted her head back to let the water clean her face of the salt and grime.

With a bar of soap and a washcloth, Jessica started at the top and worked methodically, scrubbing and sudsing each bend and curve, ignoring the sting of the cut and the tenderness of her bumps and bruises. Dirt and blood mixed with the water at her feet. By the end, her skin was bright pink from the near-scalding water and the merciless scouring, but it was a good pink, a clean pink.

The thickening steam signaled that she had forgotten to turn on the exhaust fan and that maybe she'd been in the shower for too long. Danny should be home soon, which meant it was time to get things back to normal.

The home phone rang just as Jessica wrapped her hair into a towel turban, careful to avoid antagonizing the bump on her head. She would let the call go to voice mail. As Jessica picked up her moisturizer, she heard Danny's voice coming from the bedroom.

"Hello? Hi, Rosalie... Yes, she's here... I think she's okay. Why?" He sounded confused. "Hold on. Let me get her."

Jessica's stricken face stared back from the foggy mirror. *Rosalie? Crap.* She had called Rosalie's office number on her drive home last night and left a hurried message. She couldn't remember what she'd said. Jessica threw the turban on the floor and opened the door to the bedroom.

Danny stood with a questioning look, telephone held out in his hand. "It's Rosalie."

Jessica put the phone up to her ear, all business. Danny tilted his head, staring at the cut on her arm, which had beads of blood forming on it from being abraded by the washcloth. She felt exposed.

"Jessica." Rosalie sounded panicked. "Why haven't you been answering your cell phone? I kept getting your voice mail."

"I didn't..." Jessica started. Then she remembered throwing her phone out of the shed what seemed like days ago. "Sorry."

"You've had me going crazy, Jess. I couldn't find your home number. I finally found it in an old address book on my desk."

Jessica swallowed a comment about how long it must have taken her to find it among the piles of paperwork.

"Are you okay?"

Jessica nodded over at Danny. *It's all fine.* Then she wandered into the hallway, holding the phone close to her face so she could keep her voice low. After looking back toward the bedroom to be sure Danny hadn't followed her out of the room, she responded. "It wasn't a big deal. Some idiot drunks emboldened by Islamophobia. We're fine."

"It didn't sound like that in your message. Did you call the police?"

"No. Amina insisted we not call. I'm sure you understand better than I do."

Silence filled the line for a moment. "Yes, I understand. And I feel terrible for you both. I am so sorry. I left so quickly after the meeting. I had no idea. It must have been terrifying." Rosalie's voice had increased half an octave, her words piling on each other in their apologies.

"I'm fine. Really, you don't need to worry about it." Jessica eyed the bedroom doorway, willing Danny to stay put and Rosalie to wrap it up.

"We haven't had this happen before. I mean, of course we know there is anti-Muslim sentiment in general. But we've never had any incidents by our office. Maybe that's because we have so few Muslim clients or—oh crap, the incoming refugees." Clicks on a keyboard began to accompany Rosalie's words. "I'm going to put out a memo to staff and make sure we have chaperones for people at night going forward."

Chaperones. Jessica shook her head at the irony but knew she would be taking advantage of it if she were ever up there again. She couldn't bring herself to think about that, though.

"If you think so. But as far as I'm concerned, it's over and done, and I'm fine. No need to make a big thing of it."

"As you wish." The clicking stopped. "How is Amina?"

Jessica cringed at her dereliction of duty. She hadn't tried to contact Amina. To face such hatred and violence in America must make Amina question her safety and future here. It certainly caused some second thoughts for Jessica. She felt like a coward and hated admitting that, let alone exposing it.

"I haven't been able to reach her." It wasn't completely a lie. Her phone was lost somewhere in the yard.

"As I've mentioned before, we have referrals for mental health professionals. A lot of our refugees need these services because of what they went through in their home countries. An event like you mentioned in your message could trigger a lot of fear and anxiety and bring awful memories into the forefront for Amina. Let me know if she needs a referral."

Jessica dabbed the towel at the beads of blood on her arm.

"And, Jessica? I know you said you're fine, but if you need to talk with anyone or need any help, let me know."

Jessica just needed to get off the phone and get back to Danny so she could downplay the call, the cut, and anything else that seemed awry. "It wasn't a big deal. But thanks."

Hanging up, Jessica braced herself, repeating over and over that it really was no big deal. She could convince Rosalie of that, and she could convince Danny of that, maybe even herself.

Danny was fiddling with his watch when Jessica walked into the bedroom and placed the phone on the dock. He raised his head and folded his hands in his lap. His gaze alternated between the phone and his wife. "What was that all about?"

Jessica avoided eye contact by lifting her towel to feign drying her face. "Do you mind if I get dressed? I'm not even dried off yet. Then I'll explain. It's not a big deal."

Danny raised an eyebrow, his eyes darting to her bleeding arm. "I'll be downstairs."

She could only stall for so long. Once in a pair of sweatpants and an Ocean City T-shirt that didn't quite hide the fresh bandage on her arm, Jessica walked into the family room. Danny set his newspaper aside as she sat next to him on the couch.

"So... last night, I was at the IAP offices for that refugee meeting. You know that." Best to get through this quickly. "And when I left, there were some rowdy guys out in front of the building. They were obnoxious and made some nasty comments. It's a questionable neighborhood, and I should have known better than to head out alone there at night."

It wasn't totally a lie, not really. And anyway, this whole thing might be over. She hadn't considered her volunteer position might put her in physical danger and wasn't sure she wanted to continue with it. Right now, Jessica just wanted to get the previous night's events out of her head. And if she told Danny what had happened, she wouldn't be able to do that.

His eyes squinted with concern. "You were alone?"

Jessica's stomach dropped. "Yes." *Totally a lie.*

"What happened to your arm?" He reached out to touch the bandage.

"My arm—oh, that happened this morning." She forced a laugh, though it was more of a pathetic bark. "I really should have let you help me get the trunk out to the shed. I dropped it. I fell." She folded down the elastic band of the sweatpants to show off the impressive proof of the fall. She wouldn't mention the bump on her head.

"Ouch. That looks like it hurts. I should have insisted. I'm sorry." The guilt in his eyes was unfair.

"But I'm fine, really." If she said it enough, it might be true. "And Rosalie is having chaperones at IAP now. So no worries. It's really rogue antique trunks I need to watch out for." She fake laughed again like an idiot.

"I'm not worried about rogue trunks, Jessica." He placed his hand on her head in just the wrong spot, and she jerked away with a slight yelp.

"What the— You hit your head on the trunk, too?"

She couldn't lie again, but she didn't want to alarm him. She ignored the uptick in her heartbeat as the memory of the previous evening leaked into her consciousness. "There was some pushing."

"That's a little different from 'nasty comments.'" His face hardened. "What else? What happened to your head?"

She placed her hand on his arm to reassure him and hold him from speaking. "They were drunk. They bumped into me when they walked by, and I banged my head. You can probably blame me for being clumsy, really. I mean, look at what happened with the trunk." She held out her arm and hiked her hip in his direction. "It's just a little tender. I'm sure by tomorrow I'll have forgotten it even happened." She wasn't doing a good job convincing herself.

"I don't like this, Jess." He removed her hand from his arm, gently but affirmatively.

"Like what?"

"You need to stay safe. I know you've lived in the city, but you grew up in a small town, and now you're in our safe little enclave. Maybe you should only go to the offices during the day and take advantage of that chaperone thing."

"I'll be fine."

He cross-examined her with his eyes. "Be safe. Just promise me you won't put yourself in danger for this case or some group of refugees."

"I promise."

She excused herself to go clear shelf space in the linen closet for the linens she had ironed that morning. But she ended up getting lost in her thoughts again, grasping for the calm and focus she'd left in the shed.

CHAPTER TWENTY

J essica stood at the kitchen counter and looked approvingly at her checklist, which was gloriously long and just about completed.

After her less-than-honest talk with Danny days before, Jessica had retrieved her phone from the yard to see whom to blame for the bruise on her hip, the cut on her arm, and the salt trails down her face.

Scrolling past the missed calls and messages from Rosalie, Jessica found that the culprit was her mother. It wasn't a social call. "Just checking on the boxes," her mom said. The damn boxes had half driven Jessica out of the house that morning, and their continued, unresolved status would now be another disappointment for her mother. It hadn't always been this way, the heaviness in Jessica's relationship with her mom, but its accumulated mass had loomed large ever since the boxes had arrived.

Just in case the message from her mom wasn't enough to redirect her attention, karma had also provided a message from Christine, her successor as chair for the Literacy Initiative Charity Gala. Christine had called in a panic about losing both the gala's venue to a kitchen fire and the ticket sales data to a hard-drive crash.

The best thing for Jessica to do had been to put that night on the sidewalk behind her, and Oma's boxes and Christine's call for help had been the perfect diversions.

She'd had her cry. She hadn't exactly lied to Danny about everything. The incident on the sidewalk probably wasn't really a big deal.

The images and the heartbeats wouldn't just disappear like embers in the wind, but no one had gotten significantly hurt, and she would never run into those guys again. It was a onetime thing—an anomaly. And she'd been right not to overburden Danny with the whole story or make him feel as though he needed to help her. Danny was a busy man. It was time she got busy, too.

Since crashing to the floor of the shed, Jessica had allowed herself little time for thinking or remembering. She had sliced open boxes and catalogued hand-hammered horseshoe nails, tiny leather dolls with crudely painted faces, two full sets of china, old photo albums she didn't have time to inspect, and a sizable but not yet complete pile of Oma's accumulated belongings, each with a lavender note and a story. She hadn't gotten through all the boxes, but the newly cleared space cleared her head.

She had been chief fire-putter-outer for tonight's literacy fundraiser, lining up a new venue and regenerating the attendee list the old-fashioned way—by making countless phone calls. Between all of that, finishing the trunk, and attending to a to-do list that wouldn't stop growing, she hadn't even been able to make it to book club. She also hadn't had time to contact Amina, whose one phone message asking Jessica to give her a call had come just yesterday, so Jessica had convinced herself that she wasn't yet delinquent in responding.

She would get in touch with Amina soon. But today, she would attend the gala, renewed and reinvigorated. With her volunteer duties complete, she would be able to relax and have fun with her date. It would be a fine reward for having been so busy and productive. She'd been so busy that she'd hardly had time to talk with Danny... at least that was what she told herself.

DANNY handed the keys to the valet then opened the passenger door. Jessica emerged in a burgundy floor-length gown, with simple strappy heels showing off her fresh pedicure. The dress accentuated her best features. Thin straps crossed her well-toned upper back. The loose drape below her narrow waist hid her less-toned parts as well as the bruise that had matured into a shadowy yellow. A bandage over her trunk-metal cut marred the elegance.

Standing to join her tuxedo-clad date, Jessica adjusted her dress to make sure everything was in the right place then reflexively smoothed her hair.

Danny touched the bandage softly. "I should have helped you with the trunk." Then he lit up. "You look beautiful."

She pushed aside a twinge of guilt. "And you look like you did the day we got married."

Danny cocked an eyebrow. "Yeah, I think so, too."

Maybe he doesn't deserve so much reverence. But he did look amazing. His rugged face and mussed hair, matched with his casual bearing, made him at once iconic and approachable, just as they had when she'd first seen him at that DC movie theater back when she was a young associate. But that was a long time ago.

Her preoccupation with the gala, the boxes, the spreadsheet, and the trunk had given her cover for her lingering reticence to engage. She didn't think he had noticed the distance that she had both created and suffered so acutely, but tonight offered an opportunity for them to reconnect and get back to normal.

The hotel lobby was busy. A handful of other late-arriving gala attendees in black tie hovered around the check-in table, and hotel guests dressed more comfortably spilled out of the hotel bar. The Literacy Initiative had been lucky to land this venue on such short notice, and things appeared to be moving along swimmingly.

Danny zeroed in on the place cards at the check-in table. "Here we are. Mr. and Mrs. Daniel Donnelly. Table eight. We'd better go.

We're pretty late. Sorry about that. I just haven't been able to break away from work the way I used to. I bet we missed the silent auction."

In fact, the silent auction room was empty, and black-and-white–garbed employees were hastily cleaning up the abandoned wine glasses and half-eaten hors d'oeuvres from the cocktail hour. Danny placed his hand on Jessica's lower back and guided her through the large wooden doors leading into the banquet hall.

The main hall was packed. Seats were filled with a collection of the area's education advocates, many of whom were regulars at events like this, keeping the coffers of small local charities full for another year. Binnacle had been a sustaining sponsor since the first gala six years before.

Danny and Jessica found table eight and grabbed the two empty chairs, greeting the Binnacle representatives already seated.

Jessica introduced herself to the man sitting to her left. Although they were seated at the Binnacle table, she didn't recognize the thirtysomething man in the rental tux.

It was inevitable that on first meeting, the man would ask, "So, what do you do?"

What do I do? Hmm. Let's see. I make sure all of the bills are paid, our retirement and college savings are properly invested, the house is clean, and the kids are at school on time. I have served in every capacity and on every committee at my kids' schools, and I ran this event for five years. You know those family scrapbooks that everyone else starts but never finishes? I have a cupboard full of them. I attend every single one of my kids' games and performances. I... Fuck it.

"I used to be a lawyer."

"Really? What kind?"

"Securities compliance." *And it's completely irrelevant to my life anymore. Do you want to talk about scrapbooks?* "I do some *pro bono* work now, but I'm not really practicing." She shrugged. "I guess I mostly do mom stuff these days."

Danny leaned over, gently resting a strong hand on Jessica's exposed shoulder. "Hey, Damien, good to see you here. I'm afraid Jessica is being too modest. She does a lot of volunteer work. In fact, she volunteered as a reading tutor with this group several years ago and then started and ran this gala every year until this year.

"On top of that," Danny continued, "she's the reason Binnacle Cyber Solutions exists today. I never could have pulled together such a great team and developed our products if she hadn't been carrying so much weight in those early years. All these years, really."

He gazed into her eyes and squeezed her shoulder. "And over the past couple of weeks, I've hardly even seen her. She's been so busy helping with this event, taking care of her grandmother's estate, and who knows what else, all on top of her other responsibilities. I feel lucky to get to spend the evening with her."

He really did love her. And he hadn't noticed the distance, only that she'd been busy.

Danny turned away in response to a question coming from his right, his hand trailing off her shoulder with a promise for more later in the night.

Jessica changed topics and asked about Damien's role at Binnacle. He was a new addition to a skunkworks development team at Binnacle. Jessica wasn't sure what that meant, but it sounded intriguing.

When she asked for a more detailed explanation, Damien winked and said, "Something for catching bad guys." He recounted the list of Silicon Valley start-ups where he'd worked back home in California and how he'd been involved in their growth.

Jessica drifted while continuing to nod and look intently at the developer. Maybe she'd led with law rather than household management because she was embarrassed. Or maybe she'd figured it would suck for poor Damien to feel as though he had to be in a mommy conversation with the boss's wife. Either way, that feeling of being small inched its way back into her consciousness.

Damien laughed, bringing Jessica back to the moment. She would laugh, too, then figure out what the joke had been.

———— ✦ ————

DANNY'S ARMS WRAPPED firmly around Jessica's waist as he kissed her on the back of her neck. "Good morning, hon."

Jessica tilted her head back onto his shoulder as she set the platter of pancakes back on the counter. "Good morning. Fun night."

"Great night. Why didn't you sleep in? You were sound asleep when I left for my run." He kissed her on the top of her head and let go, turning toward the refrigerator.

"I don't know what I was thinking, promising the kids pancakes this morning." She felt as though she'd been ignoring everyone lately, and pancakes had seemed like a good make-up gift. Though that was before a late night of drinking, dancing, and forgetting.

"You're a pushover. Always have been, Jess." He picked up the newspaper from the table and made himself comfortable on the couch.

The creak of the stairs meant Jessica had finished making breakfast just in time.

Mikey burst through the doorway ahead of his sister. "I smell bacon. Did you make bacon? I want bacon!"

The contagious joy filled Jessica's heart. "Of course I made bacon." She filled a plate and handed it to Mikey. "Be sure to eat some fruit, too. I don't want to be rolling you to the pharmacy to get cholesterol medicine when you're thirteen."

His mouth already full of pancake and bacon, Mikey's response was incomprehensible.

Cricket grabbed a plate from the makeshift breakfast buffet. "Did you guys have fun last night? When did you get home? I heard Gracie barking."

"Late," Jessica said. "It was fun."

Mikey had reloaded his plate with seconds by the time Conor walked silently into the kitchen.

"Morning, Conor." Jessica started to add bacon to a plate for him.

"Not hungry." Conor filled a glass with orange juice and walked back out.

Jessica sought insight from Mikey and Cricket. "What's with him?"

Two sets of shrugging shoulders answered her.

She shot a look at Danny and got a third set of shrugging shoulders in response.

Catching up with at least two of the kids made the early trip to the kitchen worth it, though. She would deal with Conor later and enjoy the Sunday-morning chatter from her unjaded children.

Cricket had a boyfriend. And based on the whack she inflicted on Mikey when he disclosed that fact through a mouthful of pancake, she hadn't wanted anyone to know. Tellingly, she blushed sweetly before saying she wasn't going to talk about it then changed the subject to swim-team gossip and her promotion from the B to the A relay team.

Mikey pulled out a copy of a field trip consent form that Jessica had apparently failed to complete and send back to school. It had been a tough last week, so she wasn't surprised she'd missed something, though it was unlike her.

"Sorry, honey. Leave it here, and I'll take care of it."

After the kids left, Jessica curled up on the couch next to Danny, who pulled her close. Taking on the asylum case might not have been the right thing for Jessica to do, but it had helped her see with new eyes what she already had at home. *This*, what she had right now, Conor's attitude notwithstanding, was just as it should be, and that should be her priority, her focus.

She had let obligations to others interfere with what was important before, years ago. She couldn't let that happen again.

She flicked on the morning news. Hundreds of desperate souls piled on rubber rafts filled the screen. She flicked it back off. She wouldn't watch the news anymore, but she did have a phone call to return.

CHAPTER TWENTY-ONE

AMINA

Bathanjaan didn't open until noon on Sundays, so it was missing the usual Spanish and Arabic chatter rising above the clanks and sizzles of the dinner rush, the fragrant smells of spices from home, and the electric tension of trying to keep up with orders. It didn't feel like a commercial kitchen on a Sunday morning, though it didn't feel like an office, either.

Sunday morning was Amina's favorite time to go to her office, which was really not much more than a desk shielded from the industrial dishwasher by two tall metal file cabinets and a sheet of plywood painted white.

She paper-clipped the week's receipts together and stacked them on her desk after updating QuickBooks then moved on to the time cards. Her job, which tended to be mostly bookkeeping, differed from the duties she'd had before she fled Aleppo, where she'd audited financial records and provided summary analyses. But once she'd adjusted to the world of American restaurants and their tax, business, and financial implications, she had added duties over time. She'd taken over accounts payable, sales, and use tax remission, and earlier in the year, she had coordinated all documentation for the tax preparer.

It hadn't taken long in her position to learn that after rent, salaries, taxes, and all the other overhead expenses, little remained for Fayiz and Sama. The longer she relied on them, the more she wanted to be able to do for them. But at some point, she would have to stop leaning on them. Though the family had not made her feel unwelcome, each additional month, week, and day was an imposition. She was tired of being an imposition and not just on family.

After that night on the street, Amina hadn't known what to expect from Jessica. The drive with her to her cousin's house had been silent. Being alone in her room that night had been silent, too, but in a different way. A cloak of emptiness wrapped the fear close around her, conjuring images from years ago and thousands of miles away, images she had successfully hidden for so long.

She didn't tell Fayiz or Sama what had happened. She didn't tell them that three men had approached her and her lawyer, spewing hateful words. Fayiz and Sama had heard those words before; they had been here long enough. She didn't tell them the men had thrown her up against the wall, pulling at her scarf and her clothes. She didn't need to worry Sama, not in her state. The incident was nothing compared to what had happened to her own brother and so many back in their home country.

She didn't tell them that her lawyer had stepped ahead of her, toward the men, speaking to them with firm authority. She didn't tell them that watching Jessica stay calm had helped keep her from panicking. She didn't tell them that she worried Jessica would want to get out of the case to protect her own safety.

The two had only spoken periodically before the incident, certainly not every day or even every week, but the pause in communication had seemed more significant this time. Amina suspected the lawyer had been unsatisfied with the case from the beginning. She certainly hadn't hidden her discomfort that first day, though she'd made up for that with her later professionalism and respect. But Amina recognized that taking on a legal case with no pay was one thing. Getting accosted on the street was another. Those men would not have confronted an American woman in that way. It was the hijab; it was the Middle Eastern woman; it was the Muslim.

For Jessica to exit the case would be a disappointment, but Amina would understand. She wouldn't blame her. She wouldn't call her cowardly or fraudulent or selfish. She would call her human. She wanted to thank Jessica for all she had done, but she'd been relieved Jessica hadn't returned the call she'd made a few days before. The chance still existed that they could continue to work together.

Then Jessica called unexpectedly during the quiet time in the prelunch kitchen. The buzz of the phone reverberating on the metal desk caused Amina to jump, sending paper clips frittering off the edge of the desk and into the bag lying open by her feet.

"I'm so sorry, Amina. I'm sorry I didn't return your call sooner. I've been... busy."

"It's okay." Amina could hardly hear her own voice.

"And I'm sorry... I'm sorry for what those guys said and did."

It was not her place to apologize. Jessica had received as much from the men as Amina had.

Jessica continued, hesitancy catching in her voice. "It's embarrassing as an American to know there are people here who do that and think that. I'm sorry."

"There is no need to apologize for them. Please," Amina said. *Please, what?* She didn't know.

"Are you okay?" Jessica asked.

"Yes." There was no way to explain how hurtful the words and the fear had been to her.

"Amina, listen—"

Amina found her voice before Jessica could back out of the case, if that was why she had called. "Jessica, can we meet? In person?" Her heart raced, thumping away the seconds it took for Jessica to respond.

"Yes. That's a good idea."

They arranged to meet again at the end of the week, and Amina hung up the phone, feeling new light and seeing new light. They hadn't talked about what had happened, yet she felt as though she had unloaded the dark memory just by connecting with the person who had been through it with her. Or at least she'd exposed it. Other memories seemed ready to come out of the shadows as well.

Amina used the two paper clips that hadn't fallen into her bag, assembled the week's paperwork into a folder, and slid that into the bottom left file cabinet drawer.

She would start on her own paperwork now. Her time with that first attorney hadn't been a complete waste of effort. His office had provided a surprisingly accurate list of what she should prepare to support her asylum claim. It was a shame he had not waited for her to complete it before he'd prepared the false filing, but maybe it had been a blessing since it meant she now had Jessica... *might* have Jessica.

Amina still had to present a supplemental filing with the USCIS, complete with dates, people, places, and events—all things Jessica had been kind enough to pull out of her gently and slowly but that, ultimately, Amina needed to provide.

The kitchen staff wouldn't arrive for another hour. She started writing.

CHAPTER TWENTY-
TWO

Golden sunlight conspired with orange and yellow leaves to beckon Jessica outside. Even if the day had been drizzly and gray, a hike might have been more appealing than the loud, stuffy school bus she found herself boarding at the curb in front of the middle-school building.

Jessica had been a familiar face at the kids' schools over the years, one of the "usual suspects" when it came to volunteering. She'd headed committees, sent in baked goods, worked at fundraisers, and laminated name tags. She did her good deeds, but she'd always managed to escape being trapped on a school bus filled with sixty loud, unruly children.

So she had missed the pumpkin-patch trips, the symphony orchestra outings, and the fifth-grade day trip to Philadelphia. But she'd never felt like a slacker for taking a pass, until this time, until she had outright overlooked a field trip consent form because she'd been distracted by an asylum case and its fallout.

The violation was aggravated by the fact that Mikey was child number three, the one who didn't see her as much in his elementary school because she had ported her efforts to the middle and high schools, where she didn't have to bake or laminate so much. It was also intensified by the emerging fact that child number one had drifted away and child number two seemed well on her way to being fully independent of her mother.

When Jessica had read the overdue consent form, she'd recalled all of those times in grade school when Mikey had batted those long eyelashes and asked if she could please please *please* chaperone. Then she'd thought of the nights this year when he had no longer needed or even asked for her help.

This go-around, she would sign up and spend some time with her little boy.

And that was how she found herself on this gorgeous fall day, heading to DC and the Holocaust Museum.

Jessica placed her hand on a cracked pleather seat back as she scanned the bus to find Mikey. She moved forward, seeing him joking around with a group of boys in the back. Mikey raised his head, waved at Jessica, and grinned his toothy smile.

A preteen, prejaded moment like this reminded Jessica of Conor as a sweet mama's boy, happily walking next to Jessica at the mall—directly next to her, not the five steps back that he did now, as though he didn't know the woman in front of him who'd just bought him the newest iPhone. Maybe she should have gone on some field trips with Conor.

As she moved toward the rear of the bus, Mikey was already back to joking with his friends. Jessica stopped short. He didn't want her back there. A needle of pain spiked her chest, then came the warm flush of embarrassment. The other two moms and the teachers sat at the front of the bus. They already knew. Jessica joined them in the mom zone.

It didn't take long into the trip for Jessica's nose to alert her to the fact that a good number of Mikey's classmates had hit puberty. Mikey wasn't fully there yet, but hauling Conor and his friends home from sports practices had familiarized Jessica with the ripe odor of boys who hadn't yet learned the utility and courtesy of deodorant. The odor would be enhanced exponentially after a full day's activities, possibly sealing the deal that this would be Jessica's one and only field trip.

Despite today's noisy passengers and poorly maintained shock absorbers, the drive flooded Jessica with memories of her commuting days. The eight lanes full of anonymous commuters jockeying for position and the unremarkable landscape of highway-adjacent suburbia remained unchanged. She'd disparaged the sixty- to ninety-minute commute when she had moved from DC. Years of carpool, however, illuminated the luxury of being alone in the car, with no kids fighting over the radio station and no one interrupting her thoughts—Jessica thought of Conor skulking out of the kitchen—and no one ignoring her.

As the bus finally started inching its way through DC's streets, Jessica turned from her memories back to the view outside her window. The sun penetrated the capitol city, but the wind seized the day. Conservative suits rushed by, the backs of suit coats flipping in the updrafts. A couple of white-haired tourists in Washington, DC, sweatshirts and fanny packs struggled to unfold their map as blasts of fall air whipped it away from their hands.

That could have been her in another life. Not the fanny-packed tourist lost in DC but the rushing suit, a partner at Highland & Cross instead of a chaperone on a yellow bus.

Her gaze fell on a woman standing on a corner up ahead. About Jessica's age, she wore Capitol Hill navy and carried a sleek black bag. Her shoes were too expensive for her to work for the government, so she must have been a lobbyist or a lawyer at one of the big law firms.

Considering the twentysomething young man accompanying the woman, Jessica went with lawyer. The young man looked eager, if a bit harried, and pulled a wheeled mobile file case. Jessica had once been that young associate. He had probably been up most of the night, getting the due diligence files organized ahead of the meeting they were on their way to right now.

Working as a young associate had been exhausting.

H&C represented Fortune 500 companies and boasted partners who had previously worked for the SEC, the FTC, and the whole federal alphabet soup. That first client meeting had been heady for Jessica, the fresh lawyer from Iowa, shifting in her chair, taking notes, and not understanding half of the discussion going on around her. But she had inhaled every sight and sound and reveled in the importance of it all. Exhaustion had been exhilarating.

The light turned green. The two maybe-attorneys crossed the street, and the yellow school bus turned left. Jessica picked at the cracked black pleather of the seat.

———————— ⟡ ————————

DISGORGED FROM THE bus, the sixth graders scrambled ahead of the adults to form a line to go through the metal detector, seemingly oblivious to the mass genocide that would be on display inside the building in front of them. Their teacher's admonitions to be respectful and quiet hadn't had any effect.

Jessica cleared security and joined the group in the atrium, relieved to find the boisterous kids had become model children, quiet and still. Turning, her eyes pulled ever upward, Jessica decided it hadn't been the teacher's words that had caused the transformation.

The atrium was large, open, and bright. But it was also ominous, with cold brick walls and exposed industrial metal braces framing the glass ceiling.

As the docents led the group toward a corner of the atrium, Jessica smiled lightly at Mikey, who listened attentively to the woman addressing the group. This wouldn't be the bonding experience she had planned. She got her own instructions from a teacher: keep an eye on wandering kids and quiet, unruly behavior, and make sure everyone returned to the atrium in sixty minutes. Her assigned group didn't even include Mikey.

The main exhibit started on the top floor, winding its way back down toward the maybe-it's-a-train-station-maybe-it's-not atrium. Stepping off the elevator on the fourth floor with her group, Jessica wilted at the huge photo of burnt bodies that faced her. She pivoted away and edged to the rear of the pack of students, which quickly dispersed into whispering clumps throughout the low-lit exhibit.

Jessica followed the students, threading her way through hushed visitors and watching for wanderers and unruliness among her charges. They, like she, were pulled to the photos, videos, and artifacts surrounding them. The babble of news reels and images of Nazi Germany blended into a harsh mosaic, ultimately distracting Jessica from her chaperone duties. She'd seen this mosaic before, in textbooks, historical fiction, and World War II movies over the years. But now modern images from her research began to flit through her mind, mirroring the destruction and human atrocities depicted in black and white around her.

Then the smell hit. Jessica could feel it in her chest before she could even process the origin of the vaguely nauseating scent. Looking around the dim room she had just entered, she saw a jumbled gray mass open to the air. Her eyes panned the length of the mass and stopped on a single item—a woman's lace-up oxford, small heel, no lace, and its original color lost to history.

Like the thousands of other shoes in the mass, this oxford was a disintegrating gray brown. Before she could envision the last wearer of the shoe, she panned out and saw a child's first shoe, a woman's pump, a man's work shoe—thousands of them, intermingled. All of them were grayed with age, and no shoe was anywhere near its mate. Each of these shoes, these dull, lifeless pieces of cloth and leather, represented a lingering and fading shadow of a life lost, a story untold. Someone had worn these shoes. Before. These shoes once had important places to go, important things to do. And now they, too, were turning to dust.

BACK IN THE ATRIUM and missing her charges, Jessica found a helpful docent who directed her to where the students had assembled, fidgeting and whispering and eyeing an empty chair sitting in front of them.

Before any unruliness commenced, an impish woman with intentional posture walked up to the chair, made a slight bow, and sat. Though delicate and slight, she faced her young audience with a commanding eye. In her brown polyester slacks, cheetah-print cardigan, and chunky necklace, she could have been anyone's grandmother. Her comfortable mall-walking shoes were all white except for the cheetah-print laces. She either loved animal prints or she always matched her laces to her top.

As the woman scanned the room, the whispering stopped, though not the fidgeting. She introduced herself. "I am Ada Rubenstein. I am a Holocaust survivor." Her German-accented words flowed clearly and slowly, sentences tending to build in a soft crescendo, drawing in her listeners.

Her calm in front of the students contrasted with the life in her eyes and in her words. Movement in the audience ceased. With a flourish of her hands to highlight a part of her story, she would draw the students in even more.

The woman started with a story about a visit to the beach with her family. "My father"—she smiled as if she were paging through a scrapbook of her youth—"he would throw us up into the air, my three sisters and me, as high and as far out in the water as he could, like we were flying. He was very strong." She flexed her arm. The kids snickered, and she giggled. "I still remember the sky that day. It was so blue, with clouds like cotton. And the sea stretched out as far as we could see. I remember the smiles on my little sisters' faces." That was the last trip her family had taken before four of them stepped onto the cattle car that took them to the camp.

Before that train ride, however, Ada and her family had watched the world around them mutate from a world the sixth graders would recognize as similar to their own—"without Snapchat, of course," she noted—to one filled with fear and confusion.

"My family had a jewelry store. The Nazis destroyed it during Kristallnacht, which you learned about on your tour. But my father was convinced the terror would pass once the Nazis felt secure in their power. Instead, atrocities became a part of life. We grew used to witnessing degradations and humiliations in the street. It became normal."

The kids listened politely. Mikey rested his chin on his left hand, transfixed, while Jessica had a growing sense of unease about what had befallen Ada's family. She had the same feeling each time she spoke with Amina, a thick dread at what she was about to hear and sinking guilt for being a mere observer.

Ada took care with her description of her family's arrival at Auschwitz. She'd clearly spoken to many groups of school kids and tailored her story for the age group in front of her. Her two youngest sisters had been hidden at a neighbor's home when the Gestapo herded the rest of the family to the trains, so they had been left behind. She spoke of her father's last words to her before guards led him away with the other men toward a brick building in the distance. She spoke of how she and the one sister with her would secretly sing Hebrew songs to defeat the guards in their own innocent way, and how a mother whose baby had died looked after Ada and her sister when their own mother died of starvation.

A warm tear rolled down Jessica's right cheek. Her nose would start running shortly, and she didn't have any tissues on her. Her sleeve would have to do, though she wouldn't be able to do anything about the splotchy face she was sure to have by the time Ada concluded her story.

"I was one of the lucky ones. I was alive when the Allies arrived. But in the chaos of the liberation, my sister and I were placed onto separate trains." Ada was adopted into a Jewish family that had escaped to Switzerland in the thirties, and they emigrated to the United States in 1949.

"I searched and searched for my father and my sisters. My father, I knew in my heart he had gone to the gas chambers, as that is what they did with the men there. But to a young girl, nothing is impossible, so I always imagined he had made a daring escape and spent the rest of his life trying to find us." Her eyes sparkled at the thought of his escape or perhaps glistened at the heartbreak of his murder.

"I never found my sisters. After the war, you see, orphans were placed with families in Europe and America. Those who had been in hiding were often given false papers and even converted to other religions to help keep them safe. The little ones sometimes never learned their true identities."

She leaned forward, gazing at the students from left to right. "But they survived. I like to think that my little sisters grew up in France, where they went to the beach every summer and had foggy but happy memories of being thrown through the air by a man with strong arms who made them feel safe. They might not know if it was a true memory or just the shadow of a dream, but they would feel the warmth of love along with the warmth of the sun."

The woman folded her hands in her lap, closed her eyes, and took a deep breath that filled her face with calm. The sixth graders glanced nervously at each other then at their teachers. There was some hesitant clapping, but that tapered quickly.

Jessica just wanted to give the impish little lady a hug. Not to make the Holocaust survivor feel better but to alleviate Jessica's sadness, to alleviate her guilt for never having gone through anything so horrific, to acknowledge that the survivor's experience was not in vain, and to promise that Jessica would have done something back then to help, would do something now. She would do something now.

As the students piled into the bus, they returned to form. Someone threw a straw that was lying on the floor, and someone else started making fart noises.

As the bus rumbled awkwardly through the afternoon traffic, every bump seemed magnified, each jolt intentional. Fanny packs and suits blended meaninglessly in the passing blur of the city. If the bus still smelled, Jessica didn't notice.

———— ❦ ————

"Mom?"

Jessica glanced over from the driver's seat. She and Mikey had been driving in silence in the ten minutes since the bus had dropped them off at school, and Mikey didn't even have his phone out. "Yes?"

"I was thinking. About the Holocaust lady and her family. It's really sad that she never found them." Mikey's mouth turned downward with concern.

"I know, honey. It's terrible what they all went through. I don't know if it's worse to know what happened or not to know."

Mikey didn't miss a beat. "It would definitely be better not to know."

"Really? Why do you say that?"

"Well, because if you know something bad happened to them, it would make you very sad to think about that bad thing happening. And you would probably think about it over and over, and that would be terrible."

"That's a good point. But some people think at least then you would have closure, meaning you can move on and not continue to worry about what might have happened." Jessica turned on her blinker and slowed ahead of the stoplight.

Mikey spoke deliberately. "But I think that if you don't know what happened, you can imagine happy things. You can have hope for their lives, you know? Like the lady said. You can have hope that you'll see them again, right?"

"What about the bad things that might have happened to them? Wouldn't you think of those, too?"

Mikey looked through the window at the cars crossing the road in front of them. "I don't think you should think of the bad things that *might* have happened. What good does that do? Thinking of good things can at least keep you happy. And maybe it would be true."

It was hard to argue with that. Mikey didn't seem so little anymore.

CHAPTER TWENTY-THREE

"**I** thought you would be done with me." Amina was uncharacteristically casual, even picking at a muffin that she let Jessica buy her.

"I wondered about it myself, to be honest." Jessica slid her chair closer to the table, wincing at the scrape of metal against the concrete floor. "I've never been in such a scary situation." She stared at the steam rising from her coffee. She hated how she sounded. She didn't know scary. She'd spent the last week and a half trying to convince herself, almost successfully, that those men had just been three idiots spouting off and nothing more. Scary or not, at least she'd had her husband to return home to that night.

Amina's face didn't reflect the anger or resentment Jessica would have expected, whether toward the men or toward Jessica's handling of the situation. "I am so sorry. I shouldn't have waited so long to see you. I should have called you afterwards. Are you okay? How have you been doing?"

Amina sipped her tea. "I'd rather tell you about my brother."

"Of course." There had been two brothers listed on Amina's asylum application, one living, one deceased.

Amina smiled, her face filling with the glow of the memory. "My younger brother was Samir. He was so good. All the people loved him from when he was a smiling baby. Even when he was a teenager, he still brought fruit to the elderly and played *hajla* with the little children in the street. He could talk with the old men for hours. He would have been the gentlest doctor, the kindest teacher."

Jessica ran her thumb down the length of her cup as she took a fortifying breath, half hoping the drone of the coffee grinder would drown out what was to come. Samir was the deceased brother.

Amina pulled her bag onto her lap and stared out the coffee-shop window. "Once, when he was around six years old, he found a baby bird by our door. The baby bird was dead, but my brother, he still tried to heal it. He wrapped it in cloth and carried it around in a tiny basket for a day to keep it warm. We tried to tell him the bird had gone, but he was so young. He felt important. He felt responsible."

Memories flickered across Amina's face, memories that softened her jaw and mouth.

"Finally, he came to my mother and me as we were preparing bread. 'Mama and Amina,' he said. He looked very serious, like a doctor delivering bad news. He said, 'The bird has died. We must have a funeral.' And so it was."

Amina's deep-brown eyes seemed to plead, "Know my brother." Her new openness disarmed Jessica, who had come into the coffee shop steeled to be patient and sensitive, to let Amina disclose at her own pace. Now she worried she wasn't ready for Amina's pace.

"We all agreed that, no, the bird did not need to be washed, which is our custom. But my brother wrapped the bird in a white cloth and placed a drop of perfume on the cloth. He then invited all the neighbors to the funeral. My mother was worried. She was traditional. What would they think if we bury a bird in such a way? But they came. All of them. The old men, the old women, the ones who never spoke but looked at you like you were a criminal. They said their prayers and paid their respects to my brother. This was not a custom, to bury dead birds. It was my brother. They loved him and respected him, even as a child."

Jessica let herself know Samir and his innocence, an innocence no different from that of Oma with her kittens and Mikey with his Lucky Charms. Jessica's light smile tasted of sorrow, though, as she recalled images of young children who had fled Assad's bombs, losing their childhood in the process.

"That bird," Amina continued. "He buried that bird beneath the earth by our home. Our home could be gone now, but I like to think that the grave is protected and the bird lies in peace. It is fortunate it did not have to witness what was to come."

Amina stopped abruptly, the muscles around her mouth tightening. She inhaled deeply, slowly, and the muscles relaxed. The glow of memory fell victim to an aura of blackest despair. Amina hadn't provided much detail on her asylum application about Samir.

"What happened to Samir?" Jessica almost whispered the question.

Amina's face flickered, her eyes narrowing as she looked past Jessica's shoulder. "He was sixteen. The men entered my parents' home. My father was not there. Even if he was home that day, he could not have helped, but he never forgave himself for not protecting his child. Samir was home, helping my mother. The soldiers mocked him for helping a woman. They said he must do a man's work and join them. My mother told the men to leave, that Samir was still a boy. They struck her down with the butt of a gun. They laughed like it was a joke and walked away. My brother packed a bag, knowing they would return. He would leave at dark to go stay with my uncle outside Aleppo. But the men knocked down the door before night and dragged Samir away."

Jessica's gasp came with a shudder. She had stopped breathing while Amina spoke, and the sudden influx of air was a shock.

"After the men took my brother, my mother walked up and down every street, asking if anyone had seen her son. She went alone. No one would talk to her. She searched for days. She hoped he was in prison and would soon come home." The muscles in the hollows of Amina's cheeks went taut. "Can you imagine wishing for prison for your son?" Her question, directed at no one, lifted into the air.

Amina's faraway look turned ice cold. She was no longer in the coffee shop. She was no longer sitting across from her American lawyer. Jessica felt like an intruder, though if she were to step away from the table, Amina probably wouldn't have noticed.

"Three days after they took him, I was baking with my mother. It was the only thing to do." The statement came out as an apology. "We heard a sound outside the door, like someone had thrown a sack of rice against the house. My mother ran to open the door, and I heard her wail. A thousand birds died of despair on hearing that sound. She fell to the ground, and a crowd of people began to gather. There was no—he was not all there. We knew it was Samir's body by his yellow football jersey and a scar on his arm from when he was a little boy."

Jessica stared at her cup. Looking directly into Amina's eyes at this point seemed voyeuristic, invasive, and tragic.

"We saw his head days later, on a fence surrounded by armed men. We saw many heads after the conflict began. Some of them we knew. But a man's head does not look like the man." Amina spoke with an air of contempt now, her nostrils flaring barely perceptibly. Jessica was the audience again but also a receptacle for Amina's rage and pain. "No, it looks like the savages who killed him—empty, lifeless, and inhuman. We did not cry when we saw Samir's head on that post, for it was not him."

Eyes welling with tears, Jessica could barely say "I'm so sorry" without choking. Amina's face was expressionless. No tears, no fiery anger in her eyes.

Jessica drove home in silence, feeling small and inconsequential but letting herself cry for Amina.

JESSICA walked into the kitchen, still feeling the heavy weight of Samir's story. It took her a few moments to notice she had walked into a standoff of sorts.

Danny faced Conor, slowly shaking his head. Conor seemed to be trying hard to look as though he didn't care.

Jessica sighed. "Hi. What did I miss?" Whatever it was, it had to be better than the conversation she'd just had with Amina.

"You can tell her," Danny said.

"What." It wasn't a question, but a statement. It was Conor being a stubborn ass again.

"You need to own it, Conor. Make decisions for good reasons and stand by those decisions. A good life compass is whether you're comfortable explaining why you made a decision. If you have solid reasoning that you can stand behind, that's great. If you don't, you need to rethink things." Again, Danny was the reasonable analyst.

"Fine." Conor turned squarely toward Jessica. "Mom, I'm not going out for basketball." He pivoted back toward Danny. "There. Happy?"

Jessica moved to Danny's side. "What do you mean? Did you get cut?" Conor was a solid player. Maybe there had been a mistake. Jessica looked to Danny for reassurance. He simply raised his eyebrows noncommittally.

"I didn't sign up for the team," Conor said.

"I don't understand. You did so well last year. I thought you were looking forward to playing varsity." Basketball was the solution to the Conor problem. Jessica didn't have the emotional energy to find another fix right now.

"I changed my mind. I don't want to play anymore. It's not like I'm going to play in college or go pro. God. Get over it."

"We know you're not going to be a pro athlete. That's not why you do sports, son." Danny seemed disappointed that Conor didn't understand why a person would do a sport, when what he needed to be was disappointed that his son was disconnecting from everything and everyone.

Jessica pursed her lips and clenched her hands. She could feel her fingernails digging into her palms. "Conor, I'm just... I don't know what to say. That was your *last* sport. Your last anything. You stopped playing piano, you quit sailing, you won't sign up for any clubs. You don't do drama. You don't do student government. What are you going to do?" If he didn't do anything, he couldn't go anywhere.

"I don't know, Mom, okay? It's not a big deal. God, just leave me alone, and I'll be fine." Conor swung his backpack over his shoulder.

"Are you doing drugs?" She didn't intend it as an aggressive accusation, though it came out like one. But if Danny wasn't going to say something, she was. Conor's lack of involvement, his cold shoulder, and his all-around attitude just didn't fit her image of him. Maybe she was overlooking something like drugs, depression, bullying, or one of the other thousand things she was supposed to be worried about as the parent of a teenager.

He turned back, and she searched his face for answers. What she saw was that Conor didn't take her question as one born of concern. "God, Mom. No. I'm not doing drugs." He pushed up his sleeves. "No track marks, see?" He unzipped his backpack and thrust the open top toward Jessica. "Wanna go through my backpack? Have you already gone through my room?"

Conor's accusation targeted her, not Danny, not even both of them. Once again, she was the shrill parent, pigeonholed as the bad guy. "Conor, *we* haven't gone through your room. Not that your dad and I wouldn't if we got concerned or thought something was going on. But you have to talk to us. We can't just watch you wander silently around this house and let it go. We're trying to respect your privacy and give you your independence, but at some point, you need to let us in. Especially if you're doing something that you don't want us to know about."

"Yes, you can. I'm fine."

"No, we can't. We're your parents." Jessica put her hand on Conor's.

He flinched but didn't pull it away.

"We love you," she said. "We're here for you. Always. No matter what it is, you can talk to us."

"I know, Mom. I just don't have anything to talk about, okay? I'm fine." He pulled back his hand.

"It's just that you used to be so involved," she said. "And then, you wouldn't take the internship at Binnacle, which I—we—don't understand. You've always wanted to be just like your dad."

"No, Mom. You wanted me to be just like Dad." His glare sliced deeper than the hinge on the trunk had. "Am I free to leave now?"

Jessica turned to Danny, who looked up from checking his phone and shook his head to indicate he had nothing to add. Jessica waved her hand toward the doorway. Conor moved out of the room with a calm that contrasted with Jessica's frustration but mirrored his father's even keel. Maybe she was overreacting.

His footsteps up the stairs and down the upstairs hallway pounded at Jessica's patience. She was rather privileged to be so outraged by her son quitting a sport, and her solitary stance intensified her discomfort. But she couldn't stop feeling the loss of the little boy who once had tagged along with his father to mend sails and who'd spent entire weekends taking apart his dad's old computers and putting them back together.

CHAPTER TWENTY-FOUR
AMINA

Amina tiptoed down the stairs into the dark living room after the house had slipped into silence. The old computer booted reluctantly, slowly filling the corner of the room with blue light. She tilted her head from side to side, feeling the tension in her neck pull through her body then slowly release as she came back to center.

After a full day of working tables, punctuated by the visit with Jessica between shifts, her body simply wanted to go to sleep. But Amina welcomed the pain in her feet and the ache of her back, wanting to feel each pang of hurt intensely. She wouldn't have been able to do that if she were asleep.

Amina slid her thumb drive into the USB port, her heart stuttering with irrational fear that the faces would stare back at her accusingly when she clicked on the photo folder. She always kept the drive with her, but she hadn't looked at the pictures since... She couldn't even remember. It was one of the only things she had of home. But even after she had deleted so many of the pictures, she was still afraid to look at the ones she'd kept. They were people she hadn't protected, people she'd left behind.

Amina had steeled herself before telling Jessica Samir's story and bringing that memory into the present. She'd feared it would bring back the terror while pushing Samir even further away, highlighting his death and his absence. She'd been closed off and hard to talk to about her parents, but it had finally felt right to talk about Samir.

She pushed aside the apprehension and clicked the folder.

She saw her mother's hands—hands that cooked and cleaned and sewed, hands that held a child's face between them when something important was being said. In the picture, her mother's able fingers were stained with pomegranate juice. The shadowing of the black-and-white photo highlighted both their strength and their tenderness.

She saw her father's eyes. A hint of a promise beamed from the deep-brown pools, boring into her very being. They were not judging her as she sat there, safe in the dark corner of the Darbis' tidy living room. No, the love was still there. She remembered the moment she'd taken that photo, when the sun was rising over the ancient city, the first rays of light meeting her father's approving gaze. This one was from before the conflicts had begun. "Baba, I wish for you that we find that promise again," she whispered, violating the stillness of the dark room. She chastised herself. She couldn't make any promises.

She saw a photo of Samir, radiating with joy while juggling a soccer ball in front of children in the street. She traced his form on the screen with her fingers, lingering on his laughing smile.

She saw a wedding. A proud groom, more beautiful than anyone or anything she had ever known, gazed at a smiling bride whom she no longer recognized as herself and who may, in fact, have disappeared.

There were others whose pictures were no longer there, others who might be gone forever. It was not right. She should not have left. Her father had convinced her in a moment of weakness to flee, and she had only thought of herself instead of all those who might never have the chance.

She'd told Jessica about Samir because she believed she owed it to her lawyer, to her case. Maybe she did. But in truth, she owed it to Samir to tell his story. She owed it to all of them.

She pulled the thumb drive from the USB port. It was warm between her fingers. She closed her hand around it and absorbed its energy. Reluctantly, she opened her hand again and placed the drive in its pocket in her bag.

CHAPTER TWENTY-FIVE

A cool breeze rustled the dried leaves sprinkled on the lawn, whipping them in a spiral before smashing them against the fence.

Jessica shielded the photos on the floor in front of her from getting flipped by the draft, but she didn't shut the windows. She had another hour or so before the kids came downstairs to scavenge for some dinner. She would close up then.

Black-and-white photos lay on the wood floor, arranged like a game of Memory. She had only glanced at the photos when she'd first opened the box after the sidewalk incident, but hearing more about Amina's irretrievable past had made her think about what she had left behind.

In one photo, a family—clearly her mother, her uncle, and her grandparents—stood in front of a movie theater. Oma looked jarringly like Jessica's mother, including the slight smirk that highlighted her apple cheeks and the thick wave of dark hair tucked behind her left ear. The title of the movie was outside the frame of the photo. It was something starring Gregory Peck. The theater had still been in town when Jessica had left for college, but it had soon become one of many casualties of the attrition endemic to rural towns.

She had been part of the exodus. Not that Iowa City was that far away, but it was exactly that—away.

163

Jessica crisscrossed her legs and placed a photo album from the box on her lap.

Twelve inches tall by eighteen inches wide, the album had a leatherlike cover with the word "Photos" embossed in gold vintage script. Inside the cover, "Our family" was written in Oma's careful hand in white ink on black paper. The brittle paper, faded at the edges where it had been exposed to light over the years, stiffly resisted then succumbed to Jessica's fingers. As she turned the first page, tiny bits of black paper crumbled and fell unceremoniously onto the wood floor.

Each page had a collection of photos, or in some cases just a single photo, with captions written in white script. An austere couple posed joylessly in chairs in front of a farmhouse. A smiling farmer flung hay with a pitchfork from atop a towering haystack.

Turning a page, Jessica caught her breath. An old woman with bright eyes sat on an uncomfortable-looking wooden chair and stared back at her. She had that old-lady matronly look about her. A shapeless homemade dress gave no indication of the figure hidden beneath. Strands of hair resisted her attempted bun and formed a rough halo around her face. It was Oma, but it wasn't. The photo was too old for it to be Oma. Jessica examined the photo, hiding the caption with her hand. The woman's round face, almond-shaped eyes, and the way she looked at the camera with utter confidence betrayed her genetic tie to Cricket. Jessica moved her hand to uncover the white script. "Gr. Margarethe," it read under the photo. *So this is you, Grandma Margarethe. Your embroidery and the quilt are beautiful. And I love your cross.*

A set of small boxes held the rest of the photos, each snapshot with writing on the back. Favorite Uncle Carl stood on his head. Dowdy Aunt Patty was dolled up like a pinup girl in her graduation photo. A lot of shots included people—relatives, presumably—she couldn't place.

Some pictures stood out more than others. In one, Jessica's mom and uncle as kids were setting off a rocket. *So very* Sputnik *of them*. Her uncle grinned for the camera, while her mom's eyes were locked on the rocket in her brother's hands.

Her mom would know who some of these people were. Jessica gathered the loose photos she had set aside, shuffling them into an approximated chronological order. That would be a good excuse to get in touch, especially since her mom had sent multiple messages asking about her progress on the boxes.

She heard footsteps behind her and turned to find Cricket, or perhaps a ghost of Margarethe's teen years. She studied Cricket's face, curious how a face could be so young but have so much history in it. Cricket knelt by the photos, scanning a selection from a pile Jessica hadn't gone through yet. She picked up a snapshot. "Is this you?"

Jessica expected to see a baby photo of herself, but instead she saw an image of her mother standing behind a four-year-old Jessica along the curb of Main Street as a parade marched by. Her mother smiled for the camera, but little Jessica's eyes were glued to the troop of men leading the parade. The men wore suspenders and beards from a different era, far removed from the 1970s. The beards were long and short, bushy and scraggly. Some men were dark haired, but their beards were gray. Some men were bald, with thick beards that, to a four-year-old, made it look as if their heads were upside down.

"No, that's my mom." Jessica directed Cricket's finger to the little girl in the photo. "That's me. Grandma is standing behind me. This was the Idaville Centennial Parade." She chuckled, closing her eyes and feeling the laughter low in her belly. "The men in town had grown their beards out for a year to celebrate the centennial. When I saw them leading the parade, I didn't know that. I thought they all had been there for a hundred years, which seemed like a million to me. I was convinced I was going to look like that someday."

Cricket joined in the laughter. "Good thing you left, huh?"

JESSICA ATTACHED THE scanned photos to the email, hit Send, then dialed her mom.

Her mom picked up on the second ring and immediately expressed surprise at the call. Jessica hadn't been the one to reach out for some time, which aggravated her existing guilt over the distance between them. Her guilt felt like interest accumulating on interest to the point that what may have started out as a small debt seemed impossible to repay.

"How is it going with Oma's things?" her mother asked.

It didn't sound like an accusation, but Jessica was embarrassed there were still stacks of boxes in her parlor. "I've been busy and got sidetracked with some other things."

"That's not what I meant. I don't expect you to be done already. Have you found anything interesting?"

"That's why I called. Cricket and I were going through Oma's photo albums yesterday, and I just emailed you some pictures I scanned."

"Hold on." Her mom's voice sounded like it was in a tunnel. She'd switched to speaker mode as she checked her email. "Oh my. What a blast from the past. No pun intended! Ha! The rocket one... I had forgotten about that. Oh my goodness, I had so much fun with the rockets. Blew up the garage once, even."

"I'm sorry, what?" That had escalated quickly. "What are you talking about?"

Her mom switched back to receiver mode. "You sure you have time?"

Jessica winced. "Yes, of course." She closed her laptop and moved to the couch. "I'd like to hear about the rocket. And the garage."

"The space program was all anybody could talk about back then, and rockets fascinated me. It was so exciting! Then one year, your uncle Robert got a rocket set for Christmas. *I*, on the other hand, got

red cowboy boots and a matching red-fringed suede skirt because...
well, I don't know why. I guess cowboys and westerns were a big deal,
too. *Gunsmoke* and all that. Oh boy, was I jealous when he opened
that rocket set."

Jessica could almost see her mom crinkling up her nose that way
she did whenever something didn't go her way. As a teen, Jessica
dreaded that expression of disapproval and dissatisfaction, but now
she wished she hadn't been away from it for so long.

"But as soon as Bobby realized he actually had to *build* the rocket? That it wasn't just a toy? Ha! I promised him he could launch it
if he let *me* build it. We didn't tell Daddy. That's why that photo you
sent shows me standing by as Bobby sets the launch."

"Did you let Uncle Robert wear your red cowboy boots and
skirt?"

"No, but I would have if he'd asked!"

Jessica could envision that, remembering how her uncle used to
sneak on a long, curly blond wig to try to convince her that eating
bread crusts turned hair curly. She had diligently cut off her bread
crusts for a year, hoping her hair would straighten, but it never did.

"I'm surprised you couldn't tell Gramps you liked rockets." Being
Gramps's "lucky charm," Jessica had always believed she could do
anything.

"At the time, you know, girls weren't supposed to be interested in
that kind of thing. It wasn't a big deal. That's just the way it was. But
I was good at math and took all the science classes. We didn't have
physics or engineering at school, so I checked out books from the library. Can you believe that?"

"You could have been an astronaut, Mom." Her upbringing
would have been unrecognizable, possibly even glamorous, had her
mom gone into the space program. Of course, Jessica probably
wouldn't even have existed in that alternate universe.

"Well, *that* was never going to happen. Not back then. Astronaut's wife, maybe. Ha! That would have been something! I was at the top of the class in all of my math and science classes. I went to my math teacher to see if he could help me find a good college for aerospace engineering. But he laughed and said girls don't get into those programs. He advised me to take secretarial classes in case I didn't get married right away. Didn't I tell you about this back in high school? I would have thought I did. Hmm. Well, anyway, as it turned out, your dad got drafted, we got married right after I graduated, I got pregnant, and that was that! Ha! But you knew that part."

Jessica couldn't reconcile her mother's lighthearted storytelling with being completely shut out of a promising future, even if it would have been a future that excluded Jessica.

"But you wanted to know about the garage." Her mom laughed. "That's where I was building the rocket. I knew the expected range of Bobby's rocket, and it wasn't going to go much higher than the house. How many chances was I going to get to set off a rocket? I decided to experiment. I took apart some mag bullets to extract the gunpowder."

"Wait—what?" Rockets and gunpowder experiments did not go along with Jessica's memories of her rather conventional small-town mom.

"Pish! It was nothing. You just use pliers to pry out the slug from the bullet, then you can get at the powder. I put the powder in an empty coffee can. I heard Daddy's car pulling into the driveway, so I shoved the empty shells in my pocket and stashed the can by a stool. You know how your Gramps smoked cigars?"

"Oh God, Mom. I don't like where this is going."

"Well, he used to smoke cigarettes. He started in the war. Lucky Strikes. That day, he parked his car in front of the garage and went in to get something. I don't know what. I was on my bike, near the garage at this point. He waved to me as he pulled out a cigarette and a matchbox before he walked into the garage. I'm sure my eyes were the size of saucers as he lit that match. He flicked it behind him. Jessie, can I take a moment to say that in my defense, who flicks a match in a garage?"

"Indeed. Objection sustained."

"And that was that."

"That's it? Boom? No casualties?"

"Daddy, thank the good Lord, was uninjured. Well, he did burn himself with his cigarette when he hit the deck. There wasn't any structural damage, just some shrapnel and a blackened corner of the garage. He thought the match landed in motor oil. He even quit smoking for a while. When he started back up, he stuck with cigars."

"And did you stop experimenting with explosives?"

"Heck no! In that photo you sent me, Bobby's rocket went three times as high as the box said it was supposed to go. Daddy just knew Bobby was a genius. Poor Bobby got science kits and erector sets for a couple more years. Ha! Daddy was really confused when Bobby became an insurance salesman."

And you got married. And then you got pregnant. And that was that. Ha.

CHAPTER TWENTY-SIX

The drive into DC for the second time in less than a month served as a reminder that Jessica had stopped taking advantage of being so close to the Capitol.

When the kids were young, she had only just left Highland & Cross, so she'd still been in the habit of heading into the District. With Danny working so much, she would often take the kids to the Museum of Natural History to see the giant dinosaur and play with the archaeology tools in the children's interactive zone. She'd taught them to fly kites on the Mall, and they'd visited the National Zoo in the summer. Eventually, though, the pull of school, local volunteer obligations, and to be honest, complacency shrank Jessica's daily orbit, and out-of-town excursions ceased.

Now, though, she had a purpose. Amina's newfound openness inspired her, and she wanted to know how much time she had to take advantage of it while preparing for the asylum interview. The alphabet soup of lawyers at her old firm just might have some inside information from their government connections that Rosalie couldn't access. It seemed auspicious that Jessica's former law school classmate and H&C colleague, Bronwyn, was free to meet for lunch that week.

Checking the mirror before she left, Jessica recognized that she had subconsciously switched into the mindset of her earlier life, putting on dark slacks, chunky heels, and a conservative blouse. It wasn't quite a client-meeting power outfit, but it was far from the boots, miniskirt, and cropped jacket she might have worn had she been meeting up with friends for their regular ladies' lunch.

Jessica's heart leapt when the pinnacle of the Washington Monument, sunlight gleaming off the white marble, appeared in the distance. Getting into the city required driving through some rough areas full of abandoned shops, boarded-up row homes, and a monotone of futility. But the stately marble of Capitol Hill spoke of America's promise.

Jessica knew not to expect to find a street spot without circling for an hour, so she parked in a garage and took a leisurely walk to the restaurant. Adopting a stride she hoped pegged her as a local and not a tourist, she nonetheless felt like an outsider.

Entering Pho 909, Jessica tried to pick Bronwyn out of the crowd of K Streeters and lawyers jockeying for a table. The place hadn't changed a bit. The decor was still humble with its chrome diner-style chairs and tables and unflattering lighting. And the lunch crowds were still big.

"Jessica Walter Donnelly!"

Jessica turned toward the commanding Southern accent that somehow found more than three syllables in her first name.

Bronwyn, whose charcoal suit was drowned out by a bold geometric scarf flowing around her neck—she never had let convention win completely—approached from behind a table near the kitchen and threw her arms around Jessica. "I'm a brunette now, so I figured you might not recognize me."

Jessica couldn't suppress a laugh. Bronwyn was Bronwyn, blond or brunette. Crow's feet graced her hazel eyes, and she had probably added fifteen pounds since they were associates together, but she had an ease of self that radiated confidence, just as she had when they'd met as first-year law students.

At first-year orientation, Jessica had finally—finally—escaped flyover country to get her degree from one of the nation's top law schools. As the fifteen aspiring lawyers in her small section had taken turns telling everyone something about themselves, Jessica could feel her spine compressing, vertebra by vertebra, a feeling of insecure panic welling up to obliterate her naïve excitement.

Jessica had never felt so unaccomplished as she had that day when she'd had to introduce herself as Jessica Walter from Iowa. "I majored in political science and came straight through," she'd said. She couldn't talk about experience in the Peace Corps, start-up businesses, military service, or advanced degrees like some of the others. She was just a girl from Iowa. But none of them had ever met anyone from Iowa, which had made her at least somewhat interesting, if a little mortified.

Bronwyn had also gone straight through from college to law school, but what had seemed pathetic for Jessica painted Bronwyn as a woman on a mission. Law school had been a necessary road bump on Bronwyn's way from Smoky Mountain county fair queen to university student body president to big firm success.

Bronwyn's huge personality, together with her story of leaving the rural South, had a gravitational pull that soon yanked Jessica out of her self-consciousness. Going from study partners to first-year associates at H&C had seemed only natural, and Jessica's admiration for Bronwyn had never faltered.

Always in control of her words and disarming with her drawl and trademark belly laugh, Bronwyn was unfailingly ready for anything. No one who met her wanted to leave her orbit.

Which reminded Jessica. "By the way, congratulations on being named managing partner. I saw it in the *Journal Law Blog*." That was just what she would have expected of her old friend—having a goal and achieving it.

Bronwyn smirked.

"Yes, Bronwyn, I read the *Law Blog* like a troll." Jessica looked around the brightly lit diner. Framed posters had faded into shadows from years of sunlight, and a scattering of replacement floor tiles didn't quite match the originals. "I suppose we should have met somewhere fancier than the Pho. I just thought 'old times' and all."

Bronwyn waved a hand, launching the glittery bangles on her wrist into a jangling melody. "Honey, I love the Pho. I still bring new associates here and tell them about those old times, fax machines, the birth of email, researching without the Internet. It's all changed. But the Pho remains the same."

A waitress approached the table, and both women placed their orders without opening the menu.

Jessica stopped the waitress before she walked away. "Does Mr. Pham still own the restaurant?"

"No. My grandfather died last year, shortly after my grandmother passed." She nodded toward a framed photo hanging behind the counter.

The young Vietnamese man in the photo resembled the older Mr. Pham, who used to greet them at the door. The petite woman standing next to him in the photo clasped his left hand tightly with both of her hands. The restaurant storefront behind them dwarfed the couple.

"My mother and father now run the restaurant." The waitress nodded softly as Jessica mumbled her sympathies.

After their server scurried toward the kitchen with their order, the women smiled sadly at each other.

"I loved Mr. Pham," Jessica said. "He was so mean to us."

"And boy, did we deserve it!" Bronwyn's belly laugh brought back memories.

"Tough love from Mr. Pham. He just didn't want us believing we were the hot shits we thought we were. But he did always make sure the H&C crew got a table."

"Ain't that the truth!"

After a respectful moment of silence, the two women fell into the conversational flow that somehow came easily to old friends whose jobs and kids and husbands and lives simply got in the way of staying in touch.

"Did you see the most recent alumni magazine? Shawn finally got his plane crash." Jessica shuddered, thinking about their old law school classmate. He had grand plans to make it rich, proclaiming, "All I need is one plane crash." Shawn had just won the second-largest damages award in the history of Florida for the families of the victims of an Everglades plane crash.

"And Jeremy—"

"CEO of a dating app!" They both blurted together. Jeremy was the creepiest—but possibly the smartest—guy in their graduating class. He'd made advances on just about every girl in law school, including Jessica and Bronwyn, on the same night, no less, and was rejected by all. Now he captained a company about to go public and make him a Silicon Valley billionaire.

Jessica continued. "I'm most excited about Amy. Dean of Stanford Law. Isn't that incredible? I always did want her in my study group. I was clearly onto something."

Jessica had been wait-listed when she'd applied to Stanford Law School. She had always attributed that to her grades from her ridiculous—and unsuccessful—attempt to minor in economics, but maybe Stanford had had some way of knowing that someday she would quit the law and just be a stay-at-home mom. She was sure that wasn't what a top law school wanted to see from its graduates. Maybe Jessica should have known she was a lightweight, too. Meeting her classmates her first year, she had felt completely out of her league. She wasn't sure she'd ever found her league.

"What have you been up to?" Bronwyn squeezed lime into one of the sparkling waters that had appeared on the table while they'd gossiped.

"Conor's a junior. He's driving now—can you believe it? Cricket's a sophomore, and I don't know how she does it, but she seems to be able to avoid all of the crazy teen drama that I remember from high school. Apparently she has a boyfriend, though I have yet to meet him. Mikey is in sixth grade, my little chatterbox. And Danny's company is doing some really exciting work in encryption. He's working on landing a huge contract with Defense."

"Yes, but what about *you*?" Bronwyn tapped her manicured fingernails on the Formica tabletop. "Why the call out of the blue? I'm always glad to hear from you, but what brings us together at the Pho today?" The tapping stopped.

"Oh yes, why I'm here. I'm doing some volunteer work. I'm sure you remember Rosalie Townsend? After she came back from that human rights thing in Thailand, she got into working with refugees, and now she heads up an immigration nonprofit in Baltimore. I ran into her at an alumni event, and somehow I ended up becoming a *pro bono* asylum attorney." She shook her head, still in disbelief. "I have one client. It's been quite an education."

"Good for you! They're lucky to have you, Jessica, and I think it's fantastic you took on something new."

"You know, me too," Jessica said. And she meant it, though she hadn't admitted it to herself until now. "I hadn't really thought I missed it. Between the kids and carpooling and taking care of the house and everything else, time passed more quickly than I would have expected. But those things have slowed down. And I have to admit that it is quite a relief to learn that my brain still works after all those years of being soft."

Bronwyn nodded slowly, as though she knew something Jessica hadn't figured out yet.

Jessica picked up a cocktail napkin half-soaked from condensation. "I thought that maybe you have someone at H&C who still has connections with the Department of Homeland Security. My client has been waiting for her interview notice, and we have no sense of timing. She's... she's from Syria." Jessica checked Bronwyn for a reaction. Bronwyn's open expression invited her to continue. "And with the way politics are going, I figure the sooner the better, before she loses her chance altogether. Maybe someone can get me some information about timing? Not for her specifically, just for the Arlington office in general."

Bronwyn tapped her nails again. "Is that all? C'mon, now. You can make those calls yourself." She eyed Jessica cagily. "I'll see what I can find out. I have to say that I was hoping maybe you were looking to get back in the game." She raised her right eyebrow, challenging the lawyer seated across from her.

Jessica's heart thumped, and her face flushed. "Oh, hmm, I hadn't really thought about that. I've been out for so long that I don't even want to say how long it's been." She looked down and found she had shredded the napkin into a soggy mass of pulp.

"It doesn't matter. Highland & Cross has a new program, and you are perfect for it." Bronwyn placed her palms on the table as though it were already a done deal.

"I'm listening." Jessica surprised herself with her statement.

"It's called ReCross. Too many women leave the law and never return, even though a lot of them want to." Bronwyn waved a hand above the table. "And I get it. Everyone needs a different balance of work and home. But the balance we need changes over time."

"Fair enough."

"We aren't the only law firm with a program like this, but ours is the best. I helped design it, so it has to be, right?" Her belly laugh turned heads at the table next to them. "We have all the training to bring you up to speed. The law stuff is easy-peasy." She waved the law stuff away with the flick of a hand. "It's the office environment, the technology, and client expectations that are usually totally alien to women coming back, especially after a hiatus as long as yours."

Bronwyn's wink was supportive rather than patronizing. "Our program goes over all of these things that might have changed since you were practicing. What client expectations are now that you are accessible twenty-four-seven via cell phone. What secretaries do now that technology has changed so much. Do you remember how Mr. Davis didn't have a computer in his corner office, even in 2000?"

Mr. Davis was a bankruptcy partner who, even back then, had seemed behind the times. She wondered about all the ways she would be considered a dinosaur in her own right if she returned to the office today.

"Well, he ended up getting a computer before he retired. It was like a two-headed chicken at the county fair. Everyone had to peek in his office to see him hunting and pecking on his keyboard. Anyway, the program works to bring you up to speed on working in the law firm today so you won't be a Mr. Davis. Then, we split trainees off into practice groups to refresh and update in your specific area of the law."

Jessica considered this. "Then what? Job?"

"In ReCross, everyone who goes through the program does an internship, kind of like the summer internships we did back in law school. We pay a stipend, but you can't expect all of the wining and dining that we enjoyed when we were interns." Bronwyn patted her belly. "Lord knows some of us don't need that! At the end of the internship, the firm determines if we have a position. Even if we don't, you've gotten the training and the experience to go out and find another firm. But we try not to admit someone into ReCross if we don't think there's a good chance we'll have a spot for her."

"Sounds interesting." Jessica's measured voice belied the somersaults churning her insides. She hadn't anticipated this offering, or maybe she had in some form, but she didn't want to seem too eager to either Bronwyn or herself. "I'm not sure if this is the best time for it for me. But it seems like a great program. The firm has certainly been the right thing for you, though. You made some good decisions along the way."

"Where will *this* moment take you? I ask myself that every single day to focus on getting to that next goal, that next moment. Hasn't failed me yet."

Mr. Pham's granddaughter returned to the table with steaming hot bowls of pho, saving Jessica from having to take this topic further. The women reverted to gossip about the rest of their graduating class, and Jessica savored the ginger-infused broth and the memories that came with it.

———————— ⬥ ————————

BRONWYN'S words replayed themselves in Jessica's head as she circled through the garage, toward the exit. "Where will *this* moment take you?" Where, indeed. This moment offered real choices, and she hadn't felt as though she'd had real choices for years.

The satellite radio kicked in as the car pulled out into the street. The newscast crackled into something about Paris, a stadium, and an explosion. And just like that, the moment changed from her own potential future to a reality four thousand miles away that could affect the future of someone connected to her, someone she cared about. Jessica turned left as she cranked up the volume.

CHAPTER TWENTY-SEVEN

J essica set down her coffee and checked her watch. It wasn't like Amina to be late, even by five minutes, and today's tardiness didn't help the unease Jessica had been experiencing since the events in Paris the prior week. One hundred thirty people were dead, hundreds wounded, and the so-called Islamic State was to blame. A significant attack in the West hadn't made the news in some time, so television news had wall-to-wall coverage, and everyone on social media was now aligned with France.

Jessica prayed Amina wasn't suffering any backlash, but her practical concern focused on potential tightening on immigration. Neither Rosalie nor Bronwyn had heard of that happening when Jessica checked in with them, though they also couldn't offer any additional information.

It only took one glance from Danny during a newscast about the attack, his eyebrows raised and a pseudo-innocent shrug of "I told you so," to trigger an internal battle. Jessica's lingering apprehensions wrestled with her indignation at her husband's opposition to her work helping Middle Eastern refugees.

To be fair, though, he didn't entirely know everything she was doing. Neither of them was guilt free, so it was best left alone. But she still resented him for his outward representation of a prejudice she had been ashamed to see in herself when she'd met Amina. Knowing Amina and hearing her stories had formed a bond that had erased apprehensions about their relationship, but Jessica would be lying to herself if she said she was completely free of biases that had surreptitiously built up over a lifetime.

The door jingled, and Amina entered. A few patrons turned toward the door, eyes lingering on the scarved woman a little longer than they might have on Jessica.

Amina breezed past them. "I am sorry for being late."

"No problem. Is everything okay?"

Exhaustion peeked through Amina's determined exterior. "Yes. Sama may deliver early, so we are busy."

"Let me know when she has the baby." Amina might be harder to get together with after that, so today's meeting was good timing.

Jessica had Amina's employment paperwork ready, with sign-here tabs, duplicates for IAP, Amina, and USCIS, and a different-colored folder for each set. It wasn't a Securities Exchange Commission filing, but it didn't seem over the top to think that a person's future and livelihood deserved as much attention to detail as a company's securities law compliance.

The USCIS was strict about deadlines, so Jessica wasn't taking any chances on getting Amina's work authorization renewed, getting the application in at the recommended 120-day mark. Plus, it was an excuse to meet. After hearing the story of Samir and sensing an opening in the Syrian's armor, Jessica hoped to take advantage of Amina's candor to build up support for the asylum case by finding more details about what had happened to her family and why.

"You didn't have to do this," Amina said. "I did the employment authorization filing the first time." But she didn't appear irritated.

"I know. But it makes me feel useful. Humor me?" Amina smiled at Jessica's weak plea, and both women laughed. The tension from their first meeting, long gone, had been replaced by a comfortable ease. Jessica handed Amina the purple folder, pointing out what to review and where to sign.

Jessica's phone buzzed. Amina was going over the documents, so Jessica opened Danny's text. Holding in a laugh, Jessica felt her face flush and couldn't suppress her smile. She'd left the Thanksgiving turkey out to thaw for later in the week, and Danny had taken some wholly inappropriate photos. They were funny, but she certainly wouldn't be showing them to the modestly dressed woman sitting across from her.

The sound of shuffling paper stopped. Questioning eyes and a tilted head from Amina demanded an explanation.

"Just my husband. He sent me a funny text." She shook her head and turned off the phone.

Amina handed over the file. "What did he say?"

Jessica fumbled. "Oh, hmm. It was, well, not appropriate for public display. They were... photos." That statement could leave room for misinterpretation. "Of a turkey." That didn't make it better.

Amina arched an eyebrow.

"Thanksgiving." Jessica sighed, releasing just enough stress to let words spill. "I think he's trying to make me feel better about it. Some of Danny's family comes every year. His parents died not long after he left for college, and somehow we ended up being Thanksgiving hosts about ten years ago. I just... I didn't want to do it this time. Yes, it's family, but I need a break from it, from them. It's like I'm the caterer every year. Maybe if they reciprocated? Or maybe not. To be honest, my sister-in-law in particular is just awful, and I don't like being around her. Danny and I had an argument about it last night since he went ahead and invited everyone without asking me." She waved away the holiday concern, especially Danny's comment that she didn't exactly have "too much going on that she couldn't host a family meal." "I shouldn't be boring you with this."

"How did you meet him?"

Amina's abrupt question jolted Jessica into the memory of the night she met Danny. Exhaustion, movies, Jujubes, and bay-blue eyes. Jessica could almost reminisce away the hurt of recent conflicts as she told Amina about that first chance meeting. Fingers touching floral fabric brought Jessica back into the moment.

Jessica pushed the folders a bit out of the way. "Tell me about your husband."

Jessica sat, quiet and attentive, as Amina wove the story of how she and Mohammed had met. Her father had encouraged her to marry for love and intellect, but her mother had looked on disapprovingly. Jessica pictured Mohammed in her mind. Lean and tall, nearly a foot taller than Amina, with curly black hair and "dancing" eyes, according to Amina, whose own eyes danced amusingly along with the story.

Amina said her mother had come around. "She never said a word of approval. One day he came for a regular visit. It was not even Eid, but she made *maamoul bi ajwa*. My brothers and I begged her always to make us our favorite cookies, but she would slap our hands away. Only for Eid, she would say." Amina opened her hands, seeing something in them that wasn't visible to Jessica. "When she made them for Mohammed, I knew."

Amina's engagement was a family affair, followed by a wedding and honeymoon on the Mediterranean coast. "Mohammed studied architecture in Damascus. It is a beautiful old city." Pain flashed across Amina's face. "Even Damascus has seen tragedy."

She tilted her head upward, breathing in deeply, as if to drown the images in a rush of air. "We had hoped to travel. Mohammed wished to see the ancient Greek temples and ruins he had read about in his books. It is good to see the history before it is destroyed by those who wish to eliminate the past."

"Danny and I have always wanted to go to Greece." Jessica regretted the banal comment immediately. Amina's eyes had stopped dancing. Jessica needed to learn what had happened to Mohammed, especially if it could support Amina's claim of fear of persecution. "I know from your application that Mohammed disappeared. What do you know about that?"

"Mohammed left for work one day and did not come home. Sometimes it can be that simple. I went to his building. My mother did not want me to go out alone, but I had no choice. When I arrived, the men would not talk to me. They would not even look at me." The flowers on Amina's scarf rose and fell with her quickened breath.

"I demanded they tell me where my husband was, but they ignored me. A child standing on the corner was watching me. He heard my shouting." Amina's brow tightened, and sadness filled her eyes. "I recognized the child. Samir had played games with him outside our door so many times. The child did not look away as I walked near. He whispered, 'They took him.'" Amina's impression of that whisper painted the tragic picture of a child who knew that some secrets led to dire endings.

"Who? Why?"

"We believed it was Assad's men. They battled the rebels in our area, and if you were not fighting with them, they assumed you were against them. It was eight days when I left. My father handed me papers and a packed bag. He told me I was registered for a conference and would visit a distant cousin who lived in America." She smiled wanly at Jessica. "Baltimore. I did not know that he had made plans for me. And I shouldn't have agreed to go so quickly. But I was..." She pursed her lips.

"You were what?"

"My father was broken. He had such guilt over Samir. But he refused to let them break me. He was to tell Mohammed where I was if Mohammed returned, but no one else was to know. And I was to come home when"—Amina's chest pulsated from either macabre laughter or sobs. Jessica couldn't tell—"when things got better."

"And did he tell Mohammed?"

Amina's blank face offered no answer. The two had never directly addressed the question of Amina's parents' survival. If they had died, they wouldn't have been able to tell Mohammed where Amina had gone. If they were alive, that would mean either Mohammed never got out, or they never connected for any number of dire reasons. Recalling Mikey's theory of always thinking the best, Jessica couldn't figure out a "best" scenario in this case, so she left the issue off the table for now.

"I am sorry, but I need to get back to the house now. Thank you for the paperwork," Amina said, her emptiness palpable. She walked away, with one hand holding an orange folder and the other hand on her bag. The void lingered in the shop even after the door jingled closed behind her.

Assad's men had assaulted Amina's mother, tortured her father, killed her brother, and kidnapped her husband. A "well-founded fear of persecution" didn't seem hard to prove. But there hadn't been any indication that her fear was based on race, religion, nationality, membership in a particular social group, or political opinion. Maybe they could make it fit into presumed opposition to Assad. And maybe there wouldn't be a tightening of reviews before the interview.

CHAPTER TWENTY-EIGHT
AMINA

Amina tucked a stuffed animal into each backpack and confirmed that each held a snack, drink, and supplies to keep fidgety little boys occupied at the hospital.

"Are you sure you don't want to come with us?" Fayiz didn't look up from the dresser as he pulled out one tiny shirt after another, examining each as though it were a puzzle he needed to solve.

Yes, she was sure she didn't want to come with them. "No, you should have time together. I will get things ready here for when she comes home." Things were ready in the Darbi home already, but Fayiz was too distracted to know one way or the other and was happy to go along with anything Amina said right now. Her talk with Jessica earlier in the week had been surprisingly comfortable, but it had caused feelings to bubble up—feelings of loss of loved ones and a family she may never have with Mohammed. She was happy for Sama and for her healthy child but needed a little more time before she could see the baby.

She never would have guessed the pulled-together American woman with her color-coded sticky notes would be the person who would make her feel normal again, but when Jessica had exposed her own cracks and struggles at home, Amina had felt as though she were commiserating with a friend rather than disclosing evidence to an attorney.

Fayiz spoke again. "We need to get the boys fed and dressed, and I don't even know..." He stared at the pile of shirts that had accumulated on the dresser. He couldn't solve the puzzle.

"You go feed them." Amina gestured toward the dresser. "And I will take care of the rest." She shooed Fayiz out of the room and picked up the shirt at the top of the pile. She set it facedown on the dresser, folded it into thirds, and smoothed the creases. She turned it over and folded it into thirds again then smoothed the creases. Falling into her mother's cadence of folding her scarves soothed her like a warm caress.

Seeing Fayiz so flustered reminded her of a day a thousand years ago when she and Mohammed had gone for a drive outside of the city to see his brother. They hadn't married yet, but she had already known they would be together forever. Forever was not a mournful concept then.

They approached an apple orchard, lush green dotted with spots of red, an oasis compared to the urban desert they had just left. Before it was in their rearview mirror, Amina asked Mohammed to "please pull to the side of the road."

When he asked her if she was okay, his eyebrows knitted together with concern, she leapt from the car, jumped the fence, and ran among the trees.

It didn't take long for Mohammed to catch her.

"Are you crazy?" he asked. "We don't know whose orchard this is." He looked over his shoulders, as if they were sneaking into Assad's compound and the guards would be on them at any moment. For some reason, his paranoia made Amina turn and run away again. She was no runner, though, so she climbed the nearest tree. She perched only a foot above Mohammed when he caught up to her.

His hair was a mess, in that way that looked as if an old woman had just run her hand through it and told him he was "such a sweet thing." He seemed vulnerable, with his head tilted up toward her and his eyes open in wonder at the woman in the tree. She would never have been able to explain it, but watching the drop of sweat trail down his temple and wind its way into the fold of his ear had sent her into gales of laughter, until she'd fallen out of the tree and into his arms.

If she had anything to give, she would have given it all to have him back and to be that girl again.

She hadn't abandoned hope, not completely. She didn't have proof her parents were dead, but the silence told her. She would have heard from them if they were alive. Her father or mother would have contacted her no matter where they had fled. But Mohammed did not know where she was, did not even know that she was still alive, and would have had no way of reaching her if he somehow, some way, had gotten out.

Despite the fears of government surveillance, she had searched for Mohammed and the others on the Darbis' old computer, late at night when the rest of the house slept, but that had been over a year ago. She had been discrete. Maybe she'd stopped out of caution. She didn't want to expose the Darbis, who had been so generous with her. But maybe she had stopped because she had been afraid to know Mohammed's fate. While her parents' death seemed certain, his didn't have to be if she never confirmed it.

Learning his fate didn't seem as daunting anymore, though. In fact, she wanted to know. She might not have been able to be that girl again, but she could be herself again, whoever that may be. The library had computers. It was probably closed for Thanksgiving today, but she could wait. She had experience with waiting.

She folded the last shirt and moved to tidy the loose Lego bricks that surrounded a multicolored reproduction of the ruins at Palmyra, which the boys had built for their plastic dinosaurs to attack. Poor Syria wasn't even safe from extinct animals.

"Amina? Are the boys' clothes ready?" Sounds of cabinet doors closing and silverware hitting the counter came from the kitchen.

Amina closed the drawer. It was time for two little boys to go meet their new brother.

CHAPTER TWENTY-NINE

The robust smell of Danny's freshly ground coffee filled a room that would soon smell of turkey and pies and, if it stayed chilly, charred oak.

Jessica had grudgingly crawled out of her warm bed along with Danny early that morning. She would have loved to sleep in on Thanksgiving just once, but a turkey had to get in the oven, potatoes had to get peeled, and so on. She'd resigned herself to another thankless Thanksgiving, not quite forgiving Danny for forcing the event on her again but willing to set aside her frustrations in the interest of harmony. She was being selfish, but Danny just didn't seem to get that he was pushing things a little too far.

Pouring herself a cup of coffee and greedily inhaling the aroma, Jessica peered out the window. Trees blocked the sunrise, but an otherworldly red, ripped by thin clouds, infused the morning sky. It just might be a beautiful day.

The back door opened, and Gracie ran into the kitchen to alert Jessica that she and Danny were back from their run and say "Hey, where is my breakfast?"

"Good run?" Jessica asked.

Danny's face was flushed, even through his perpetual sailor's tan. "Yes. Great weather for a run." He filled a tall glass with water from the fridge. "Did you see the sky?"

"Gorgeous. What time is everyone getting here? I sent out the emails, but no one got back to me. Yet again. I don't know what time anyone is coming or if anyone is bringing anything." She didn't hide her judginess of the ungrateful guests.

Danny set the empty glass on the counter. "Calm down, now." His tone was a little too condescending. "They'll be here the same time they get here every year. And you always assume they'll bring nothing, so you should be all set. Oh, and Sean texted me that he'll be bringing the kids and his girlfriend—"

"Wait, what?!" Jessica set down her coffee too hard, and brown liquid spilled onto the counter. "Why didn't you tell me? Every year, it's either extra people or no-shows. It would help not to find out the day of. Just what I need. Both of them." The sister-in-law and the girlfriend were almost more than she could handle.

He held his hands out, palms forward, as if he were being stopped by the police. "Whoa. I got the text after you fell asleep last night. It'll be fine. It's just a few more people, and..." He scanned the counters and kitchen table. Jessica had already laid out all of the casserole dishes and serving dishes she would be using. Potatoes, bread rolls, and various cans lined the counters, ready to be prepped. "We have plenty of food. You always figure out how to manage things. The more the merrier, right?"

Jessica pursed her lips and slowly shook her head.

Danny came over and wrapped his arms around her, nuzzling his sweaty face up against hers, seemingly oblivious to her stiffened body. "Thanks for putting up with my family for these things. I know they can be a pain in the ass. But they're family."

Jessica could still taste the salt from his sweaty kiss after he walked away. She wiped it off with the back of her hand. The pile of russets forced her to admit that she did have plenty of potatoes, but that was beside the point.

Her phone buzzed with a text from Amina. *Sama had her baby. You said to let you know.*

Jessica thumbed her response. *Good news! Are you at the hospital?*

No. Fayiz is taking the boys today.

R u going, too?

No. Just the family.

Jessica stood with her thumbs resting on the edge of the phone. Before she knew it, her thumbs were moving, and they hit Send.

Will u join us for Thanksgiving dinner?

It couldn't be unsent. Jessica watched the screen intently, wondering what the hell she had just done and what Amina was thinking at the other end. Yes, the relationship had thawed since that first, uncomfortable meeting, and she and Amina had even had some casual conversations interspersed among their serious talks about the asylum application. At that last meeting, they had really connected, though. But it would have been a lie to say that was why Jessica had invited her. Danny's holier-than-thou attitude about this whole day may have tempted the devil on her shoulder. It might feel good to see him feel uncomfortable for once. *What am I getting myself into? Is this even ethical?*

The screen remained static. Amina must have also thought she was off base. Jessica relaxed a bit.

Just as her phone went black, it lit up again.

Yes. Thank you.

JESSICA stepped back from the dining room table and stood next to Cricket to survey the results of their efforts.

An estate sale find, the cherry barn-style table had been one of Jessica's early refinishing successes. Today, it anchored the room and held its own against the heirlooms arranged on top of it.

The silver had been Danny's grandmother's and was one of the only things they had of his family's. Jessica didn't even mind polishing the striking and intricately carved pieces, and she always put them out for the holidays. But this year, she had to decide on plates due to Oma's boxes, which had offered up not one but two full sets of dinnerware. Going back and forth between Oma's floral china and Oma Bee's clunky plates, between memories of Oma's roast Christmas duck and her great-grandmother Oma Bee's lazy summer afternoon rhubarb pie, she made the natural decision, alternating place settings around the table.

"What do you think, Crick?"

"It's a little crowded. Who are all of the extra plates for?"

"Uncle Sean's kids." She tried not to sneer. "And girlfriend."

"I didn't know they were coming. We haven't seen Colton and Elana much since the divorce. They're always with their mom anymore."

Jessica bit her tongue so she wouldn't say something she would regret.

"But that's only thirteen," Cricket said. "Who's the other one for?"

Danny had just walked into the room, drying his hands on a fifty-year-old tea towel embroidered "Thursday." She would have to tell him at some point, and it wasn't a big deal anyway. After all, Danny's brother was bringing last-minute guests. Sure, they were family, but it was Jessica's home, and she had every right to invite a guest. A flash of dread shot through her gut nonetheless. She suppressed it. Danny was always cool. This would be fine.

"I invited my asylum client."

"Nice." Cricket pulled her phone from her pocket as she walked into the hallway.

Danny looked dubious. "When did that happen? You didn't mention that this morning." He put the towel in his back pocket.

Jessica pretended to arrange the plates on the table. "Oh, right. You were in the shower, and then things got busy with all of the prep." She opened her mouth to mention the baby and the hospital and try to explain this client about whom he knew nothing, but Mikey interrupted, poking his head through the doorway.

"Hey, Mom, why is the turkey in the oven if the oven is turned off?"

———— ⟋⟍⟍⟋ ————

MIKEY two-finger typed on the laptop, researching furiously.

Jessica reassured him. "It'll be fine, Mikey. We're not going to get salmonella." They would have to nuke the bird later to get it completely cooked, but it still had a bit of time to bake the old-fashioned way. She shoved the half-baked bird back in the now-heated oven and posted a sticky note warning everyone—especially the unknown culprit—against touching any of the oven's control buttons.

She'd been right about Danny. He didn't seem to mind that there would be an extra body. The extra body's identity might be more of a challenge, but if Danny was anything, he was unflappable. She didn't even know where he'd gone, but probably to his office to respond to emails.

"Close that thing and help me get the appetizers ready. Cricket, can you get off your phone and go make sure the bathroom is tidied up?" She turned to her oldest, so helpfully lounging on the couch and clicking through the football pregame shows. "Conor, I think we should move the couch so we can bring in some more chairs by the fire. Can you take care of that?" He could still watch his shows while helping. She was meeting him halfway, though his grunted response didn't seem to acknowledge her accommodations. Under ordinary circumstances, she would be all over the sulky teenager to get in line for guests, but today she just couldn't find the reserves for that. As long as he didn't do anything to offend Amina, she would be happy.

The dog started barking before the doorbell rang. That would be Amina. Jessica had asked her to come a little earlier than the rest of the crew, thinking it would be less crazy than walking into, well, all the crazy. "Mikey, can you put Gracie in the mudroom? I don't want her jumping all over our guest." Jessica rushed to the front door as her youngest grabbed Gracie's collar and started leading her to the back.

Cricket jumped in behind Jessica as she opened the door. "Hi, Amina," Jessica said. "Happy Thanksgiving! We are so happy you're joining us. This is Cricket. Come on in."

Amina's eyes, tentative but curious, scanned the space, darting up the stairway and down the hallway then stopping on the remaining pile of boxes in the parlor.

Jessica gestured at the boxes. "Remember how I told you my grandmother died last summer? I'm almost done working my way through all of her old things. It's been a bit of an adventure." She reflexively rubbed her upper arm. The bandage was gone, but the memory of that day lingered.

Danny walked in from the dining room directly behind Amina, his face hardening upon seeing their guest. Jessica's stomach dropped the way it had the time her dad walked in on her and a friend smoking cigarettes in junior high. She might have miscalculated Danny's likelihood of being chill about this after all.

"Amina, this is my husband, Danny."

Danny welcomed her, but his smile didn't reach his eyes.

"Crick, can you take Amina back to the kitchen and get her something to drink?" Jessica gave Cricket a look that she hoped her bright daughter would understand meant, "Don't ask the nice stranger any questions."

Amina's eyes darted from Jessica to Danny and back again before she turned to follow Cricket.

Danny watched his daughter and the scarved stranger walk past the stairs and into the kitchen before he dropped his already weak smile.

"I thought you were representing some kid from Latin America."

"I never said I was." Although that was the truth, Jessica knew she sounded a little defensive.

"Okay. But that was the original plan, wasn't it?"

"Yes, but IAP assigned me to Amina." Jessica shrugged. "Is that a problem?" Her tone was too sharp for someone who hadn't been totally forthcoming in the past couple of months.

"And where exactly is she from? Clearly not Guatemala." The bite in his words, so unfamiliar coming from Danny, didn't feel good, and she regretted the accusatory tone she herself had taken.

"Syria."

"Right. And you invited her here today right after all that shit in Paris? And you know my brother was in the navy, Jessica. Jesus Christ." He squinted his eyes. "Did you invite her just to spite him for the last-minute change?"

Jessica's eyes shot wide open. "No! Oh my God, Danny, of course I didn't invite her to irritate Sean. I'm sure he can handle a young woman from Syria." Truth be told, she hadn't considered that. She wasn't worried about Sean's feelings, but she didn't want to introduce another trigger for Amina.

Danny squinted at her as if he were trying to place someone he might not even know. "I don't think you thought this through." He didn't say anything else, not verbally.

Their silent conversation ended abruptly when the front door flew open and Danny's brother barreled through with his kids, just beating the youngest of the three Donnelly brothers and his own family to the door.

CHAPTER THIRTY
AMINA

Amina had never been in an American's home. She had seen magazines, and this home looked a lot like some of the pictures she had seen, just with a remarkable amount of dark woodwork.

Large, framed photos of a smiling family lined the entryway—straight, centered, symmetrical, and flanked by a large letter D. In perfectly focused portraits against soft backgrounds of the waterfront, the artificially posed family wore genuinely happy smiles. A model sailboat perched in an alcove opposite the stairwell, and books lined bookshelves end to end. They were probably alphabetized.

It looked as if nothing was allowed to move.

The curly hair in front of her bounced as Cricket led her into a kitchen thick with golden aromas. Amina inhaled deeply. The layers, from yeasty to savory to peppery, meant the chef had been busy today.

A tall young man sat on a chair in the adjacent room, his feet propped up on an old trunk as he watched American football. He did not look over when they walked in. The square jaw and sharp cheekbone matched Jessica's husband's profile.

Cricket, her eyes sparkling even when she was turned away from the fireplace, asked, "What can I get you to drink?"

Before Amina could answer, a loud male voice boomed from the front of the house, then rushing footsteps competed to see who would reach the family room first. Children soon swarmed through the doorway, two racing for seats on the couch and the others drawn to the plates of cookies on the kitchen counter.

"No cookies yet, guys!" Jessica walked toward Amina, not breaking eye contact, even as she waved the kids away from the counter.

Five adults followed Jessica, including her husband, who was leaning in to talk with a broad-shouldered man with close-cropped hair.

Jessica stopped next to Amina and waited for everyone to settle into the room.

"Everyone, this is my friend Amina."

Amina memorized the American names. First came broad-shouldered Sean and another brother, Patrick, who was a shorter version of Danny. Sister-in-law Claire looked about Jessica's age and wore maroon lipstick that matched her sweater, and a girlfriend, Tina, seemed closer to Amina's age but was blond and wore a skintight knit dress that accentuated every curve. Each nodded in turn when introduced then splintered off just as the kids had.

Jessica had told Amina that no one there would know anything about her. That included Jessica's husband, based on the icy courtesy that couldn't quite veil his surprise upon seeing her.

Cricket had bounded into the family room and was now hugging the other kids. Amina couldn't hear their words amidst the crescendo of noise, but their animated gestures made it seem as though they hadn't seen each other for a while.

The kids didn't look twice at her, but the two women had already snuck glances, each time shifting their eyes to the side when Amina made eye contact. *I know you're looking at me,* she wanted to say. She could brush it off, had to in a country in which she stood out. She could at least stare back at the ones who didn't look away, smile even, and divine their thoughts, good or bad.

Jessica moved about the kitchen, arranging food on plates and taking out glasses for the guests. The men stood behind the couch, each already with a can of beer in his hand, glancing at the TV occasionally while they talked. Claire and Tina now lingered off to the side, leaning their heads together and alternating between eye rolls and sharp laughter.

Amina turned to see Jessica pull a tray of tiny toasts covered in cheese out of the oven then scan the countertops. There wasn't a bit of open space. Amina set her bag on the floor out of the way and rearranged some of the dishes until Jessica could set the tray down. Her grateful smile came with a hint of anxiety.

The two other women acted like customers at the restaurant, happy to be away from home and unconcerned with what was going on in the kitchen. Jessica had mentioned feeling like a caterer, but she seemed more like a cook and hostess, perhaps even a server soon. Amina had some experience there.

Jessica didn't ask Amina to help, but the two fell into a natural rhythm. Amina delivered plates of starters to the family, catching two or three of them staring at her then looking away quickly. The kids were typing on phones, even as they chattered with their cousins, hands flying up from devices occasionally to emphasize a point. Jessica's son Conor stood out as more focused, quietly removed from the activity.

Something about the broad-shouldered brother reminded her of the large man who had led the attack that night in Baltimore, except the brother had a kind calm that didn't set her internal alarms ringing.

She smiled to herself at the irony of being the observer, fascinated by this family's dynamic, not because it seemed unusual but because it seemed so ordinary.

The "loud American" reputation seemed to be earned, though, if this group was representative.

But that would mean there should be a "loud Syrian" reputation. She silently chastised herself for the quick judgment.

The debates led by her own father any time he'd had a guest or family member in the room with him had taken on an air of supreme importance, regardless of whether the topic was Assad's ascension to power or why the Syrian soccer team had never qualified for the World Cup. Voices would rise, dismantling arguments, disputing facts, and questioning logic. Only thick cigarette smoke had rivaled the competing voices in filling the room.

Her mother had never joined in, but the kids knew to look at her to get an indication of whether their own argument was strong. A slight bow of her mother's head would fill Amina's heart with confidence, encouraging her to stand behind her words. At the end of each debate, her father would rise from his chair ceremoniously and look up at a ceiling blackened from years of debates and cigarettes. Then, in his professorial manner, he would pronounce "the truth."

Amina removed an empty plate and crumpled napkin from a side table near the sister-in-law and girlfriend, who were sneering at the mention of "his ex."

"Oh, hi. Was it Amina?" Claire didn't wait for a response, jutting out her lower jaw and displaying a smudge of maroon on her front teeth. "You shouldn't be doing this. You're a guest." She turned her head toward the kitchen, asking over her shoulder, "Hey, Jess, you need any help?"

Jessica looked up from filling a bowl with green beans, her eyebrows raised in skepticism, but Claire was already back to gossiping with Tina.

It was doubtful the sister-in-law would have been helpful even if she really had wanted to be. Jessica's dance in the kitchen, from stove to counter to table, was as familiar in an American kitchen as it was in a Syrian one. She was separated from the cheering coming from in front of the TV as well as the cell phone activity of the kids, and a feast magically materialized before her, ready to be carried to the table.

Considering Jessica had not wanted to do this, she sure put her all into it. Amina noted the parallels between Thanksgiving dinner and Jessica taking her on as a client. But she felt she was more than that now, more than a client, and she was happy to help when the others weren't.

Jessica put her hands on her hips almost triumphantly. She picked up a large tarnished bell and swung it from a cracked leather handle. The sharp clang brought all of the noise, except for the banter from the sports announcers, to a halt. Attention focused on the apron-garbed woman in the kitchen.

Jessica smiled and shrugged, holding the bell aloft. "It's from one of the boxes. Dinner bell from the farm. Thought I'd give it a try. Guess it works! Okay, folks, it's time to eat! Go grab a seat."

Jessica placed her hand on Amina's shoulder. "You too. Thanks for your help. I feel bad! You work in a restaurant, and then you come over here and get put to work. Danny will get the turkey, and I can handle the rest."

Amina washed her hands. Even the sink was sparkling clean.

Heads turned when she entered the dining room, but kids and adults alike resumed their conversations quickly. The chairs at either end of the table awaited the host and hostess. One other chair was empty.

Sean stood and pulled the chair out for her. "We're pretty jammed in here, ma'am. Good thing you're small."

She slid onto the ladder-back chair and unfolded the white linen napkin, lightly running her thumb across the embroidered bird's nest in the corner.

As the broad-shouldered brother removed his own napkin from his plate, the candlelight glinted off of a blue stone on his elaborate gold ring. She'd seen a ring like that before. A regular at Bathanjaan had also attended the US Naval Academy there in Annapolis. Perhaps the man who'd attacked them on the sidewalk was military, and that was the similarity she sensed between the two. It could have been a fine discussion in her father's den, debating the American military, comparing the vulgar man on the street to the soft-spoken man who pulled the chair out for her.

On the other side of her sat the quiet son.

"Ready for some nuked turkey?" Jessica walked in from the kitchen and stopped, a stricken look taking over her face as her eyes panned from Amina's left to her right. Amina's heart jumped, her mind racing in concern that she had, perhaps, violated some Thanksgiving convention.

CHAPTER THIRTY-ONE

Following Danny into the dining room, Jessica dismissed their earlier interaction over the surprise entrance of Amina. He'd been his placid self since the minor scene in the entryway. He'd had his say and had moved on, so she would, too. Seeing the room before her helped.

With the food in place and the candles lit, the table looked like Thanksgiving. In fact, most of it had far more Thanksgiving experience than she did. Between the silver and the dishes alone, there were over a hundred Thanksgivings represented.

Danny set the turkey on the table and moved toward his seat. Jessica froze. There was Amina, squeezed between Conor and a former Navy SEAL. She should have used those place tag holders she'd found in one of the boxes. Even a seat between Tina and Claire would have been better than sitting between a special ops officer who'd fought in Afghanistan and a teen whose capacity for positive human interaction had been lost somewhere between getting his first pimple and getting his driver's license.

Everyone now stared at Jessica, except for Mikey, who had already begun serving himself.

"Mikey, wait until everyone is ready to eat," Jessica snapped just as Mikey's forkful of potatoes was about to enter his mouth.

He lowered his fork ever so slowly. Danny shot an admonishing glare in her direction before turning toward Mikey.

"Mikey, would you like to say grace?" Danny asked.

Jessica's head shot up. *No, no, no.* "I'm sorry, Amina. I don't want to make you uncomfortable."

Claire rolled her eyes.

Amina smiled softly. "Please continue with your traditions. I, too, am thankful for many things."

Bless her. Jessica nodded at Mikey while avoiding Danny's stare.

"Bless us, O Lord, and these your gifts which we are about to receive from your bounty. Through Christ our Lord. Amen." Mikey had his forkful of potatoes in his mouth before the chorus of "Amens" from around the table concluded.

Danny glared at Mikey. "And I would like to thank Amina for joining us. It's an honor to share our meal with you." Danny smiled tightly at Amina and glanced almost imperceptibly at Jessica, a reminder of his earlier irritation but also, hopefully, an indication that he'd moved on from his surprise at Amina's identity. He shifted his focus to his brother Patrick, who was sitting next to him. Jessica loosened a bit and joined the others to fill her plate.

Claire picked obsessively through the carved turkey before selecting a few pieces of white meat. "Remember that year you overcooked it, Jess? We must have gone through twice as much wine just to make up for how dry it was! So funny that this year you undercooked it."

She wasn't saying it as if it were funny, and Jessica didn't laugh. "It all worked out, thanks to Mikey," Jessica said. "We had a lot going on, getting ready for things. Someone pushed the wrong button."

Claire nodded, her mouth full of a dinner roll, a bit of butter stuck to her lip. "You know, I really wish I could do Thanksgiving at our house. It's just, you know..." The sincerity of her reasoning dripped like weak gravy. "I work."

"Yes, you've mentioned that. I'm sure it keeps you busy." Jessica stopped herself before falling down a well of sarcasm. "We're always happy to host Thanksgiving." She shot Danny the same hollow smile he had just used with Amina. *See? I can move on, too.* She passed the corn to the left and accepted the potatoes coming from the right.

Jessica caught Amina regarding a plate of canned cranberry sauce, her head tilted just so. Jessica couldn't imagine Thanksgiving without it. Growing up, it was always the only thing on Oma's floral plates that hadn't been made from scratch.

Amina decided to take a small slice, placing it delicately on the edge of her plate, one of Oma Bee's. Oma Bee, Oma's mother and "Bee" for Bertha, had been as sturdy as the acorn-and-oak-leaf–adorned plate in front of Amina. She'd survived polio and had kept the farm going through droughts and depressions. The sight of a hijab-clad woman at the dining table might have shocked her, but Oma Bee would have appreciated the Syrian's resilience.

Jessica asked after the cousins' recent sports activities. Steering the conversation to something neutral would avoid uncomfortable topics. But side conversations took over, and Jessica found herself straining to hear what was happening at the other end of the table. Fortunately, things seemed quiet down there. Amina poked at the cranberry sauce before deciding to try the mashed potatoes. Conor was building himself a dinner roll-and-turkey sandwich, and Danny was engaged in a discussion with his younger brother.

Claire eyed Amina as though wondering whether the woman in the headscarf would be able to pull off the trick of using both a fork and a knife.

"So, Amina," Claire asked. "Where are you from?"

"Syria." Amina took a sip of water.

Claire looked around, her eyes wide, as though making sure everyone had heard the secret she'd just exposed. "We have an Arab at my office. I think he's from Pakistan."

"Then he's not Arabic." Jessica couldn't keep from jumping in.

"Pardon me?" Claire didn't disguise her annoyance at being corrected.

"Pakistanis aren't Arabic," Jessica said, searching her memory and praying for accuracy in whatever source had fed her this information during her Internet research. Pakistan was next to Afghanistan. She turned to her left. "Sean, you served over there."

Sean's low voice drifted across the table. "I served in Afghanistan, right next door. We worked with a lot of Pakistanis." He nodded appreciatively.

"Well, it's all the same, right? Arab, Pakistan, Afghanistan." Claire laughed and motioned with her hand to charade a headscarf around her head.

Jessica wanted to feel morally superior, but she couldn't. She had used that same gesture.

"Actually," Amina said, rather patiently considering the conversation going on around her, "my headscarf is part of my family's Muslim tradition. An Arab comes from the Arabian Peninsula or speaks Arabic, as I do. But Pakistan is in South Asia, and they speak..." She turned to Sean for assistance.

Sean obliged with information earned from direct experience, not Wikipedia. "Urdu is the national language. But Punjabi, Pashto, some others. Depends on where you are. We had Pakistani interpreters who spoke five or six languages, including Dari and others we needed in Afghanistan. We never would have made it through alive without those guys."

Amina picked up her fork and her knife, and Claire glowered from across the table.

Sean was not the trigger she should have worried about. Jessica opened her mouth to change the subject, but a high-pitched beeping beat her to it.

Burnt rolls set off the fire alarm, and soon she was attending to frozen pies that hadn't been put out to thaw. Running back and forth between the kitchen and the dining room, Jessica managed to shove some turkey and mashed potatoes in her mouth. She couldn't, however, keep up with the conversations.

Bringing out more corn casserole, Jessica noticed Amina sitting quietly, watching the discussions going on around her. Cricket's voice rose as she animatedly told a story of some crazy thing that had happened in her science lab. Danny held down the other end of the table. Although he exuded calm, he was still as taut as one of his sailing lines in a strong wind.

What sounded like a plate of food hitting the floor came from the kitchen. *Damn dog got out.* Jessica glared at Mikey then hurried into the kitchen to see what Gracie was now thankful for.

Returning to the dining room after cleaning up Gracie's impromptu Thanksgiving meal of half-thawed pumpkin pie, Jessica saw Amina and Conor talking quietly. *Conor, I hope you aren't saying something I'll regret.* Amina wore a smile that reflected a youthfulness Jessica hadn't before seen in her. Jessica strained to catch some of the conversation but couldn't make out any words over the increasing volume of the argument on the other side of the table about whether the Baltimore Ravens needed a new coach.

"Jessica, can you help with this?" Danny had overshot his busboy abilities, attempting to carry the turkey tray, the dish of sweet potatoes, and a couple of wine glasses. As a wine glass bobbled, he seemed to be calculating which serving piece would be least worst to drop.

With a lingering glance at Conor and Amina, Jessica reluctantly grabbed the turkey platter with both hands and followed Danny into the kitchen.

JESSICA carefully placed the last clean plate on the drying rack, double-checking to ensure it wouldn't slip and cause a cascade of shattering china. She wasn't going to be the generation that destroyed these dishes.

As daunting as it had seemed to have to hand-wash the pieces by herself—after all, Claire worked and needed the break, and Jessica had insisted Amina take a tour of the house with Cricket instead of being stuck as kitchen maid—it had proved to be a rather calming activity. In fact, she only now processed the raucous laughter coming from the family room.

Shouts of "he's bluffing" and "show me your cards" brought a warm smile to Jessica's face. *Tradition.* Danny and Sean were talking off to the side of the room, but the rest of the crew were busy at cards. Except Conor. He was missing. So was Amina, not that she would play poker. *Do Muslims gamble? Is that a Claire question?* But Amina had been getting a house tour. The house was not huge, so that tour had to have ended.

Her hands dripping with soapy water, Jessica snatched a tea towel and dried them as she searched the other rooms. The dining room was empty, and the table was clear. It didn't look as though a twenty-four-pound turkey and fifteen pounds of potatoes had just been devoured there. No one was in the parlor, just those remaining boxes. The one marked "Betty" was barely hidden anymore by the few remaining.

Sounds of murmuring and clicking on a keyboard came from the small office off the parlor. The door hung open, and the glow of the computer screen outshone the dim lamplight.

Amina was in front of the computer, and Conor sat at a respectful distance to her right on a stool he must have brought in from the parlor. A young man's face filled the screen. His hair was as black as Amina's, and the joy in his eyes and round cheeks could have pulled Jessica through the computer screen.

Her brother?

Amina clicked on the mouse, and another photo popped up. This one was of an older woman standing next to a man seated in a chair. The woman, wearing a red headscarf embroidered in black with an elaborate floral design, stared into the camera, pain in her red-rimmed eyes. The man's eyes showed no emotion, no life. He looked away from the camera but not really at any particular place, it seemed. Jessica couldn't help but think the photo had been taken after Samir's death. She pushed the door open a bit more. Amina and Conor turned at the door's squeak.

Conor stood, his body angled between Jessica and Amina. If Jessica didn't know any better, she would have read his positioning as protective.

Jessica cocked her head. "What's up?"

"Amina was showing me photos of her family. All of her family photos are on a single flash drive. She doesn't have a backup, which is crazy."

Jessica glared.

Conor cringed and turned to Amina. "Sorry. No offense."

Amina's lone freckle disappeared under her left eye as she smiled forgivingly at Conor. "I agree it is crazy. I should have a copy. It is almost all I have of home."

Conor continued. "Anyway, I was making her a copy on an extra flash drive before her taxi gets here."

Mom tears threatened to flow. He'd done something right, which meant that maybe she had done something right, which meant that maybe everything would turn out fine.

Danny's voice carried through the house, announcing that the ante was being raised to a minimum of five M&M's. Then he asked, "Hey, where's Conor?"

CONOR helped Amina with her coat and said goodbye before heading back to the family room, where the poker and the noise hadn't let up.

Jessica walked Amina to the door. The taxi was already waiting out front. Amina placed Jessica's hand between her own. Her hands were small but warm and soft.

"Your son."

"Yes." Jessica hastened to apologize. "I hope he was polite. American teenagers can be..." Jessica couldn't narrow down the adjectives.

Amina shook her head. "He reminds me of my brother Samir."

"Oh, you're talking about Mikey."

"No." A smile touched Amina's lips. "I am talking about Conor."

Jessica felt as if a piling had been shoved into her chest as Amina's words of her brother flashed through Jessica's mind. *Sweet and dear as a child. Dead and decapitated at sixteen.*

CHAPTER THIRTY-TWO

The front door closed behind the last of the extended Donnelly family with a definitive click. Jessica let out an exaggerated sigh as Danny turned the dead bolt. "Well, we made it!" She started walking back toward the kitchen to put away the rest of the dishes and glassware.

Danny's glare stopped her. "That night in Baltimore."

"What night?"

"You fucking kidding me?" A rare darkness emanated from his bay blues. "When you ran into some 'rowdy guys' at IAP. Was she with you?"

"Yes."

"You said you were alone." Disappointment clouded his face. "And the rowdy guys. Any chance they had an issue with her?"

The discomfort of discovery swelled within Jessica, obviating any response.

"Jesus Christ, Jess. The cut? The bruise? Your head? Was that all really from the trunk?"

"The cut and the bruise were. I hit my head on the wall of the building. They pushed me. But that was it. It wasn't a big deal." Her voice sounded unfamiliar in its meekness. She couldn't convince even herself anymore about the triviality of that night's events.

"It was a big deal. It *is* a big deal. You lied about it. You lied to *me*, so clearly you thought it was a big deal. How in the world could you think it's okay to bring her to our house?"

Dark walls closed in on his raised voice. Jessica glanced up the stairs, where the kids were hopefully behind doors and plugged in. "How could I think it's *not* okay?"

"You've already been through enough because of her. And continuing to represent her should be more than enough of a sacrifice for a stranger. Do you want our family to be targets now?" He'd finished with the sidewalk incident.

She found her voice again. "You've got to be kidding me, right? I hardly think that having her over for dinner will result in bands of roaming Islamophobes descending on our house."

The condescension on his face, so rare, so damning, made Jessica waver between feeling as if maybe she were the worst person in the world and maybe he was being a complete jerk.

He barreled forward. "We don't even know if *she's* someone we should worry about. You do know Binnacle creates products to defend us against enemies from her part of the world, right? You are unbelievable."

Jessica pulled Danny into the parlor and lowered her voice to a forceful whisper. "I've spent enough time with her. I know her story. We faced... a bad situation together. I would know if we needed to be concerned with her."

"Why?" Danny didn't feel the need to lower his own voice. "Because you have extensive training in psyops? Because she tells you a story, and it must be true? Just because you've Googled Syria and ISIS doesn't mean you can spot a terrorist. And you definitely can't spot a terrorist's sister or daughter or cousin. Who knows if she's a sleeper agent or if her family here is. Look at what happened in Paris. Canada. Australia. Nobody knew. Because you just can't. You have to take responsibility and stay safe. And you definitely have to keep our family safe."

"God, Danny. I'm no bleeding heart. You know that. And I'm not blind to the politics or the dangers. But you're right. I do have a responsibility, both to our family *and* to Amina. I'm not going to show the kids that it's okay to take on something as important as helping someone escape persecution and then just give up because it's uncomfortable or scary. What kind of message does that send? What would that make me?"

Danny took a breath, poised to challenge Jessica's declaration. Instead, he forced air out with a huff and narrowed his eyes. "Just keep her away from the house. And the kids. I don't want them involved. I was not a fan of Cricket showing her around the house, and I'm definitely not happy with whatever the hell she and Conor were off doing."

She met his challenging stare. "Good God, Danny, he was copying some family photos for her."

Danny dismissed her explanation with a shake of his head. "I was okay with you doing this."

"Okay with me doing this? What's that supposed to mean? I didn't ask your permission."

"No," he said. "You didn't."

Jessica's jaw dropped. "I'm sorry. I think I missed the memo that I need to get your permission to do volunteer work." The temperature in her core rose, making its way up toward her face. "Are you kidding me?"

"God, Jessica. I wasn't talking about permission to do volunteer work in general. This has to do with our family's safety. And your safety. You have no idea who you're dealing with. I don't care how many times you've talked to her or what she has told you. It *is* my business if you are exposing us to a risk."

"Because she's from Syria."

"Of course."

"Oh my God." Jessica threw her head back. "Danny, I have never questioned whether what Binnacle is doing is exposing us to danger. You hire foreigners—"

"Who are fully vetted and pass background checks. We'd never get our security clearances otherwise."

"And Amina has been fingerprinted and has had background checks. But what I was getting ready to say before you cut me off was that you are involved in dark areas of the Internet, encryption, government stuff. All of that, by definition, presumes bad guys—bad guys who would probably love to get access to the inner workings of your code. I don't know what your government contracts cover. I trust you are looking out for us. For all I know, this new contract with Defense is providing encryption technology for military bases, and Binnacle will be a target for espionage and its principals targets for kidnappings."

"You are grasping. And anyway, you don't need to worry about that. We didn't get the contract."

Jessica had just been ready to fire back with a challenge on who was grasping, but her emotions took a left turn on seeing the veiled but clear defeat in Danny's eyes. "What? When did you hear that? I thought you had an inside track and things looked good?"

"I did, and they did. Defense hasn't issued the award yet, but my contact let me know yesterday we are out." Danny suddenly stood up a little straighter and cocked his head.

Jessica didn't like the way his mouth twisted. "What?"

"Nothing," he said.

"No, really, what? Why the look?"

"Nothing."

The sudden passive-aggressiveness contradicted the heat in his eyes.

He continued. "I'm just still wondering why Defense went with someone else. It was an airtight bid. No one can compete with us on product or price. It must have been something else from their due diligence." He arched his eyebrows. "They find things."

He thought it was Amina. She knew it. But she wouldn't give him the chance to feign personal offense and deny it. She recalled Amina's concerns about government surveillance of her Internet use. *They find things.* "Well, she's still my client, and I'm committed to getting her through the process."

"Is there anything else you haven't told me?" The comment was offhanded but biting.

The whole "permission" thing still rang in Jessica's ears. It was her turn to sound offhanded. "I guess maybe I didn't mention that I'm going to apply to enter a program to go back to work at H&C. Or do I need to ask permission for that, too?"

CHAPTER THIRTY-THREE

It had been quiet around the house since Thanksgiving the prior week. Emptiness hung in every room, even when people were home. Mikey and Cricket were tied up in winter sports, and final exams loomed for all three kids. Even Conor seemed to be paying attention to his books up in his room, though the glimmer of normalcy she had seen from him on Thanksgiving hadn't reappeared since.

Book club tonight would be a welcome distraction. Jessica stoked her newly lit fire, watching the flames lick the cured wood. It was the perfect night for a fire, and she looked forward to the arrival of the girls, to the laughing and the clinking of glasses, and to the thoughtful arguments over plot points and character flaws. She didn't even care if they didn't talk about the book. She just wanted her people here, people who would support what she was doing.

Danny's out-of-character fury from Thanksgiving had vanished. In its place was a coldness that even the old fireplace couldn't thaw. She'd been tiptoeing around despite the fact that she had every right to volunteer with the IAP and every right to invite Amina to the house.

Little splinters of guilt fought to work their way into her head, but her anger at his treatment of her, as if she were a naïve child, wasn't going to let them have their effect. Neither had broached the toxic subject, though it clung to the edge of Jessica's mind. But she wouldn't press, because that anger from Danny had scraped her soul.

She would make it through this case and focus on repairing things when it was over.

The clock was closing in on 7:00 p.m., with her guests due to arrive at 7:30. The kids had rushed up to their rooms the moment Jessica brought out the party set of wine goblets. Based on the bounty of snacks and drinks they'd smuggled upstairs, none of them would be back down tonight. As for Danny, now that the Defense contract wasn't on the table, his late nights should have been over. But he'd already told the kids he wouldn't be home until after they went to sleep tonight.

She would have to explain away his absence to the girls. Danny was the exception to the "Avoid book club at all costs" mindset among the book-club husbands. He actually seemed to enjoy the gatherings, finding that if he silently refilled everyone's wine glasses, he could avoid getting put on the spot with uncomfortable questions. And the ladies loved him for it.

Jessica would be refilling the wine glasses tonight.

A light crackle from the fireplace accentuated the quiet. The stack of wood looked a little small, though, and hopefully the girls would linger.

The floodlights flicked on automatically when Jessica walked out the back door. The wood pile was hidden in the shadow of the light directed toward the yard.

An unanticipated chill ran up Jessica's spine. A nor'easter had pushed the temperature below freezing, but that wasn't what caused the chill. Jessica glanced up at the dark rectangles of glass of the master bedroom then picked up a couple of choice logs and hustled back into the warmth.

"Aren't you worried about having her around your kids?" Manicured fingers held an empty wine goblet aloft. Ever-loyal Mary Anne, never

one to hold back her opinions, started to go off track with her loyalty to Jessica after learning of her association with a Syrian.

Jessica carried a bottle of merlot over to rescue the empty glass. "No, I'm not. Why would I be?" She filled the glass, already rethinking her decision to tell the group about her latest volunteer efforts.

"Well, I mean, you don't really *know* her. She's from Syria, and they all hate us over there. How do you talk to her, anyway? Do you have an interpreter?"

Jessica set the half-full merlot bottle on a coaster on the trunk. "To be fair, they don't *all* hate us over there. Most of them just want to be somewhere safe. And no, no interpreter. She speaks English like a lot of Syrians. She went to college. She's an accountant. She's a normal person." She hoped she didn't sound preachy, but really, her friends should have been taking her side on this.

Addie piped up from the couch. "But I've read about how these Muslim women are recruiting kids to join militant groups. The teens are buying tickets to, like, Turkey then walking over the border to Syria or wherever to become fighters or jihadist brides."

"Yes! I've seen that on the news." Mary Anne was getting riled up, her already weak filter failing. "They target kids who have no social ties and somehow convince them the West is evil and they can be warriors and martyrs. Can you imagine waking up and finding a note? 'Mom and Dad, I left to fight for the caliphate.'" She shivered ominously and took another sip of wine, as if a good merlot would solve the worldwide terrorism crisis.

Jessica hadn't mentioned to the girls how Conor and Amina had been huddling in the dark, scrolling through photos from Syria. And she wouldn't.

"I'm not worried about that with the Donnellys!" Finally, someone was on her side.

"Thanks, Kai." Jessica smiled in appreciation of the rescue.

Kai continued. "I'm worried about something happening here in America." She sipped her chardonnay. "I won't let the kids go hang out at the mall anymore or even go to the movies without me, and they hate me for it, but"—she shrugged—"they're bringing in thousands of refugees, you know, and we don't know anything about them. Add that to the gun violence we already have, and it's scary."

Some rescue. Jessica hadn't mentioned Danny's response yet, but all signs pointed to her friends siding with him. She couldn't bear that.

"Hey, Jess," Denise said. "Is this trunk new? I mean, not new, of course—it's old. But have you always had it? Has my move to Bethesda completely disrupted my brain?"

God bless. This was a better line of questioning. "Yes!" Jessica said. "It was my great-great-great-grandmother's. Came over on the boat. It had been in an attic for years. I can't even tell you how filthy it was." Jessica reflexively rubbed the tips of her fingers together. She could still feel the dirt on her hands.

"Well, I love it. I'm so envious. You always do such great work with these old things. I don't know how you have the time. Of course, now that I don't have the kids half the time, I guess I need to find a hobby, too. I'm going crazy."

She hated any implication, even if unintended, that she must have all the time in the world to be able to take on frivolous pursuits. It was more than that. "It does take time, but it's pretty Zen in my workshop, like time doesn't even matter." *God, that sounded cheesy.* "But I agree. Find a hobby that you love." Jessica flipped her hand up to change both the tone and the focus of attention. "And come back to Annapolis more often, for God's sake. We'll keep you busy!"

The group chimed in with offers of yoga classes and lunches. A stray suggestion to try an Internet dating site was met with quick and universal condemnation but then a small reconsidered chorus of "well, maybe..."

The sound of metal hitting a wine glass brought the rising volume of chatter to a halt. Eight women turned to the fireplace, where Dina, the month's researcher, stood holding a wine glass in her right hand and a fire poker in her left.

"Quit your gabbing and grab a seat, girls!" The group's book researchers had to be authoritarians, or the girls would never get to the book. The wine and the gossip were always too good.

The rest of the women squeezed in on the couch or pulled in a chair from the kitchen while Jessica weaved through the room with a bottle of red and a bottle of white to top everyone off.

Jessica finally took a seat herself, but her attention drifted away from the discussion as she replayed the earlier conversation. Her friends' words about Amina and about Syrians in general—tinged with prejudice as they might be—needled her. She hadn't really paid attention to Conor's social life lately, but he had holed up in his room a lot. And he certainly had issues with his parents. Then there was that unexpected connection Conor seemed to have made with Amina at Thanksgiving. Jessica had thought that was a good thing.

The girls weren't always right about plot points and character flaws. Even surrounded by her good friends, Jessica couldn't help but feel even more isolated. She needed someone to be on her side.

CHAPTER THIRTY-FOUR

The flank steak was marinating. Conor liked it medium rare. A huge bowl of blueberries, raspberries, and strawberries, in just the right proportions to meet Cricket's exacting specifications, was chilling in the fridge, ready for the freshly whipped cream Jessica had made as a special treat.

It would just be her and the kids again tonight. Not thinking about Amina and Thanksgiving was easier when Danny wasn't home, and his work schedule seemed to respect that. She needed to wrap up some open questions with Amina next week but should be able to keep things low-key and prove Danny wrong.

Cricket rushed into the room, her jacket on and backpack buckled. "Hey, Mom!"

"What's up? Dinner will be ready in about forty-five minutes." Jessica set the just-scrubbed potatoes on the counter. Silver on Cricket's chest caught her eye. "Your grandmother's necklace brings out your Irish. I'm glad I surrendered it to you."

"Thanks!" Cricket rubbed the pendant and smiled. "I'll grab some dinner if I'm still hungry when I get home." She seemed to recognize confusion on Jessica's face and cocked her head. "Lit project. Remember?"

"Oh, right, of course." She didn't remember. "Do you have to go? Can't you do it all online?"

"Mom. You realize you're encouraging more screen time?" Cricket shook her head in mock disappointment. "No, we have to make a video, so we all need to be there. But if it's important to you, I'll be sure to be on my phone and my laptop while we're working on things."

Jessica wiped her hands on her pants and opened the fridge door. "Very funny. Let me get you a bowl of berries to go." She took the bowl out then went searching for a plastic container.

"I'm good. Thanks, though!"

Conor poked his head in the room. "Let's go." His head vanished as quickly as it had appeared.

"Where are you going?" Jessica asked, her question tinged with a sense of abandonment.

Conor's voice came from the hallway. "A friend's."

"He's dropping me off at Caitlyn's, and he's going to some friend's house."

But I made dinner. But friends are good. *Deep breath.* "Okay. Have fun on the project." She set the empty plastic container on the counter. "Drive safely, Conor." The door shut just as the words left her mouth.

The kitchen seemed bigger than usual. *Mikey.* The potatoes were for Mikey. She could still salvage the night, but she needed the fry cutter.

She pulled open the drawer full of kitchen tools, but it wasn't there. It wasn't in the utensil drawer, either. Nor was it in the kitchen crock with the serving spoons or the container cabinet. Jessica stood with her hands on her hips, channeling her memory and mentally combing through each bag she'd ever taken to Goodwill. Where the hell was it?

Soon, every drawer and door was open, and she was on her knees, digging in the back of the corner cabinet.

Relief overtook irrational panic just as Mikey came in and asked why the kitchen looked like Conor's bedroom. There it was, among an avocado slicer, a strawberry huller, and assorted kitchen accessories that had migrated to the very back of the cabinet.

"Hi, Mikey. Can you help with the potatoes?"

Looking at a son on the cusp of adolescence, who was game to help make dinner, Jessica could see shades of a younger Conor. Though Conor favored his father physically and Mikey his mom, they'd both had an infectious enthusiasm for life at Mikey's age. Maybe Mikey's enthusiasm would survive puberty.

She gripped the cold gray of the rectangular potato cutter, with its stiff wires crisscrossing to make perfect squares. It was a Presto French Fry Cutter, to be exact—old, metal, and effective. And stolen. She smiled, remembering that trip in the eighties.

"Watch and learn." Jessica selected a potato, placed the Presto above it, and sliced through cleanly, creating twenty-five raw French fries. "Your turn." She handed over the cutter. "Do you know where I got this, Mikey?"

He shook his head while positioning the Presto above a potato carefully balanced on its end.

She smiled slyly. "You know, I just might be the criminal ancestor you wished you had."

"Yeah, right." He pushed down, pressing a little harder on the right than on the left, and the cutter went into the potato flesh at an angle before wedging itself in place midtuber.

"You want to use equal pressure on each side," Jessica suggested.

He adjusted his hands to try to salvage the first batch of fries.

"My dad took me and my brothers camping up in Minnesota one summer. I was probably ten." God, she missed him. And Mikey had never even gotten a chance to meet him. She shook away a twinge of guilt.

"Things aren't too close out in the middle of the country, not like here on the East Coast. We drove maybe eight or nine hours to one of the ten thousand lakes. I can't remember which one. We didn't have electronics like you have now, so we passed the time counting train cars, playing license plate bingo, and seeing who could stuff the most cheese puffs in their mouth." Jessica shuddered at that latter memory but still retained a small bit of pride that she had been the victor.

"The pike were running thick that week. We caught a bucketful on our first day. My dad skilleted them over a fire, and we ate fish every day." Thinking back on it, Jessica figured they most certainly did not have a fishing license. They had probably been fishing in a national park and could have gotten a pretty hefty fine. Maybe a healthy streak of petty criminality did run in the family.

Mikey's pile of fries grew slowly, the latest additions significantly straighter than the first. "I don't like fish," he said without losing focus.

"You would like to eat fish that you just caught. Especially if my dad cooked it. But we didn't just eat fish. We ate potatoes. You would have loved that. Lots and lots of potatoes." She smiled at the memory of those piles of potatoes sliced up in precise columns using a Presto cutter, heated in oil on the skillet, and eaten with just a sprinkle of salt.

"Well, maybe I'd eat them if there were a lot of potatoes," Mikey conceded.

"It was such a great trip. We climbed trees, caught frogs, made campfires every night."

While Mikey kept at the potatoes, Jessica reassembled the kitchen and fast-forwarded mentally from camping in Minnesota to finishing her first year of law school. She'd conquered the self-doubt from that first day of orientation and had the grades and a summer internship to prove it.

She'd only had a few days between her last exam and the start of the internship, but she had promised her mom she would come home. She arrived, exhausted from finals and travel, to a mostly empty house. Her brother Kenny was busy with a wife and baby, and her younger brother, Jason, was working long hours at the ethanol plant, hoping to save up for college.

Early on the day she had to leave, her dad took her to the pond outside of town. They didn't catch anything, but the still of the morning, rippled only by the light splash of hook and bait hitting the water, almost made her want to stay forever. The fear she'd had in that moment of comfort and the risk of staying—of being stuck—haunted the beautiful memory.

She studied the uncommonly focused Mikey. She didn't even know if they owned any fishing poles.

Mikey straightened up, visibly satisfied with the pile of raw fries in front of him. He set the cutter down. "So how exactly are you a criminal?"

After she and her dad had gotten back from fishing that morning and he'd gone to get her suitcase, she'd spied the Presto in the kitchen and pocketed it. Maybe she'd known then she wouldn't be coming back. It had never seemed like a conscious decision not to return. Exams then law review then multinational closings then babies—there was always something that kept her from going back. Mikey held the Presto in his hand. He couldn't possibly understand the crime.

"Oh, you know, we caught all those fish without a fishing license. And we ate way more than a license would have let us keep anyway."

"That's your story? Are you kidding me? We are so boring."

Jessica playfully knocked him in the shoulder. "It's a federal violation! I can't go back in time and become a bank robber. So sorry."

He set the Presto on the counter. "Am I all done? Can I go? My science project is due tomorrow."

She let him head upstairs after extracting a promise that he would be back down when dinner was ready. But she felt a pang of devastation at the prospect of a day when he couldn't, or wouldn't, be there because he had his own life, and she would turn into her mother, pining for his return.

Jessica took the Presto to the sink, wiped each crisscrossed wire free of potato remnants, then dried it with an old towel. After she moved some tongs and a garlic crusher, the Presto fit perfectly in the drawer next to the sink, where she could find it whenever she needed it.

CHAPTER THIRTY-FIVE

Jessica's phone lit up.

 Danny: *Turn on CNN now.*

 Cricket: *OMG! R u watching news?*

 Danny: *Are you seeing this?*

 Conor: *Mom - check on Amina.*

Jessica clicked on the TV.

The onscreen images were familiar, a bad kind of familiar. Police in riot gear, holding a line. A row of people with their hands in the air, walking past a Starbucks and a Bank of America building. A man and woman holding each other silently. Debris on a desolate street lined with palm trees and abandoned shopping bags. People—some first responders, some not—on their knees, bent over bodies with unseen faces. Men, women, and children walking slowly, splattered with blood, eyes vacant. A White House spokesperson announcing that the president would have a statement in minutes.

The crawl at the bottom of the screen told the story succinctly. "Explosions rock California shopping mall and financial center. Scores dead."

Please don't be Muslims. I'm sure it was Muslims. She was the worst. *Wait for the evidence.*

September 11, Katrina, and the 2004 tsunami had taught Jessica that she lacked the self-control to avoid the news stream that would soon engulf the airwaves and rage about this tragedy for days or weeks to come. Adrenaline had already taken hold, her heart palpably making that known. *Wait for the evidence.*

Jessica clicked through the channels to see who had the latest news. It became clear that a lot of people weren't waiting for the evidence.

"This is what happens when you have open borders and welcome *so-called* refugees." *Click.*

"This has all the hallmarks of an Islamic extremist attack: Targeting symbols of the West. Targeting innocent populations. Using suicide bombers." *Click.*

"Our current administration is to blame for these attacks by not being forceful enough in its opposition to terrorist groups. If we were doing more to take them out overseas, they wouldn't have the resources to commit acts like this here at home." *Click.*

"The terrorists are simply responding to our own intervention in the region." *Click.*

"The first thing we need to do is close the borders and block further immigration from the region." *Click. Mute.*

Jessica hopped online. Themes and memes with "#KeepThemOut" and "#LoveNotHate" had already flooded social media. It was a helpless feeling to watch people in despair on television and know there was nothing one could do to ease their suffering or bring back their dead. Merlot didn't work to solve society's problems, but she doubted hashtags would, either.

Jessica left the TV on, with the audio off, and busied herself around the house. A dark emptiness grew in her gut as she caught headline updates on the screen.

Wipe down the kitchen cabinets. "Forty-three dead and forty-nine wounded."

Fold the laundry and pay the bills. "Unexploded suicide vest found. Separate attack apparently abandoned."

Dust the ceiling fans. "Terror group claims credit for coordinated attacks."

Jessica was rearranging the framed photos on the mantel when she heard the front door close. She switched off the TV.

Cricket flew into the family room, wide-eyed, dropping her backpack at her feet. "Did you hear the news? You didn't respond."

"I did, Cricket, and please tell me why you were on your phone in the middle of the school day." In-school texting was a minor infraction but something over which she had at least a little control.

"Well... we were... on break, and I thought it was important?"

Jessica could see the wheels turning in Cricket's head, reprogramming herself to remember that maybe she shouldn't have been sending text messages to her mother from school.

"I thought the school made you keep your phones in your lockers, but considering I got more than one text"—Jessica glared at Conor and Mikey, who were lurking in the doorway, to confirm to them that Conor wasn't off the hook and Mikey had better be paying attention—"I'll assume the school made an exception today."

Conor stepped into the room. "So, Mom, did you talk to Amina?"

"Not yet. Are you worried about something?"

"No. Yes. I don't know. Shouldn't we be worried? I mean, the attacks were by Islamic extremists. She's Muslim. I don't know. It just seemed like something you would do."

"We don't know for certain it was Islamic extremists." Three faces with eyebrows raised stared back at Jessica. "Okay, someone has claimed responsibility. I get it. But this *just* happened, and it's important that you guys learn that you have to wait for the evidence. Don't jump to conclusions. The way media works anymore, it's all about who can post the headline, rather than the truth, first. Please don't fall into that trap."

The three murmured their possibly sincere agreement and left for their respective study bunkers.

Jessica couldn't disagree with Conor's thinking that she should contact Amina. She needed to think through how this might affect the asylum case. It really shouldn't, but there was bound to be blow-back against local Muslims. She pulled out her phone.

The call to Amina's cell number went straight to voice mail. She sent a text instead. *Can you meet with me tomorrow?*

Jessica lingered to see if Amina started to type. There was no response. But she knew Amina didn't use her phone while she was working.

— ❦ —

THE KITCHEN COUNTER commanded Jessica's attention, daring her to find space to prepare dinner. She'd recently tried some cupboard reshuffling to accommodate Oma's and Oma Bee's kitchenware and assortments from the boxes, but she'd ended up with cabinet doors that barely closed and a countertop cluttered with random platters and small appliances. With fewer opportunities for family dinner anymore, maybe it didn't matter if the kitchen was a disaster.

She moved a slow cooker and a stack of salad plates to the table so she could chop vegetables. People still needed to eat.

Gracie started barking and ran toward the front door. Danny's footsteps then a jingle of keys hitting the table soon followed.

"Hi, Danny. Does chicken and roasted veggies sound okay for dinner?" Jessica didn't look up from the squash, not expecting much of a reply. The space between them had thawed a bit, but it was still icy.

Papers rustled as Danny rifled through his bag. "Do you remember Damien? You met him at the gala."

Jessica confirmed, relieved at the possibility of conversation about something other than terror attacks, any conversation, really. Then she remembered Damien... from California.

"Oh no." She spun, holding the knife in her right hand. "Did he know anyone who was there?"

"He doesn't know yet. His family is okay, but things are crazy there right now, and he's still trying to get in touch with friends and former colleagues." Danny seemed distracted, searching for something in his bag.

"It's so scary. Sometimes I wonder why it doesn't happen more often, especially when you see how easy it seems. I tried to call—" Jessica clamped her mouth shut.

"Call who? Amina?" Whatever Danny had been searching for lost all importance now. He scrutinized her, eyes challenging and unwavering.

Jessica averted her own eyes, turning back toward the counter. "Yes, Amina. I'm sure this upsets her as much as us." She resumed her slicing.

"You think so?" He didn't sound convinced. "I don't want you meeting up with her anymore except at the IAP offices. You shouldn't even have to do that. Can't you do it all by phone?"

"You 'don't want me to'? What's that supposed to mean?"

"Exactly what you think. You shouldn't be out walking with her in the street. You shouldn't be meeting with her at coffee shops."

Jessica set the knife down and turned slowly. "I'll be fine."

"You don't know what some wacko is going to do in the name of 'Murica when he sees a Muslim walking down the street right now. I'd rather not have you become collateral damage or even the target when that happens. I don't know exactly what happened that night in Baltimore, but it may be that you won't get off so easy if it happens again."

"I'm not going to be worried about that."

"Well, you should. On the radio on the way home... people are out for blood in a way I've never heard before. Plus, to be fair, you don't even really know Amina."

"Here we go again. Come on, Danny, you've met her. She is not a suicide bomber."

He rubbed his temples. "No. I have no idea. Nor do you. Be honest with yourself, Jessica. Even if she's not a potential threat, she knows and lives with others from that area. Don't forget that I'm still hoping to work with the Department of Defense, despite losing that last contract. The skunkworks project Damien's working on might give us a new opening. Though that ship may have sailed."

"I'm less worried about Amina's risk to us than the possibility that this attack will make it harder for her to get asylum."

"So, wait, according to what I heard on the news, a Muslim woman walks into a crowded food court in California and blows herself up with a bomb filled with shrapnel in order to cause as much carnage as possible. And your concern is that now some stranger won't get a free ticket into our country."

"That's not what I said. And it's not a 'free ticket.' And who knows if what you heard is true?"

The air hung thick, Danny's words piercing through with laser precision. "I don't think I'm being unreasonable to say that you—we—all need to be vigilant. Can you deny that?"

Jessica couldn't bring herself to deny it, but she didn't want to admit that.

Danny continued. "And can you deny that you do not, and cannot, truly know that Amina and her family here have no inclinations toward terrorism? That you've never even wondered about it?"

Who's the lawyer here?

She left his questions hanging in the space between them that had grown so heavy. No answer she could give would satisfy both of them.

———— ⟋⟍ ————

JESSICA awoke with a start. Darkness engulfed the bedroom, and tiny pellets of sleet sprayed at the window. Danny faced away from her, his breathing slow and steady. He was oblivious to the vivid images just now burned into Jessica's mind.

A dark sidewalk. A cigarette flicked into the street. Two open hands clenching into fists. Memories of that night had invaded her dreams before, causing her to wake to a familiar heaviness on her chest. But this time, as her dream-self had turned toward dream-Amina, she saw the Syrian staring at her with eyes that seemed to bore into her soul. Those eyes saw weakness. They saw inadequacy. They shone with the knowledge that the Syrian was the stronger of the two.

Jessica pulled the covers up to her chin and rolled over into a fetal position, wrapping the blanket tight to hold in her limbs. She stared out the sleet-shot window into the darkness.

CHAPTER THIRTY-SIX
AMINA

Amina waved at a lost-looking Jessica from her table by the Jobs section of the library. She probably didn't need to wave to get her attention. The scarf could do that, but sometimes she forgot, though the past few days had been a solid reminder. The furtive glances were not as furtive, and strangers added inches, feet, and sometimes an entire street between them and her. She didn't feel the same sense of wariness or fear from the patrons in the Enoch Pratt. But that wasn't why she was here.

Jessica joined her at the table. "This place puts my local library to shame. I've never been." She pulled her notebook out of her bag and scanned the room before pulling her chair closer to the table. "How are you doing?" she asked, her face tense with concern.

Fayiz had been worried there might be a drop in business after the attacks earlier in the week, but traffic had been steady. Out in public, the silent slights and occasional comments might have increased, but there had been nothing violent. "We are doing well. It was such a tragedy."

Squeaky wheels interrupted the quiet conversation as a librarian pushed a book cart past the table.

Jessica fiddled with her pen. She didn't have a coffee in her hand today. "I spoke with Rosalie this morning, and there are whisperings about possibly putting a temporary moratorium on processing asylum claims of people coming from—" The pen stopped moving until Jessica seemed to overcome the invisible force that had stopped her mid-sentence. "From Muslim countries. Even if this doesn't happen and they don't freeze claims, we know that the USCIS review is going to be more intense than ever, considering what just happened in California."

Amina reached into her own bag. "One reason I wanted to meet here is that I am putting together information for you—names, dates, and anything I can remember. I created a timeline and used information I found online here at the library. I could only find so much." *And I could not find my people.* She pushed forward a folder.

Jessica scanned the typed timeline contained on the first page. "This is perfect. We'll file it as soon as you get your interview notice. It really could be any day. Do you have any paperwork, letters, something that you or your family mailed to the United States or posted on the Internet somewhere? Photos, videos, anything that we can use to supplement this? I know I've asked before, but maybe while you worked on this, some things came to mind."

Amina shook her head. Jessica still didn't get it. "I have told you. We did not send anything to America, and when I left, my father packed little. I was to be here only a short time, and my father did not want to raise suspicions. I have some photos, the ones that Conor copied, but I do not think the ones I kept will be helpful."

Jessica closed the folder and started to put it in her bag. "Wait. What do you mean by 'the ones you kept'?"

"I had other photos on my flash drive, but I deleted them before I left Aleppo."

"Where? Where did you delete them?"

"I'm not sure I understand the question. They were on my flash drive, but I deleted them so the wrong people would not discover them. Some were horrible photos anyway. I'm not even sure why I took some of them."

Jessica had her phone in her hand, typing on the screen.

A loud bang caused both of them to jump. The reverberations in the cavernous room turned heads, and many eyes stopped on Amina. It had only been a book hitting a table, though, and a red-faced woman was the culprit. Eyes quickly returned to their own books.

Jessica's phone lit up, and she smiled. "I need your original flash drive."

"Why?"

"I just texted Conor. We might be able to recover the deleted files. Maybe there will be something there that could help your case. It's worth a shot."

Amina bit her lip. She reached into her bag and handed a black flash drive to Jessica. "I don't want to see any of the deleted photos you find."

CHAPTER THIRTY-SEVEN

J essica felt like a voyeur, scrolling through someone else's photos. She had already seen plenty of images of Aleppo online and on the news. Whole sections of the city had been utterly destroyed by Assad's mortars and ISIS's bombs. Skeletons of exposed concrete had been crushed as though stomped by a giant. Piles of unidentifiable debris clogged narrow streets between hollowed-out buildings. Residents wandered like ghosts among the devastation, gray from the dust, gray from the despair.

In Amina's photos, however, she got to see the city through Amina's eyes. The family home had a shockingly purple front door, vibrant rugs, and walls lined with books and abstract artwork, a family's history. Amina's brothers, with their million-dollar smiles, athletic pants, and Nike sneakers, looked like collegiate rugby players, ready on a moment's notice to play ball or party hard. Many of the women in the photos kept to dark-colored clothing. The woman who appeared to be Amina's mother, however, had a different colorful hijab in every picture.

The front door creaked open, jolting Jessica out of the slide show. Then came sounds of backpacks hitting the floor. All three kids were in the kitchen in a flash, their heads in the fridge, fighting over the last Gatorade.

Jessica zeroed in on her oldest. "Hey, Conor, when you're done, can you come over here? No rush."

After Cricket and Mikey went upstairs, Conor approached the table, holding a sandwich and that Gatorade. Just a couple of weeks ago, he would have sulked his way over, whether or not he'd scored the last bottle. Today, he made eye contact and seemed curious.

"Can you help me with the flash drive? I got it from Amina. She said she deleted a bunch of photos, and who knows, they could help her case."

Conor set the bottle and the sandwich on the kitchen table. The sandwich didn't have a plate or a napkin, and Jessica could see the crumbs already accumulating on the wood. She stood to let Conor take the chair.

It only took him a few minutes.

"Here you go," he said, pointing to a new folder on her computer. "They're all in this folder. I named it 'Amina.' All of the files—the ones she didn't delete and ones she did—are all mixed in with each other. The flash drive still just shows the undeleted ones."

"Thanks. Oh, um, can you name it something else? And..." She hesitated, hating what she wanted to ask of him.

"And don't tell Dad? No problem." Conor's response was so casual but somehow supportive. Apparently, the kids weren't completely oblivious to the friction between Danny and Jessica.

Conor picked up his Gatorade and sandwich and was gone. Jessica brushed the crumbs into her palm as she listened to his footsteps going up the stairs. She would have to go through the deleted photos, but she wanted the table to be clean.

The first photo she opened stopped Jessica cold. The young woman looked familiar—the curve of the jaw, the freckle under her left eye. Her black hair was long and full, tendrils flying freely in the wind as she laughed at something happening off camera.

Without the hijab, Amina was a different person, stripped of her Muslimism, her heritage, and her hometown. No. She was the same person. It was Jessica who looked at her differently, Jessica who had cloaked Amina in expectations and limitations unfairly. She tried to read the woman's mind through the photo. The laughter spoke to a now-abandoned optimism, an optimism left trampled and destroyed like young men and concrete buildings.

Jessica clicked through the familiar smiling faces, the purple door, those photos she'd viewed before Conor did his magic. Then came more of the recovered, never-before-seen photos. Amina stood in front of a man who must have been Mohammed. He was not as tall as Jessica had imagined, but she could almost see his eyes dancing. His arms were wrapped around Amina, their hands intertwined at her waist.

In the next photo, Amina sat among a group of women. They were young and old, covered and uncovered. Unsmiling faces didn't tell the whole story. A middle-aged woman rested her hand on the shoulder of a younger woman with glistening eyes. A blue-eyed woman held the hand of the woman next to her. Amina sat in the middle, daring the camera to capture the moment with accuracy.

Continuing to scroll, Jessica found fewer and fewer images that she had already seen. The sorority appeared a few more times, with some changes in the faces. But quickly, the purple doors and smiles gave way to crumbled concrete and faces buried in hands.

One photo showed a body covered in a white sheet, a crowd of mourners surrounding it. Amina's father stared into the camera with despair.

Jessica dropped her head to the table and groaned.

"What's up?" Conor's voice jolted Jessica upright. "Were you able to see all the pictures?"

"Yes, I think they're all there." She shivered at the sadness of seeing ghosts on her computer.

"Are they going to help her case?"

"I'm not sure. I don't know what I'm looking for, to be honest."

Conor sat in a kitchen chair and set his phone on the table, pushing it away just a bit.

Jessica checked her watch. It would be quite a while before Danny got home. "You see, to get asylum, Amina has to present her case in an interview. She has to demonstrate that she's been persecuted or has what they call 'a well-founded fear of persecution' based on one of five grounds—race, religion, nationality, membership in a particular social group, or political opinion. A lot of that will be telling her story, which is pretty horrible, but which is also pretty common. When you think about it, anyone could put together a story of persecution. Just go online, and you can find all sorts of material you could work into your own narrative."

Conor hadn't moved and hadn't glanced at his phone, which had buzzed twice already.

Jessica continued. "Amina also has to provide documents and evidence to help support her claim. When Amina left Syria, she didn't exactly bring affidavits attesting to all of the things that happened to her and her family—where things happened, when they happened, stuff like that. She has no documentation, no evidence. It just makes the process more difficult for her."

"What about the pictures?" Conor asked.

She didn't think he was looking at her as though she had stupidly missed potential evidence, but his tone said otherwise. "Well, photos are great, and we can definitely use them, but they just prove that she has pictures of people who look like they are of Middle Eastern descent in a place that looks like it's probably in the Middle East."

Conor nodded anxiously. "Okay, but what about the metadata?"

She didn't know what the hell he was talking about. "Go on."

"Well, there's going to be EXIF data associated with each image. Of course, depending on what device they used to take the pictures, like a DSLR versus a cell phone, the data will be different. But there should definitely be time and date, and probably a lot of them have geotags, so we can know where they were taken. It's how people can stalk you online, Mom." There was a little bit of playful condescension in that last comment, but he was on to something, so Jessica let it slide.

"That could be helpful." *Understatement.* "Can you show me how to access this, uh, stuff?"

"Metadata, Mom. Jeez. You are so old. Here, I'll show you."

Danny's admonitions not to get the family involved in Amina's case fought to change the direction of the moment, but Jessica brushed them aside. Her son was working with her, and that was a good enough reason to make an exception. Plus, it was just for a minute as he showed her how to do something on the computer.

Standing behind Conor as he started in on her laptop, Jessica saw a young Danny tapping away, making the laptop do his will.

⎯⎯⎯⎯ ◦✎◦ ⎯⎯⎯⎯

DANNY had gotten home after she'd fallen asleep and was out the door before she rolled out of bed the next morning. She wouldn't even have known he'd been home if Gracie hadn't sounded the alarm when Danny creaked up the stairs around midnight. But his late night had allowed her to go through the files without fear of confrontation, though confrontation might have been better than the lonely chill.

Conor had been right—there was data. But the blur of numbers and meaningless file extensions meant little to her. Jessica didn't know how Danny and his team could stand looking at computer screens of code day after day. It would take a lot of searching and tracking to match up times and places to Amina's history, not to mention ibuprofen for the headaches likely to result from staring at the screen. She would dig into that today.

Conor sidled up next to Jessica as she poured her second cup of coffee.

"So I was wondering..." Conor stared at the counter.

She watched him fidget, seeing a rare glimpse of the little boy who still resided within. "Yes? What were you wondering?"

Conor stretched out his fingers, clenched his fist, then did it again. Looking right in Jessica's eyes, he asked, "Can I help with Amina's case? I mean, I can help go through the metadata. Maybe do some Internet searches to try to get the evidence you need."

Jessica was dumbfounded. And torn. But the sincerity softening his face softened her. And he hadn't looked her in the eye like that in she didn't know how long. She would love for him to help her with something, but this? *Confidentiality, beheadings. Danny.*

"There are some things I'll need to investigate. There are confidentiality issues to consider."

Conor's expectant expression began to morph into one of defeat.

Jessica couldn't let that happen. "But I think we can work it all out. Let me talk to Rosalie and Amina, and we can figure out what you can do to help."

The hug caught Jessica off guard. She hadn't realized how tall he'd gotten, but she softened into his six-foot frame, the frame of a young man.

CHAPTER THIRTY-EIGHT

Jessica handed Amina the flash drive as though it were a precious family heirloom, which in a sense, it was, one probably more valuable to Amina than any of the items from Oma's boxes were to Jessica.

"Thank you." Amina squeezed the drive and placed it back in its refuge. "And please thank Conor for his help." She didn't ask about the deleted photos.

The coffee shop was busier than usual, but the elevated lunchtime chatter blended with the smell of roasted coffee to create a comforting buffer around the two women.

"Amina, I'm curious. I saw photos of you without the hijab." She motioned toward Amina's red headscarf. "Why... I mean, when did you start wearing one? Or stop wearing one?"

"I did not always wear a hijab in Syria. It was my choice. We had that freedom until ISIS invaded and extremists started beating women with bare heads."

Jessica wanted to ask, *Why, then, when you're living in America, would you wear something that you wore in Syria to avoid getting beaten? Something that, in America, almost got you beaten?* But damned if she was going to be Claire.

Amina seemed to read her thoughts. "My family. My past." Her fingers graced the fringe of the scarf, which surrounded her face with elaborately embroidered black flowers.

The realization struck Jessica like a jolt of caffeine. The scarf was Amina's mother's, the one from the photo she'd seen on the computer on Thanksgiving. Amina's photos and Jessica's meetings with Amina flashed like a slideshow in her mind. All of the scarves were her mother's, and scarves in a suitcase leaving Syria wouldn't raise suspicion.

The drone of the coffee grinder overwhelmed the background noise. The two sipped their drinks, gazing out the window at the pedestrians rushing past in the pre-Christmas craziness.

"There were some other photos," Jessica said. "Women."

Amina set her cup down. Her deep breaths slowed. "Those women, those photographs, must be protected." She searched Jessica's eyes, securing another promise, like she had on the night of the attack.

"Who are they?"

Amina folded her napkin and pressed the crease before folding it and creasing it again. She had deleted those photos for a reason, even though they weren't horrific photos of the aftermath of bombings or beatings, nor were they photos of the dead. At least she hoped they weren't photos of the dead.

"I was part of a group of women. It was... a study group."

Jessica pictured the women from the "study group," the wide range in ages, the different dress, the apparent bond. Amina had mentioned the study group on her original application, and only now did it trigger Jessica's lawyer impulses and the reference to "groups" in the asylum rules. She'd written it off originally as a school thing, nothing of importance. She was an idiot for not asking about it earlier. "Can you tell me about it?"

"There was a bookstore near my home. We met there. The owner let us use a small room. There were university students, a pharmacist, an engineer, women who did not work but were intelligent and wanted to challenge their minds. Sometimes we would discuss a book. My father read a lot, and we would sometimes try one of his books, but they were usually so boring." She placed her hand across her face and laughed then sighed. Her hand fell to her chest, rising and falling with each breath.

"We talked about our lives. We talked about what lives we wanted for our children. We talked about how we could continue to work in our professions or continue our educations when the fighting came and it became dangerous. Some women were afraid to speak. I learned from my father, so I spoke extra loud to speak even for those who were afraid. We trusted each other." Amina's burst of words stopped abruptly.

"It sounds like more than just a study group."

"We were there for each other and helped anyone who came, in the time we had."

"What kind of help?"

"Some women wanted contraception when medical services were disrupted. Other women just needed someone to listen to them. You have to understand that the Assad regime does not allow private organizations, only government. Maybe a study group is accepted." She twisted her mouth as if to admit even this must be approached with paranoid discretion. "But not what we were doing. After the fighting began, what we did was against what the strict Islamists were trying to impose in areas around us. Our study group was something these two opposing groups would have been happy to destroy together. But that is the story of what is happening in my home. Many opposing factions. And their common ground is that they want to destroy everything in their path. But we still did some important things."

Amina paused for what appeared to be an internal debate as she unfolded her napkin. "My friend Najlaa. She was a doctor. Her husband beat her. And then he began to beat their older daughter. War brings out evil in men, even in their own homes. She did not gather clothing or any other items. We prepared a suitcase for her. Each of us put in some of our own things. Some put in some of their daughters' things for Najlaa's girls. We each gave some money, even from the little we had. One in our group had a relative in Lebanon. Najlaa was a doctor, so the village would welcome her. Another woman found transportation. We were so careful. If anyone found out, it would mean death for Najlaa and maybe all of us. The day came, and Najlaa and her two daughters went in the back of a truck.

"The next day, the husband and a group of men ran down the street. They were yelling and pounding on doors. They were polite to the men they encountered but rough with the women. 'Where is she? Where did she go?' It was frightening, but the flames in the husband's eyes and the hard words from his mouth made me know we had done the right thing."

The faces of the women from the pictures flashed through Jessica's mind, and she wondered which had been saved. "Were there others?"

"Najlaa was not the first; she was not the last. It became more difficult, and we knew we would not be able to continue forever. But we always would say, 'Just one more.'"

Jessica wrapped her hands around her coffee, absorbing the heat.

Amina closed her eyes and whispered, "I shouldn't have left."

"Syria? Of course you should have left. Your father had been imprisoned, your brother murdered, your husband taken away, your city bombed. Who wouldn't want to leave?"

"A stronger person. A less selfish person." Amina's dead stare filled with tears that wouldn't fall. "I knew. I could have done something."

"You knew what?"

"When my father handed me my bag, he told me. He knew, my father did. He knew about our group, what we did. He'd learned that others knew, others who would... who would end it, who would end me and end them. But Mohammed was gone, and I was—" Her sharp inhalation shuddered her chest. "No. I should have stayed. Women suffered and died. If I had stayed..."

"If you had stayed, you would have suffered the same fate. But your father arranged for you to leave so you didn't have to stay. You are very fortunate you got out. Do you know how they found out? Was it the store owner?"

"It doesn't matter."

Jessica agreed it didn't matter, at least not for the asylum claim. But the rest of the story, the possibility of Amina facing violence due to her involvement in a women's support group, did matter.

"Amina, I'd like to add this information to your paperwork. We'll need to get some dates and whatever information you can provide. I'll add it to the file for the amendment we're making to your application."

CHAPTER THIRTY-NINE
AMINA

Since Amina's last meeting with Jessica, the cold had truly arrived. Amina cleared away the condensation on the bus window, exposing the passing buildings. A woman wearing a red coat and furry black boots walked down the sidewalk. Her long strides and apparent lack of regard for the slushy sidewalks complemented her deliberate posture. Other pedestrians hurried past, their shoulders hunched up to their ears to keep out the cold. This sort of weather must have existed solely to allow the woman in red to wear those boots, and the others would not have been happy to learn this.

Amina exhaled, and the window clouded over again.

While pulling together the information Jessica had recommended to back up her story about the study group, Amina had redirected her search efforts from her family, which had been unsuccessful, to the women from her group. Yesterday, the day she also had received her long-awaited interview notice, a face on the library's computer screen had matched one from the group. Amina's nervous anxiety over the upcoming interview in just a few weeks had been replaced with tear-filled relief that someone had survived.

Najlaa, the doctor, was working in a mobile medical unit with an international relief group in Lebanon. Amina had discovered her name listed among the international collection of physicians assisting refugees. The images from Lebanon haunted Amina almost as much as images from Syria. Over a million refugees from Syria had gone to Lebanon, a staggering number that was hard to wrap her head around.

She wondered if ghosts of the other women from the group circled Najlaa's head as they did hers or if the distractions of the still living, the barely living, around Najlaa kept the ghosts at bay. A nervous hollow in Amina's gut warned her not to be optimistic that the relief group would respond to her inquiry about how to reach Najlaa.

The bus stopped, and two of the shoulder hunchers from the sidewalk boarded. The seat next to Amina was the only seat open, but they walked past without making eye contact. Allowing a woman her privacy back home might have been seen as a sign of respect. Here, it was a distancing, a stigma.

She closed her eyes.

If only she had stayed. But she had been thinking only of herself.

If only she had stayed. She would have talked to her friend Rasha, who had been part of the group from the beginning. Rasha would have told her husband she had made up what she'd said about the group, that it really *was* just a study group and nothing more.

Amina's father hadn't known which of the women had been at the bookstore when the men came. But Amina could have warned them. Somehow, there would have been a way. Instead, those women were forever silenced.

And she was in America.

She'd seen the images on TV of the refugees—thousands, millions, numbers that seemed unreal. She'd seen the images of men, women, and children crowded on plastic boats, some souls never making it to shore. She'd seen images of thousands of families suffering in refugee camps.

And she was in America.

She folded the interview notification letter and hesitated before putting it back in her bag. Jessica had told her she must tell the interviewer about the study group and what had happened when they were discovered because it could be the most important part of her history. But it was the most shameful to Amina because she was safe and would be using their suffering to support her claim.

She reflected on Rasha, her friend. Rasha had been quiet but always there to laugh and cry with the women. Rasha had packed a child's dress and a pair of her own shoes in the suitcase for Najlaa. The empathy and fear on Rasha's face at the moment the doctor had escaped—and at that moment only—had revealed the horror that Rasha and Najlaa shared, the horror Najlaa was escaping and Rasha would continue to endure. And in the end, Rasha had betrayed them all.

But it was forgivable.

It was forgiven.

Amina missed having sisters.

CHAPTER FORTY

"Hey, Mom. I've updated the research files." Conor plopped into the chair on Jessica's right and plucked a red apple from the bowl. A green apple tumbled onto the table. "Sorry." He put the fallen apple back into the bowl.

Jessica pushed the laptop away. "Did you find anything?" There hadn't been a lot Conor could help with due to confidentiality restrictions, but his research since Christmas on country conditions and news stories that tied to Amina's timeline could bolster her credibility. With no official documentation to support her story, Amina's credibility was critical to her case.

Conor pinched the apple stem with two fingers and spun the apple with the other hand, staring intently at the process. When the stem finally broke away due to the strain, he looked at what he held in his two hands.

"Well?" Jessica asked.

"It's gone."

"What's gone?"

"Amina's house. Her parents' house. The whole neighborhood." He set the apple on the top of the pile, keeping the stem and rolling it between his fingers.

Jessica groaned, placing her face in her hands. "When? Are you sure?"

Conor pulled the laptop closer and started typing. "I accessed satellite photos of the area. See here?" He pointed at a bird's-eye view of buildings and streets.

"These photos are publicly available?"

"Don't worry. I didn't hack into military servers, Mom. The United Nations released these."

The image on the screen was pretty clinical. There were no visual enhancements, just a freeze-frame from a satellite or drone passing overhead while time- and date-stamping each shot. "This is where they lived." He pointed at two red circles he had added to the image. The circles highlighted two gray squares among rows of other squares lined up along crisscrossed streets. "Here's another shot. And another. " He scrolled through images that showed the same area, red circles highlighting Amina's and her parents' homes. "Then, here." He stopped scrolling.

Entire streets were gone, replaced by unrecognizable rubble. No gray squares remained. Jessica touched the screen. "This is the same place? Are you sure? Where are the red circles?" She struggled to find a purple door.

"Nothing left to circle. But here"—he moved the cursor to a spot left of center on the screen—"here is where their house was. You can tell by the coordinates and these landmarks here. But look at the dates in the corners." He clicked through the photos again, slowing to point out the date of the most recent predestruction image and the date of the first postdestruction image. "Now..." He clicked open a different tab and pulled up a news article.

"What's this?" Jessica leaned in to scan the words on the screen.

"English-language newspaper in Turkey. I cross-matched dates on the images with news articles. See here?" He scrolled down and highlighted a portion of the article then pointed out the matching dates on the newspaper article and the satellite images. "Amina's entire neighborhood in Aleppo was destroyed in a massive attack. At least three hundred fifty people were killed. There is a mass grave over"—he clicked back to the satellite images, scrolled through a few, then pointed—"over here." He zoomed in. The dark misshapen rectangles lay on the gray ground like columns crafted by an inept builder.

"By whom?"

"The regime blames the rebels. The rebels blame the regime. Does it matter? I can do some more research."

"No," Jessica said softly. "It doesn't matter." She clicked through the images, back and forth, from life to destruction. She closed her eyes. Amina's timeline was seared in her memory. Amina had last spoken to her father the day before the attack.

— ❧ —

"Looks like you still have a lot to open, Rosalie." Jessica motioned to-ward a small Christmas tree sitting atop one of the stacks of banker's boxes in Rosalie's office. "I don't think we had that many packages under our tree last week."

"Funny, Jessica. If you want to be cute, our 'packages' are the refugees arriving this week. And thank you so much for your help with preparations for that. I can't even tell you how busy it's been for staff here. It's been a relief to have an extra body to help coordinate communications and resources ahead of their arrival."

"No problem. I'm impressed with everything that's available. Considering the angry talk on TV, you wouldn't know there are so many people ready to help the refugees integrate. By the way, Amina will be able to come with me on the thirty-first when they get here."

"I was hoping to hear that. Having another Syrian there will help make the arrivals more comfortable. And we can use all the inter-preters we can get."

"Actually, I'm thinking of it as being something to help Amina ahead of her interview in a few weeks. She feels guilty, ashamed even, for leaving her family and friends behind. It'll be good for her to be with people who shared her experiences, to remind her that no one would question her decision to leave."

"Agreed. And regarding the interview, the timing isn't great, of course, but I wouldn't recommend requesting an extension. The whole moratorium thing is still floating around. The political pressure is so high right now in opposition to refugees and asylum, especially Muslims. By the way, how are things working out with your new paralegal?"

"Ha ha. Thanks for not totally browbeating me on that. I know it's discouraged, but Amina was so supportive of having him help, and really, what teenager volunteers to spend Christmas break doing research? He's cross-referencing dates and GPS coordinates with news reports and images online. It's all matching up with Amina's story, so it should really help with credibility. I'm pretty sure Conor will end up being an expert on the Syrian crisis before this is all over." She could hear the pride in her own voice.

"Her credibility will be key, yes." Rosalie removed her red-rimmed glasses from atop her head and held them like a dagger. "Bronwyn called me."

Bronwyn hadn't called Jessica, and based on Rosalie's follow-up, that must have shown on Jessica's face.

"She said she would have contacted just you, but this was something she wanted to get to IAP right away. She has some back-channel information—not official and not for certain—that while existing claims won't be affected by any moratorium or ban if those do happen, they will be treated with unofficial and unadvertised heightened review, effective immediately. Any credibility you can establish is great, but you really need to have documentation to back up her claims—affidavits, letters, official reports. A lot of claims use letters from family, which aren't incredibly strong because of the family connection—"

"That's not going to happen anyway, Rose. Amina hasn't been able to find any of her family, and Conor just found evidence that her parents, who are the ones who know everything, are probably dead. Amina didn't say anything when I told her, but I'm sure she's devastated."

Rosalie set her glasses on a pile of papers and frowned. "It would be even better if you had official documents or affidavits and letters from someone in a position of authority. I didn't see any of that in your report."

Jessica threw her hands up, her voice rising with them. "We've got nothing like that. That's crazy they would require that from these people."

Rosalie glanced at the open doorway.

Jessica lowered her voice. "Anything else?"

"Have you scheduled Amina's interview prep session yet? It's intimidating to sit in front of an interviewer and talk about your intimate and personal history."

Jessica remembered feeling intimidated sitting in front of *Amina*, waiting to talk about Amina's intimate and personal history. "I haven't coordinated a time yet, but we'll get on the schedule for a prep session. This was supposed to be an easy case. I can't imagine what the hard ones are like. You know, I'm not sure how people with real jobs take on these *pro bono* cases."

Rosalie perked up and put her glasses back on. "Speaking of which, by the way"—her hands flittered over to a short pile on her right—"I received a request from Highland & Cross for a referral letter, and of course Bronwyn mentioned it on our call. I do hope that if you end up back in the big leagues, you won't leave us behind. H&C has a strong *pro bono* presence, so I know they'll support you. And I'll want you to keep taking on cases. This case will end, one way or another."

"Let's see how it ends, then I'll get back to you."

"So, enough of the law stuff and back to the packages. How was your Christmas?"

"Kind of quiet this year. The kids are getting older, you know. It's not the same as it used to be." Jessica forced a smile. "Cricket's been out with her boyfriend, whom I've only met once. Danny's busy with work. Mikey has been tied up on social media since the social butterfly can't see his friends in school. Having Conor help has been the Christmas miracle, I guess." It had, in fact, been the bright spot that had distracted her from the silent chasm between her and Danny.

In a way, though, the quiet seemed as if it had allowed the chasm to start to close. At least that was what Jessica hoped the lack of direct confrontations between her and Danny meant. New Year's Eve, just two days away, was always a special night for them, and it could be the chance to reconnect and make things the way they used to be.

CHAPTER FORTY-ONE

The brake lights in front of Jessica flashed on, then off, then on again.

She seethed. *A little early to be drunk, even for New Year's*. She checked the clock on the dashboard. Well, it wasn't that early. The ball would be dropping soon enough. She had fully intended on being home earlier, but the refugee planes had been delayed, and she hadn't wanted to leave until each of the families safely connected with their support worker.

Danny hadn't said goodbye when she told him she was heading up to Baltimore to take care of some IAP business. The arrival of refugees had been big news and not universally popular. She hadn't told him her full involvement, but he was no dummy.

Before leaving, she'd told Danny she would be back in time for their annual New Year's Eve date. Even the kids had New Year's parties this year. But Jessica and Danny had stayed in together ever since the year they'd first met.

It had been another year in a string of holidays after law school, and she hadn't gone home from DC, though that hadn't fully achieved its sense of normalcy yet. There were always deals that had to close before the end of the year, and that year had been no different. The moment the bank had confirmed the wire transfer on the very last deal, the pressure that had built up through the month burst through. Adrenaline, exhaustion, and emotions she hadn't wanted to admit to having all collided in a rush and a crash.

The partners went home to their families, and the other associates dispersed like captured squirrels suddenly set free from their cage. With her heart and brain both racing toward an invisible and possibly nonexistent finish line, Jessica couldn't bear the thought of going back to her empty apartment. She needed to decompress, defocus, and escape herself. She gave the cabbie a different address, not caring that she was alone, in a suit, and carrying a briefcase.

The stress had eaten away at her stomach, but she saddled up to the theater snack bar anyway to order some Jujubes because, well, when in Rome. She didn't have to battle any crowds at the theater that night. It was New Year's Eve, after all. But she still managed to bump into the guy with the bay-blue eyes standing behind her. She smiled through her apologies before going to the theater to find a seat.

Maybe it was the lack of strength that weakened the usual barriers, or maybe it was the Jujubes. For whatever reason, Jessica welcomed Mr. Bay-Blue Eyes to sit next to her in the theater, to walk the city sidewalks in the cold moonlight with her, and to talk her down from her postclosing rush.

Every year since then, the two had found a movie and stayed in. Jessica brought the Jujubes.

Shit! The Jujubes! She checked the time again. She was late as it was, and she only knew of one place where she could still find what was apparently considered a vintage candy. They would have to skip them this year.

Jessica's headlights lit up the SUV parked by the garage as she pulled into the driveway. The kids were probably already out. Mikey had a sleepover, but the other two had curfews, and Danny and Jessica would be up late waiting for them. Until then, though, they could have some much-needed alone time. They didn't need Jujubes, just the tradition, the togetherness, and a movie to fill the space in which words weren't working. If they could get that feeling back, she could work on the words later.

Gracie met her at the door, and Jessica called out to announce, and apologize for, her late arrival. Blue light flickered in the darkness of the family room. Jessica hung her coat on the newel and set her bag next to the stairs. Danny must have run upstairs and left the TV on.

She hollered up the stairs. "Hey, hon. I totally forgot to get the Jujubes. Do you think we can manage without them this one time?"

She walked back to the kitchen to open a bottle of wine and jumped when she glanced at the couch. "Oh. Hi."

Danny wasn't upstairs.

"Sorry I'm late," she continued. "I forgot to get the Jujubes. I'm so sorry. You wouldn't have believed the traffic."

Danny set down his beer. "No worries."

"So, what are we watching?" The faces of Julia Roberts and Hugh Grant filled the screen. Danny was well into *Notting Hill,* a longtime favorite.

Danny gestured toward the screen but said nothing.

"Oh. You... started already? No problem. Just let me pour us each a glass."

Danny shrugged. "Wasn't sure when you'd be home. Thought I'd go to bed early tonight, anyway."

He downed the rest of the bottle and flicked off the TV, leaving Jessica standing in the dark, holding a corkscrew and a bottle of cab.

Her eyes strained to find his face in the dark. "But we always watch..."

"Movie's almost over."

She could make out his form but only saw the back of his head. "Can't we just have a quiet night?"

"Hard to do when you're not here."

"When *I'm* not here?" She set the bottle on the table. The tension from traffic and being late and everything else found its way into her grip, and she didn't let go of the neck. Tension also found its way into her rising voice. "I'm always here. That's what I do—I'm here. You're the one who's been missing so much."

He turned to face her. "Is that a problem all of a sudden? I have a job, a company, employees. I support a family, put food on the table, a roof over our heads, give you the opportunity to do your volunteer work." He gestured casually toward what she assumed was Baltimore and refugees.

"Is that what this is about? That I'm not contributing enough? Or is it that I'm working with Amina? Or that I might just have a life of my own?" She was borderline screeching, which made Danny's unwavering calm all the more disturbing.

"No, Jessica. You didn't think about how what you do affects others, and you lied about it. I'm done. I'm going to bed. You can watch the rest of the movie yourself."

Jessica released her grip on the bottle and felt warm blood surge into her fingers as Danny left the room. They had never had these arguments before this case began. She wondered if this was how Denise's marriage had started to unravel. No, Denise's husband had been cheating on her. Still, the tension between Jessica and Danny was not sustainable, and she didn't know how to fix it.

She poured a generous glass of wine and clicked on the TV but couldn't stomach watching the happy ending of a romantic comedy. Instead, the national news was running tape of the refugees' arrival. They appeared more fearful on the news than they had in real life. On the screen, their faces spoke of pain and exhaustion. Before she'd left for home earlier, those same faces had smiled in relief and gratitude, each one hugging Amina as though she represented both everything they'd left behind and everything they had to look forward to.

It was anyone's guess what those faces would look like after the glow of arrival wore off and they faced the onset of reality.

She flicked off the TV and listened. Walking through the doorway, toward the front door, she strained to hear a word or a creak on the stairs but heard nothing. Danny wasn't coming back down. Jessica ran her hand along the handrail then picked up her laptop bag from the bottom of the stairs.

She hadn't planned to finish her ReCross application until next weekend. But she wouldn't be able to sleep until the kids got home safely, and she wasn't going to lie in bed for the next couple of hours.

Jessica set her wine glass on the trunk next to the laptop. After opening the computer, she curled up in the corner of the couch to watch the screen light up and the Wi-Fi connect.

She logged into the ReCross application page to see where she had left off. Her work history was ancient, and leaving that huge "raising kids" gap in the résumé portion was a gut punch. But they knew they were hiring people who had been away from the law for a while.

She'd completed the writing task and technology test already. That left just the personal statement. Bronwyn had told her this was the most important piece of the application. According to Bronwyn, H&C had started the ReCross program not out of charity but to leverage the skills of highly trained lawyers who were motivated to succeed. The program also served to add female leadership to a firm top-heavy with men in a business environment that mandated female faces. But they weren't going to make it easy, and they only wanted the best.

Jessica scrolled down and read the personal statement prompt. "Please describe your professional goals and your motivations for returning to the practice of law." The text box was big. And empty.

An email alert popped up, pulling her eyes to the corner of the screen. It was from her mom. The subject line read, "A memoir-y thing I wrote."

She clicked to open the email, which was blank except for a Word document titled, "Rocket Girl." Jessica laughed with rueful commiseration. Her mom, the rocket girl wannabe, was stuck in Iowa, and she was stuck alone on New Year's Eve. At least the two of them had one thing in common, though Jessica was surprised to feel that being stuck alone tonight was the worse of the two fates.

Working at H&C had gotten Jessica out of Iowa, and it had been sexy and impressive and had made her feel as though the world wasn't just passing her by. She'd been a part of it and had loved it... until events had conspired against her and she'd missed her last chance to see her father and be by her mother's side. Perhaps she shouldn't have blamed the situation on that deal that had had one problem after another and had demanded all of her attention. Perhaps she should have looked within and recognized that she'd made her own decisions. She clicked from the email back over to the application and the empty text box.

Before she could move forward with ReCross, or any more personal pursuits for that matter, she needed to fix the things she had broken. She didn't want to be stuck in place while the world passed by, leaving her in the rearview mirror, but she couldn't leave anyone else behind, either.

There was still one unopened box in the parlor, the one with her mom's name marked in black Sharpie. She'd left it, a prickly bit of unfinished business that marred an otherwise back-to-normal room, thinking it shouldn't have come to her in the first place. She had decided it would be intrusive to open it since she'd distanced herself from her mother most of all. But the box was there and would be until she did something about it. She closed the laptop. She would open her mother's email after she finished with Oma's boxes.

Jessica knocked her wine glass against the metal edging on the trunk, producing a dull clang, and quietly gave a toast to a new year that would, hopefully, be better than the last.

CHAPTER FORTY-TWO

Jessica lifted the cup, only to find it empty. She'd started using Oma's coffee cups despite their daintiness and the fact that they predated the concept of venti-sized coffee mugs. Something about the bone china and memories of it coming out after big holiday meals at the farm kept her in the moment instead of her usual focus on what she needed to do next.

In this New Year's Day moment, categorizing receipts and bills wasn't providing the fulfilling sense of accomplishment it had in years past. Scanning, shredding, and filing away the prior year in anticipation of the one ahead had always made Jessica feel as though she were moving forward. This year, though, even a sense of stasis would have been better than the feeling that she was regressing.

Mikey poked his head through the dining room doorway, a phone held to his ear. "Mom, you wanna talk to Grams?"

Jessica nodded and closed her laptop.

"Bye, Grams. Happy New Year." Mikey passed the phone to Jessica then called to Gracie and raced her out of the room and up the stairs.

"What's going on in Annapolis today? Mikey told me Conor and Cricket are still in bed."

Jessica snorted. "Yes, the life of a teenager. I expect Mikey will crash soon, himself. He was up all night at a sleepover."

"And Danny?"

Her mom's tone didn't indicate that she knew of any marital discord, but Jessica bristled nonetheless. "Danny's getting ready to head over to our neighbor's man cave for football. And I'm doing paperwork." She picked up her empty cup and stood. "I *was* doing paperwork." She moved to the kitchen and refilled. "I read your essay."

Her mom let out a puff of air, as if she'd been holding her breath. "Jessica, when you sent me that photo... and we talked, I decided maybe I should write my stories down. Someone might be interested in them someday."

"It was really good, Mom. I especially liked the description of your old house, with Oma's window boxes and Gramps's tools in the yard. It's like I was there." The wood crackled in the fireplace as Jessica added a log.

"Hush. I know it needs work. I even signed up for a class at the community college. Memoir writing. Two classes, actually. That and a technology class. You know, whenever I need computer help, I call Conor. Some rocket girl. Ha! I think I just need a boost to get caught up so I can figure out these things myself. But don't tell Conor. I'll still call him to ask for his advice."

Learning that her son and mother had maintained a strong relationship despite her own failings left Jessica disappointed in herself for not even knowing. "The classes sound great."

"I already have a title for my memoirs: *The Girl Who Wanted to Go to Space but Went to the Kitchen Instead.*"

"Could be either a tragedy or a comedy, Mom." Jessica picked at her fingernails. "Do you feel like you missed out on doing something big? Do you have any regrets?"

"No."

Jessica envied her mom for being able to answer in the negative with such authority.

"You know, when I was growing up, things were starting to change. Girls didn't have the options boys did in Idaville, but I at least had the option to *think* about going into engineering. My mom, my grandmother, I doubt it ever would have occurred to them that they could do something other than be housewives. I just happened to be the transition generation. And then I got to watch you go past your dreams and into reality. If I'd wanted to go to law school, my math teacher would have said the same thing to me that he said when I wanted to be an engineer. But for you, it was so simple. You wanted to go. You worked hard. You went. You became a lawyer. I was so proud. We both were, your dad and me."

Jessica could almost feel her mom sitting next to her on the couch, each of them silently sipping coffee from Oma's china. Even an uncomfortable quiet was tempting. There was no need to dredge up the past and taint the moment. But memories of getting news about her dad's cancer and pushing them aside, leaving her mother to handle the sickness and the loss, and leaving her father to die without one last goodbye flooded her mind, disrupting any ease she might feel.

She'd thought that surely he would make it through New Year's, and then she would be free to make a trip back. She hadn't understood how fast a killer pancreatic cancer was, but that was no excuse. Some end-of-the-year deal had closed before the ball dropped, and some nameless people had made millions, but her dad hadn't made it past New Year's that year.

"I'm sorry... about Dad's last Christmas." Her voice cracked. "I should have been there for him. For you."

"That was a tough Christmas." Jessica had to strain to hear her mom now. She didn't sound so close anymore. "The next Christmas was harder. It eventually got easier. But I do wish you'd been back."

"I thought you were mad and..." She started to say she thought her mom didn't want to see her or talk with her, but she knew that wasn't the case. It was all Jessica. She didn't want to feel uncomfortable about her choices and the fact that she had compounded the problem by choosing distance over connection.

"No, never mad. But I've been lonely, and I think that might be worse. I've got your brothers and the grandkids, and Facebook and Instagram to keep up with everyone, but I felt abandoned by my little girl. I tried to convince myself it was because we were so successful in raising you, that you had too many important things going on."

"No, Mom, that's not why. I mean, yes, you were successful in raising me. You were great parents. But I was selfish and blind to what was important. I think I believed staying home—in Idaville—would hold me back. That's why I left, but then I got so caught up out here with work then my own family on top of that, and I thought I had really pulled off having it all. When Dad died, though, I knew right away I was wrong. That's why I quit. I saw what I missed with you, with Dad. I was mortified thinking about what else I might have missed and what I would miss in the future. But I didn't know how to fix what I'd already broken."

"I think you just did."

The new log settled into the pile, fresh embers from an old log pulsing as they fell beneath the grate. Jessica wasn't feeling as forgiving of herself, at least not while there were other things to fix in her own home. "I wish I had another chance with Dad. He must have hated me when he died."

"Your dad loved you so much, Jessie." Her mom's tone had shifted, almost scolding her for disparaging her father. "The guys down at the lodge would throw pretzels at him as soon as your name came up. He bragged about you so much."

"And then I wasn't even with him when he was sick. And I wasn't there for you."

"Honey, you were always with him. And you are always with me."

The line went quiet again, but it wasn't a distant quiet. This time, it really was more like they were sitting together, sharing a cup of coffee and watching the fire.

Finally, her mom spoke. "You haven't mentioned anything about Mom's things for a while. How did that all end up?"

"Not as planned, to be honest. I figured I would get things lined up for consignment after New Year's, but I pretty much kept all of it. I'm not sure where it will all fit, but I just couldn't get rid of things. If only I hadn't been an attorney, Oma would have given the job to someone else and I wouldn't need to find the space."

"Oh, honey. She didn't ask you to handle her things because you're an attorney."

Jessica frowned then laughed at herself. "That sounds about right. I guess she was a wily one. That suede skirt, by the way. The red one you got instead of a rocket. I have it."

"What!" The sudden increase in volume caused Jessica to pull the phone away from her ear.

"Yes. It was in the last box I opened."

"How about the boots?"

"No boots. But Oma left a note: 'Tell your mom I knew she was the one who built the rocket.'"

CHAPTER FORTY-THREE

A whisper of cold slipped through the poorly sealed window in the kitchen. Jessica wrapped her hands more tightly around her coffee as she marveled at the view. A translucent layer of frost covered every surface in the backyard, turning each blade of grass into a tiny, alluring dagger.

She glanced at the couch. "Can I get you a refill, hon?"

Danny shook his head, not looking up from his Sunday paper. "I'm good."

Jessica wanted *them* to be good. After talking with her mom, Jessica had been emotionally spent. She hadn't realized the guilt and anxiety she'd repressed over the years, but her mom's forgiveness had started to wash it away. She had a new fullness that steeled her to do the same with Danny.

Since the New Year's Eve movie debacle three nights before, Jessica had set the stage for reconciliation, removing potential obstacles in hopes of creating the right moment, a sort of protective bubble around them. She hadn't mentioned Amina or the refugees. She'd made sure Danny's newspapers were on the kitchen table for him, and she had even gotten up early that morning to get the coffee started. She could do nothing about the lost government contract, though.

Today was the day. The kids were likely to sleep in, a winter break bad habit that had fully taken hold, and if the draft from the window were any indication, no one would want to leave the house.

Jessica flicked on the local news to check the weather forecast, just to be sure. An obnoxious mattress ad blared from the television speakers, garnering a cautionary frown from Danny.

She wouldn't let his attitude burst her bubble. "Sorry. Just watching for the weather." Jessica adjusted the volume all the way down.

"G'morning." A yawning Conor stumbled into the room, his bedhead raging and mocking her for thinking he would still be buried in his blankets. His too-long flannel pajama bottoms were ragged at the hems, and he had no concerns about walking on them. Jessica had offered to shorten them, touting her minimal sewing skills, but had been rebuffed.

"Morning. How was last night?" Jessica tried to act nonchalant about Conor going out again the night before. Conor had checked in—early, even—when he'd gotten home, then he'd gone straight to bed. She was glad he was finally being social again, but it did open up a world of potential landmines.

"Fine. Kind of boring. What's for breakfast?"

"Same as always."

He made no effort to move, looking expectantly at her.

She gestured toward the kitchen, not taking his bait and not offering to be a short-order cook this morning. "I think you can manage."

He hiked his eyebrows and grinned. "Worth asking."

Jessica glanced up at the TV. "Oh my God!" She scrambled for the remote and turned up the volume, ignoring the glare from Danny.

The caption at the bottom of the screen read, "Local restaurant vandalized." The reporter was talking, but Jessica was too distracted by the scene to process what she was saying. Behind the reporter stood a three-story brick building with a fading watch shop advertisement on its side. The restaurant windows were smashed, and the restaurant name lay scattered in shards on the ground.

Bathanjaan. Jessica moved directly in front of the TV. The reporter was wrapping up, but Jessica caught enough to understand that someone had vandalized the restaurant overnight. As the cameraman panned the scene, Jessica spotted the back of a small woman in a gray-and-white hijab, speaking to a police officer. *Amina. Shit.* She had to get up there.

Danny looked over the top of his newspaper, appearing more curious than annoyed but still annoyed. "What's going on?"

"Bathanjaan—Amina's cousin's restaurant—was vandalized last night. In Baltimore. Some kind of anti-Muslim attack. I just saw her on the news. She was talking to the police. I need to get up there." Jessica looked over at the coffeepot to see if there would be enough for a to-go cup.

"Wait. What? Why do *you* need to go up there?" Full annoyance filled Danny's rising voice.

"She's my client."

"Hold on," Danny said. "Let's think about this first."

"What do you mean, 'think about this'? There's nothing to think about." Indignation rose in Jessica's chest, pushing away her earlier plans.

"What I *mean* is don't go out of your way to insert yourself where you don't need to. You aren't her cousin's lawyer. You aren't her caretaker. You are her asylum attorney, and this"—he waved his hand at the TV—"this has nothing to do with that. I told you this kind of thing was going to happen. And I don't want you or us involved."

The protective bubble burst. "I'm going. She has a problem with the police. Don't look at me like that. That's not what I mean. You have to understand that her life, her family in Syria... The police there do awful things. I can't even tell you. Plus, she worries that having any involvement with the police could jeopardize her asylum claim." *And that's why all the mess from that night in Baltimore. And why I didn't tell you.*

Danny rose from the couch, his chest puffed out and his shoulders back, leaving his discarded newspaper askew on the coffee table.

Jessica moderated her tone, remembering the task she still needed to accomplish when she got home. "I'll be fine, Danny. The police are there. It's probably just some stupid kids who got kicked out of the bars after last call, not a vast anti-Muslim campaign that's going to end up on our front porch. I'm just going to lend some moral support. Amina is already worried because of the bombings in California and all of the crazy talk." Her eyes locked with Danny's, and she strained to maintain softness in her own to counter the bitter anger in his.

Danny tensed, clenching and unclenching his fists, either preparing for or fending off an explosion. But it seemed as though he also thought it was something to put off until later. "Fuck. Fine. I'm coming with you."

"I'm coming, too."

Jessica and Danny swiveled in unison. She had forgotten Conor was in the room. He stood there, his hair a mess, with milk dripping from his cereal bowl. Of course he would want to go. He had a stake in what was happening with Amina, and Jessica wasn't going to tell him no. Apparently, Danny wasn't, either, but he glared accusingly at Jessica for getting them all involved in something he thought had nothing to do with them.

THE drive into the city was an exercise in silence, broken only when Jessica gave clipped directions to Danny for when to turn. On a Sunday morning in Baltimore, finding a parking spot should have been a breeze, but the fire trucks, news trucks, and onlookers forced Danny to park around the corner from the restaurant. As they approached, Jessica couldn't even see the restaurant through the crowd of people that seemed drawn, as if to a train wreck, despite the bitter cold.

Jessica needled her way past rubberneckers, bumping into a local news cameraman. The on-the-scene correspondent Jessica had seen on the news earlier was reviewing her notes. Jessica's stomach turned in disgust as she looked past the bleached-blond reporter and scanned the storefront. In blood-red spray paint, someone had written, "go hom muslims." Dumb bastards couldn't even spell. A swastika marked the doorway. Always a nice touch.

The police tape blocked her from getting close to the building. Darkness hid most of the restaurant's interior, but judging from the tipped tables by the gaping windows, the vandals had gambled that they had a few extra minutes to do damage inside before someone walked by.

She stopped herself from gawking like the other bystanders and turned to scan the crowd instead. The old woman she had seen in the restaurant, reading a book, a few months ago, stood on the corner, speaking close to Amina's ear. As Jessica approached, the two parted, and Amina thanked the woman.

Amina turned to Jessica, surprise apparent on her face. "How did you hear?" She grabbed Jessica's hands.

"The news this morning. I am so sorry."

Amina opened her mouth to respond, but her eyes suddenly shifted away from Jessica, and she shut her mouth.

Out of the corner of her eye, Jessica saw Danny approaching. "Danny and Conor insisted on coming. We all feel terrible. Is there anything we can do?" It was such an empty question.

"I don't know. I—" Amina stopped as a familiar-looking bearded man in a heavy wool coat and knit hat approached. "Fayiz, this is my attorney, Jessica Donnelly, and her husband, Danny, and son, Conor. This is my cousin, Fayiz Darbi."

The flipped-up collar of Fayiz's jacket hid part of his face, but the waterfalling smile would have been enough to remind Jessica of the hospitable restaurant host she had met on her first visit to Bathanjaan. After Fayiz thanked each of the Donnellys for coming, a man holding a clipboard emblazoned with an insurance company logo called him away from the small group.

Just past the insurance guy, Jessica noticed a woman holding an infant and standing next to two small boys. The boys were spitting images of each other, one just inches shorter than the other. Both had jet-black hair that fell in soft curls, and each of them was wearing a fire-engine-red ski jacket and black snow boots. Jessica caught Amina's attention and tilted her head in the woman's direction. "Sama?"

"Yes. Please, let me introduce you," Amina said.

Jessica smiled apologetically at Danny and excused herself.

She was already feeling the effects of the cold. It wasn't the lightning-quick, piercing cold she remembered from her childhood when she would step outside and instantly feel her lungs contract to the deepest well of warmth within. Instead, this was the type of cold that seeped in slowly, almost taking her unawares, but sticking out barbs once it got inside so it was hard to shake off.

In her haste to get to Baltimore that morning, Jessica had not thought to bring a hat. Precious body heat escaped as the Maryland cold took advantage of her vulnerability. She eyed Amina's scarf with envy.

Sama nodded when introduced then spoke with the hesitant English Jessica recalled from the restaurant. "I am sorry this is how we meet."

"So am I. But I'm glad to meet some of Amina's family formally. I hope you're able to get the restaurant back in shape quickly. I don't know if you remember, but—"

"Yes, I remember. I was pregnant." Sama cooed at the bundle in her arms. Tiny eyes and a tiny nose barely peeked through the blanket protecting the baby from the cold.

"It's freezing out here," Jessica said. "Can we take you home? All four of you?" Jessica lowered her voice so little ears wouldn't hear her. "Aren't you worried that your boys will be scared down here?"

Sama shook her head emphatically. "No. Thank you. It is important they see that a few cowards in night can do hate, but in daylight, today, many good people help. They learn what is right." There *was* a lot of support on such a frigid morning, idle onlookers notwithstanding. Jessica could see it was a good message for anyone to take away from such a hateful event.

Jessica bent down toward the boys and asked them how old they were and what their favorite games were. They excitedly told her about dinosaurs, and Jessica had to make a quick trip back into her internal archives to remember the difference between an iguanodon and a stegosaurus so she could engage in a pretty high-level discussion about giant, extinct lizards. She straightened back up after being corrected regarding T. Rex, which was not the largest dinosaur, as that would of course be the Titanosaur.

Words started to form in Jessica's mouth as she faced Sama. Words about how this was all contrary to American values and that people do change, but sometimes acceptance takes time, and blah, blah, blah. She rolled her eyes at the mere idea of such a condescending platitude and placed her hand on Sama's shoulder. "Sama, anything you need, please let me know. I will be bringing the family for kibbeh and kababs as soon as you're back open." That is, she would if Danny let her out of the house again.

Jessica turned back toward where she had left her own boys. True to teenage form, Conor stood off to the side, with his eyes glued to his phone. Danny, on the other hand, appeared to be deep in discussion with Fayiz, probably trying to use his personable charm to un-cover evidence that Fayiz was an ISIS plant.

Walking past the yellow police tape toward Danny and Fayiz, Jes-sica hoped to intervene in case Danny had overstepped his bounds. Her lungs emptied in an uncontrollable rush when a quick glance through the open restaurant window led her eyes to a burly, irregular slab of wood, centuries old, bleeding with red spray paint. The shat-tered glass, the busted furniture, and the vandalized walls were just broken things. This, however... this was a desecration. She stood, mourning a dead tree and a lost sense of faith, until the cold barbs pricking her fingers and Danny's continuing conversation with Fayiz, spurred her to move forward.

Fayiz motioned toward Jessica as she neared. "And her?"

"Ah, no. Poor Jessica is a Vikings fan." The men looked at each other with feigned pity. "We tried to convert her, but she's too stub-born." Danny winked.

This wasn't the Danny who had driven her there, and it didn't seem as if he were performing a covert interrogation.

"We were just talking about the playoffs, hon. The Darbis are Ravens fans."

Fayiz smiled. "Good reason to emigrate to Baltimore, no?" He seemed impressively at ease, all things considered.

Jessica looked over at her other Ravens fan, wondering why Conor wasn't part of this conversation. Her son was still on his phone. If she weren't in public right now, Jessica would have sent that phone flying down the street, shattering it into a thousand pieces. She snapped her fingers at him discretely but got no response. Hiss-ing came next. Finally, she walked over. "Conor—"

Conor pushed past her, seemingly oblivious to her presence, let alone her irritation. "Mr. Darbi, have you checked your restaurant's online reviews?"

"Conor, Mr. Darbi doesn't have time for that right now." Jessica looked at Fayiz and mouthed, "I'm so sorry. Teenagers."

"No, Mom, look." Conor handed his phone to Jessica, who held it so both she and Fayiz could read it.

Danny followed the interaction with interest but didn't speak.

As Jessica scrolled slowly through the page, they saw review after review of messages praising the restaurant, the food, and the owners.

"Best kebabs in the Mid-Atlantic."

"The owner always makes you feel welcome and encourages you to try a new recipe—which you never regret doing."

"Baltimore is lucky the Darbis decided to establish their restaurant in our town."

And the rave reviews continued.

"Okay, Conor," Jessica said. "Great reviews. It really is a great restaurant, and I'm sure Mr. Darbi has seen these. What am I missing?"

"Check the dates."

She obliged. Positive review after positive review had been posted that morning.

"That's not the only review site, either, Mom. I pulled up some others, and the same thing is happening."

"Well..." Fayiz nodded to Danny as though concluding an unfinished conversation. "I guess we need to get cleaned up and opened again so we can thank all these people with some good food."

"We're not all bad," Jessica said softly, mostly to herself.

"I know," Fayiz responded. "Neither are we."

Danny pursed his lips and ran his gloved fingers over his hair, matting it awkwardly. Before Jessica could pass the phone back to Conor, a text popped up then popped off. *Heat is on delete ur texts no pix.*

Under no circumstances could that be good.

"Mom?" Conor reached out his hand. "My phone?"

"Oh, sorry. I spaced out." Jessica clicked the phone off and handed it over.

CHAPTER FORTY-FOUR

T he ride home was as silent as the ride to Baltimore, quieter even since Jessica didn't have to give directions. Danny didn't speak a word and kept his eyes firmly focused on the road ahead. Jessica wasn't sure what to make of it, or what to make of anything, really. Her plan for the day had been flipped on its head.

Shoving all of this in Danny's face—Amina and more broken, shattered pieces of violence connected to her—was not the context Jessica had wanted for the conversation she had crafted in her head.

The Darbis had seemed ready to get back to work, though. Fayiz had assured her they should be back up and running in about a week and that everything could be replaced.

Almost everything.

Jessica peered over her shoulder into the back seat to get her mind off the table and off her disrupted reconciliation plans. Conor was typing away on his phone, oblivious to her stare.

Heat is on delete ur texts no pix. Jessica's imagination coursed through its full creative scope to come up with what that could mean. Visions of every movie, TV show, and newspaper article about teenage bad behavior flashed through her mind. *Break-ins, stealing booze, sexting, meth labs.* Conor was no criminal mastermind, and surely he was too awkward for sexting. But maybe his friends were... and weren't. *Who are your friends? Why haven't I insisted on meeting them?* All he'd had to do was help her out for her to let her guard down and forget he was a teenager who had, practically yesterday, been a huge pain in the ass. If he was in trouble, Danny would likely blame her.

After finally arriving home, Conor got the welcome from the dog and instructions from Danny to go feed her. Jessica took the travel mugs to the sink to wash them, letting Danny resume his interrupted newspaper ritual. But there was no sound of rustling newsprint.

"Conor." Danny called his son over when he came back into the room. "When you duped those photos from Mrs. Hamid, did you keep a copy of them on our computer?"

Conor looked at Jessica with wide eyes. He hadn't kept a copy of them on their computer... the first time he'd copied them, anyway.

Jessica stepped in. "I have a copy of them. Why?"

Conor's eyes said, "Thank you."

Jessica wasn't ready to go after him about the text, but he would have to answer to her later.

Danny squinted, his deep thoughts turning into slow words. "We've been working on a new biometrics platform, and it needs to be tested. If I can get those photos, we can see if we can match up any of those faces with images across the Internet."

"I don't understand," Jessica said. "Match up faces?"

"We might be able to find her family. Fayiz told me Amina hasn't been in touch with anyone."

Conor caught Jessica's eye, silently asking his mother who was this strange man offering to help.

She shrugged at Danny, not wanting to jinx the goodwill by over-reacting, but she was still wary that this was somehow a trap. "Okay... I'll check with Amina to get her sign-off. I'm sure she'll be fine with it."

Danny continued. "And, Conor, would you like to come in to the office to help with this?"

"Great, Dad. Sounds good. I'm gonna go work on my home-work."

Danny smirked in self-satisfaction that he'd so easily convinced their reluctant son to help.

After Jessica heard Conor step on the uppermost creaky stair, she broached the subject of the baffling change in Danny. "What's up with the photos? Why the offer to help?"

"Fayiz." Danny approached her. "He seems like a good guy."

"Why wouldn't he be?"

"Well, of course he would be." He ran his fingers through his hair, leaving portions sticking straight up this time. "But I was really impressed with him. Not just from talking with him. It was the people coming up to sympathize and offer help with cleanup. He and his restaurant are a part of the fabric of that neighborhood. He's gener-ated a lot of goodwill, and that's not easy in any business. I can't even imagine accomplishing that as a foreigner."

Jessica quietly pulled out some ground beef and turned on the stovetop, letting Danny talk while she made chili.

"You know all of the news stories about the refugees? So many dying when boats sink or when they're packed into vans going over the border?"

Jessica nodded.

"He told me he learned that his sister and her family finally left Syria, but he hasn't heard from them in months. He's afraid he's go-ing to see them dead on a beach on TV."

Jessica had no idea. She had never considered asking about Fay-iz's family. Yet another thoughtless failure to add to her list.

Danny continued. "So I'm standing there, talking to this man, a good man, who doesn't know where his family is. And I own a busi-ness where my team and I have been busting ass building software for the government to catch bad guys, but at its core, its purpose is to find people. I have to see if we can find somebody."

"Mm-hmm. That would be helpful. I think this is great, but what—I mean, why... why are you trying to help? You said you didn't want me to be involved, and now you *and* your company? And Conor?"

"I've been a prick," Danny said bluntly but confidently. He wrapped his arms around her, reminding her of the icy barbs she'd collected standing outside. She wanted to stay in his embrace until his warmth permeated every cell in her body. He obliged.

"Just be careful, okay?" Danny finally untangled his arms and looked her in the eye. "I also need to tell you that I spoke with my Defense contact a while ago. It turns out the company we lost our contract to, they worked some back doors. There were some campaign contributions. It had nothing to do with Amina, you, or Syria. I was out of bounds. I'm sorry."

"I'm sorry, too." She grabbed his hands, still warmer than hers, and laced her fingers through his. "That night in Baltimore..."

Danny's head tilted, nonthreatening, nonjudging.

Their eyes didn't break contact even while Jessica described the three men, her terror, and her dreams. Jessica only broke eye contact when she started crying. The fear, guilt, and shame ran down her face. "I'm so sorry, Danny. I should have told you, but—"

"No buts. I understand why you didn't tell me. It's all in the past. We don't need to dwell on it."

"No, I should have told you. And after I didn't tell you, I should have talked to you about what was going on. I—we—can't let ourselves get to that place of parallel living. We have to talk. As long as we're talking, I know we'll be okay. We may say some things we regret or that come out the wrong way, but it's better than silence."

Once again, Danny wrapped his strong, warm arms around Jessica. She tilted her head up to see two glistening blue eyes just before they closed and the embrace tightened.

CHAPTER FORTY-FIVE

The last words Jessica heard from Danny before she fell asleep replayed in her mind when she opened her eyes to the darkness of early morning. "I don't want to go to sleep tonight because I'm afraid I'll let go of you."

Her right arm was now draped over his chest, their bare legs tangled together. She hated to move, wondering how long he had held her close after she'd drifted away.

She tilted her head back and found him gazing peacefully down at her. "Hi."

"Hi."

He kissed her softly on the lips then pulled her in close and tight. "I wish I didn't have to go to work, but I do," Danny whispered.

"It's probably for the best. I feel like I just came out of a fog. I'll be able to take a fresh look at everything today. Amina's interview is in a week and a half, and I need to get her prepped and any final paperwork together."

Danny stretched his way out of bed, and she silently thanked him for bypassing his morning exercise routine. "I'll be home for dinner tonight. Be sure to make something good." He winked then hollered when Jessica batted him with a pillow. "How about I bring something home?"

A Monday morning blur followed. None of the kids woke on time, and all of them were out the door without so much as a "see ya."

Conor acted as though no heat was on, but she would talk to Danny about it that night, and they would handle it together.

———— ⌒⟳⌒ ————

DANNY, HOME EARLY FOR the first time since before Thanksgiving, pulled Jessica's attention away from the laundry piled in front of her in the family room.

"I brought Italian Market for dinner." He placed paper to-go bags on the counter. "The kids all home?"

She affirmed and noted the restaurant bags were rumpled in just the right way to indicate that Danny had picked up some wine to go with the lasagna. They would probably need it after talking with Conor.

"I meant to tell you something last night," she said. "But, well, we got a little distracted."

"You're right. We did." His grin gave Jessica the flutters, but she pushed them aside.

"Yesterday, at the restaurant, when I was handing Conor his phone, a text popped up. Something like 'the heat is on, delete your texts, no photos.' I don't know who sent it. It looked like it was part of a group chat."

"Okay..." He tilted his head, as if waiting for the punchline.

"Okay? Someone was asking the group to delete all of their texts and photos because the 'heat' was on." Jessica hoped to see some kind of glimmer in Danny's eyes that would indicate she wasn't making crazy leaps of logic. "He was busy on his phone the whole ride home. I want to know what happened, what the heat is, and what's in the photos."

"What's your concern?"

"He was out with three of his friends Saturday night—three friends we don't even know. He hasn't been social in such a long time, and as you well know, he hasn't exactly been a golden boy for the past year. I totally dropped the ball on finding out who these new friends are. He goes out, comes in super early—isn't that odd for a teenager? And then we don't see him the rest of the night? Is it totally implausible that he snuck back out to join up with the guys? Or they did something so bad they had to split up early?"

Danny didn't look at her as though she were an alarmist, but he didn't look concerned, either. "Let's ask him."

"Conor, can I see your phone?" Danny's blank face didn't betray any suspicions or accusations. For all their son knew, his dad could have been simply asking to see what brand of case Conor had.

Conor had walked into the kitchen to grab a bite before dinner but immediately switched from food mode to defense mode. "No. Why?" He didn't move.

"Hand it over. Now." Danny's sharpened tone shocked both Conor and Jessica. Maybe she would get to play good cop for a change.

Conor glared at Danny but relented, passing his phone as if he were surrendering a pistol.

Danny pressed the home button. "What's the password?"

"Why? What are you looking for?"

"Just tell me the password, Conor. You know I can get into this phone if I want to. I don't care what Apple tells you."

Jessica considered writing the password down as Conor reluctantly recited the numbers, but she knew the code would change within a minute after Conor got his phone back.

"Can you tell me why you're violating my privacy rights?" Conor's indignation seemed to be a last-ditch effort to regain control of a situation he knew he couldn't escape.

Just then, Mikey skipped into the room, stopping abruptly upon seeing the standoff. Jessica shooed him away, and he backed out on his tiptoes, grimacing for his brother.

"Don't go all ACLU on us, Conor," Danny said. "You have no rights under this roof."

"Give me a break," Conor mumbled under his breath, resigned but still resistant.

"I hope we don't have to. What did you do Saturday night?"

"What? You know I went out with the guys and came home at ten. I was early. Jeez."

Jessica pulled out a chair and sat. This dynamic between Danny and Conor fascinated her, and she wondered how Danny had viewed her in prior encounters when she was the one on the offensive against their older son.

"What did you guys do?"

"Just hung out. I got bored, so I came home."

As much as she enjoyed being a bystander, Jessica couldn't make Danny carry their side of the confrontation alone. She had raised the alarm, after all. "We just want to know what you guys did while you were out. Playing video games? Poker? Watching TV? We're just curious. We're not trying to get anyone in trouble."

"Just hanging out. I don't know." Conor also didn't know where to direct his eyes. Anywhere but his parents' faces, it seemed. They moved from the laundry to the floor to a crab-festival print on the wall.

Danny rubbed his chin with his free hand. "Then why would you get a text on Sunday morning, telling you to delete all of your texts and photos because the heat was on?"

Conor froze. He looked from Jessica to Danny and back with startled eyes then returned to indignant form. "Why were you checking my texts? That's not cool." With his hands flinching by his sides and his jaw swiveling, Conor couldn't mask his agitation with feigned teenage indifference any longer. "That's not cool."

Jessica sighed. "We weren't checking your texts, Conor. It popped up when I had your phone at the restaurant. *You* handed *me* the phone, remember?"

"Here's the deal, son," Danny said. "You are going to tell us what was going on that night. Then you are going to tell us what was in the texts and photos."

Conor tapped his right hand against his thigh in a syncopated rhythm, his eyes flickering back and forth between his parents. "Nothing was going on. Feel free to frisk my phone." He gestured toward the device in Danny's hand. "No texts, no photos. Nothing to see here, folks."

Danny shook his head. "Conor, I'm not stupid. I know you would have deleted any incriminating texts or pictures by now. But I also know that I can access all of that stuff. I'm not the FBI, but well, let's face it. I'm better than the FBI. Don't you think it's better if you just tell us now?"

Conor closed his eyes and tilted his head up toward the ceiling, letting out a muted but extended grunt. His fists clenched, and he gave in. "Fine. We were at Lucas's, and we were playing Xbox, and his parents were gone, and his brother showed up with some weed. Everyone was, you know, just goofing around." He stared at the ground and put his hands in his back pockets.

"Did you try the pot?" Jessica tried to keep the tone conciliatory, straining at the unfamiliar role of good cop.

At first, Conor didn't respond, then he gave a slight nod.

"And then you drove," Danny said, shaking his head in disappointment.

Conor's nod was smaller this time.

"Why did you come home early?" Jessica asked.

"Zach, that's Lucas's brother, his friends showed up, and they were getting, I don't know, they were kind of crazy. I just wanted to get out of there. So I came home."

Jessica wanted to plant her hands on Conor's shoulders to steady him. His fidgeting was making her nervous. "Did you go back out after you went to bed?"

Conor's head jerked up, and he looked at Jessica squarely. "What? No. Why would I go back out? Why are you asking that?"

"Just curious," Jessica murmured.

The fidgeting had stopped, and Conor's eyes glistened the same as they had last month when he'd asked if he could help with Amina's case and the same as they had ten years ago when he'd told her how much he loved their new puppy. The sincerity in her son's eyes told her he was telling the truth.

Danny took back over. "So, who's the heat? And what was in the pictures?"

"I guess after I left, Zach's friend brought out some more shit. Sorry, I mean stuff, like drugs or whatever, and it got stupid. Lucas's parents started asking questions in the morning. He was already in trouble and didn't want to get completely grounded." Conor kicked at an invisible rock on the floor. "Those guys are idiots."

Jessica stood and reached for Danny's hand.

"I just thought we were going to play Halo," Conor mumbled with a slight whine that reminded Jessica of a time he had gotten a green gumball instead of the red gumball he'd wanted out of the machine at the mall.

Jessica stifled a laugh, drawing a cautionary hand squeeze from Danny.

Danny nodded toward the doorway. "You can go up to your room."

Conor eyed the phone in Danny's hand then looked up at Danny's face. He paused then turned to walk out of the room. "I'm really sorry." He didn't turn around.

Jessica waited until she heard the last creak on the stairs before turning back to Danny. "I can't believe I'm so relieved to learn that our son *only* tried pot last night, not to mention grateful for our creaky, old house. I forgot that Conor couldn't have snuck out without triggering the Gracie alarm."

Danny spun the phone on the counter. "So, what do we do with Conor?"

"Let's let it sit for a little while. I don't want to make a decision when I'm all worked up from the vandalism and hearing about the pot."

Danny's face lit up. "I'm impressed, hon. Reasonable and devious all at the same time. We'll let him squirm while he wonders what we're going to do."

⁂

JESSICA watched Danny from under the comforter as he set out his clothes for the next morning. "Conor was unusually chatty tonight at dinner. I'm impressed he made a showing, though he does love lasagna."

Danny hung a tie on the rack. "Yes, I noticed. Maybe we just hold off on meting out a punishment and enjoy the nervous chatter."

"I think we should give him a pass," Jessica said. "Just this once."

Danny raised his eyebrows. "Really? I'd expect to hear myself say that but not you."

"We know he's going to make mistakes. Watching him over the past several weeks, I can see that he's improving. I mean, aside from the trying-drugs thing. But that's normal. He's a teen. You know what's not normal? He opened up to a stranger, who probably felt very uncomfortable at our table. He recognized that he could do something to help her protect all she had left of her family. And he even helped me with figuring out some technology and research things so I could do my job."

"Shit."

"What?"

"You're reminding me that all this time I've been sulking about the whole Amina thing, I've been missing out on your life."

She smiled. "I've been here, honey. You see my life every day."

"No, really. Tell me about what's been going on. What's happening with that H&C program? We've never even talked about it. What is it?" The room went dark as Danny flipped the light switch.

"It's a training program for former lawyers who want to go back into law. It's called ReCross."

He stood by the bed, adjusting his clock alarm. "Clever name."

"It was probably Bronwyn's idea. Ha!" She covered her mouth in shock. "Oh my God, I sound like my mom. Please don't let me do that." She grabbed Danny's arm in exaggerated pleading, pulling him fully onto the bed before snuggling into him. "It's been great to reconnect with Bronwyn. I really cut that whole life away when I left the firm. Anyway, if they accept you into the program, you do the training, and then maybe you get a job."

Danny brushed the hair away from her face, tucking it behind her ear. "Is this something you want to do?"

Jessica searched his face for an indication of what he meant, but the darkness hid everything but the familiar curve of his jaw. Did he want her to maintain the status quo, holding down the fort? Did he think she wasn't up for such a challenge but was willing to humor her?

"I don't know. I think so. What do you think about it?"

"I think you should go for it if it's what you want to do."

"But it would upend everything around here. The kids are used to my availability."

"The kids can adapt to anything, Jessica. Conor drives, and they can all take on more responsibility. I'll do whatever you need me to do. You just decide what *you* want to do first." He sounded sincere, and he was right about the kids. Maybe she wasn't actually worried about it not being right for the kids.

CHAPTER FORTY-SIX

Amina stood just far enough away from their regular table to make it clear that she didn't plan on sitting today.

"Is everything okay? Did something else happen?" Jessica reflexively checked her phone to see if she'd missed a text.

"This. Us. Here." Amina seemed to be at a loss for words, despite her fluency.

"Here? You don't want to meet at the coffee shop anymore? That's no problem. You tell me where."

Amina closed her eyes. "That's not what I mean."

"Please, sit. Let's talk about it." Jessica pushed the other chair away from the table with her foot.

Amina waved off the chair and clutched her bag. "I've been thinking... about everything. My cousin, he will not say this, but I believe I'm the reason for what happened. I am in the restaurant in hijab. I am the Syrian. He and Sama were punished because of me."

Amina's statements could have been true. Jessica had no idea one way or the other but didn't care. "First of all, you are not allowed to blame yourself. Period. End of story. I'm sure Fayiz and Sama are happy to keep you with them for as long as you need."

Amina sighed. "I know you're right. They're good people. They will help me. And that's the problem with them and with you. I need to do this on my own. Because otherwise, I will cause more problems."

"I don't follow."

"When I left Syria, my father thought it was right that I come to America. I did not. But Mohammed was gone, and I—" Amina bit her lip, her chin quivering. "I was pregnant."

"You never told me that." The paperwork hadn't mentioned any baby.

"I only thought of me when I left. That is what I did wrong. I should have thought of Mohammed, my family, my friends. But I came to America, and bad things have followed. I was punished, and Mohammed, too. I lost my baby, his baby, shortly after I arrived."

Jessica's head was spinning. "Amina, I am so sorry. But you were not punished. There is no punishment going on here. I think you're just getting nervous about the interview, and the whole restaurant thing was scary." The espresso machine hissed, reminding Jessica they weren't alone in the shop.

"I have put you in danger already. I caused problems between you and your husband. Now my cousin and his family are suffering because of me."

"Wait a minute." Jessica stood and moved closer to Amina, lowering her voice. "I took this case willingly, and we are in this together."

"When we first met here, in this coffee shop, I said I would work with you. Do you remember?"

She hadn't forgotten. The hangover, the intense eyes from the small woman who'd sat across from her, and her own insecurities were fresh in her mind.

"And you said I could change my mind."

"I don't understand."

"I could change my mind about working with you. I have changed my mind."

"But your interview is next week."

A nearby patron swiveled her head at Jessica's sharp tone. Amina consented to move to a back table for more privacy.

"You have been a great help, but I will do this by myself now."

"We've put a lot of time in this. I can't even count the hours of research, just to understand what's going on in Syria. And Danny offered to search for your fam—"

"This isn't about you or the amount of time you put in. Did you ever really want this case? Why did you do it? To make yourself look good? To feel good about yourself? For me, this is about survival and living with myself. This is my decision."

The drone of the coffee grinder reverberated through Jessica's bones, amplifying the gut punch of Amina's words.

Amina's hands pressed against the table, her resolution clear.

"Okay," Jessica said. "I will get you the paperwork we've finalized, and you can move forward yourself. I don't have anything from Najlaa, though. Were you able to get through to her in Lebanon and send her the information I prepared so she can provide an affidavit?" Amina had insisted on handling communications with her doctor friend.

"I did reach her, but I will not ask her to do that." Amina's hands relaxed on her lap. Hearing Jessica back off seemed to calm her. "She's already doing so much for our community. So much, and I am doing nothing." Amina cut off Jessica's attempted interjection about Amina's help with the refugees and the need for some documentary support for her claim. "Najlaa is in a delicate position as an outsider in Lebanon. You know they do not have official refugee camps. Even though she has a position in the medical clinic, she is still a refugee herself."

"But she can help your case, even if you don't want me to anymore. Can she send a letter even if she doesn't want to go to the embassy to get the affidavit notarized?"

"You are not hearing me. I don't want to endanger her situation more than it is. I will succeed or fail on my own and will not be contacting her about this again."

"I advise you not to sever ties," Jessica blurted. "It's not worth it."

The intense eyes from her first meeting with Amina made an appearance. The suspicion deep within them returned, cutting to Jessica's core. The message was clear. *"How dare you advise me about severed ties?"*

JESSICA THREW HERSELF on the bed in exasperation. She'd told Danny she would stay home tonight and watch a movie with him, but he had insisted she go to book club after he'd seen how stressed she was from her meeting with Amina. He'd taken the news in stride that she hadn't gotten to talk to Amina about using her photos for a search, assuring her that things would all work out. Then he'd said, "Please, go have a glass of wine with your friends."

Danny looked up from his book. "You're home early. How was group therapy?"

Jessica splayed her arms out and squinted at the ceiling. "Very funny. It was fine. It started to sleet, so I left before it got too icy. Good book, but we didn't really talk about it much."

"That sounds normal."

"Yeah, but I felt kind of like I wasn't there tonight." Jessica reconsidered. "No, I felt like I was there but that I was there just to watch."

Danny marked his page and set his book on the bed next to him.

"And when I'm just watching, it seems... really... petty? Small? Self-indulgent? I don't know. Something. A bunch of women griping and gossiping and enjoying. I don't know. I just think how ridiculous we would seem to outsiders, especially someone who has lived a truly challenging life. I didn't even bring up what's been going on with my asylum case, or lack thereof. I couldn't bear the thought of complaining about getting fired from a volunteer gig, again, and them possibly saying it was probably for the best." She closed her eyes, covering her face with her hands.

"A person doesn't have to live a challenging life to have value, Jess."

"I know. But it felt so meaningless."

"Meaningful relationships can grow from small conversations."

Jessica whacked him with her pillow. "You sound like those inspirational quotes that get passed around on Facebook. I hate those!" She plopped back down on the comforter. "You're right, though. And I'm being a little bitchy about it because I'm usually part of all of that, and I will be again. It's just a weird time right now. I didn't feel like I quite fit in tonight."

"I have good news." The bed creaked as Danny leaned back against the headboard.

Jessica peeked between her fingers.

"I contacted Fayiz, and he sent me a couple of photos of Mohammed. He asked me to see if I could find his cousin-in-law."

Jessica pulled her hands from her face. She got his implication. Fayiz had asked Danny to do something for him. Jessica wouldn't be in violation of Amina's request for her not to help with the case.

"I can't promise anything, though. We don't even know if he's alive."

CHAPTER FORTY-SEVEN

The sandpaper was worn down to bare, so Jessica folded it over to the unused side and sanded away the rest of the water damage on the windowsill. She wiped up the sawdust, admiring the exposed woodgrain. Old windows had old leaks and needed a little TLC every now and then. So did her mind, and this process, these motions, this focus somehow did the trick.

"Mom." Conor's footsteps were soft on the parlor rug behind Jessica. "I think you should go check on Cricket."

"Okay... Is there anything I should know?"

"Just—I don't know. Just go check on her."

Jessica wiped her dusty hands on her thighs and stood, her knees cracking in protest. She would apply the wood stain later.

It seemed odd that Conor would be openly worried about one of his kitchen-table sparring partners, but he had been on his best behavior since the other night, especially after he'd learned he wasn't being grounded.

Jessica made her way up to Cricket's room and knocked softly on the door. "Crick? Can I come in?" The indistinguishable mumble sounded close enough to "yes" for Jessica to open the door.

Cloud-filtered sunlight filled the room, which had nothing out of place other than a quilted bundle on top of the bed. The quilt was bathed in stained-glass watercolors and quivering from silent sobs.

"Honey, what's wrong?"

Cricket pushed her phone out from under the quilt. Jessica read the social media post in the middle of the screen.

"Guess what ladies your dreams have come true and i am a free man stay calm theres enough too go around." It was posted by ach14. *Who's ach14?*

"Who is this grammatically challenged guy?"

The quilted mound progressed from the light quiver to an increasing pulse of audible sobs. "He didn't even tell me to my face! I'm so embarrassed. Everybody saw this."

Ah. Aaron Herndon, number fourteen on the lacrosse team. When he'd picked up Cricket the day after Christmas, Jessica had wondered if that confident smirk on his face leaned a little too close to Eddie Haskell, but she had been too preoccupied to make further inquiries. *Little prick broke up with my daughter via social media.* "I'm so sorry, honey. I do have to say, though, that he's the one who looks bad. I mean, the grammar alone—"

"Mom! Oh my God! You don't understand!"

Jessica sat on the edge of the bed and placed her hand on top of the mound. "I do, Crick. I was a teenager once. Nothing has changed. I had huge crushes and got crushed and had my share of embarrassing moments."

Cricket's head burst out from under the quilt. Puffy red flesh ringed her bloodshot eyes. "Things have changed. It's not the olden days. This is On. The. Internet. Everybody saw it. Arrrrr!" She threw the quilt back over her head. But she had stopped crying, and anger was better than despair.

Jessica pulled up her leg and folded it under herself to get comfortable. "I was a sophomore and made the varsity basketball team. I was the only sophomore and got to hang out with the juniors and seniors on the team. I thought I was the shit. I was in love with this guy, Marcus Danneberg. He was a god. Dark hair, high cheekbones, deep-brown eyes. He was my Jake Ryan from *Sixteen Candles.*" She tilted her head. "You do know who Jake Ryan is, don't you?"

The mound spoke. "Are you kidding? You and Dad made us watch all the John Hughes movies."

"I guess we did *something* right. Anyway, I seemed to be fitting in with the upperclassmen, and I happened to mention after one of our first practices that I had a crush on Marcus."

Jessica must have paused to lament the error of that decision for too long, because Cricket prompted her with an elbow to her thigh. "And?"

"Well, I didn't know if he even knew I existed. But the girls were so supportive. 'I definitely think you have a chance!' 'You guys would make such a cute couple!' And so on. Little did I know that Melissa Hagge, the team captain's best friend, had her eye on Marcus. And she was a senior. And a cheerleader. And a little slutty. Not that there's a connection, of course.

"I was really excited for the first boys' basketball game. It was the first time that my parents were going to let me go out to the pizza place after the game. I had picked out this great—oh, I'm not even going to describe that outfit because you never approve of my clothing suggestions, but I can say that I made my hair extra big that night."

Jessica could recall that night with uncommon clarity. It had been a visceral thrill to walk into a high school gym buzzing with teenage hormones and the excitement of a big game. The squeak of the shoes on the court, the enveloping stuffiness of the shared air, the pulsating sounds from a not-terrible high school band added up to pure adrenaline.

A head emerged from the mound. "I've seen pictures, Mom. I know you were a complete nerd."

"I was not a nerd! That is how we looked back then. I was perfectly fashionable."

"Mom. Just having the words 'I was perfectly fashionable' come out of your mouth tells me that you were the nerdy girl in the John Hughes movie."

Jessica chose to ignore the insult. "They announced the starting players, and the crowd went crazy when each of them ran out onto the court. The cheerleaders had a cheer for each of the guys, holding up signs with their names on them. Marcus was last. When he ran out, the cheerleaders held up his sign. Apparently, Marcus did know I existed because he looked over at me, right at me. Then he and the other guys started laughing. The cheerleaders turned around with the sign. 'Jessie loves Marcus,' with a giant heart and a crude drawing of a pimply face and big hair." In that moment, in that gym, the fear that she would always be the girl in the poster had engulfed her. Jessica felt sorry for that young girl now, the one who had believed she could be defined by someone else's crude image of her.

Cricket had rolled over and was peeking out from under the quilt. Her lower lip protruded, and her eyes dripped with pity. "That sucks." Then, she added, "I didn't know they called you Jessie."

"I left it in Iowa when I went to law school."

"Yeah, I like 'Jessica' better. It sounds more adult."

Jessica rubbed Cricket's back. The muscle memory from soothing Crick as a crying baby filled Jessica with a warmth she wished she could capture and pack away in her trunk. Cricket's stuttering, post-cry breathing had eased. *In and out. In and out.* Jessica found herself falling in with the soothing rhythm. She pulled up her other leg and stretched out along the edge of the bed.

"So what happened with you and Marcus?"

"What do you mean?"

"I mean, what happened? After the game?"

"Nothing. I never spoke with him."

Cricket's face fell. "I thought maybe he felt bad they did that, and he, like, asked you out after the game when he saw you at the pizza place, and you ended up sitting on top of a table eating a pizza together."

"Honey, life is not a John Hughes movie." Jessica twisted a lock of Cricket's curls around her finger. "The drawing on the cheerleaders' poster wasn't *entirely* inaccurate, and I certainly couldn't compete with a blond cheerleader with a C cup. And I didn't go to the pizza place that night, anyway. It was hard enough to go to school the following Monday. I kept my head down. There were a few snide comments, but by the end of the week, something else had grabbed their attention, and life went on. Lesson learned."

"Right. Don't tell anyone who you have a crush on."

Jessica released the curl, and it restored itself to its original form. "No. That's not the lesson. I learned that bad things happen and I could survive them. I know that was a very minor bad thing, but it seemed like the end of the world at the time."

The two lay there silently, breathing in unison. As Jessica closed her eyes, the concept of time evaporated. Today didn't exist. It was the day Cricket was born, and she was lying in the hospital bed. It was a night when Cricket was in third grade, and they were snuggling with each other under the covers while the rest of the house had the flu. It was someday that hadn't yet happened, but it would be warm and loving and forever.

CHAPTER FORTY-EIGHT

The phone buzzed, and Jessica checked it when she stopped at the light. It was a group text to her and Conor from Danny: *Found him*

Jessica typed back, ignoring the green light and the honking from the car behind her. *U sure?*

Danny: *90.3%*

Conor: *Where?*

Danny: *Will get u info when home*

It didn't take long for Jessica to get home and unload the groceries, moving from the laundry room to the kitchen to the office, trying to keep busy. She picked up the phone three times to call Amina but stopped herself from dialing, wanting to have more certainty first.

If she were in Amina's place, Jessica would want to know, despite that missing 9.7 percent, but she held back. Amina had been clear that she didn't want Jessica involved anymore, and Amina didn't even know about Danny's search for Mohammed. Plus, Danny hadn't mentioned anything about where Mohammed might be or if he had any indication that Mohammed was alive. Jessica wouldn't further jeopardize her relationship with Amina without more information.

When Danny finally walked through the door, Jessica beat even the dog to greet him. Conor followed close behind.

With three expectant faces before him, Danny came through for Gracie first, giving her a good scratch behind the ears. Then he tilted his head toward his office. "Let's go in here."

Conor took a deep breath and clenched his teeth against apparent nerves. Jessica grabbed his arm to steady both of them as they walked through the parlor.

"I know I've explained the software to you," Danny said. "Most of it is nothing special, just the same as the facial recognition that gets used online, by police departments, and so on. But we aren't trying to match up against social media postings or criminal records or other defined collections. In order to get the largest reach, we scrape the Internet of billions of images. For most companies, this would be too much data and would trip up the system. But we aren't most companies. The same code we use to handle huge encryption and decryption events, we've refactored to manage huge data stores in a fraction of the time and without the risk of server overload. And Damien's team has improved our biometrics algorithms to reduce false positives better than any technology out there. That makes a big difference when you're searching billions of images. Got that?"

Surely he didn't think his wife and son "got that."

But Conor bobbed his head vigorously. "Yes. So cool, Dad."

Danny raised his eyebrows at Jessica, seeking confirmation.

"Uh, no. Can you give me the dummies' version?"

"We put in Fayiz's pictures of Mohammed, and we got a match."

"A 90 percent match, you said in your text."

"A 90.3 percent match," he corrected. "But that's the programming talking. We need to get eyeballs on it. I haven't had a chance to review any of this. Damien did the tech monitoring and passed this all off to me when I left the office." Danny typed at lightning speed as he spoke. Screen after screen popped on and off the monitor as he bypassed the security features to access the program.

A familiar round face appeared on the screen. It was a picture of a smiling Mohammed. And next to it was a photo of another black-haired man with heavy eyebrows, but the man in that picture had cheekbones seemingly carved by sand instead of the fuller face in the first photo. This second man stood in the back of a delivery truck distinguished by a dirty tarp in place of a metal door. He was lifting a shrink-wrapped case of plastic water bottles. A crowd of people with outstretched arms were assembled in a kind of distorted mosh pit behind the truck.

"Is that him?" Conor leaned in closer to the screen, placing his hand on Danny's shoulder. "Can you enlarge it?"

"Sure. This is the match." He took a moment, staring intently at the screen, as though he were trying to capture that remaining 9.7 percent. "It's really a clear photo. You can see most of his face, his eyes, ears, the shape of his jaw. And we even get enough for skin-texture analysis." Danny started typing again.

"But it might *not* be him." Jessica could see the resemblance between the men, but it wasn't a dead match. The man in the truck had the dark, curly hair, but his eyes didn't dance as Amina had described. The man with the water bottles had deep lines across his forehead and outlining his mouth, lines absent on Amina's photos of her husband. This man seemed to have a war etched on his face. She wasn't sure she would have picked him out of a crowd. But Danny seemed pretty confident. "Now what?" she asked. "Where is this picture from?"

"Hold on." Danny was still typing. A small window appeared on the screen. Danny clicked on the embedded link and landed on a website for an international aid agency. The photo of the maybe-Mohammed had been pulled from their blog. And the blog post had been posted only a month before.

"He might still be there!" Jessica's wheels were spinning. *Contact the aid group. Find the guy.* "What time is it in... Where was the photo taken?"

"The blog says the water was being distributed in Greece." Conor typed on his phone. "Looks like it's three in the morning over there."

Danny swiveled around, a big grin on his self-satisfied face.

Jessica rolled her eyes but couldn't hold back a matching grin. "You're just happy that you have a new product for Binnacle and that it might actually work."

"You got it from here, Counselor?"

"I got it from here." She would reach out to the aid agency and try to track down this man, whose name was not listed in the caption or the blog post. But she couldn't keep this from Amina, not after seeing that face on the screen.

⸻ ৩ ⸻

IT WAS JESSICA'S THIRD surprise visit to see Amina at Bathanjaan, but this was something she needed to do in person. She'd expected that by one thirty, the place would be emptying out, the lunch crowd dispersing to get back to the office. But the place had just reopened, and the crowd seemed eager to support it, just as the reviews had indicated. The restaurant looked great, with new glass and no graffiti. A casual visitor wouldn't have known the place had been vandalized. But the chairs in the middle of the room surrounded an empty space. She knew.

Fayiz caught Jessica's eye. She had let him know she was coming, to be sure Amina would be in the restaurant, though she was reserving the news for Amina's ears first. He motioned for her to follow him back to the corner, the one in which she had seen the old woman reading during her first visit.

Fayiz must have read her mind. "Mrs. Baum wasn't in today. She had a doctor's appointment, but I saved her table, just in case. I think it's okay if you sit here." He winked. "Can I get you something while you wait?"

She'd been so nervous this morning that she'd forgotten to eat lunch. "You know, I've been craving your kibbeh since my first visit. I even tried to make it myself." She stuck out her tongue and laughed. "Won't try that again! Can I get that with some of the bread and hummus?"

"My pleasure. What would you like me to tell Amina?"

Her mind went to her first surprise visit. "Tell her a friend is here to see her."

He smiled and gave her a slight bow before walking toward the kitchen.

The clinking of silverware hitting plates and indistinct conversation, which might have served as calming white noise in a different moment, only heightened her nerves. Danny had assured her that his tech was good, but she would never forgive herself if she showed Amina a photo that wasn't her husband.

"Hi." Amina approached the table, stealing Jessica's attention away from the unknown. "Fayiz told me to take a break, but I really should get back quickly."

Jessica pulled a chair over to her side of the table and patted it, motioning for Amina to sit. She understood Amina's questioning eyes. "I'm not here to change your mind," she reassured her. That wasn't what was important right now.

Jessica opened her laptop and logged into Bathanjaan's Wi-Fi. "I've got something to show you."

During the drive to Baltimore, Jessica had raced through countless scripts of what to say to Amina. She could cut straight to the chase, give an explanation and context, or prepare her for the possibility it wasn't Mohammed.

Seeing her friend sitting next to her, Jessica knew she didn't need to say anything at all. She simply clicked open the blog page.

The gasp caught in Amina's throat, and tears started flowing without giving her eyes a chance to well up first. Her shaking fingers pressed to the image as if she were attempting to make the man emerge from the screen.

Jessica didn't need to ask. The certainty was 100 percent. "Well, it looks like he finally got to go to Greece."

Levity seemed to be lost on Amina. "Greece? Where? Can I go there? How can I talk to him?" She turned to Jessica for just a moment, her fingers never leaving the screen.

"No, absolutely not," Jessica blurted, instantly regretting her abrupt response upon seeing Amina's stricken face. "Go to Greece, I mean," she corrected. "If you leave the US before you're granted asylum, there is no way you'll get back in. Technically, you are allowed to leave the country, but..." This was a bit uncomfortable but true. "Seeing as you're from Syria, and there are so many political barriers right now for refugees or even visitors coming from your country, if you leave to go to a place where there are a lot of Syrian refugees and then try to return... well, it might not look good with all of the unvetted people over there, recent terror attacks by people who had traveled back and forth to the Middle East... you know." Jessica grimaced. "Even though you would be going to visit your husband." The words rushed out as Jessica attempted to soften the ones she'd just said.

"Am I guaranteed for him to be given asylum if I get it?"

"Well, no, not guaranteed. There's a process, but it's different from what you're doing. You can look into it if, I mean when, your asylum is granted. I could help. If you want, I mean."

Amina overlooked Jessica's fumbling words, and Jessica didn't bother explaining derivative asylum status, which she had researched before she left home. Watching Amina trace the photo of a younger Mohammed on the screen then trace the match to his right was peaceful, serene. Amina's tears hitting the table brought Jessica back to the present. She placed a hand on Amina's free one.

Amina's gaze didn't stray from the screen, but she spoke as though in apology. "I thought he was dead. I thought there was no way he could have survived when no one else did. I believed I would never have anything from home again. That's why I never asked you about bringing him to America." An imploring silence grew at their table, competing with the "goodbyes" and the scrape of chair legs coming from a group of departing patrons. "To have him with me will be to have home with me."

Jessica wanted to temper her expectations. "I know you reached Najlaa fairly easily, but she was employed by a prominent aid group. Mohammed was photographed in an unofficial camp and isn't connected with the aid group that provided the water you see in the photo. We don't know much else yet. But we are doing everything we can to track him down. And then... just know that it can be hard to get into America."

Jessica squeezed Amina's hand, her head turning toward the empty space in the middle of the room.

CHAPTER FORTY-NINE

The snowflakes fell with gravity-defying lightness. They were the big fluffy kind, the ones that stuck to every branch and transformed lifeless winter trees into soft white sculptures. Jessica tightened her grasp on a cup that still had residual heat from the remnants of her morning coffee.

Danny put his warm hands on her shoulders, and she melted into them. "Hi," she said without turning around. She didn't want him to move his hands.

"It's cold over here, hon. Why don't you move over to the fire?"

"No, that's okay. I'm just thinking."

"I think pretty well by the fire myself." He removed his hands, pulled a chair next to hers, and sat.

A fat snowflake stuck to the window, slowly melting from its edges inward.

"Remember when I stopped working after my dad died? I thought leaving the firm was what I needed to do to not screw up anything else. I thought I couldn't do the big, important job and take care of the family all at the same time." She shivered as a gust of wind swirled the snow. "I didn't consider that maybe things aren't all or nothing. That having it all and being successful doesn't mean you can't make mistakes." The fat snowflake, now a drop of water, slowly slid down the window, picking up smaller drops on its way and leaving a meandering trail behind it.

"The law firm got me out of Idaville, but that wasn't exactly an accomplishment." She leaned her head on Danny's shoulder. "It brought me to you, of course. And now that I'm here, I need to decide what I want to do next. I want to make choices going forward that mean something to me and to us. I want to choose things that complement our life together and fall in with my own goals."

"What are those?"

"That's the problem. I don't even know right now. It's been so long. I feel like I haven't set any personal goals in ages."

"Then maybe that's the first thing you need to do."

"I think you're right."

"Usually am. Not always but usually." He winked. "Gotta go pick up a package. Should be back in an hour and a half."

"Thanks for doing that."

"You ready for it?" He nodded toward the shed, which glistened like a freshly frosted gingerbread house in the snow.

"It's one thing I am both certain I want to do and completely ready for."

JESSICA reached her stocking feet out and put them closer to the glowing logs. Danny was right. It was easier to think by the fire. The crackle and the sweet smell of burning oak also beckoned Cricket and Mikey, who labored at second-semester assignments near the hearth.

Jessica scrolled through her own homework, an email from Bronwyn about ReCross interviews. Bronwyn had forwarded the names of all of the partners doing interviews. Jessica had worked with a few of them. One of them had even been in her first-year associate group. That lawyer, like Bronwyn, had stuck it out and risen through the ranks. Jessica supposed she could have been one of them, could even become one of them.

Two blasts of a horn outside interrupted her research, and Jessica's heart jumped. She didn't hesitate to put her laptop aside and throw on some boots and a jacket.

Danny pulled up in the SUV and parked it just outside the garage before opening the driver's door.

"Do you have it?" Jessica rubbed her hands together, jumping up and down to ward off the cold. The oak and laptop heat had already dissipated.

"Yup." Danny slammed the door and headed toward the back of the car.

Jessica followed him, nodding to Conor, who was opening the tailgate. Danny motioned with his hand for Conor to take the lead. Conor climbed in and positioned himself behind an object wrapped in a faded red blanket tightly secured by at least half a roll of packing tape.

"Push it toward me, and Mom and I will help ease it onto the ground," Danny said.

Jessica braced herself, but it was even heavier than she had expected. They set it on the ground and waited for Conor to jump down and join them.

"Can you get the door, Jess? We've got this." Danny and Conor loaded the cumbersome package onto a dolly. Jessica led the way to the shed, her feet crunching through the frozen crust hidden under the layer of giant flakes.

She had spent the weekend getting the shed ready, including buying a space heater to keep away the cold. A Shop-Vac had taken care of any remaining evidence of the trunk work. She wanted the space to feel fresh so she could focus on this one project.

Jessica pointed at a clear space on the floor, and the boys maneuvered the object through the door and into place. There was barely enough room to move around it, but it would work.

The three stood there, hands on hips, staring at the red blanket. Jessica broke the trance with a smile. "Thanks, guys. I've got it from here."

"You sure? I can help with the tape," Conor said.

"I can go get a box cutter," Danny offered.

"No, I'm good. I've got brisket in the pot for dinner. Why don't you guys go watch some basketball? I'll let you know if I need any help." She rubbed her healed hip through her puffy jacket. "I'm probably good until I need to move it somewhere."

As father and son walked across the snow-covered lawn to the house, Danny casually set his left hand on Conor's shoulder, leaning in to say something that Jessica couldn't hear. Conor nodded then quick-stepped to get to the back door first and opened it for his dad. Jessica smiled then surveyed the unwrapping that needed to be done. This time, she knew what was in the package.

With a pair of utility scissors, she battled the industrial-strength tape, leaving the blanket in a mess of strips and shreds. After she pulled away what now resembled old bandages, three hundred years of Syria stood before her, crisscrossed in red paint. Amina might not have needed her help anymore, but this table did. And Jessica might actually get to learn some of the stories the old olive tree had to tell.

CHAPTER FIFTY

The text message Jessica received from Amina the day before had not come completely out of the blue. The two had maintained contact since Jessica's third surprise visit to the restaurant, a communication opening that had grown along with the unsuccessful search for Mohammed. While Jessica had asked about the pending interview, she'd held back from giving too much advice, respecting Amina's independence. Then a text had arrived with an unexpected request.

Amina: *Will you come with me to the interview tomorrow?*

Jessica: *Only if you let me drive.*

Jessica immediately worried her attempt at a joke had come off as bitter snark, but then Amina sent the first emoji Jessica had seen from her— ;-).

It was also the first time an emoji had made Jessica cry.

Danny handed Jessica the car keys. "Good luck, Counselor."

Jessica had woken up before even Danny that interview morning, but he had the coffee ready by the time she had her things pulled together.

"Thanks, hon. We'll take all the luck we can get." They were as prepared as they could be at this point. She couldn't help but wonder what her inexperience had caused her to overlook, and she didn't want to think about the fact that they might have to wait up to sixty days for a decision.

Conor, who Jessica had allowed to skip school when Amina followed up her emoji with a request that Conor join them, fumbled to readjust his tie around a shirt collar that gaped at his neck. She'd told him he didn't need to dress up. After all, this wasn't a court hearing. Only Jessica would be allowed in the interview room with Amina, and even then, the interviewer would be addressing all of the questions to Amina. But Conor still emerged from his room looking more like a paralegal than a varsity basketball dropout.

Stars still filled the sky when they picked up Amina from the Darbis' home. The predawn departure didn't help with conversation, but a later start to an interview for which lateness could result in denial would only have added to the stress.

The buzz of rubber tires on concrete filled the otherwise-silent interior of the car. Jessica spoke only once, to point out the shadowy Washington Monument in the distance as they passed by the District. Conor sat obediently in the back seat, probably more nervous than the women sitting in front. He didn't even take his phone out of his pocket.

Walking from the parking garage to the Arlington Asylum Office was not an awe-inspiring American moment. Though modern, the building was a rather unremarkable structure for one that could have such a profound effect on people's lives.

Jessica's and Amina's reflections jumped from window to window as the two walked toward the building's entrance. Strides aligned, the American and the Syrian didn't look anything other than confident. The windows, however, didn't capture the fullness of the nerves throbbing in Jessica's chest.

Conor beat the two women to the lobby receptionist, who directed them toward the elevators. Conor held the elevator door to allow a Hispanic-looking woman and her three children into the elevator first. When the woman's husband nodded to Conor in appreciation, Jessica's stomach flipped. If simple courtesies performed by her son had that effect on her already, it was going to be an emotional day.

Silence accompanied the group to the third floor and hovered in the background as they waited their turn to go through security. Amina held her bag close before giving it up to the guard.

After checking in, the trio hovered by the chairs, not wanting to sit down because they'd been sitting for so long, or maybe because they were too nervous to sit still. A hushed jumble of languages mingled in the air as heads huddled together in consultation here and there. Fears and desires were reflected on faces of every skin tone Jessica could imagine. The world was seemingly represented in a single room with only fifty chairs.

"Do you want to review any of the materials? We can go over the questions he's likely to ask." Jessica opened her bag and shuffled through the paperwork.

Amina shook her head then smiled and arched an eyebrow.

"What? Is there something in my teeth?" Jessica maneuvered her tongue around her teeth to find any stray remnants from breakfast.

"You're wearing that American TV lawyer outfit."

"Yeah, but I switched shoes." Jessica hiked up her right pant leg, showing off a pair of low-heeled loafers. It seemed the right compromise: look the part and be comfortable all at the same time.

Conor stood, tapping his hands on his thighs rhythmically, his nervousness starkly exposed against Amina's calm.

Rosalie had warned Jessica that, even with a scheduled interview, the wait could be long. For Conor's sake alone, Jessica hoped they would be spared.

Mercifully, a voice soon broke both the room's quiet and Conor's tapping. "Amina Hamid?" A male interviewer stood next to one of the rooms flanking the waiting area, his eyebrows raised. His dull gray hair hung a touch too long over the ears, and his sallow skin begged for a trip to the beach for an infusion of sunlight. He had a slight paunch, which contrasted with his otherwise-slight frame, further indication that he spent too much time inside. It seemed funny that a seemingly untraveled man had such a position over people who'd traveled so far.

"Here we go." Jessica stuffed the file back in her bag and took the lead in moving toward the interviewer.

Amina rested her hand on Jessica's arm, halting her. "Thank you." Amina pressed a small envelope into Jessica's hand.

"Save your thanks. We haven't won yet."

"I know. But thank you for everything." Amina smiled then turned toward the fidgeting teen. "Thank you, too, Conor. I don't think I would be in this office without your help and support."

The color rising in Conor's cheeks betrayed his youth despite the pressed shirt and shined shoes.

The officer repeated Amina's name. Jessica shoved the envelope into her jacket pocket and felt Gramps's coin, which she'd grabbed from her jewelry box that morning in a last-minute moment of anxiety. "I don't need this." She held it out to Conor.

Conor stopped tapping his thigh and took the coin, turning it over and back.

"You were my lucky charm, hon."

Amina took a deep breath. "Jessica? Let's go." She grabbed Jessica's hand, and they followed the officer into the interview room.

CHAPTER FIFTY-ONE

AMINA

The officer leading them into a small office wasn't wearing a uniform like the guard in the entryway or the one at the security checkpoint, but that almost made him more ominous to Amina. It was harder to read his purpose when he was wearing a white button-down shirt, geometric tie, and gray pants.

Jessica placed her hand on Amina's arm, guiding her into the chair directly facing the officer's own behind the desk. Jessica moved one of four empty chairs and sat against the wall, a reminder that the officer would be interviewing Amina, not her lawyer.

Jessica had been so understanding at the restaurant when she'd shown Amina Mohammed's picture. Never had Amina felt so exposed, not when she'd submitted to the USCIS's fingerprinting and background checks, not when facing the questions from Jessica, not even when those men on the sidewalk had torn away her hijab.

The tears, the sobs, and the intimate stories about her life with Mohammed had exposed her, showing her weakness of love and loss. She and Jessica had talked for over an hour at the restaurant. Actually, she had talked for over an hour. Jessica had hardly said a word while Amina poured out all of the memories of Mohammed she had kept hidden since she'd left Syria.

But the exposure, so raw, had surprised her. Shame, guilt, and embarrassment had been absent. Instead, a sense of openness had filled her, reminding her that people were resilient and there was space for her to be close to those who wanted to help her. Having Jessica with her at the interview, even if all she did was sit in a plastic chair under a photo of the US president, made Amina feel wanted.

"Ms. Hamid," the officer said, squinting with a tight smile. "We will take our time and go through your paperwork. If you need a break, just let me know." He patted both hands on a small stack of folders and a blank pad of paper, indicating the work ahead of them. "I'll start with your I-589 form."

He reached, almost with ceremony, to the black pen in his shirt pocket. The click with his thumb, simply engaging a small bit of plastic with another small bit of plastic, resonated like a starting gun.

Who she was—Amina Hamid, accountant from Aleppo, Syria—was spelled out on the form, and the officer quizzed her on her own biography. They were easy questions, but she felt relieved that she had reviewed the document the day before.

She had also pulled together updated country condition documentation. Human Rights Watch reports and US State Department reports on Syria read like demented caricatures of her home, but everything was true, an accurate portrait. When the officer paused to turn over a page, she asked her own question. "I provided updated country reports. Can I tell you about them?" She could demonstrate her knowledge and show her seriousness.

"I don't need to hear from you about Syria," he said curtly, as if he were the expert on her country. "I want to hear about *your* experiences."

Of course. His rebuke sent her heart galloping, and she willed it, unsuccessfully, to slow. He tapped the black pen on her open file. She found herself distracted, trying to read the writing on the pen, but his fingers blocked her view.

The tapping stopped. "Why did you come to the US?"

She blinked her eyes away from the pen. "Pardon me?"

"When you arrived. When you left Syria, why did you leave?" The officer leaned back in his chair.

"I came to attend a conference on international accounting. I am an accountant."

"Yes. We already established that you are an accountant. Did you attend?"

"The conference? Yes. Yes." She exhaled in relief over having the right answer.

"Do you have proof?"

Amina's head swiveled toward Jessica, whose expression of guilt shattered Amina's confidence. "No, but—"

He raised his hand, telling her to stop, then leaned forward and wrote something on his paper, but she couldn't read it from her seat. He moved on before she could decide how to rectify the error or figure out what the error had been.

"Your husband is an architect, right? You say here on the form you don't know where he is. You haven't seen or talked with him?"

"No. I have seen his photo. He may be in Greece."

"Wait, so you do know where he is?" His squint didn't come with a smile this time.

"No." She glanced at Jessica again but didn't receive anything beyond a hesitant shrug in response. "I don't. We found a picture on the Internet of him at a refugee camp in Greece, but we are unable to locate him."

The officer scribbled a note and circled it, pushing down hard enough with his pen that she could hear the scrape of the ballpoint against paper.

After listening to Amina detail her father's detention and torture at the hands of the regime and her brother's murder, the officer paged through photos that depicted her father's injuries. "Regarding your father, I didn't see any paperwork. Do you have any official documentation or other corroboration?"

"No." She didn't have any more words to talk about her family. She certainly didn't have documents.

"Your brother Samir. Do you know who murdered him?"

She felt herself sinking into her plastic chair. "No."

He made another note then thumbed through the remaining papers from her file.

Panic welled in Amina's core. The pile of paper was too short. *How many pages do those other people from the waiting room have? How many do I need?* She turned to Jessica to see if the lawyer was also worried about the thickness of the folder but only saw kind eyes promising that she was doing fine. Amina didn't believe her.

"Let's move to the women's support group." The man's slow cadence only heightened her anxiety. "You called it"—he flipped some pages—"a study group when you initially filed, but in your amendment, you call it something different."

Is he implying I lied? Was Jessica right to focus on this? The fear of being exposed as a liar when she wasn't a liar threatened to burst her chest. She pressed her palms together to harness energy and told him everything she had told Jessica, measuring her tone in an attempt to maximize believability.

"Do you have any support for this story?" he asked. "I assume from your earlier answers and the files here you don't—"

"Yes," she almost barked. "I have this." She opened her bag, pulled out a yellow folder, and thrust it at the officer while avoiding Jessica's puzzled expression. The papers had only just arrived the day before, and she'd been too nervous to talk about anything since. "One woman we helped escape, Najlaa Mustafa, she is the doctor I mentioned in the amendment. She is in Lebanon now. She runs a mobile medical clinic for World Relief Group. She provided an affidavit." Amina opened the folder and pressed her finger on the top page. "There is also an affidavit from another woman, Rasha, also in Lebanon, who was part of our group." Amina slid the top document over and pointed to the second affidavit. "She was in Aleppo when the men came to punish the group. They only cut her face, leaving her scars as a warning to others not to subvert the regime."

When Najlaa had told Amina that Rasha, the one who'd betrayed the group, had arrived in Lebanon, her husband having died in the conflicts, Amina cried tears of joy that Rasha had survived. Rasha had insisted on sending her own statement before she'd even learned Amina had forgiven her.

The officer stared intently at the stamped documents. He made another notation on his pad, the pen moving across the paper and leaving marks that would affect her future.

Amina took a deep breath, emboldened by her sisters in Lebanon and those that remained in Syria. She wouldn't let that pen dictate her future. She would give it all the words it needed to ensure she could stay here and lay the path for Mohammed to join her in safety.

CHAPTER FIFTY-TWO

J essica emerged from the interview room, feeling as if she had newly witnessed Amina's harrowing last years in Syria.

In the waiting room, Conor stood out like a well-dressed junkie in need of a fix, fidgeting and rubbing the coin between his fingers. "Well? How did it go? Did she pass?" His eyes skipped back and forth from his mom to Amina.

Jessica smiled. It wasn't quite pass-fail, but then again, it kind of was. "She did great." She nodded reassuringly at Amina, who maintained a calm exterior but whose eyes showed an understandable anxiety. She didn't need to hear anything other than that she did great.

A pit in Jessica's gut grew heavy with her failure to get information about the conference and to ensure the officer knew about the recent location of Mohammed. She was responsible for putting Amina in a defensive position and could only pray it hadn't killed her chances.

She hadn't been able to get a read on the officer—whether he'd found Amina credible, whether he'd thought her fear was well-founded, whether he'd thought the women's group satisfied the law's requirement regarding social groups or political opposition, or whether he was a jaded employee who had seen too many fraudulent claims to be generous in his approvals.

"Now we wait." Amina didn't have to say "Again," but she had to be thinking it.

"Okay, so what now?" Conor stared intently at his mom. "Did he say anything? Will it still be up to sixty days before we hear?"

"No, he didn't say anything about timing, and yes, up to sixty days. But if he refers the case to the immigration court, we're looking at maybe another six months or more."

"But that would be better than a 'no,' right?"

"Right. But we want an outright 'yes.'"

"With a 'yes,' it would be done? Like done done?" It was as though Conor was trying to find the question that would trigger an automatic "yes," and asylum would be granted immediately.

"Pretty much, yes." She squeezed Amina's hand. "Done done sounds good, right?"

Amina worked up a smile.

"Amina, do you remember the first time we met? At the IAP offices?"

"Of course," Amina said. "I walked out. I'm sorry about that." Amusement pulled at the edges of her smile.

"That's not why I mention it. I don't blame you. You asked me why I volunteered to take your case. I gave you some BS answer about giving you the help you deserved or something like that. But really, I didn't know myself."

Jessica had long been myopic to believe she'd been so independent in achieving the life she had. She now recognized that there were postmen and embroiderers and would-be astronauts—some of whom never knew her but who would live on through her—who had opened paths she could travel. She was merely an extension of them, a bridge to those who would follow. Amina was a part of that now, even more so as an extension of Amina's own family. But the reason for taking on Amina's case didn't need to be profound or even enlightened.

"It was the right thing to do. Thanks for letting me"—she grabbed Conor's hand—"us be a part of it."

———— ❧ ————

BELTWAY TRAFFIC HAD fed on already-frayed nerves, and Jessica's mind and body were depleted as if she'd done a couple of all-nighters in a row by the time she dropped off Amina and arrived with Conor to a darkened home. Danny had said he would pick up Cricket from swim practice. He must have taken Mikey with him.

Jessica threw her briefcase on the kitchen table and collapsed onto the couch. Gracie leapt up next to her and started licking her cheek.

"Thanks, girl. I needed that." Jessica could hear the crinkle of paper as Gracie stepped on her jacket. She had forgotten about the envelope from Amina.

Jessica removed the contents and set the envelope on the trunk. In her hand was an index card enclosed in a note.

"To Jessica Donnelly. Thank you for helping us, and thank you for helping Amina. Peace be upon you, Fayiz and Sama. PS, I wish you could try my mother's. She used bitter oranges from her own tree. I have never been able to make it like her."

And on the index card was the recipe for kibbeh arnabieh.

CHAPTER FIFTY-THREE

AMINA

The smell of sweet cinnamon and smoky firewood snuffed out the cold that accompanied Amina into the Donnellys' entryway. Conor closed the door and took her heavy jacket.

It seemed like a year since she had visited the home as an outsider on Thanksgiving, yet it hadn't even been three months. The slow drag of the three weeks since the interview magnified the time warp.

Jessica offered to let her use Danny's office for the call so she could have a level of privacy she wouldn't have been able to have at the Darbis' home.

While searching for Mohammed, Jessica had communicated with the aid agency in Greece and even the man who'd taken the photo. But it wasn't until she'd contacted an architect in the town near the camp that she had found Mohammed. Amina's attorney was clever. Of course, Mohammed would have sought out a Greek architect to tell him about the structures in the area.

Finding her husband and knowing she would soon talk with him had kept Amina's mind off the constant worry about words she had not said in the interview and words that she *had* said but could have said differently. Since the interview, she had been searching for accounting positions to force optimism about the asylum decision that hadn't arrived yet, but job hunting hadn't suppressed the anxiety. Today pulled her out of her loop of anxiety, if only momentarily.

Jessica and Conor smiled and sneaked wordless glances at each other like nervous schoolchildren. Amina almost wished for the loud and the busy from back in November.

Left alone in Danny's office, Amina swiveled slowly in the chair. She hadn't paid attention to the items on the wall the last time she was in this room. Photos showed sailboats crashing through waves and tanned men grinning and holding up large trophies. What looked like half of a sailboat named "Wild Goose" was mounted on brown wood. Anchoring the array of boat prints, dead center on the wall, was a large photo in a dark wood frame. It was Jessica, beaming as a white veil whipped in the wind around her face, and a handsome Danny kissing her on the cheek.

Amina swiveled back and faced a blue-and-white screen. She waited.

The call was set for 10:00 a.m. She checked the time. It was 9:59.

Staring at the clock in the corner of the computer seemed to make the time go by even more slowly. But the seconds could not hold off forever. The screen lit up, begging Amina to accept the call.

Mohammed said nothing, but his smile told her he could see her face.

She traced a scar on his face that hadn't been there before. "My love. It is you." She pulled back her hand so she could see all of him.

"My heart. I have been waiting for this day. You brought me through. You brought me here."

His eyes spoke words she had not allowed herself to dream.

Their silence sent the minutes flying past, and there was so much to say.

EPILOGUE

The Smoky Mountain twang in Annapolis's new fair-trade coffee shop turned more heads than just Jessica's.

Jessica covered the microphone on her phone. "Bronwyn!" She waved her friend over from the server she'd been questioning. The law partner was in her civilians today—charcoal linen slacks, a silk turquoise blouse, and a fantastic necklace. Bronwyn still rocked the power heels, though. *You can take the girl out of the high-powered law office...*

"Gotta go, Mom. We'll see you in two weeks. I promised Mikey I'd take him fishing. Hopefully, Kenny has the old poles. I didn't catch anything with them last time, so they owe me." Jessica clicked off the phone just as Bronwyn walked up to her.

After the obligatory hugs, Bronwyn cut to the chase. "Grab your coffee, and let's go. I need to see what was so great that you passed up the opportunity to come back to Highland & Cross. I've got ninety, and then I have to get to a soccer game. Damn travel teams. But at least I had an excuse to see you while I was in the area."

Jessica eyed the Louboutins. "You always wear kick-ass heels to the soccer pitch?"

"Honey, I ain't no soccer mom. Now show me what you got."

"Right next door, my dear." Jessica found herself somehow following Bronwyn as she led her out of the globally eclectic shop to a locally dull building just down the block. It didn't look like much. In fact, it looked like a candidate for demolition. The aged sideboards reluctantly showed ghosts of white paint that had lost its fight against the elements ages ago, and high, cloudy windows didn't let in much light, even from the blazing summer sun.

"Don't tell me. You're a slum lord."

"Very funny, Bron. This used to be a boat repair shop. We got a great price, mostly because the family of Danny's old sailing coach owned it but partly because it's a dump. The pier has collapsed, and the building itself, well, I don't know how it was still standing before we put in some temporary support beams. But this neighborhood is on the rebound. It's hard to tell quite yet, but it's happening. I'm not sure what I'm going to do with it long-term. For now, though"—Jessica slid the barn-style door open—"it's my studio."

Opening the door triggered a flurry of dust that threatened to engulf the women. It took a moment to fan away the cloud and let their eyes adjust to the darkness so the interior could reveal itself.

Jessica flicked on caged lights that hung between exposed wooden beams overhead. She stood grinning as Bronwyn scanned the mostly empty space, a single room with ample space for a boat or two and lined with large metal hooks and mostly empty wooden shelves.

Bronwyn tapped the toe of her Louboutin on the aged, wide-plank floor. "You're gonna have to explain, honey. You said you took a pass on the internship so you could pursue some passion. I figured you were going to work full-time with Rosalie at IAP."

"I am absolutely continuing with that! I'm just volunteering part-time there, though. Working on getting derivative asylum for a spouse right now, in fact. And Rosalie strong-armed me into taking on another case on top of that." That wasn't true. Jessica had solicited the new case, emboldened after Amina's asylum approval. Getting the USCIS news about Amina had been better than any corporate transaction closing. No one got rich, but lives got richer.

Jessica walked toward a large workbench that stood between two of the new support beams in the middle of the space. "This is my new workshop. I rehabilitate old trees. Old furniture and wood fixtures, really, but they were all trees once, right? I don't have much yet, but some of the sponsors of a gala I used to run stepped up to be my first customers."

Next to one of the beams sat her current project. "Isn't this gorgeous? It's an antebellum bed, walnut." She traced the carvings on one of the seven-foot-tall bedposts. "See how the posts are warped? The original owners threw it in a lake near their home during the Civil War so the soldiers and looters wouldn't pillage it. It's been passed down through the family ever since they pulled it from the water."

Bronwyn ran her hand down a post, her ring sparkling in the dusty light. "So, how do you unwarp it?"

"Shut your mouth! I don't unwarp it. I'll refinish this bed, but for everything I work on, everything I've always worked on, in fact, I leave the life, the soul. The warping is part of the bed's history but also the family's history, our country's history, even. Without that, it's just another bed and means nothing. You might as well chuck this back in the lake and buy a new bed from Pottery Barn."

Jessica moved to the other side of the space. "You'll appreciate this, too. A state senator brought me his grandfather's desk. His grandfather was a judge. Look at this here." Jessica pointed to thousands of tiny pockmarks scattered atop the right side of a desk that should have looked stately in its solid construction, except that a destroyed finish marked it as a flea market castoff instead.

Bronwyn ran her hand across the scarred wood. "Do tell."

"When the judge got stuck on a point of law or struggled with a decision, he sat at his desk and tapped it over and over with a letter opener." Jessica mimed the tapping. "The senator thinks that this area over here..." She pointed at a particularly worn area where individual indents gave way to a small crater. "He thinks this happened during a case involving an elderly woman accused of killing her severely disabled son. She was afraid she would die before him and he would be left with no one to care for him. The senator has wanted to refinish this desk for years but worried a refinisher would buff away his grandfather's marks. He said these scars remind him that things aren't always black and white and that he should take the time to work through the facts to get to the right resolution."

Bronwyn tapped her impressive wedding ring in agreement.

"That's the grand tour," Jessica said, spinning for effect. The supplies that had crowded the backyard shed took up no more than one of the shelves that ran the length of the space. The workbench and two pieces anchored the room but left plenty of unused real estate. To Jessica, the open space promised opportunity.

"Bron, do you remember telling me how you always ask yourself where 'this moment' will take you? I found myself in a moment, restoring a table—a scrap of trunk and root from a tree from halfway around the world. That tree represented a family and a business, a journey, a conflict, a resolution. I was on my knees with a tiny brush, removing red paint, and that moment took me to each one of those things. And it was exactly where I wanted to be."

"And Danny's on board?"

Jessica walked back to a small desk by the front door and opened the top drawer.

Bronwyn accepted a small white card from Jessica. "'The Old Wood Company. Jessica Donnelly. Everything.'" She tilted her head. "Everything?"

"That's all Danny. I don't need business cards, but he insisted. He says that now, when anyone asks what I do, I can say 'everything,' and I have the business card to prove it."

"I always did love Danny. And this"—Bronwyn waved her arms—"this is fantastic. In fact, I could probably get some business for you. We have some pieces at the firm, and oh, the congressional offices are full of historic pieces. All of our contacts on the Hill? Honey, I'm on this. Don't you worry."

The open space, swimming with dancing dust, suddenly seemed too small for Bronwyn's aspirations.

Jessica laughed. "All right. I'll be waiting for a call from the White House furniture director. Surely there's one of those, right?" Jessica flipped off the lights. "Listen, I have an important appointment this afternoon, and you've got soccer, so let's go grab a quick lunch. There's a great new bistro just down the street. We would have loved it when we were associates."

JESSICA pulled her car in front of the IAP building. Amina stood in front, wearing canary yellow and a wide smile that belied the dark night the two had experienced there the prior year. A balding man in his fifties wearing a button-down dress shirt and no tie stood next to her. He said goodbye to Amina and slung the strap of a leather suitcase over his shoulder when Amina headed toward the car.

"Hi, Jessica! Thanks for picking me up." Amina tossed a bulky bag in the back then sat in the passenger seat, buckling in before Jessica pulled away from the curb.

"Who's the guy with the briefcase? How was the meeting?"

"Gary, my new boss. When I told him about my idea to provide financial literacy classes for IAP clients, he offered for the firm to defray the program costs, so he came to the meeting today. Rosalie signed off on it, and I'll start leading the classes in two weeks."

A break in pedestrians crossing the street permitted Jessica to turn right.

"I'm even starting to learn some Spanish," Amina said.

"*Si?*"

"*Si, un poco.*"

"That's all the Spanish I've got, Amina. When you end up being able to speak four languages to my one, well, I guess that proves I'm a total slacker." Jessica checked her GPS. They were fifteen minutes away. She turned on the radio. Skipping past the news channels, Jessica decided on a throwback music station.

Changing lanes on Baltimore's one-way streets was a gladiator sport, and today's bumper-to-bumper traffic left little room for maneuvering. Jessica checked her mirrors to find an opening so she could make a left turn ahead.

Amina humming along with the radio snapped Jessica out of her focus. She looked over to see Amina mouthing the chorus to "Oops!... I Did It Again." Jessica couldn't contain herself and blurted a laugh.

Amina stared at Jessica blankly. "What? I can't know American music?" She smiled with a hint of mischief. "I was here in 2000, remember? And we do have radios in Syria. That Britney Spears. Wow. Am I right?"

A buoyancy had emerged in Amina since her asylum had been approved, even more so after they'd filed the petition for derivative asylum for Mohammed. The worry lines prematurely aging her face had already softened, and a new light in her deep eyes brought optimism for the future to balance the pain of her past.

Finally getting out of Baltimore downtown proper, Jessica followed the GPS to a quieter street. Tidy brick-row houses set back from the street looked like old Baltimore but were newly renovated.

Jessica pulled up to the curb. "Here we are."

Amina had signed the lease but had only seen a model unit. Today, she was moving into her very own place.

After getting out of the car and grabbing her bag, Amina held her meager belongings at arm's length and laughed. "Fayiz will bring over the rest of my things later, but it still won't be enough for a whole apartment. I think I could fit in a closet with all of my things!

I feel a little bad that I'm taking some of the furniture that the interfaith group is providing to refugees. It's just me." She smiled then clenched her teeth nervously. "Hopefully not for long, though."

Jessica joined her on the walk up the stairs to the entrance. It would be many months before Mohammed's approval could possibly come through, but Rosalie was optimistic about the process, and Amina would be able to get their home prepared in the meantime. She handed the key to Amina ceremoniously, and Amina led Jessica up to the second-floor unit.

Fumbling with the key in the lock, Amina couldn't see Jessica shaking with anticipation behind her. Finally, the key clicked, and the knob turned.

Amina walked in and... silence.

Jessica stood back in the open doorway. Amina ran her hand along the small kitchen table then walked over to pick up a TV remote control sitting on the arm of a navy twill couch. She gestured toward the bedroom. Jessica nodded and followed her into the room. The overhead light illuminated a queen-sized bed with a seagrass headboard and a white down comforter. Amina peeked into the bathroom to see plush towels hanging from the towel bar and skin care products lined up on the counter.

The women returned to the kitchen. "This seems like more than what the interfaith group said they would provide," Amina said.

Jessica tilted her head toward the cabinets. "Take a look."

Amina opened the cabinet above the dishwasher. Sturdy cream dishes adorned with acorns and oak leaves filled the shelves.

"Jessica. What..." Her eyes welled, threatening to spill over when she shook her head in disbelief.

"No interfaith donations here. It was my book club. Everyone pitched in. After they met you..." Jessica had underestimated her friends. She'd brought Amina to book club the previous month, and it was as though she'd brought a long-lost little sister. They had been as open to helping her as they would have been with anyone in the group. "Nari sent over the couch. It's used, but it's in really good shape. I doubt anyone ever sat on it. Mary Ann, well, you'll recall from her scrutinizing your pores that she's a skin care consultant. You got her complete lineup. Kai is an interior designer, so she made sure everything coordinated, but she wanted to keep it neutral so you could still make the place your own." Jessica ran her hand over the smooth maple of the table. "This great table just needed to be refinished. I'll let Denise tell you its story."

"And the dishes? I remember them."

"They were my great-grandmother's. I left my grandmother's note on the shelves. I even added a note from me. You can read about the happy family memories that come with the dishes. I hope you'll add your own."

Amina took Jessica's hands in her own. "I already have."

Dear Reader,

We hope you enjoyed *Unbroken Threads*, by Jennifer Klepper. Please consider leaving a review on your favorite book site.

Visit our website (https://RedAdeptPublishing.com) to subscribe to the Red Adept Publishing Newsletter to be notified of future releases.

AUTHOR'S NOTE

When I started writing this book, I thought surely that by the time it was published, the war in Syria would be over. At the date of publication, however, the destruction and killing in Syria continues, and the challenges faced by refugees in the US have increased. When the war does end, the effects will last within Syria and throughout the Syrian diaspora for generations as people attempt to heal and rebuild. While I did significant reading and research about Syria and have included factual information in this book, it remains a work of fiction. *Unbroken Threads* barely scratches the surface of what Syrians have gone through in their home country and, for those who have left, abroad. I hope readers will seek out Syrian and Syrian-American writers of fiction and nonfiction to learn more about the ancient and beautiful country of Syria and the people who call it home. Their voices are strong and unique and add an element that is often missing from today's news coverage.

For a discussion guide and further reading, please visit www.jenniferklepper.com[1].

---

1.   http://www.jenniferklepper.com

ACKNOWLEDGMENTS

An unexpected joy of writing this book was discovering the vast and supportive world of writers. Without these groups, I never would have published *Unbroken Threads*, and I wouldn't have the network of friends I now have all over the world.

The Women's Fiction Writers Association (WFWA) was my first foray into the world of writers' groups. I have never seen a professional organization so uplifting and so generous with their time and wisdom in furtherance of fellow members' career goals. Maybe I've been sheltered, but maybe writers are special. The Annapolis Poets and Writers group was the first group to hear or read any of my manuscript, and they wholly set me straight on a few things this novice writer didn't yet know. Authors 18, a group of novelists debuting in 2018, inspires me daily with its talent, candor, generosity, and humor. I cannot imagine going through the publishing process without them, and I wish them all huge success.

My early beta readers provided valuable feedback as well as much-appreciated support. They were Julie Kyle, Asli Stewart, Amy Van Slyke, and the most well-read person I've ever known, James Buttinger. My mom and sister were early readers, and I wish every writer had such an enthusiastic family.

I never would have gotten to the point of writers' groups and beta readers, though, if it weren't for author Julie Lawson Timmer, who told me that I wrote upmarket women's fiction, insisted I could call myself a writer since I was writing, and introduced me to WFWA.

The Red Adept Publishing team could not be more supportive or professional. Erica Lucke Dean has been author mentor extraordinaire. My editors, Alyssa Hall and Neila Forssberg, were invaluable in helping me transform and polish my manuscript. Their patience astonishes me.

A special technical thank you to Zach Zayner for providing input on biometrics technologies for a book that won't be on the SFF shelf and to the software development team at Workbench Education for making me believe that anything is possible on a computer if you have good developers.

It's important to note that, while I spoke with real people and researched Syria, refugees, asylum law, and technology, every factual error and every misstep in this book is on me.

Thank you also to my neighborhood book club. These women love their wine, love to talk, and love books that promote discussion. They are also generous and giving, both within the group and in the greater community. I hope to write the kind of books that keep my book club talking late into the night.

Thank you to my family—my mom, my dad, my sister, my grandparents, my aunts, and my uncles—for providing a framework of family and tradition that influenced this book so much. I was lucky to marry into a family that has the same values, though perhaps that's one of the things that drew my husband and me together in the first place.

Finally, and most importantly, thank you to my children, who watched me write, edit, and promote this book all while telling them to please be quiet. And to my husband, who has always supported anything I've wanted to do, 100 percent, and would do anything to make sure it happened. I am so very, very fortunate.

About the Author

A Midwest native, Jennifer Klepper made stops in Dallas, Charlottesville, and Boston before settling in Maryland. While she has an appreciation for the expansive beauty of the plains states, she hopes never to live landlocked again.

Jennifer attended Southern Methodist University and the University of Virginia School of Law. Her law degree has guided her through the worlds of corporate law, tech startups, and court advocacy for foster children. She is an ardent consumer of podcasts and books that challenge her with compelling and unfamiliar topics. When she's not writing, she's crossing things off a never-ending to-do list and hoping to catch that next sunset. Jennifer lives with her husband, two kids, and a dog who looks like a Dr. Seuss character.

Read more at https://www.jenniferklepper.com/.